The Legend of Jesse Smoke

On the Way Home
The Lives of Riley Chance
Almighty Me
The White Rooster and Other Stories
A Hole in the Earth
The Gypsy Man
Out of Season
Far as the Eye Can See

The Legend of Jesse Smoke

A Novel

Robert Bausch

BLOOMSBURY

NEW YORK · LONDON · OXFORD · NEW DELHI · SYDNEY

Bloomsbury USA
An imprint of Bloomsbury Publishing Plc

1385 Broadway	50 Bedford Square
New York	London
NY 10018	WC1B 3DP
USA	UK

www.bloomsbury.com

BLOOMSBURY and the Diana logo are trademarks of Bloomsbury
Publishing Plc

First published 2016

ISBN: HB: 978-1-63286-397-3
        ePub: 978-1-63286-399-7

LIBRARY OF CONGRESS CATALOGING-IN-PUBLICATION DATA

Names: Bausch, Robert, author.
Title: The legend of Jesse Smoke / Robert Bausch.
Description: New York : Bloomsbury USA, 2016.
Identifiers: LCCN 2015047028 | ISBN 978-1-63286-397-3 (hardcover) |
ISBN 978-1-63286-399-7 (ebook)
Subjects: LCSH: Women football players—Fiction. | Sports stories. | BISAC:
FICTION / Literary. | FICTION / Sports.
Classification: LCC PS3552.A847 L44 2016 | DDC 813/.54—dc23 LC record
available at http://lccn.loc.gov/2015047028

2 4 6 8 10 9 7 5 3 1

Typeset by RefineCatch Limited, Bungay, Suffolk
Printed and bound in the U.S.A. by Berryville Graphics Inc., Berryville, Virginia

To find out more about our authors and books visit www.bloomsbury.com. Here
you will find extracts, author interviews, details of forthcoming events and the
option to sign up for our newsletters.

Bloomsbury books may be purchased for business or promotional use. For
information on bulk purchases please contact Macmillan Corporate and Premium
Sales Department at specialmarkets@macmillan.com.

For Denny, again, wherever we are . . .
And in memory of George Garrett,
"He was the best of us . . ."

The work is all . . .
—Roland Flint

Truth is better offered in disguise . . .
—George Garrett

One

THE FIRST TIME I saw Jesse Smoke throw a football I knew she was going to be a miracle. I never saw anything like it, and I'd been in the game, professionally, more than thirty years; I saw John Elway, Dan Marino, Peyton Manning, Tom Brady. Hell, I remember films of Johnny Unitas and Sonny Jurgensen. I'd been a scout, an assistant, and even for a very short time, head coach. (Interim, for a failing team, but still, head coach.)

I was working at my natural position the first time I saw her, as an assistant. I wasn't scouting. I was on vacation, traveling in Central America on a brief cruise between the end of the first minicamp and the start of the scouting combine, in February. I wasn't even thinking about football.

It was on a beach, in Belize. That part of the story everybody tells about us is absolutely true. I was watching some hotdog jet skiers skewer the water in front of the beach, hopping over their own waves, throwing plumes of white water in the air. And then I noticed her, standing just out of the water, on dry sand, in a one-piece bathing suit.

She was tall, for a woman—about six feet one or two maybe—lithe and wiry, small breasted, and not too wide in the hips either, but definitely a fine-looking woman. She was mixed race maybe, a little on the brown side, maybe some Spanish or African in her background. Maybe even some Indian. She had long, powerfully built legs and wore a yellow bandanna around her neck that bounced when she ran. Her hair was black, curly in a wide variety of ways—I mean she had waves, and small twists and little curlicues that made her whole head look like some fully blossomed, half-tended garden. And she could throw a football a fucking mile.

I mean it. She stood on one end of this beach, in a small turn of the shore, and she threw a full-size football across the water to the other side, where a young man about four inches taller than she was caught it. He didn't try to throw it back, he just came running around the turn, howling his approval. She'd done it to prove she could, it seemed. I swear that football hadn't even arched that much—she heaved it on a line about fifty or sixty yards. A perfect spiral.

Others there wanted to see her do it again. So the hell did I. See, she was standing in sand. Sand! You can't get enough footing on sand to whip a ball that far. She didn't even take much of a stride in the direction of her throw, either. Not that her form was bad. She released the ball quickly—snapped it off the end of her arm is more accurate—and she leaned into it the right way. I know it was only the first throw from her I'd ever seen, but I noticed everything about it because it was so amazing. I can't believe she didn't fall down, or recoil in the opposite direction from the throw, given the velocity with which the ball had left her hand; something about the laws of motion, of action creating an equal and opposite reaction.

She was with a lot of young men her age. They surrounded her and it was hard to tell if she was among them or they, too, had just discovered her. The guy she threw the ball to was with her, I could see that, and he was waving everybody off, shouting out something about betting money she could throw it even farther.

I would not have gone over there, but I was by myself as usual and had nothing better to do. Besides, I thought they might be impressed to meet the offensive coordinator of the Washington Redskins. Forgive me if that sounds like pride.

I didn't announce myself right away. A couple of the men wanted to challenge her. All of them wore bright-colored Speedo outfits, their muscular, oiled bodies looking positively shellacked in the glare of sand and sunlight. In my khaki shorts, sandals, purple-and-yellow Hawaiian shirt, and Panama hat, I felt middle-aged and bloated (so much for pride). I approached, stepped a little to the side, and watched from under the shade of a scruffy palm tree a short distance away. Nobody would have noticed me anyway, except perhaps to remark that even older people liked this little beach.

"I bet she can't hit a moving target," somebody shouted. She held the football in both hands, flipping it up and down a little, catching it in front of herself, without ever throwing it more than a few inches in the air. I noticed that each time it left her hand it spun exactly one revolution so that it always came down with the laces in her right palm. She knew what she was doing with that ball.

"Give me something to hit," she said.

One of the men picked up a piece of driftwood. "I'll put this over there on the other side."

"That's nothing. Come on," she said.

"Like you could see that thing lying in the sand all the way over there?" the guy protested.

Then somebody else had the bright idea that she should hit one of the jet skiers.

She scoffed at that, too.

"Can't do it, huh?" another said. "Too far away for you."

"Oh, I can *do* it. Long's I know where he's going."

"Hell *they* don't know which way they're going," the big guy with her said.

"You could guess," the first man said.

She looked at him, letting the ball sit still a moment. Then she turned and watched the jet skiers. The men around her didn't take their eyes off her, but she studied the jet skiers a while, until she picked out one that was doing figure eights, way out in the water. She sort of limbered herself, and let the ball down a bit, and the men all backed away. Then she pointed at this guy—I mean he was at least sixty yards out—and her big companion said, "That one?"

"Exactly," she said.

"Get back," the big guy said to the rest of them.

She took a few steps back, pointed her foot exactly as a quarterback should, even though the terrain was slightly downhill, and whipped the ball across the water on a line toward the jet skier. He moved through the water and the ball became a smaller and smaller black shadow of a dot as it moved in a slight arch to a point at which the jet skier would be when the ball got there. It zipped past just to the right of the guy's shoulder and hit the handlebars in front of him. Scared the living shit out of him, you could tell, and he lost control for a moment, but it was a perfect pass. If he'd been running down a field and looked back, he could have caught the ball with one hand; the ball zipped just over his neck and his shoulder. Sixty yards.

The men surrounded her, cheering and screaming. That's when I walked right up to them and took off my hat. A couple of the men quieted down when they saw me, but the general ruckus around her continued until she looked at me and put her hand up to the rest of them. Sure enough, they all stopped.

"Hello," her big boyfriend said to me.

"I'm Skip Granger," I said. It didn't seem to make much of an impact. "Ever hear of the Washington Redskins?"

"Of course."

"Well, I coach for them—I'm an assistant."

"Really," the big boyfriend said. The others started whispering. The girl just stared at me.

"I wanted to tell you, that was one hell of a throw."

"Thank you," she said.

Somebody had gone out to retrieve the ball and brought it back. I heard laughter about how unhappy the jet skier was; how he'd threatened to beat somebody's ass until he saw the crowd standing on the beach, waiting for the ball. He wasn't about to challenge what looked like an entire football team. The fellow who retrieved the ball threw it over a few heads and she caught it.

Her boyfriend told me her name. "She's a great quarterback," he said.

The men started crowding in closer to hear what we were saying. Some of them were whispering. I heard the word "coach."

"Where'd you learn to throw a football like that?" I asked.

She shrugged. "I always knew. Played for my father when I was in school."

"Where?"

"Guam."

"Really."

"He coached high school there, on the base."

"So you're military."

"*He* was. Coached for the American high school."

"So you played on the high school team, then?"

"Not with the boys," she said.

I'd never heard of a girl's football team anywhere, much less in Guam, but I didn't tell her that. I was curious to know if she played tackle football and asked her if she'd ever worn a helmet and equipment.

"Nah," she said. "We played flag football. Didn't need a helmet. But it was pretty rough anyway."

"Well, it's really something the way you can throw that ball. Can I see it?"

"You want to see me throw it again?"

"No, the ball. Mind if I take a look?"

She flipped it to me. An NFL football is eleven inches long and twenty-eight inches around the middle; it weighs between a pound to a pound and a half, depending on the weather. In cold weather it's a bit light. In wet weather it can be almost a pound heavier. The ball she was throwing had been dry before she threw it at the fellow on the jet ski, and it was definitely a regulation ball.

"Play anywhere now?"

"She's going to try out for the Divas," her boyfriend said.

"What team is that?"

"You ever hear of the IWFL?"

I hadn't.

He scoffed a little, clearly pleased to know more than an assistant coach for the Washington Redskins. "The Independent Women's Football League."

"Hunh," I said. "Not familiar with it."

"It's professional football. Jesse's going for a tryout next week."

"Well, I expect she'll make the team," I said.

She smiled.

"Where do the Divas play?"

"In Washington," she said.

"D.C.?"

She nodded. I couldn't believe my luck.

"Where exactly?"

"I don't know. I think at a park or sports complex?"

"They're having tryouts this time of year?"

"They play eight games a year," her boyfriend said. "From late April to June."

"How can I find out where they play? I'd like to catch a game, maybe."

"Go on the Internet," Jesse said. "That's how I heard of them."

"Really."

"Yes, sir."

I turned to her boyfriend. "What's your name?"

"Nate. Everybody calls me Nate. We're on vacation."

"She's your wife?" I asked.

She laughed. "Ah, no!" she said.

He was laughing too. "We're just friends," he said. He was a little taller than she was—built very sturdily, solid as a jeep, and none of it fat. But he couldn't throw the ball nearly as far, he admitted, or as accurately.

"Jesse," I said. "You think you might come to a Redskins tryout?"

"Right," she smirked, flipping the ball over to Nate.

"Not a proper tryout, I mean, but a minicamp. Sort of a practice session the team puts on every year." I had the craziest idea right then, see—the craziest idea I ever had in my life, and the most creative. Whatever it cost me, it would be worth every penny. I had plenty of money at the time; we got paid very well in this profession. I was single, with no obligations of any kind except to Coach Jonathon Engram and the team, and I always, always enjoyed a good practical joke. I had this instant picture of showing up at minicamp with all the undrafted rookies, and a player named Jesse Smoke. I'd figure some way to get her throwing a ball in front of a few of our more "primo" players. And when I say "primo," I don't mean "prime," I mean *primo*donna.

Are you beginning to figure it out? I recruit players on the spot for tryouts in my job, so I'd just claim I'd invited this new guy. Then I'd figure a way to spring Jesse on them. I could already imagine their faces when they saw her throw a football. I might even be able to make them all believe I'd actually signed her. It would kill Coach Engram. It really was just a whim.

"I'll pay you," I said. "Just for fun."

"I don't understand."

"Put it this way: There's a few players at your position in this game I'd, ah, like to humble a little bit."

She had nothing to say to this, and we stood there quiet a moment. Nate said, "And what'll you pay her?"

I put my hands on my hips, screwed up my face a little to think. "When do you try out for that women's team?"

"She's got to be there next Tuesday." He put the ball back in her hands.

And then she smiled at me, a broad, innocent show of white teeth. Everybody on earth knows that smile now, and it was just as disarming and pretty back then, scrunching up those brown freckles spattered across her broad, flat nose. She was definitely striking to look at with those white teeth, those large, sea-blue eyes.

"Can you throw a ball with somebody in your face?"

"She's a scrambler," Nate said.

"Ever been knocked down?"

"Sure. Lots of times. That's how you play flag football. You tackle the ball carrier and then pull out the flag."

"You want to have some fun?"

They both waited. A few of the men standing around, getting impatient with this little interview of mine, started urging her to throw at something else.

"You'll be in Washington anyway." I took a card out of my wallet and handed it to her. "I get back in town on Monday. Soon as you get in, call me."

"Really?"

"I'll pay you for your time."

"What is it you want, exactly?" She tilted her head. Nate moved a little toward me, waiting for my answer.

"I'd just like a few of the players and coaches on the team to see you throw a ball. And I really will pay you."

"How much?"

"You tell me."

"Five hundred?"

I laughed. "Honey," I said, "you got a deal. And let's call it seven."

"All right, then," she said.

I grabbed her hand and she gave me a very firm handshake. I couldn't help feeling like I'd hit some sort of jackpot.

I had no idea.

Two

As everybody knows, Jonathon Engram was the head coach of the Washington Redskins back then. An All-Pro quarterback before he went into coaching, he had been almost unstoppable—like Joe Montana. Average size for a quarterback, and not that strong of an arm either, maybe fifty yards tops, but the guy could win games, knew just how to get a team down the field and score. He threw accurately, with the right touch on the ball: When he needed to fire it, he fired it; when he needed to lob it softly and drop it over a guy's head and shoulders, he did that. He knew the game as well as anybody ever knew it, and then some.

He was a winning coach almost from the start. When he took over the Redskins, they had been losing for almost a decade. Middle-of-the-pack losers. They went 8 and 8 a few times, but mostly they were in the 7 and 9 or 6 and 10 neighborhood. The NFL switched to an eighteen-game season in Engram's first year coaching and he won 10 and lost 8. It was a pretty impressive turnaround for a guy's first year, because they won their last nine games straight, after starting out 1 and 8. The next year they won 11 and lost 7, then went into the playoffs as a wild card team and made it all the way to the NFC championship game. They lost (badly) to the Arizona Cardinals. (The Cardinals won the Super Bowl that year for the first time in their history.)

The next year the Redskins went 12 and 6. They lost again in the NFC championship, this time to the Eagles. Coach Engram said we'd win it all the next year, and we almost did it. We went 14 and 4 and made it to the Super Bowl, but lost to the Cleveland Browns. (31–30; it was a hell of a game.)

Then the year before I met Jesse, we lost the final four games of the year to finish 9 and 9. A lot of players were getting old or leaving for other teams in free agency, and we'd had a few drafts that didn't pan out. (We drafted one guy, a running back, who would have been a great player if he hadn't drowned in a freak accident before the season started. He was offshore, somewhere a hundred miles east of Buxton, North Carolina, fishing as first mate on a charter boat, trying to gaff a fish, and the line got tangled around his wrist. The fish—a huge blue marlin—still pretty strong after a long struggle to get it near to the boat, sounded and took him with it. The last time anyone saw him, he was struggling to get his glove off and unwind the line, even as the fish disappeared with him into the darkness.)

The whole year we had that kind of luck. No deaths besides that one, but freak accidents that robbed the roster of some very fine players. A blown knee, a blood clot in somebody's lung. Before the season was over, we had three players from our practice squad starting. It was a bad year.

That year I met Jesse Smoke, we ended up with three quarterbacks on the team, not one a rookie. We had a promising draft of other position players two months after I went on vacation, and Coach Engram said he was "cautiously optimistic" about the coming year. "It will be tough, though," he said. "I'm going to have to be tough on everybody. These men *will* be ready to play."

One of the top draft picks you may remember was a defensive end named Orlando Brown. That's right, the great Orlando. He was a rookie that year, a little heavy for a defensive end—315 pounds—but at six feet eleven inches tall, he looked lean as a racehorse. And he could run almost as fast. He'd played wide receiver in high school, so he could catch a ball if you wanted him to, though all anyone wanted to see was him on the defensive line, charging a quarterback or rooting through offensive linemen to find a runner. He was definitely a kind of freak, and that became a theme for us because, hell, we had a few on the team.

We had a guy named Daniel Wilber, a center, who was only five feet eleven inches tall and weighed 342 pounds. He looked like one of those old minivans in his uniform, but there was not an ounce of fat on his body and he was probably the best center in all of football. You couldn't budge him, and if he wanted you out of a play, you were gone. He made All-Pro in his second season and would continue to make it every year he played after that. What the guy did in his spare time was—are you ready for this?—he taught yoga classes. I'm not kidding. It was really funny watching him doing some of those stretches, pointing his toes like a goddamn ballet dancer.

Drew Bruckner played middle linebacker. He was an artist, you know, a painter, with a canvas and a palette and brushes. He could produce the most beautiful pictures of birds and foxes; mountains and lakes. Didn't do many people. He said he thought folks were mostly either ugly or too pretty to be interesting. As for football, he played like a man who wanted to end it all. At six feet and 250 pounds, he wasn't as big as your average middle linebacker, but he was twice as mean on the field. Didn't care who he ran over, or what kind of collision he caused, he just went after it. That's what he called it too, "going after it."

You remember Darius Exley, our tall, lithe, unbelievably fast wide receiver. Guy could leap as high as a pole-vaulter and snatch the ball out of the air almost from any angle around his body. If you got the ball near him, he would get it. He collected action figure dolls. Like hundreds of them, with all their various weapons. He was proud of that collection. Guys on other teams would tease him about his "toys," but he said nothing, quiet as a stopped clock, like he couldn't care less what anyone called him. He could move so swiftly, he'd catch eleven balls and score four touchdowns and have nothing whatever to say about it. Nothing excited him, it seemed, but that doll collection.

Lined up on the other side of the line was our so-called possession receiver, Rob Anders. Rob was gay, one of the first players to admit it while still playing the game. He was only five feet eleven inches tall, and weighed barely more than 170 pounds—pretty slight for a wide receiver—but he was a great roll blocker. He could put a bigger man on his belly so quick you'd think somebody blew off the guy's legs. He never put anybody on his back, but if a defender was running forward, coming up to tackle a runner on Anders's side, it was really something to see how fast Anders would make him disappear. From the opposite side it looked like the guy fell into a ditch or something. Anders could also catch anything near him, sometimes with one hand. He scored so many touchdowns leaping parallel to the ground and grabbing a ball just before it hit the ground with the palm of one hand, and flipping over on his side before he landed—he could roll in the air like a fish in water—that after a while, folks stopped calling him anything other than "Porpoise."

At running back, of course, was Walter Mickens, from Georgia. He was six feet, weighed around 220, and could run as fast as anybody in the league except maybe Darius Exley. He could also move diagonally, or sideways, and even jump backward and come down still moving; he hit the ground full speed from any angle. He was hard to bring down, too. He had a little twist he'd make with his hips and if you had your hands there trying to drag him down, he'd throw you off like water from a bucket. The fans called him "Mighty Mickens." He was a religious fanatic. Had one cross tattooed on his neck and one on each arm. He believed god was a football fan and kept a little shrine to Christ in his locker.

Don't worry, I'm not going to go over the whole roster—that would take too long, and to tell the truth, not all of them are that interesting. (There's a roster in the back of this book that you can consult if you need to, along with a schedule and some other things.) Just the superfreaks, most of whom, by this point, were fully established players you knew would make the team. And the rookie, Orlando Brown, was a shoe-in. Unless he turned out to be weak in the knees, literally—because at his height just about everybody who tried to block him would be at his knees—he would definitely be what Coach Engram and everybody else called an "impact player." If we could only get these guys to play together—to work together and become one beast—it seemed like nobody would be able to whip them.

The truth was, I looked forward to the year. I knew Engram was probably a little worried about his job because it had started to look like we were slipping, and the owner—well, I don't want to get into talking about him yet. He's not really as cold-blooded as everybody thinks—I mean he's got his loyalties and attachments just like anybody else, but he's not the kind of man who can tolerate a downward trend in anything. Coach Engram never spoke to me about it, except to mention that things were going to be tough this year, but I had the feeling he'd been given the impression that our owner was getting impatient.

See, for the past two years or so our one real problem was, as you might have guessed, at quarterback.

Now, we had a great player there. Corey Ambrose had proven himself over and over to be a winner. He could throw the ball reasonably well—accurate from forty or fifty if you gave him time to throw—and the other players liked playing for him. He had what the receivers call a "soft ball." It came in spinning just right, and without too much steam on it, usually out in front of them, easy enough to snatch out of the air. In tight situations, he could stand up to the pressure as well as anyone, and he almost never threw the ball so that his receivers had to stretch out and reach for it in traffic—what players call being "hung out to dry." You could get a few smashed ribs that way, and both Exley and Anders, and the other men who were responsible for catching what Ambrose put up for them, appreciated his accuracy.

But he was always getting hurt. The kind of small nagging injuries that weren't so bad for somebody who plays linebacker or center, but ones that cripple a quarterback. The year before, he sat out five games because of a broken middle finger on his throwing hand. Do you know how many times a guy in any other position breaks his finger in a given year? How many men play with multiple broken fingers? Nobody talks about it, but believe me, most of the lineman have broken fingers at least once or twice in the course of a season; some, in the course of a game. The year before that, Ambrose developed a severe case of laryngitis; couldn't raise his voice above a whisper. It hung on for two weeks and just to be safe, the doctor ordered another week of silence after that. He missed three games because he couldn't call the signals. None of that would have been so bad, but he always acted like some kind of dispossessed royalty. The guy was good and he knew it. So he would damn well stay on his ass until he was good and healed, never once fearing for his job. He knew it was his. (And let me tell you, I hate that kind of certainty.)

The guy we had playing behind him was another freak. A tall, lanky kid from Oklahoma named Ken Spivey who could whip the ball far enough and, when he was on his game, throw pretty accurately, too. Only he was erratic. He still had not fully grasped the playbook, and what was worse, he let things upset him—had a terrible temper—and when he got angry he'd lose concentration, which is to say, he'd lose his talent. I mean *all* of it. Hell, he'd lose the ability to *hold* a football, much less throw the damned thing. You could tell when he was getting upset, because his face would turn bright red. And you know *what* upset him? He didn't like it when somebody pushed him or knocked him down. Which tends to happen a lot in football, especially when a fellow is playing quarterback.

The third-string guy was Jimmy Kelso. He's a head coach now, but back then he was one of those fellows you like to have around because he was plenty smart and plenty willing. He played well in college, showed he could lead a team downfield. His passes were unerringly accurate—I mean he could drop the ball over a guy's shoulder and into his arms before he had time to look for it. Problem was, he couldn't throw the ball very far. The arm strength just wasn't there. We used him in practice a lot, especially when we wanted our defense to be ready for a short, quick passing game, but even then you have to be able to really fire the ball sometimes. For a quick-out pass, where the wide receiver runs five to seven steps and then breaks toward the sideline, the quarterback has to be able to put the ball in the air, on a line, with little or no arch, twenty to twenty-five yards, before the receiver makes his cut toward the sideline. When he does make his cut and turns his head to look for the ball, it's supposed to be right there in front of him. Half the time Kelso couldn't even make that simple pattern work. He'd throw it quickly enough, but the ball wouldn't have enough steam on it and a lot of the time the defensive back or even a linebacker would simply knock it down, or worse, intercept it. When you intercept that kind of pass, there's only three people who can stop you from taking it back all the way "to the house," as the players still like to say: the receiver you jumped in front of to intercept it—and he's usually moving pretty fast in the *other* direction, and therefore isn't likely to catch up to anybody; the quarterback, who generally isn't very fast, or likely to be able to tackle a coatrack; and the referee, who is usually racing down the field next to the interceptor so he can signal touchdown. So an interception under those circumstances is a pretty grim development—

and, unfortunately, what you could frequently expect with Kelso leading the charge.

The truth is, in spite of the All-Pro talent at starter, and the almost prissy cockiness of our bench, we were considered pretty weak at quarterback.

I got back from my vacation on a Thursday, but I didn't go to Redskins Park right away. I had another few days to relax before I had to get back, and I wanted to do a little scouting.

This was a joke I kept up for myself: that I was actually scouting Jesse Smoke. The truth is, I wanted to see her in a real football situation, so I got on the Internet and looked up the Washington Divas. Turned out, they played an eight-game season, and though they were located out in Prince George's County, Maryland, in Ruby Park, they played their games at Spellman High School in D.C. Tickets were all of five dollars. Their first game was three weeks away, on April 1, a Friday night.

So, they were a professional team, I guess, but three weeks to get ready for a season wasn't a lot of time.

I went to the "tryouts."

I saw Jesse zipping a few balls here and there and a lot of long, lanky women dropping most of what she threw. I saw her lighten up a bit, take it more softly, and gently lay the ball out there. After a while, she looked like our third stringer, Kelso, and the girls were catching it now. It was clear Jesse was going to make the team. The coach—a big burly-looking fellow who wore horn-rimmed glasses, hollered in a very high-pitched voice, and used his whistle way too much—kept her in for almost every drill. When one of the other Diva wannabes tried her hand at it, he would soon have Jesse talking to her, showing her where she needed to improve.

I was kind of sorry to see that she had to soften her throws, though. I really was. Seemed a shame to take somebody down from such a great height. See, the ability to throw a football forty to fifty miles an hour, it's the equivalent of a ninety-nine mile an hour fastball.

The thing I noticed about Jesse's play, though, wasn't so much her arm. The coach had her holding back on that talent pretty quickly. No, what I noticed was her footwork. Only five quarterbacks in history, maybe, had perfect footwork: Bob Griese, Joe Namath, Dan Marino, Tom Brady, and Jonathon Engram. Don't get me wrong—there have been truly great quarterbacks who just didn't happen to have very good footwork. Johnny Unitas always looked like he was trying to get his feet out of horseshit when he dropped back to pass. Sonny Jurgensen skipped in a little backpedaling semicircle, like a boxer retreating from an especially capable and damaging left jab. Brett Favre seemed to shimmy back, as though his pants were full of ice cubes. Joe Montana crossed his legs like a ballet dancer, not a quarterback, and sometimes he planted both feet and seemed to hop a little before he made up his mind where he was going with the ball. Peyton Manning backed up or retreated sideways like a man trying to keep his feet dry by dodging an oncoming wave on a beach. A lot of great quarterbacks just couldn't master the footwork. Somehow each of those guys managed to over-come bad form, and perhaps that is why they were such memorable players—for all they managed to do in spite of their poor footwork. But Griese? He set the standard. The rest of those guys—Namath, Marino, Brady, and Engram, too—perfect footwork. I can't describe it exactly, but I know it when I see it. And Jesse had it. When she dropped back to pass it was like watching a cartoon of perfection; like some instructional video from on high on the art of quarterbacking.

She also had an unbelievably quick release. Once she made up her mind to throw it, the ball left her hand nearly instantaneously.

When the tryouts ended, after Jesse had put her equipment in a big bag that Nate hoisted on his shoulder, I walked over and made my presence known to her.

The coach knew exactly who I was, and told me he was honored to meet me.

"I just thought I'd come out," I said. "You know, see what's going on here."

He laughed. Then he told me he'd played for the University of Pittsburgh. "I was a guard." He smiled. "Andy Swilling. I was pretty good, but I didn't get drafted by any of the NFL teams. I couldn't even draw their interest as an undrafted free agent. Too small."

He'd made up some ground on his size, I saw, though not necessarily the right kind, so I didn't say anything. Jesse motioned for Nate to put down the equipment bag. When he recognized me, he came over and took my hand. "How you doing? Come to see Jesse play?"

The coach looked at me. "You know Jesse?"

"She can throw a football," I said.

"I know. I think we're going to have a pretty good team this year."

I asked him how long he'd been coaching the Divas.

"Since our first year."

I waited.

"Six years ago."

"It's a whole league and everything," Nate said.

"Who won last year's championship?" I asked.

Nate looked over to Andy who answered for him. "The Philadelphia Fillies. They're pretty tough."

"Really."

"Yeah. They've won it every year since they came into the league. Before that it was the Cleveland Bombers."

"So the Fillies new to the league?"

Andy shrugged. "There's a few women's professional football leagues, believe it or not. The Fillies came from the WFA—the Women's Football Association."

"And your league?"

"We're the IWFL. The Independent . . ."

"*Women's* Football League." I finished for him and he looked a little embarrassed.

"Right."

"Strange, I don't understand why I never heard of—" I stopped. "Anyway, it's news to me. Isn't that something?"

"Yes, sir."

"Women's professional football."

"There's also the WPFL, the Women's Professional Football League, and the—"

"No, I get it," I said.

Jesse, who had not said a word up to this point, now moved a little closer to me. "What are you doing here?" she said, looking into my eyes.

"I wanted to see you throw a ball to somebody, you know, with folks chasing after you."

"Why?"

"I told you."

"You were serious?"

"You think I wasn't?"

She looked away.

"I'd hoped you'd call me." I tried to keep it easy, cheerful. "Thought we had a deal."

"Seven hundred," she said.

"Sure, why not?"

"Seven hundred for what?" Andy said.

"This fellow wants to use me for some sort of practical joke," she said. Then she turned back to me. "I was going to call you."

"It's not a practical joke exactly," I said.

She smirked, stepped back a little, then still looking at me said, "Let's get going, Nate."

"Seriously," I said. "I'll pay you."

"Hey," Andy said. "What *is* this?"

I looked at him.

"What's going on? Are you trying to . . . What's going on?"

"Nothing complicated. Really. I just want her to come down to Redskins Park when we have our second minicamp."

"You want her to try out or something?" He said this with a half smile.

"Right," I said. "Because that makes a hell of a lot of sense."

"Well what do you want her for, then?"

"I guess I'd like some of our more complacent players to see her throw a football."

"I'm sorry. But she's not going to be able to do any of that until the end of our season."

"Fine. The hell with minicamp. She can come to our first real camp, in July. Your season ends the first week in June. I looked it up."

He looked at Jesse. Everyone was quiet for a moment. Then I said, "It would sure be something to see Jesse throw the ball to Darius Exley."

That did the trick. "Okay, then. You get me in to watch her there," Andy said, "and I'll help arrange it."

"I'd be glad to."

"Nobody needs to help arrange anything," Jesse said.

Andy reddened slightly. "No, I just meant I won't stand in the *way*."

"That would be great," I said, feeling good about where we were leaving it.

As I was turning to leave, Andy touched my arm. "And maybe tickets? If you could spare a couple of tickets every now and then?"

"Sure," I said. I had an allotment every year, and no family to speak of. I could always give away a few tickets if I needed to.

Three

COACH ENGRAM WAS in his office as usual when I finally reported back to Redskins Park, but I didn't want to let him in on my little joke yet. I was pretty confident I could arrange the thing as long as I didn't get into gender. He was on the phone when I stepped into the room, but he motioned for me to sit down. I glanced at the sports page a while, trying not to overhear the conversation, in case it was private, but then I realized he was talking to the Minnesota Vikings general manager about "upgrades" at various positions, including quarterback, but none of it seemed to go anywhere. When he was done, he hung up the phone and smiled. "Enjoy your vacation?"

I told him I'd had a great time.

"You go with anybody this time?"

"Nope."

"Okay," he said, again with a smile. "So what's with the shit-eating grin? What's on your mind?"

"I found a quarterback."

"Really."

"You're not going to believe it."

"Try me." He sat back and relaxed in the big black leather chair he almost never used. He looked just then like an owner, not a coach. He had put on weight since he quit playing—not enough that you'd call him fat, but he was definitely pushing the limits of his belt back then, and wasn't near so lean as he is now. He had dark brown hair, slicked straight back off his forehead, and a wide, jutting jaw edged in short gray stubble. From the neck up he looked like a cross between Vince Lombardi and Don Shula. An imposing kind of thing sitting across from him, I gotta tell ya.

"This particular player has no college experience."

"Where'd you see him?"

Now I was about to cross into the realm of fiction. I had to lie a little, see, and leave out gender, but I told myself it was innocent enough—just a small lie of omission. "In Belize, first, on the beach."

He looked at me as though something had erupted from my forehead. Stumbling on a player when you're not actively scouting and going through the considerable work and vigilance of the scouting department tends not to inspire a lot of confidence.

"Trust me, Jon. This player throws the ball as well as you ever did. I've seen scrimmages with—I saw this player in action against others, okay? I saw the footwork, the mechanics. Mechanically, she's perfect." I felt my blood turn up in the creases of my neck as I let out that word. But he didn't seem to notice.

"You've talked to the kid?"

"I did. And I extended an invitation to camp this summer."

"Why not get him in here in the spring? Or hell, next week?"

"I was lucky to get a commitment for this summer."

"You believe in this guy?"

"Absolutely. You got to see for yourself."

23

He shrugged. "All right. Go talk to Charley and get what you need from him. If it's not going to break the bank to bring the kid in, I don't see why not."

I got up to leave. "You won't regret it, Coach," I said.

"What's the kid's name?"

"Jesse," I said. "Jesse Smoke."

He said nothing, but the name had to have gotten stuck in there under his scalp. It's a pretty hard name to forget, ain't it?

So I went to Charley Duncan, our general manager. Charley doesn't like to spend a lot of time talking to assistants until after draft day, but once he confirmed with Engram, he told me to go ahead. I could sign Jesse Smoke for the minimum NFL salary, which was over a half a million dollars a year back then. Charley even told me I could give the kid a signing bonus if I wanted. "No more than sixty-five or seventy K," he said.

"Absolutely."

"And I'll pray your boy can throw the ball better than Corey Ambrose."

"Just has to throw it as well, right? Then we won't worry if Ambrose gets a run in his hosiery or breaks a fingernail."

"Very funny."

He didn't know how funny it was. Come to think of it, I didn't either, until I was out the door.

You might think I should have been a little worried about folks not taking my idea too kindly; I mean, I really did half believe it was only a pretty elaborate joke. I was famous for that kind of thing anyway. But once I had permission to actually sign somebody? I started believing it. *Why not?* I found myself thinking. Why can't we do the unthinkable and sign the first woman to an NFL team? I knew folks would say it was against the rules, but I couldn't remember seeing anything about that one.

Well you know, I started doing a little research into the rules, and like everything else that is written down, the rules are subject to interpretation. They really are.

Case in point: The first forward pass was thrown not by somebody who knew the rules, just by a man who thought it might work. And when nobody could find anything in the original rule book preventing it, they simply added a few rules to govern it.

Legend has it that Knute Rockne of Notre Dame was the first to try it when he was a player there, but that's not really true. It was Pop Warner, coaching in Carlisle, Pennsylvania, who started using it pretty regularly and was beating people with it in 1907, long before Rockne helped beat Army with it in 1913. The Carlisle team was made up of American Indians—among them, Jim Thorpe—and they perfected it, the forward pass. Eventually college football changed the rules to make it more acceptable as a strategy in a game. All of this was before pro football even got off the ground, so the forward pass did begin in the college game. Before Pop Warner used it, only a few teams tried one or two of them in a game every now and then, but it was considered a "sissy" move by just about everybody. Then Pop Warner started killing other teams with it.

The new rules the leagues originally put in were pretty strict and forbidding. If you tried a forward pass and it fell incomplete, it was a fifteen-yard penalty. Also, one of your players had to touch the thing when you tried it. If you threw the ball over his head and he didn't touch it, the defense could recover it and take it back the other way. Finally, you had to throw it over the middle only—a ten-yard space in the center—or you were penalized. For a long time that was all the rules said about it.

When pro football got going, they pretty much adopted the college rules. By that time Warner had so popularized the forward pass, other teams, including Notre Dame, were also using it and the rules had changed to accommodate it. No more fifteen-yard penalty. An incomplete pass was just that. Nobody had to touch it and it didn't go over to the other team. Of course the rule book says all kinds of things about throwing the ball now, and hundreds of rules developed over almost a hundred years of playing. But for sure the first time anybody did it, there was nothing in the rules about it one way or the other.

There's nothing to prevent a woman from playing in the NFL either, if you read the rules with the idea that all references to "man" or "men" are generic rather than specific. Like when somebody says, "The rights of man" or "All men are created equal," they're not talking about *just* men, right? I mean, that's how they interpreted it in the beginning probably, way back there when the Frenchmen and Americans were writing all that stuff down. But nobody today would dare suggest that's what it actually means. Similarly, in football the rules make all kinds of references to eleven men to a side, man-to-man, when a man does this or a man does that, and so on. But there is no rule, specifically, that says only men can play in these games and that no women are allowed. None. Go ahead, look it up.

You know, it's funny now, but even way back then I was starting to believe in it. I'd remember what the ball looked like sailing off the tip of Jesse Smoke's arm, and think, *Why the hell not?*

Four

A LONG TIME ago, quarterbacks called their own plays. They would take time as they played to set up certain strategies, or they'd go for it all right off the bat just to set the tone of a game. A lot of them practiced every day with the same receivers and learned speed, quickness, stopping ability, cuts at every angle, and just about anything else they could about a receiver's movements. Most of the time they "looked" for a receiver running a planned route, and when they didn't see him, they "looked" for another one running a different route. It was all done with sight; with what the quarterback could see. The great ones had terrific vision—from sideline to sideline. I'm talking about peripheral vision as well as twenty-twenty. They could pick a guy out when they weren't actually looking his way, turn to him, and release the ball with a snap to get it to him. Since a receiver always knows where he is going and the quarterback has rehearsed the same play with him over and over in practice, it worked pretty well. Guys like Raymond Berry and Fred Biletnikoff who couldn't outrun a tree sloth but who had great hands and could cut (change direction) on a dime caught enough balls to get to the Hall of Fame. The quarterback knew how to find them and hit them as they moved.

Over the years, a lot of that changed. But those changes were not brought about simply by altering the rules; strategy, how the men played the game—that changed as well. Even so, here, very basically, is how the defense on a team lined up on the field back then:

```
      SS                          S

              LB      LB      LB
      CB          DE DT  DT DE          CB
_____
```

SS = strong safety, S = safety, LB = linebacker, CB = cornerback, DE = defensive end, DT = defensive tackle

The defense above is called a "four-three" because there are four linemen and only three linebackers. Lots of teams played this defense, including Engram's Redskins.

Some play what is called a "three-four." They look the same except they've got only three linemen and four linebackers, like this:

```
      SS                                  S

              LB   LB  LB  LB
      CB          DE   DT  DE                CB
_____
```

The linemen and the linebackers concentrate mostly on stopping the run and getting to the quarterback before he can throw the ball. The cornerbacks and safeties are called "defensive backs," and they try to "cover" the receivers to keep them from catching the ball. They either play "man-to-man," which means they take on one of the receivers and go with him wherever he goes, or in what's called a "zone" defense, in which they take an area of the field and cover that whenever anybody ventures into it. Sometimes if the offense is running plays with three, four, or even five receivers, defenses will take out linebackers and replace them with extra defensive backs. One extra defensive back is called a "nickle" defense. Two, is called a "dime." Four extra defensive backs is called a "quarter defense." (I'll explain the offense in a bit.) Sometimes a defense will play zone on one side of the field and man-to-man on the other. All of the possible combinations of those defenses come into play with the sole purpose of confusing a quarterback. Defenses always try to disguise what they are doing.

Over the years, combination zone defenses and man-to-man variations got pretty good at slowing down the receivers who could speed past a defensive back and break into the open, often by bumping the receiver and knocking him off his path while he passed through their zone.

Eventually defenses got so quick and so complex that the coaches themselves started calling the plays instead of the quarterback. This didn't start until the early to mid-eighties or so, but it caught on and now we haven't seen a quarterback who calls his own plays since Peyton Manning with Indianapolis and later the Broncos.

But that does not mean the quarterback doesn't have real hard things to do. He's got to be sure of himself without being cocky; he's got to think fast and make decisions in a fraction of a second; he's got to read what defensive players are up to—both recognizing align-ments (how men are placed on the field, how they are moving when his own men move) and also characteristics of individual players he's studied on film. (He might know something about a middle line-backer that the middle linebacker himself doesn't know.) He has to know when a defensive player is feigning a blitz—that is, rushing the passer—and when he's really coming.

Now I don't want to bore everybody with a lot of football terms or strategies. But this much is important to know if you're going to appreciate what Jesse Smoke accomplished in her short career: A quarterback has got to see the whole field as if it was vertical in front of him instead of horizontal; as if he was looking down on it from above. Now, he's got what's called a "passing tree" for each receiver in his head and in front of him. A receiver has a wide variety of moves he can make and patterns he can run. But all of them come off his position on the field and the initial path he might take, and when you draw it all up on a board it looks like a tree. It really does. Here's a partial map of some of the moves a wide receiver on the left side of the line might be asked to make. Bear in mind, these are "routes" he would run as fast as he can immediately after the ball is snapped by the center to the quarterback.

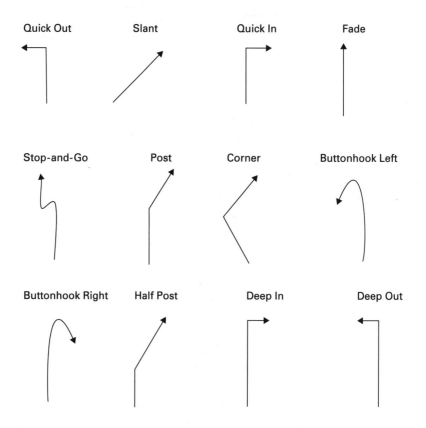

A "quick out" goes only five to seven yards. Same thing with a "quick in." A "deep out" can be the same move but much deeper down the field—fifteen or twenty yards or more. There's a wide variety of other moves—the "come back," the "curl-and-go," the "in-and-out," which combines a "slant in" with a "corner" route. If it's an angle in geometry, football's got a name for it and you can draw it on a board. Now each player who is eligible to run a pattern and catch a pass is assigned one of the above moves on any given passing play. Put all of the possibilities for one receiver together, and they look like this:

A Typical Passing Tree

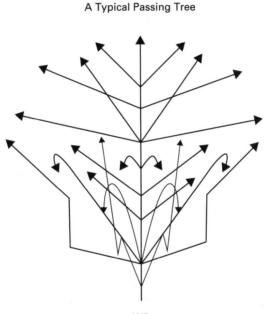

WR

That's a passing tree for just one wide receiver. In the playbook, each one of those little arrows has a number or a name. When the quarterback calls a play, like "66, yellow 40, 22Xgo," each one of the receivers has a designated path to follow (one of the little arrows above). So as you can see, everything is done as precisely as possible. Each receiver has his own passing tree, the quarterback calls plays based on the pattern from the tree that he wants from each receiver, and each one knows where he's supposed to be on every play. That's his responsibility. He must cut left or right at precise angles, all of them identified on paper and practiced over and over again in drills on the field. The quarterback, then, has to know where every one of them is supposed to be, and he has to do this with as many as five different players at once.

So now here's how an offense lines up on the field:

WR............................TE...LT...LG...C...RG...RT............................WR
QB

FB   HB

WR = wide receiver, TE = tight end, LT = left tackle, LG = left guard, C = center, RG = right guard, RT = right tackle, FB = fullback, HB = halfback or running back, QB = quarterback

The quarterback takes the ball directly from the center in this formation. That side of the line where the tight end lines up is called the "strong side." The tight end can be an extra blocker on running plays or a receiver who runs one of the patterns on the passing tree. The dotted line is the scrimmage line. The center lines up directly over the ball at the beginning of every play and play begins when he "hikes" (snaps) it to the quarterback. There must be seven men on this line at all times before a play—you can have more than seven, but not less. The rule says, "Eligible receivers must be on both ends of the line, and all of the players on the line between them must be ineligible receivers," that is, they cannot catch a pass or take a hand off from the quarterback. There are a wide variety of variations on this rule, however. Some teams will use what is called a "slot receiver" and replace the fullback with another wide receiver and place him just behind the line of scrimmage but split wide between the tackle and the wide receiver on a given side. Sometimes they'll use four wide receivers, no tight end, and one running back; or even five wide receivers. Here's an example of a three-wide-receiver formation. In this set, a running back is replaced with another wide receiver and he lines up in the slot, between the right tackle and the wide receiver on the right side. So on this one play, the quarterback would have this kind of set up, and expectation.

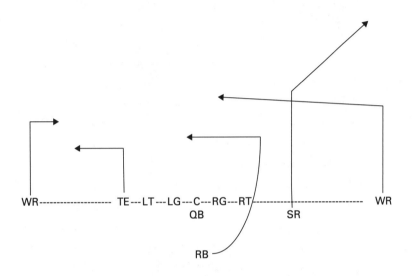

On most plays there are five men on offense the quarterback can throw to: two wide receivers, two running backs, and a tight end. With the above play, there is only one running back and three wide receivers, the two on the outside lined up on the line of scrimmage and the slot receiver.

In four-wide-receiver sets, there is no running back, but an extra slot receiver who would line up on the left and parallel to the slot receiver on the other side. In a five-wide-receiver set, teams take out the tight end and split a wide receiver out five yards or so from the line like this:

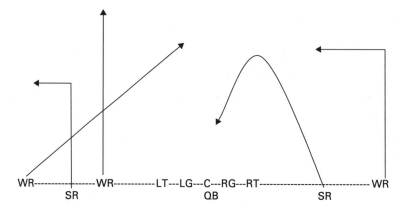

WR----------+------WR------------LT---LG---C---RG---RT----------------+-----------WR
      SR   QB   SR

What you see here are individual plays, with one of the moves on the passing tree assigned to each player. When the quarterback calls a play like this, he knows each of these paths or routes that his receivers will run. And when there are four or five wide receivers, the defense puts in extra defensive backs and takes out linebackers.

That is, very simply, how it works. Now remember, each of these is one play, and there are hundreds of plays, all predicated on the single moves possible in each receiver's passing tree. Each of the receivers in the plays above, according to the design of each particular play, must make one of the moves on the passing tree. It just depends on which play the quarterback has called.

Above all, the quarterback's got to release the ball quickly, once he knows where he's going with it. All of this he's got to do in less than four seconds, while men twice his size are fighting furiously to get to him and knock him down. When a quarterback can do all these things with absolute calm, without dancing on his feet, or "stuttering" as some coaches call it, and throw the ball exactly as the situation demands—either lofting it gently and letting it fall softly over a receiver's shoulder and into his hands as he runs, or firing it on a line, with almost no arch in its trajectory whatsoever, to an instantaneously selected spot on the field no larger than the hole in a tire, so that a receiver running full speed runs into it precisely as he turns, and snatches it out of the air—then, well then you've got something.

Those quarterbacks of the past who called their own plays, who planned an offensive strategy while they were doing everything else; who adapted to the game as it developed and altered their play calling to suit the situation on the field—they had to have been geniuses. I know I couldn't do it. Coach Engram is one of the most intelligent men I've ever met, and he never did it.

Five

FAR AS I know, not one single person who has written a book on Jesse has ever *seen* a women's game. Well, I went to every Divas game I could that spring. They were all at night, these games—under very poor lights with fewer than a thousand fans watching. The girls had old, discarded high school equipment, but the jerseys and helmets were new, so they looked more or less like a team. But they were slow, too. I have to admit that. Jesse moved around in the pocket, though, like a pro: She read the field, saw receivers, and easily flipped the ball over defenders into their arms. When she was hurried or flushed out of the pocket, she showed that she could throw on the run. She was never terribly rattled.

I noticed just one weakness. In a game against the Philadelphia Fillies—who were tougher and faster than any other team she faced—she started throwing off her back foot as she fell away from the pass rush. That's a bad habit. She could still throw fairly accurately that way, and remember she was always taking something off the ball—I mean she wasn't ever trying to throw very hard, so it wouldn't hurt her arm to be doing that a few times—but if she let it become habit, and then kept doing that when she *was* trying to throw hard, it would ruin her perfect form, to say nothing of her arm.

I hung around after each game to talk to her. Sometimes the four of us—Jesse; her coach, Andy; Nate; and I—would go get something to eat downtown. I always paid for dinner. That night she played the Fillies was a hard time for all of us. Bigger and faster than the Divas, the Fillies didn't throw the ball much. All they did was run it, really, up the gut. Play after play. They had a huge offensive line—women who could probably play college ball—and they just pushed their way down the field. They kicked to the Divas and Jesse started a pretty good march down the field with a few passing plays, but then she got sacked for a ten-yard loss and the Divas had to punt. The Fillies used up the entire first quarter to score one touchdown. Jesse drove the Divas down the field in five plays and threw a 15-yard touchdown pass to her favorite target—a tall, lean, bony young woman named Michelle Cloud.

But when they kicked it back to the Fillies, the Divas didn't see the ball on offense again in the first half. Starting at their 18-yard line, the Fillies drove the ball downfield in eighteen small-yardage running plays and scored another touchdown just before the half.

The Divas had to kick it to the Fillies to start the second half, and it was all over after that. The Fillies took it down the field again, bulling their way in for another touchdown, and even though Jesse hit Michelle with a 45-yard bomb and another touchdown, the Divas could not stop the Fillies' offense. Their kicker made every extra point, while the Divas missed one, leading to a final score of 28 to 20.

At dinner everybody was a little down. The Fillies, big and clumsy as they were, should not have bullied the Divas so completely. At least that's what Coach Andy said. "We've got so much more finesse than they have."

"I thought we'd have time to come back," Nate said. He always talked about the team that way, as if he'd been right on the field beside them. Of course, most football fans do that. "We'll get them next time," they say. It's always a game "we" play, fans and players alike.

Jesse herself was not too glum. She always seemed to maintain the most even disposition, like an airplane that flies above the storms. She had cut her hair pretty short for the season, and it stuck up now a bit in the back. She wore no makeup, but she didn't really need it with those naturally dark eyebrows arching perfectly over her deep-set blue eyes. Her lips, too, were naturally red tinted. I already mentioned the brown freckles that ran across her lovely broad nose. And when she smiled, her cheeks themselves seemed to light up.

In the fourth quarter of the game, when the score was 28 to 14, she drove the Divas down the field with a series of short, quick passes. (The Fillies, having wised up to Michelle, always had two defenders following her now at all times.) Finally realizing the drive was taking too much time, Jesse decided to try one last deep pass. She wanted to go to the other wide receiver, Brenda Smalls, who could catch the ball nearly as well as Michelle, though she was not as tall or fast. She might have gotten open, too, but the play took too long to develop, and before Jesse could let the ball fly, a big defensive end knocked her flat on her back. I saw her head bounce off the turf. She rolled over and seemed to stare at the ground a few inches from her nose, then she got herself back up, and though she was a little wobbly, went back to the huddle and called the next play. I could see she had a bloody lip. The defender had put her helmet right under Jesse's chin and driven her to the ground. It was a miracle she hadn't fumbled.

Now, at dinner, she seemed a bit groggy. I asked her if she was all right.

"I'm fine."

"You took a good hit there near the end."

"I'm all right," she said. "Really. Bumped my head. That's it."

All of them wanted to know what was going on with the Redskins, how the preparations for the new season were going. I'd been working ten hours a day, watching film and grading players, both ours and the ones from other teams we might be interested in. I scouted players being phased out or in danger of being cut by other teams; I even paid attention to players who might want to make a move through free agency the following year. I studied films of college players who'd not been drafted. We were always looking for new talent.

My job, though, involved finding offensive players. If I happened to notice a guy playing great defense against the people I was looking at, then I'd let somebody on the defensive side know, of course. We were also evaluating our playbook, looking at film from last year's games and grading those plays that worked most smoothly and the ones that had a higher percentage of screwups.

Nothing is more continually evaluated, designed, and redesigned than an NFL team. Trust me. Nothing on earth. Not even the most complex surgical unit goes under so much self-examination and retooling as we do. And now, almost nothing is more expensive. The annual payroll of the average NFL team would supply the entire U.S. Army.

Anyway, I told them a little of what I was doing, and then tried to turn the conversation back to the game. I wanted to see what Jesse thought about losing; how it affected her.

Nate made a few remarks about how great she had played, completing 14 of 18 passes and throwing for 3 touchdowns. He was amazed by how well she stood up to the pass rush. Then he began talking about how tough the Fillies were.

"It's always either you guys or the Fillies, isn't it?" I said to Andy.

"The Cleveland Bombers are tough, too. But yeah. It's going to be between the Fillies and us. Their coach is a woman, too."

"Does that make a difference?" I said.

"No," said Jesse.

"They play a different kind of game, though, don't they," I said. "What'd they throw, two passes all day?"

"Three," Nate said. "I counted 'em."

"And they completed all three of them," Jesse said.

"Something's good about that brand of football," I said. It was true, of course. As anybody who follows the game knows, if you've got the ball on offense and you can keep it a long time, the defense gets tired, time begins to run out. And if you can score at the end of a long drive, it takes something out of the other team; they get the idea they can't possibly stop you.

"Our defense played pretty well," Andy said. "They fought it out. Just the Fillies play like men."

Jesse looked at him.

"I mean—sorry. I didn't mean that the way it sounded."

"You'll get a chance to play them again," I said to Jesse, "if you make the playoffs."

"If I had a choice about it," she said, calmly, "I'd line up on the field right now and play them again."

"That's the spirit," Andy said.

That was the spirit all right. He had no idea what it meant to hear her talk like that. She may have been on the losing side, but she was absolutely undefeated.

Even that early on, I wanted to spend as much time as possible watching Jesse. I wanted to get to know her better than you generally want to know even a top prospect. What kept going through my mind was, *What if she really has what it takes?* Without ever really making a choice one way or the other, I was getting more and more serious about her. She seemed to like me, although she was not particularly open about anything other than football.

I only saw her play in four games, and except for the loss to the Fillies, the others were a breeze. She threw seven touchdown passes against the Baltimore Beauties. Six against the Pittsburgh Bombshells. Not once did I see her lose her cool. The only time she faced any real pressure and got hit hard, she got back up and kept playing. But even in that game she hadn't allowed herself to be

40

pushed too much. She could get rid of the ball so fast, a pass rush couldn't agitate her.

She did start throwing off her back foot against the Fillies, like I said, but the next time I saw her play she stepped into each throw as perfectly as always. Still, I was worried about that little kink in her delivery, because against a real pass rush it would be the end of her. I wondered what I should do about it.

I knew if I brought her to camp and let Engram see her throw, he'd be impressed. But what then? I realized I was worried about how she would do in camp. Not for the little joke I wanted to play, but because I was beginning to see that she really was a damn good football player. But when Coach Engram saw her against the men—against that massive charge of flesh and bone—she absolutely could not fall away from it and throw the ball. They'd spot it in an instant and that would be that. Rather than try to work with her, they might laugh. A man, they'd work with—they'd drill him and strive through practice and repetition to get the kinks worked out. A woman, though, would be a different animal altogether. To win Engram over the way I was won over, she had to be perfect already, in every possible circumstance of the position. Even then, thinking about all these things, I insisted to myself that it was only a joke I wanted to pull; a shock to the system of some of the more comfortable fellows in camp.

And at the same time, I wondered what she might be able to do with our playbook.

One early morning, I called Jesse and asked if she'd meet me at the Divas' practice field. To be exactly polite about it, I invited Andy Swilling as well. Of course, Nate showed up and so did Michelle Cloud, who looked at me as though I was a rapist.

I had a playbook with me, and a bag of footballs that I'd brought from Redskins Park.

"What's the drill?" Jesse said.

I gave her the playbook. "Study this."

"What is it?"

"Our playbook. You know how to read one?"

She held it in her hands and opened it as though it was some sort of ancient text. More than three hundred pages, it featured a wide variety of plays from almost every conceivable formation. "I can read it," she said. If she was in awe, it was not because anything in the book was too complex for her, but simply because it was a real play-book from an NFL team.

"Study it carefully, then—memorize it if you can."

"I can *have* this?"

"Well, I'm lending it to you. I want it back when you're done."

"Why are you doing this?"

For a moment I was uncertain how to respond. "I really don't know." Everybody looked at me. "I just want you to show up at that camp, you know, as prepared as I can get you."

"Awful lot of work for a practical joke, isn't it?"

"I'm going to sign you," I said now. All four of them looked at me as if I'd just announced my intention to part the waters of the Potomac River. "You'll make a lot of money for it."

Jesse looked at the book in her hands. Then she closed it and held it against her chest. Her face was expressionless.

Andy said, "Can I see it?"

She handed it to him and he flipped through it while we all stood there awkwardly. Then I told Jesse what I'd noticed about her delivery. Andy piped in that he'd noticed it too. Nate and Michelle said nothing.

Jesse mulled it over a bit. "Off my back foot."

"It's pretty well-pronounced. I wish I had film so I could show it to you."

"No. I've seen it on film," she said. "My dad worked with me on it all the time. Said it was my worst flaw."

"He noticed other flaws?"

"Sure."

"Like what?"

"I used to tap the ball before I threw it."

"A lot of quarterbacks do that."

"My father said I did it every time, right before I let the ball go. As soon as I made up my mind where I was going to throw it, I'd tap it, with my left hand, then throw it. He said I was telegraphing my throw, and eventually folks would notice it and then they'd know when to jump to try and knock it down."

"How'd he break the habit?"

"It was hard. First he tried to make me quit by forcing me to throw with one hand, leaving the other one taped to my side. But that was just too awkward. I needed to feel the ball in both hands when I was dropping back. Oddly enough, it helped my form when I run and throw."

"But if that didn't work, then what'd he do?"

"He made me hold a second football under my left arm. My hand was still free to tap the ball I was going to throw, but every time I did, I'd drop the other ball. That worked for a while, but eventually I figured out how to hold the ball under my arm just right so that I had flexibility in my wrist and I could tap the ball again, without dropping the one under my arm, so he gave up on that. He didn't want to, but he did. He sometimes used that football under the arm thing with the wide receivers; he'd make them hold a ball under both arms, run down the field, and catch a third ball without dropping any of them. You try that sometime. But . . . it worked. Made them sure-handed as hell."

"That's what I did with Michelle and Brenda and all the others," Andy said. He had the playbook under his arm now. "Jesse told me about it. I used smaller balls, but it worked."

"I've noticed," I said.

He smiled with pride.

I turned back to Jesse. "So then, how'd your dad beat your habit of tapping the ball? I haven't seen you do that once."

"He rigged up a black rubber glove with a bladder in the palm that made a loud squeak whenever it was pressed. It didn't take long

43

wearing that thing. I'd hear the blare of it every time I tapped the ball, so I'd throw passes until I didn't hear anything anymore. Then I didn't have the habit."

"Your father knew what he was doing."

"He did. Taught me a lot." It was quiet for a beat. Then Jesse said, "Anyway, I've seen myself on film. I know when I'm forced to throw before I'm ready for it I sometimes let it go from my back foot. I don't do it often, though."

"If you were a man, you could do it a lot if you got the ball off under pressure and hit what you were aiming at. Nobody'd care. I'm afraid when we get to camp, though, and let the others see you throw, you can't afford to do that even once."

"You're really serious about this?" she said.

"He must be," Andy said, holding up the playbook.

"I am dead serious." I realized the truth of this even as I spoke the words. I did not want to mislead Jesse, and the joke was not going to be on her. I had a really nervous, kind of scary feeling all over. The way you feel when you're standing on a balcony, fifty floors up, and you look over the edge—the thrilling kind of rush that, for a moment, makes you breathe differently. I was really going to do it; sign her and try to get her a tryout with the team.

I opened the bag of balls and let them out on the ground. It was an absolutely beautiful spring day. The last game of the Divas' season was coming up in a week, but Jesse had no practice until later in the after-noon. Anyway, her coach was right there and we were on their field, so it wasn't as if she could be late.

"What's your dad doing now?" I asked Jesse, flipping her one of the balls.

She held the ball tightly in her hands, looked at Nate, then to the ground. "He passed away my senior year of high school."

I told her I was sorry.

"It was a heart attack," she said, looking back at me.

"He was only fifty-three," Nate said.

"Well, he sure would be pleased to see you play now," I said. I waited a bit, then said something stupid about her mother handling things on her own. It wasn't a question, just an expression of hope that she was all right and all.

Jesse's face lost some of its luster then; she didn't exactly scowl, but something went out of that usually bright demeanor. "I don't know my mother," she said. "She left when I was too young to remember her."

"And you've never seen her since? Never heard from her?"

"No. I don't want to, either." She flipped the ball up and let it spin. Caught it again gently, then flipped it up again—just the way she had that day on the beach when I first saw her.

Andy looked at me. It was clear he'd never heard her talk about her mother or father. This was all news to him. He looked sad to me.

"So what's the drill?" Jesse asked. "You going to teach me something here or what?"

"I'm going to try to."

She flipped the ball again. She looked a little bit like a tall, teenage boy with those brown freckles across her pretty, broad nose.

"You've got to learn to do one of three things when you're under pressure," I said. "Step up, in between rushers and blockers; step to the side a bit and throw, leaning toward your front foot as you should; or take off with it, and throw on the run. What you cannot do is step back and try to whip it off at the same time."

"All of this I know," she said. "But you left out one other option my father taught me."

"What's that?"

She took the ball into her stomach and doubled up, her head down in front of her knees. Then she straightened and looked at me. "Fold 'em. Take the sack."

"Absolutely, he was right about that."

"That's what I can't seem to learn to do, you know? Whenever, I *should* do that, I just end up stepping back and throwing the damn thing."

45

"Well, right now I don't want to drill you on taking sacks. I'd like to see if we can work on the other three options."

"Okay."

So that's what we did. All that morning and even into the afternoon we worked on it. By the time we quit, the other Diva players had arrived for practice and were stretching on the sidelines.

In the first drill, I had Nate and Andy rushing at her, with me and Michelle in front, blocking them, which formed what is called a "pocket." I showed Jesse how to "step up" in the pocket. I could tell she was just humoring me. It was a move that came naturally to her, though I hadn't had a chance to see her do it in a game. She moved forward easily, planted, and threw. Then we stood in front of her and waved towels in her face, overhand, fast and hard so she could feel the wind of them, and she'd step to the side, left and right, plant, and throw. Finally, I had her drop back to pass while Nate, Andy, and I threw footballs at her, not exactly trying to hit her, just having them in the air all at once, coming toward her, while she had to plant, look for Michelle in various pass routes, and hit her on the move. Every time she shied away from one of those footballs, I blew a whistle. A few times she got hit, but we weren't throwing them hard, and after a while, she didn't even flinch.

We repeated the last drill, relentlessly, every chance we got, over the next few weeks, hefting footballs at Jesse, and as far as I could tell she'd stopped throwing off her back foot. She got a bloody nose once (after that I put a helmet on her) and had the wind knocked out of her a few times, but as long as she had the ball in her hands, she never ducked or shied away. Jesse learned and adapted as swiftly as any player I'd ever coached. (We like to call that, "coachability.") But the thing I remember most from all those drills was her power of concentration. After a while, it was as if only she and Michelle were on the field, playing catch. Michelle didn't drop many balls, and Jesse didn't miss once. It really was delightful watching her play.

At the end of one of our little practices, after I had gathered all the balls and bagged them, and we'd all drained a bottle of water or two, as we were walking off the field, Jesse said to me, "You remind me of my father a little bit."

Even back then I was a little portly in the middle, though at six feet four, I suppose I had the height to carry it. I said, "I feel sorry for your father."

"No. I mean the way you coach me."

"Really." I was moved by that, if also a little disappointed. I didn't feel old enough, yet, to be completely eliminated from the romantic arena. Jesse was beautiful. I had been admiring her beauty in just the way a potential suitor admires that sort of thing. But I was just being an old fool, I see now. At twenty-four to my fifty-one, she was almost thirty years younger than me. I guess I was just coming to terms then with the notion that I was too old for a lot of the women I saw and admired. At any rate, it was a high compliment she'd given me, and I was moved when she expressed it. I reached over and tapped her on the shoulder. "He would be very proud of you."

I saw Andy's pace shorten a bit ahead of us, as though he had to avoid stepping on something in front of him.

"You've coached them up well, Andy," I said.

"Thank you. They're a great bunch of gals."

Jesse shot him a look.

"A great bunch," he said again. "Terrific women."

I laughed a little, and Jesse said, "I hate being called a 'gal.'"

"Come on! It's just the opposite of 'guy,'" Andy said.

The truth was Andy had done a good job getting them all to play together, taking advantage of the talent he had on the team. The Divas finished the season at 7 and 1, first place in their division. (They beat the Cleveland Bombers 34-0.) And so they did indeed get a chance to play the Fillies one more time—this time for the championship. I was as excited about that game, I have to say, as any in my own professional career. I couldn't wait to see it.

Six

I SHOULDN'T MENTION my own professional career as if it meant anything. What I mean is, I was not ever a first stringer on any pro team. I played well at the University of Illinois and got enough recognition to be drafted in the fourth round by the Atlanta Falcons. I even got a bit of attention my rookie year because I showed so much "promise," as the sportswriters like to say. In one exhibition game—teams only played two in Jesse's day, but back when I was playing, they played four—I threw three touchdown passes to rally our third stringers to a victory over the Bears' third stringers. That won me a spot as the third-string quarterback that year. I carried a clipboard and studied the playbook and watched a lot of football. In practice I sometimes got to run the "scout" team. Those are the second and third stringers who pretend to be the opposing team of the week and run that team's plays against the first-string defense so they can recognize them in the game. When you are running the plays of the team you're about to play, against the first stringers of your own defense, you don't learn a hell of a lot about how to run your own offense. I was always pretending to be the opposing team's quarterback and sometimes that was fun. I would never admit this to anyone back then, but I got a kick out of beating the defense in practice. You could tell sometimes that it pissed them off, too. They'd make a little more noise when they rushed at me. I used to hear the word "kill" a lot.

Anyway, I ended up playing for half a dozen teams—or, I should say, ended up on the roster of half a dozen teams—and then one year nobody wanted me. In my entire NFL career I threw only twenty-two passes that counted and completed twelve. I never threw a touchdown pass in a regular season game, though I did have a couple of spectacular interceptions, one of them run back more than a hundred yards. It was Reggie Clovis's last interception as a matter of fact, and he is now in the Hall of Fame. The other was only technically an interception. I was playing for the San Diego Chargers at the time. Second-string quarterback behind none other than Jonathon Engram. (That's how we met and became friends, and how I eventually got into coaching.) We were on top in a huge blowout when the coach took Engram out and put me in to "mop up." It was a simple shuttle pass to the halfback—a glorified draw play, really—where you drop back like you're going to throw the ball, then flip it underhand a few feet in front of you to the halfback, who takes off up the middle. Well, I flipped it to the guy and he fiddled with it a bit, almost gently, before a defensive lineman from the other team picked it out of the air in front of him and went the other way with it. In the replays it looked like I'd shuttled the ball to the running back so he could lovingly hand it off to the opposing lineman. Anyway, on his way to the end zone for his big moment in the limelight, the lineman ran right over me and shattered my collarbone.

That was my last game. I got put on injured reserve and spent the rest of that season in a sling. I was released during the off-season, and that was that. Like I said, nobody wanted me.

So, I got into coaching. I started out as a special teams coach with the University of Maryland, then moved to Atlanta and caught on with the Falcons as quarterbacks coach. I stayed in Atlanta a few years and worked my way up. I was offensive coordinator when the head coach got fired and I was asked to serve as interim coach for the last six games of the season. I did pretty well. Coached them to three victories, but at the end of the year, the owner and general manager started their search for a permanent coach, and as the owner said to me, I wasn't "in the mix." That's when Jonathon Engram called. He'd been hired to coach the Redskins and wanted me for his staff. I jumped at the chance, of course; we were already friends, so I knew I could work with him, and I knew I'd probably learn a whole lot about coaching, too.

At any rate, I'd been involved with a very good team or two but had never won a championship. The Redskins had come close that one year, and there was talk that we'd have to make good the year I met Jesse or Jonathon would be out of a job, which of course meant so would I. As they like to say in every sport: The pressure was on.

But with all that stress, you know what I was worried about that spring? The championship battle between the Divas and the Fillies; it really had me tied up in knots. You'd have thought *I* was their head coach, not Andy Swilling.

I stayed away from practice the week before the championship because I didn't want to know Andy's plan for the game; I wanted to watch the thing unfold without the knowledge of how it was supposed to. It's sometimes very rewarding to watch a game that way.

The championship was played at Claremont High School in Northern Virginia—a pretty good field, with far better lighting than they'd had for any of the previous games played in D.C. and freshly limed lines that made it look like the proper venue for a championship. The stadium even had assigned seating in real seats, rather than just elevated boards. There was a pretty good crowd there, too. It wasn't a sellout, but the stands looked pretty well full. I'd say maybe fifteen hundred to two thousand people.

Of course I was invited to watch from the sideline if I wanted, but I preferred watching from the stands, so I bought a seat high up, near the 40-yard line. When I got to the game I stopped near the sideline and waited until a few of the players noticed me. I waved to Jesse and a few of the girls to let them know I was there, then climbed up to my seat. I got up there just in time to see the opening kickoff.

The Divas won the toss but elected to let the Fillies have the ball first. As they had done in the first game, the Fillies started pushing their way down the field. They started at their own 28-yard line, and thirteen plays later were on the Divas' 11. Only this time the girls on defense came on a hell of a lot stronger. On third and 3, the Fillies tried to run it up the middle; one of the girls broke through low and fell in front of the running back, who tripped over her for a 2-yard loss. They were close enough for a field goal, but the kicker missed it. The Divas had stopped the Fillies without a score. Three minutes left in the first quarter, and the score was still 0 to 0.

Andy's game plan became apparent on the Divas' first possession. Everything Jesse threw would be from what they like to call a "quarterback waggle"—rolling slightly to her left or right as she dropped back to pass. Either she'd dump the ball off short or she'd fire it to one of the outside receivers. Andy put Michelle Cloud in motion on almost every play, too. The women's league doesn't use a lot of motion before a play, because that takes so much practice to get right, and the league just doesn't have the facilities or the money to devote that much time to practices. But Michelle was perfect for it. She was smart and never made a mistake. She would move from the left side of the field to the slot position and then, just as the ball was snapped, she would disappear in the confusion for a second before coming open 5 or 10 yards downfield, where Jesse would hit her. The play looked like this:

51

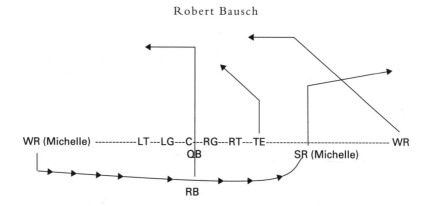

Michelle began the play on the left. As Jesse called the signals, Michelle would go in motion to the slot position on the right. She timed her move to the slot position perfectly. Each time they ran this play, she was in that position the instant before the ball was hiked to Jesse. Jesse would fake a handoff to the running back (who would then run through the line and become a receiver), only to fall back and throw it to Michelle on the outside. Also, they worked out a kind of passing tree for each receiver; I could see that Jesse was throwing to a place on the field. Many times she dropped back, looked to her left, then to her right, then she'd throw the ball 15 yards to what looked like an open space until Michelle or Brenda Smalls would suddenly emerge out of the pack into that area, take the ball from the air, and keep going. Jesse's release was so quick, and the plays developed so quickly, that the Fillies' pass rush was useless. Jesse threw it a lot harder than she had all year too, though still not as hard as she could actually throw it. Michelle didn't drop one ball. Neither did Brenda.

The Divas didn't run the ball much, but they had a dainty little halfback named Cissy Davis who could run and catch. On the last play of their first possession—after they'd driven a little more than 50 yards downfield with quick, short passes to the wide receivers— Jesse threw one of those dump-off passes to Cissy in the flat just to the outside of the pass rush, and she took off like some frightened Pekingese and ran 25 yards for a touchdown.

A flat pass looks like this:

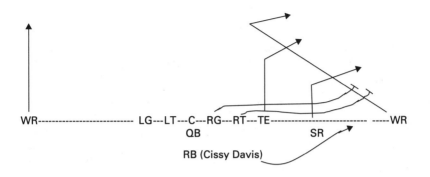

When Cissy got to the "flat," which is just to the right of Jesse in the backfield, a few yards behind the line of scrimmage, Jesse flipped her the ball. The right guard, the tackle, Michelle Cloud, and Brenda Smalls were all in front of her to block, and nobody could catch her.

On their next possession, the Fillies, slow and plodding as always, couldn't even get a first down. The Divas defense, in a kind of frenzy, stayed in their positions, held on to their blockers, and went down with them if they had to. It might have been luck the second time the Divas stopped them, when the Fillies running back fell down trying to cut through a gaping hole in the line, but they went three and out and had to punt from the 50-yard line.

On first down, Jesse flipped another flare pass in the flat to Cissy and she ran for 16 yards. Then on the next play, Michelle went in motion to the strong side, and when the ball was snapped, she took off down the middle of the field. Jesse lobbed it over everybody and hit her on the run for a 69-yard touchdown.

Just like that, the Divas were up 14 points. I could hear the girls screaming and cheering down on the sideline. The crowd got into it too. It was pretty damn noisy and exciting throughout the stands.

The Fillies started getting careless now. When you're trying to catch up, you want to move the ball a little faster and you get nervous about letting your opponent have it back, since another score might finish you. They even tried a few passes—including one that went for 12 yards. But they kept stepping on their own hair, as the saying goes in the women's league. By the end of the first quarter, they were down 21 points.

Jesse was something to watch. She was so sure of herself directing the offense, pointing to places on the field where she wanted folks to move. And I really admired the way Andy Swilling had coached his team for the game. I mean he really *coached* them. They were playing like one beast, every move exactly choreographed as though the plays were rehearsed, rather than practiced. Even the defense played with more confidence. The Fillies pushed them around, as they had before, up and down the field, but every time it looked like they might bully their way into the end zone, the Divas would manage to stop them. The Fillies kicked three field goals out of five tries, but the half was winding down now, and they were getting more and more frustrated. The very thing they were used to exploiting as a weapon ran out on them: time. Though they had the ball for most of the first half, by the time it ended they were down 27 to 9. It was something to see.

I was as deeply involved in that game as any I had ever watched from the stands, or anywhere else, for that matter.

With four possessions in the first half, the Divas scored four touchdowns. (Their kicker missed one extra point.) They had the ball for less than 6 minutes in the entire half. I wanted to go down there at halftime and hug every one of them, including Andy.

It started to rain in the second half, and it was all pretty sloppy after that—sloppy and scoreless. By the end of the game, everybody was making a mess of things. The Fillies started trying to throw the ball even more—they had to catch up, after all—which was something pretty comical, really. I'm sorry to say this, but to put it mildly, their quarterback threw the ball like a girl. And nobody on the Fillies could catch all that well either.

The Divas had their share of mistakes in the second half, sure— dropped balls and fumbles. At one point, when Jesse threw a pass to a spot where Michelle was supposed to be, Michelle fell in the mud trying to make her cut and the ball hit one of the referees right between the eyes. He fell straight back into the mud and just lay there. Everybody thought he was dead. But it was just a broken nose. And a severe case of male humiliation. Coming to, apparently he said "Mommy" real loud and a lot of the folks attending to him heard it and started laughing. I felt sorry for the guy.

When the game was over, I went to congratulate Andy and the team. The school was kind enough to let the Divas use their gymnasium and locker rooms, although all athletic equipment was off-limits. Andy had the players gather in the gym so they could celebrate a bit.

It's a different thing when women celebrate. They aren't as noisy or physical with it somehow. I can't describe what it was like in that gasping crowd of tired, muddy, bruised women, as they looked at one another and embraced with these deep sighs. It was a celebration of something almost spiritual. That's all I can say about it. I'm not a poet or anything, and I don't want to get sappy, but . . . you should have seen it. They weren't just high fiving each other and grabbing one another around the neck; they didn't howl or shout or slap anybody on the ass. They were just joyful together. Does that describe it? You have to see it to believe it, but it was almost as if they could know each other's thoughts without words, so it was all conveyed through tearful smiles and knowing glances.

They had a few bottles of champagne—courtesy of Andy and the team owners—but they drank the stuff, you know? They didn't pour it over anybody's head or anything. The owners were a couple of government lawyers whose names I've long since forgotten, but they congratulated each of the players who had made "impact" plays, and of course they were all over themselves in their praise of Jesse. Then Andy introduced me to everybody and I shook hands with the two lawyers, and one of them, who wore a long dress and very pointed black shoes, wouldn't let go of my hand until she'd finished telling me all she remembered of that season we went to the Super Bowl and lost. She was pretty sure we'd have won that game, she said, if we'd only used the clock better. (We lost by one point, remember.) When she let go of my hand and held her champagne glass high, Andy and all the players cheered. In spite of the lack of horseplay and rowdiness, it was a genuine championship celebration and I was suddenly very proud to be a part of it—if only a very small one, admittedly. I put my arms around Jesse and said, "You played a great game."

Then she said something I couldn't hear very well because of the noise. I shouted, "How's it feel to be a champion?"

"I like it."

"You really were terrific," I said.

Then I figured out what she must have said before, because she said the same thing, only a lot louder: "I was good in the *first* half."

"You controlled the team, Jesse. You led them."

She smiled, then tipped her glass to the women behind her. "Here's to a great bunch of gals," she said, allowing herself a moment of merriment. Everybody cheered.

"I thought you hated that word," I said, elbowing her.

She winked at me. "For Andy's benefit."

And then Andy hugged her, leaning back and lifting her a bit off the floor, getting mud all over the front of his Oxford shirt. When he put Jesse down, she accidentally spilled a little of her champagne on him.

"Oops. I'm sorry," she said, laughing, trying to brush it off the front of him, whereupon he took the glass from her ever so gently, held it up high, and poured it over his own head. Everybody cheered. "*This* is how you celebrate," he said, the bubbly dripping off his brow. "God bless all of you. I love every one of you." It really was a triumphant moment.

A lot of the players were crying now. Hell, I almost got a few tears in my eyes. I looked at Jesse, at the way she stood there, her legs slightly apart, her arms dangling now by her sides, the light glittering in her eyes, and knew I had to do everything I could to protect her from any sort of harm. She was fatherless in a big world and people would want to exploit her and use her. She was so damned bright-eyed about everything. She loved football, and maybe didn't even know just how talented she really was. It was all just competition to her, and fun. She didn't know how cold it would get when the world knew what she could do.

And it was right then when I realized how damn serious I was about her; it was then that I made up my mind that I would bring her to camp and some way, somehow, get her on the field to let everyone see what she could do. If I had told anyone what I was thinking at that moment, they would have thought I was crazy. Probably I was.

And suddenly the whole future seemed in equal parts frightening, exciting, and, though I wouldn't have been able to say quite why, sad.

Seven

I'D GOTTEN TO know Jesse pretty well during our drills, but I was so wrapped up in the mechanics of how I was going to show her off to the guys in camp, having her run a few plays against the men, that I'd forgotten one important skill necessary to play quarterback. And then, when I heard her yell during the celebration, it hit me. Her voice. I'd never paid much attention to it. From the stands I hadn't been able to hear it, and she never called signals when we practiced. (I started every play by hollering "Go," which is pretty stupid, even for an NFL assistant like me.) Her form was so good—the whole picture she presented when she dropped back to pass and let the ball go, the accuracy of every throw one after another, the way she handled the ball, faking a handoff to the running back—it filled everything I thought and believed about her. So I'd never really thought about calling signals. The thing is, you got to shout pretty loud to do that. And when you do, you better have a voice men respond to.

Jesse had a pleasant voice when she talked, but I have to say, when I heard her during the celebration, when she hollered so she could be heard above all the others, it sounded a little too much like a bleat—like somebody just stomped down on a guinea pig. Hearing that, I got this sudden blast of fear that cramped my heart, and maybe that is what got me started; maybe her high-pitched voice prompted me to think about the future with such nerve-racking anxiety. I didn't want her to be hurt by any experience I might be setting her up for.

Others in the loud celebration talked to me and hugged me, but my eyes never left her. I saw how her eyes lit up for every face, how she pulled her teammates together for photographs and videos, the way she refused to hog the limelight. She drank a toast to Michelle, Cissy, and Brenda. Then to the defense. Then she yelled again, a god bless to her coach, Andy Swilling. He picked her up again and then the other players joined him and they held her over their heads.

I drove home that night with the contract I was supposed to get her to sign still in my pocket.

Now I'm telling you, it was not my conscience that plagued me. I didn't think I was actually doing anything wrong. I just got cold feet thinking of all the cards stacked against what I knew for sure now I wanted to do. And I felt as though I might have manipulated Jesse somehow—okay, that would involve my conscience, sure. But it wasn't that. I can't really explain how I was feeling except to say that she was young, and she trusted me—working together I'd even gotten to know her a little—and I couldn't help realizing that, on some level, I was engineering this situation in which she would very likely be totally humiliated. More likely than not, they'd laugh her off the field. She was a woman, and football is a man's game. No matter how well she threw the ball, they wouldn't let her do enough of it to really see it; she would be this freak in a football uniform, a curiosity. And I didn't want that for her. I could just imagine the offensive linemen laughing at that high-pitched voice of hers as she called signals. I even wondered on some level whether they'd be willing to block for her, to give their best effort in protecting her when she dropped back to pass. And would any of the men be willing to play for her? Follow her?

Thinking about all of this made me more than sad. I was already grieving a terrible loss and nothing had even happened yet. I kept asking myself what I was trying to do. What was going through my mind when I told Coach Engram I had found a quarterback; when I bothered to get a contract for her? It hit me, then, that the whole thing might very well cost me my job—especially if I spent any of the team's money to sign her.

I could pay her out of my own pocket, I supposed, but what if she got hurt? What if somebody fell on her and crushed her rib cage? Who would be liable for that?

The more I thought about it, the deeper I got into it, and by the time I got to insurance policies and injury clauses, I realized I was driving myself nuts. I took several deep breaths every morning for a while, concentrated on only the good things: Jesse's form, her footwork, that quick release. By the time I got to work I'd feel a little better. And nothing had happened yet. That, too, was one of the good things.

A week or so after the championship I asked Jesse to meet me at the practice field where we had run all those drills. I asked Andy and Nate to join us. I was going to tell everyone what I was planning. Also, I wanted to see what Jesse sounded like when she called signals. That was the thing that had got me all discouraged and panicky about things, and I'd never actually paid any attention to it or listened for it.

I told Jesse what I was worried about, then asked her to call some signals. "Do it as loud as you can make it," I said.

She was embarrassed. "You didn't hear me in the games?"

"I guess I did, but I never paid any attention to it."

She was reluctant, but she bent over like she was behind center and started barking signals. It wasn't that bad. She sounded a little like

Neil Young, belting out a high note and, at the very top of her voice, it crackled a bit, and I thought it must be awfully painful. But she said it was nothing. It was how she always called signals.

"That's not bad," I said.

"I can make it louder, too, if I have to."

"No, that's fine. We use a silent count if it's too noisy in the stadium. For most situations you're plenty loud enough."

I can't describe how relieved I was. I was still worried about what might happen and all—I mean it still felt pretty crazy to even think about what I was trying to do—but it was easier to ignore it for some reason. We practiced a while with the footballs—I lobbed them at her while she stood there ignoring them and throwing the ball—and then we called it quits. As we were leaving, Jesse looked at me then said in a low voice to Nate, "I wish I knew what he's got up his sleeve."

Another week went by and I was so busy at the Park I didn't have time for much of anything else. But I'd lay in bed all night thinking about the problem. How was I going to get her into camp? I'd watched so much Redskins film that week and slept so little, my eyes felt as if somebody had sliced them and then slapped them back together in the sockets. I didn't go anywhere on Sunday. I told Coach Engram I had a wedding to go to, but I just stayed home and slept most of the day. And that's how I discovered the answer. In a dream.

The next morning I called Andy and Nate and asked if they could meet me for a late dinner. I still had plenty to do with the team, and I knew I'd be all day at it, but they agreed to come by the practice facility around seven. I promised to give them a tour before we went out to eat.

Everyone was gone when they got there that night, except Coach Engram, who was working, as usual, in the film room. I gave them a quick tour, insisting that they be quiet throughout.

"Man that was something," Nate said, when we got back to the parking lot outside.

"Yeah. It's one of the best facilities in the league," I said.

"Imagine if the Divas had something like *that*," Andy said.

"Yeah," I said. "Imagine."

"I'd sure love to work on one of those machines in that weight room," Nate said.

"Well," I said, "I got a way where I think you can, actually."

In all my recent anxiety about Jesse, what always ran through the back of my mind was the certain knowledge that if I could only get her enough time out on the field with the men, they would see what I had seen. I just had to get her to the place where she could perform against the men long enough that the men could not only see her play but find themselves challenged by her. She wouldn't be throwing to Michelle and Brenda—good as those girls were at catching the ball— no, she'd be firing it as hard as she could, right into the broad, flat, strong, soft hands of Darius Exley, Rob Anders, and the other wide receivers on the team.

"Where we going?" Andy said.

I stopped in front of my Chevy Suburban and looked at Nate. "Mind if I ask you something?"

"Go ahead." He was wearing blue slacks and a sweatshirt. His hair lay flat on his head, almost like a painted surface, and he had a small gold earring in his right ear. And as I said earlier, he was tall and fit, without an ounce of fat on him.

"You ever play football?" I asked.

"Not so anyone would notice."

"How'd you meet Jesse, anyway?"

"I told you. We were in school together, all the way from elementary school."

"You've known her that long?"

"Sure."

I opened the door of the Suburban. "I'll drive. Get in."

"Where to?" Andy repeated as he climbed in the backseat.

Nate got in front and I started the engine. "A hamburger joint I know."

It was a place out near Dulles Airport called Benny's that had pretty good burgers. While we waited for our food, I decided to see what they thought of my idea, because I'd need both of them to pull it off. "Listen," I said, "You know it's going to be pretty hard to get anybody at Redskins Park to watch Jesse long enough to assess the quality of her play."

"But can't you do something about that?" Andy said, surprised. "You're the offensive coordinator."

"Yeah, and that won't mean a whole hell of a lot once they know she's a girl."

"*She* would probably use the word 'woman,'" Nate said, perfectly serious.

"I know. So would I. That wasn't me talking. It's how *they'll* think of her, see, and how they'll talk about her."

"So what do we do about that?" said Nate.

"I have an idea. And it's easy enough to pull off if you guys will support me on it."

They were quiet for a minute, watching me.

"What if I show up the first day at camp with you, Nate."

"With *me?*"

"Yeah."

"I don't get it."

"I told Coach Engram I'd found a quarterback, see. So on the first day, when we have all those meetings and such to run through, there's so many players there, he won't know who you are from Adam. You just answer to the name Jesse Smoke." I turned to Andy. "I'll get a uniform—all the equipment she needs, pads, flak jacket, helmet, pants, shoes and socks, jockstrap, everything—and you take it home with you. Then that first day, Nate, when we're ready for passing drills, you stand in and throw the ball."

"I can't throw anything like Jesse."

"It won't matter. You can throw it. I've seen you. You got enough on it to throw it a perfectly good distance. And they won't pay much attention to accuracy in the beginning. All we'll be looking at the first day is conditioning, release, and arm strength. You've certainly got that. And between now and then, I can show you a few other things."

He nodded. "Okay."

Andy said, "I think I see where you're going with this."

"Then, the first day of contact scrimmage, Andy, you bring Jesse here and I'll get her out on the field. In uniform, nobody'll even dream she's a woman. She's tall enough and solid enough they won't think twice about it. She'll just be a number. And then I'll get her in the scrimmage."

"Look," Nate said, "isn't it just the coach and a few assistants you need to see her?"

I nodded. "And then if *they* buy into it, we can work on the players. Why?"

"So why do we have to do all this scheming to get her on the field. Why not just set up a meeting with the coach and a couple of the receivers, maybe a center, and just let her show them what she can do?"

It wasn't a bad idea. I couldn't believe I hadn't thought of it. I didn't need to sell the players and coaches all at once. I only had to get her in front of Engram and let her throw the ball. He'd see what I saw. Jesse could throw it better than he ever had.

Nate said, "You could set something like that up, right?"

"Yeah, I think I could."

"You're really serious about this, aren't you?" Andy said.

"No joke," I said. "Not anymore, anyway. If I can get her on this team, I'm gonna do it."

"What about *my* team?"

This took me by surprise. "*Your* team?"

"We've signed her to play four years for us."

"You did what?"

"The owners signed her the day after the championship."

I sat there with my mouth open. I didn't know what to say. I'd never expected Andy to be a problem. I thought we were in this together. Now there was something out in the open we had to deal with and of course I had gotten it there with my big mouth.

A waiter brought out our food. I went to the condiments bar to get some extra mustard and when I started back to the table Nate and Andy were talking quickly and quietly until they saw me.

I sat down and took a big bite of my burger. It was juicy, and charcoal-broiled, but I was so steamed I couldn't enjoy it. All three of us chewed in silence. Both of them were staring at me. Finally, I said, "How much are you paying her?"

"Thirty thousand a year. Highest contract of any player in a women's league that I know of."

"Really."

"That's almost $4,000 a game."

"Do the Divas even bring in that much?"

"They do okay. Paying customers, every game."

"Andy, I can pay her over half a million dollars. That's the minimum contract for an undrafted rookie in the NFL these days."

"I knew it was a lot. I didn't know it was that much."

"You'd stand in the way of her making that kind of money? What the hell did you think I was working on here?"

Andy picked at his burger, removing bits of lettuce, but he didn't take another bite of it until he'd completely swallowed what he was chewing. I could see his mind working.

Nate was silent. It wasn't obvious whose side he was on.

Finally Andy said, "It's like this. You're having your fun—don't get me wrong now. I'm grateful for your help and it's been nice getting to know you, it really has. But you're slumming with us—"

"I'm not slumming. I'm serious."

"The Divas. They're not exactly the NFL," he said, flatly. "Are they?"

"No."

"This little operation in the suburbs is not even NCAA, or high school, right?"

"It's better than high school," I said. "And maybe some colleges."

"Whether you're slumming or not, what happens if you get this chance for Jesse—if you manage to get them to really evaluate her as a player? No matter how good she is, she will never make it. You know that, and I know that. She'll never make it. I mean, hell, man, this whole thing started out as a joke, didn't it? So . . . what's changed?"

"I've seen her play. So have you."

"And you think she'll make it," Andy said. "You really think that?"

"If she *doesn't*, it won't be because of her talent."

"But the odds are so brutal. And how much of her half a million dollars will she even collect if she's laughed off the field the first day?"

"She'll collect $9,900 dollars a week," I said. I knew what I was talking about. "And there's a $70,000 signing bonus. She'll keep that."

"Even if she gets by the first day, they could cut her the second week, or the third week."

Now Nate was interested. "Yeah, and if she makes it through three weeks, that's thirty thousand *more* than thirty."

"Right, and don't forget the $70,000 dollar signing bonus," I said. "She gets that, no matter what."

"But if they cut her," Andy protested, "—and you and I both know they will—then she's out of football. She's violated her contract with the Divas, and—"

"Wait a minute," I said. "You put a clause in her contract about playing for other teams?"

"*I* didn't. The owners did. They *are* lawyers, you know."

I shook my head.

"Well, I guess that settles it," Nate said.

"Not necessarily," I said. I didn't want my hamburger anymore. It's funny, up until that evening I'd been suffering from stage fright. Thinking about all the ways I could fail made me not want to try, but the knowledge of this technicality that might prevent me from doing what I was so nervous and sad about doing made me suddenly as determined as a turtle set on laying her eggs on the other side of an interstate highway.

"Look, I'm sorry," Andy said. "The Divas need her and the owners weren't about to risk losing her."

"Did you tell them about me?" I asked.

Andy focused on his plate.

"I wonder how the other girls are going to feel when they find out how much Jesse is making?" I said.

"They'll be okay with it. They like winning."

"Well, I'm going to have a talk with her."

"Feel free," said Andy, finishing the last of the burger I'd just paid for.

Barely containing myself, I said, "I gotta tell you, I don't appreciate you letting all this happen without telling me about it."

"Well," he said. "It's my team, too. And, hell, I want to win just like the next guy, right?"

The three of us were quiet a while. Then I said to Nate, "I liked your idea."

"Yeah," he said. "How I would've liked to see Coach Engram's face once he saw her throw a ball."

"You still might. I'm gonna have a look at that contract."

"Lawyers drew it up, man," Andy said. "It's airtight."

"We'll see." Jesse was the furthest thing from my mind at that moment. All I wanted to do was beat Andy at his own game.

In the car on the way back to Redskins Park, Andy said, "Hey, you have any luck getting me tickets?"

I couldn't believe his nerve. "What tickets?"

"To a game?"

"You want to go to a Redskins game."

"Remember? You said you could get me some tickets."

"Well, maybe that's one to negotiate," I said. "What do you think?"

He fell silent, understanding the point I was making. I swear, some folks will stick a blade under your heart and ask you for a letter of recommendation. The only tickets I could imagine getting for Andy were traffic tickets.

Eight

WHEN I ASKED Jesse if I could see the contract, she didn't hesitate to show it to me. We were in her apartment, which was almost completely unfurnished, except for a fifteen-speed bike, a black lounge chair, a pile of books with no bookcase, and a portable TV. She wore a flannel shirt and sweatpants, with a gold chain around her neck and, as usual, her hair was a cute tangle of tight curls all over her head.

When I knocked on the door, she swung it open and stepped back behind it so only her head peeked around. "What are you doing here?" she said, not unhappy to see me, just surprised. I stood there on the doorstep a while, feeling slightly awkward for both of us. But then she backed away, saying, "Sorry—come on in."

I'd never been to her apartment before, so it was kind of painful at first. We stood there silently a moment or two. "I'm not really settled in yet," she said when she saw the way I was looking around at all the empty space. "I mean, I've been here for a few months now, but . . .

it's all been so hectic. I was actually going out to buy some furniture this weekend."

"Heard you signed a new contract."

She motioned for me to have a seat in the lounge chair. "I did. They gave me a raise."

"Really."

"Thirty-seven fifty a game."

"Unless you go into the postseason."

"Well . . ." She wasn't sure what I meant.

"Does the contract say anything about the postseason? For instance, what if you win the championship again?"

"Oh. I think it's just a yearly salary. I'll have to get a job, I guess, during the off-season."

"Who's going to hire you to work only forty-four weeks of the year?"

I sat in the lounge chair and leaned back. She perched on a stool she'd brought in from the kitchen. She said, "You can get that to recline, if you—"

"Can I see it—the contract?"

She went right into her bedroom and got it. I took it out of its little green folder and started looking it over. It was one of those standard contracts lawyers draw up, printed on impressive-looking paper, with two holes punched in the top and a metal binder holding it fast to the top edge of the folder. I had not read many of these word for word, but I was pretty used to looking for headings and clauses. She sat watching me. After a while, she asked me if I wanted something to drink. I told her a glass of water would be nice.

When she brought the water back, I noticed a look of worry on her face, so I said, "Did you have someplace you need to be?"

"Look, Skip, I appreciate all you're trying to do for me—all you *have* done for me." She paused. I took the glass from her and set it down on the floor next to the chair. She sat on the stool again—directly across from me. "I hope you don't mind my asking, but why is it you wanted to see that? I mean—"

"I have a little experience with these things," I said. "I'm just trying to see that you're being treated right." Instantly I realized the lie I was telling her. I don't know about you, but that happens to a person sometimes, right? Your mouth just starts going off and what comes out is letter-perfect—and not at all accurate—as if your brain has been hardwired for dishonesty above all else. Something must have changed in my face when I realized what I was doing, because her eyes fixed on mine, stopping me cold. I didn't allow what I'd said to hang between us long. "Look, Jesse. That's not entirely true. I mean I *do* want to look out after your interests, but . . . I have other concerns here as well."

"Wanting me to play for the Redskins?"

"Yes."

And then this knowing smile settled over her face. I can't tell you how old I felt right then—like a senile old man being humored by his lovely caretaker. "You're not really serious about that, now *are* you?"

"What do I have to do to convince you people?"

"You people?"

"No, I'm serious. You think I'm slumming? Like Andy does?"

She had no response to that and averted her eyes, though only momentarily. Then she looked back at me. "I've studied the play-book. And I learned from all the drilling and practice. I really did. I even think for a while there, *I* believed it, too."

"You *should* believe it."

"I am grateful to you, Skip. But now it's time to look at things clearly, you know? Logically."

"I *am* being logical. I may be the only one who—"

"But it's *not* logical," she said. "What you're thinking is crazy."

"Goddamn," I said. "Who've you been talking to, anyway? If they could just see you play. The Jesse *I* know . . ." But I didn't finish the sentence, frozen again by the look she gave me—not stern so much as sad, disappointed that I had interrupted her.

"Will you just listen for a second?" she said.

I nodded.

"I had a dream a few days ago, okay? It was about my father. He was laughing and for the longest time I couldn't figure out why. I couldn't get him to tell me, or to stop laughing. We were in a grove of trees, and the sun was shining bright and warm through the leaves, and at first I was glad he was laughing. But then it got awful—you know, the way dreams do—and I couldn't get him to talk to me. These awful black clouds started racing in front of the sun—not like they do in real life, but like, fast and mean, and right into the sun. I kept trying to get him to listen to me, you know, to stop laughing. I was afraid it would kill him, like he wouldn't be able to breathe or something. And then it was like a horror film. I was screaming at him to stop laughing. He hadn't laughed that much the whole time he was alive. I felt evil listening to it. Evil. Finally, I reached out to put my hand over his mouth and then I noticed I had a burgundy sleeve. Then there was a bar across my vision and I realized I was wearing a Washington Redskins uniform." She paused, looking at me. "*That* was why my father was laughing."

"It was just a dream," I said.

"Except in dreams is where we find out sometimes what we really think, you know? I mean, it's so crazy it's kind of funny. You *know* they'll just say I'm not big enough or strong enough."

"Jesse, I've scouted thousands of players. I've seen most of the great, the good, and the not-so-good quarterbacks in the league for more than twenty years now—I watched the great ones when I was a quarterback myself. I've spent a lifetime studying the position and the folks who've tried to play it, and I'm telling you: You're *as* good or better than all of them."

"What about trying to call the signals? I know you think I don't have the voice for it."

"What?"

"Isn't that what your little test was about the other day?"

"You did fine, Jesse. It's not a baritone, but Christ, everyone would be able to hear it. You passed that test with flying colors."

"You really *don't* see how silly this is, do you?"

"The women heard you, didn't they?"

"*I'm* not worried about it," she said. "I know I can yell loud enough. But *they'll* say I can't . . ."

"Look, Jesse—how well you scream is the least of our problems."

"I know," she interrupted me. "Silent signals. I've studied them, too."

"So what are you worried about then?"

"I don't want to be a goddamn joke."

"You're not a joke," I said. I leaned forward now and looked into those dazzling blue eyes to let her know I was serious. "It started out like that, Jess. Okay? Maybe it did. But it's gone way beyond that now. I've seen you play."

"Against women."

"Sammy Baugh weighed exactly ten pounds more than you do and he was only an inch taller. Eddie LeBaron, who also played for the Redskins—my father saw him play as a boy—weighed ten pounds *less* and happened to be seven inches shorter. Jonathon Engram weighed exactly one hundred eighty pounds, and he's an inch shorter than you are."

She started shaking her head. "They were men."

"So?"

"You're just gonna get yourself in trouble. Both of us. I've been down this road."

"What road?"

She waved her hand. "Nothing."

"What do you mean you've been 'down this road'?"

"This is just going to be trouble for you and—"

I held up the contract. "*Here's* trouble. This."

"What do you mean?"

"If this is as airtight as Andy says it is, we're arguing over nothing. This contract here may very well put an end to the whole idea."

"Why?"

"You may have given the Divas exclusive rights to you for the next four years."

"I didn't do that."

"Really? Andy says you did. He says it's right here in this contract."

She reached for it, but I held it back. "At least let me finish looking at it."

"I didn't sign anything that says I can't play for somebody else," she muttered.

"How do you know? Did anybody mention it to you?"

"No."

"You read this? All of it?"

"No, not really. Nobody does that."

"Lawyers and agents do it, that's for damn sure. You have an agent with you?"

"Nate was there."

"Did he read it?"

She shook her head.

I continued paging through it, looking for the rights clause. Finally, on the last page, I found it. "Here it is."

Jesse got off her stool and sat on the arm of the chair, looking over my shoulder. The contract did say that Jesse was obligated to the Divas for four years and that playing for any other team during the life of the contract was strictly prohibited. Later in the same clause, however, it defined "team" as "any entity in the various women's professional football leagues, to include other women's teams that might be initiated or formed in the future."

"And right there's our loophole," I said.

"What?"

"It seems to define 'team' as a 'women's' professional league entity. See here?" I read the line to her again. "Nothing in the contract specifies that you can't play for a men's team."

She went back to her stool and sat down, letting her long arms dangle between her legs. I did not like the look on her face.

"Sure this isn't just stage fright?" I asked.

"I don't know." She was frustrated. "I just . . . *don't* know."

"Come on—I'm just as good as any pro scout," I said. "I'm telling you, Jess. This can be done. You just have to believe in yourself. And pay more attention to the dreams you have when you're awake. I mean, haven't you dreamed of this, even a little bit?"

"I know I've got the talent," she said.

"Damn straight, you do."

She leaned forward and rested her chin in the palms of her hands, her long capable fingers flat against each side of her face, as if she was trying to recall something she had certain knowledge of but could not remember. "They'll just laugh at me, though," she sighed. "That's the thing."

"No, they won't, Jess. I'm going to make this real simple. I'll arrange a session with just Coach Engram. I'll ask Darius Exley, Rob Anders, and maybe our center to join us. They will see you throw the ball. And I *promise* you, no one will laugh."

One brow lifted and her eyes widened a bit. "You think so?"

"Honey," I said. "I know it completely."

Nine

MAYBE I *WAS* going crazy. But here's the thing: I knew what I saw. I'd watched her flick a ball sixty yards in the air with a motion that was so natural it looked like she was a machine and not a human being at all. I'd seen her in game circumstances, rushed and harried, knocked to the ground with incredible force. Look, a 240-pound female lineman running at you full speed makes about the same impression on your chest as a 315-pound male lineman, because 240 can run faster than 315. I had no reason to believe she couldn't take it. She'd need special equipment in certain forward areas to protect her, sure, but she wore a pretty hard-shelled set of pads in the women's game and seemed to hold up well enough. She was six feet two inches tall and built wonderfully, with the quickest release I ever saw; the only thing she didn't happen to have was a goddamn penis.

Some days I couldn't get her out of my mind; no matter what I was involved in, I kept seeing that ball sailing off Jesse's fingertips, the way she carried herself while we threw footballs at her, the uncommon poise she demonstrated in games. I felt not only completely sane but truly excited about showing her off. I was, and remain, perfectly happy taking the credit: I was the one who discovered her.

A lot of what we do in the coaching profession starts with respect, and to be respected you have to have credibility. Players will listen to a coach if they think he knows what he's talking about, if he's straight with them. Unless you're the head coach, you don't often have to work with all fifty-three men, but you certainly know them all, and they know you. As the offensive coordinator, I'd had to earn the hope and belief of every single man on the offense. That's twenty to twenty-five men. (There are about the same number on the defensive team. The kickoff and punt teams, the so-called special teams, take many of their players from the offense or defense.) So I began wondering now what I'd say to Darius, Rob, and Dan to get them to help me out. But then something happened that set the whole thing in motion before I could even begin to manage it. *The Washington Post* got involved.

The only newspaper left in town that still had a print issue also had several sportswriters covering the Redskins. The venerable old man of the group was a sixty-year-old, pipe-smoking Irish paunch named Colin Roddy. Roddy hung around Redskins Park every day, even in the off-season. Everybody knew him—the secretarial staff, scouts, coaches, equipment men, medical staff, conditioning coordinators, and so on. Everyone talked to him. It was almost as if he was his own department at Redskins Park.

The only people who regularly avoided him were Charley Duncan and me. Charley didn't like him because he was always criticizing the Redskins organization for letting Coach Engram have the last word on players, and Charley resented being referred to as a general manager "in name only." Me, I stayed away from Roddy because I didn't think he could write a damn story without looking for the worm in the apple. His angle was always such that something is not what it seems, you know? Something is rotten in Denmark. He didn't often find much to exploit along those lines, but he was always looking, and it was the angle of just about every question he'd ask. A young player would be striving to catch on with the team and another player would get injured and rather than ask the young player how he felt about getting an opportunity to play, Roddy would wonder if it wasn't a cause for secret celebration that the other player got hurt. He once asked Coach Engram if he thought I'd make a good replacement for him; if it wasn't pretty clear that I wanted to supplant him and manage the team *my* way. That kind of thing.

One other fellow, it turned out, didn't like Roddy much either. Our number one draft choice, Orlando Brown, said to me one day that he had to avoid all members of the press, and Roddy especially, because reporters seemed to incite his natural homicidal tendencies. "If I have to listen to that dude for five minutes, I'll kill the son of a bitch," Orlando said. I believed him.

But everybody else at Redskins Park tolerated Roddy; some even enjoyed having him around. He was easy to tease and he had a kind of charm and humor that put a lot of people at ease. Coach Engram said he was harmless enough and I think he even got a kick out of having Roddy there at his press conferences. He told me once that he sometimes called on Roddy for a question simply because he knew it would be fun to answer and would be sure to distract everybody from the day's hot issues.

Anyway, Roddy wrote in the Sunday *Post*, in a column he called "It Has Occurred to Me," that the Redskins might be interested in a new quarterback who not only threw the ball better than anybody on the roster but could also probably charm the opposing players into letting the Redskins have their way. "I'm talking real charm," he wrote, "the kind that causes Trojan Wars and Greek tragedies. In short, I'm talking about a woman." Then he named me. He wrote,

I have it from a good source that offensive assistant Skip Granger is working with a young phenom who is *really* phenomenal: the starting quarterback for the Washington Divas, a (believe it or not) women's professional football team. This source also says that Granger is working behind the scenes to sign this player and bring her to Redskins training camp late this summer. Except somebody ought to tell Coach Granger that women are not allowed to play in the National Football League, charm or no charm.

I knew I had Andy to thank for that one. He really was looking out after his own interests, and clearly didn't care if he hurt Jesse or me in the process.

The funny thing was, Coach Engram just thought it was a joke; he didn't call me in or anything. We were in a meeting with one of the offensive-quality-control guys, looking at film of all our offensive plays from the year before and mapping out our tendencies in various down and distance situations, when he seemed to recall it suddenly. Stopping the video machine midplay, he looked over at me. "You see Roddy's column Sunday?"

I nodded. I'd been toying with the idea of bringing it up myself, uncertain how to handle this latest development.

"What the hell happened to that guy? Has he lost his mind?"

"No."

It was quiet a moment as he reached over to reset the video back to where we'd just been. Then he said, "That son of a bitch'll write anything to get attention."

I was silent, couldn't think quite how to begin.

Then Coach Engram laughed. It was a good solid laugh, as though he remembered a great joke. "I swear," he said, "you don't let anything bother you, do you? He wrote something like that about me, I'd kick his ass."

"Only it's true," I said.

But that just got him laughing harder. He really thought I was kidding. He pressed play and started studying our offense again.

Others, though, did believe it. A few reporters asked me if it was true—I said I had no comment—and worse, some tried to get in touch with Jesse herself. It wasn't like hundreds of them descended on her. One reporter telephoned her on Monday afternoon. He wasn't even a Redskins beat reporter. He worked for the *Post*, though, helped write some sports stories as well as interviews and features for the Style section. He wanted to know if she was the starting quarterback of the Washington Divas. She talked to him for a few minutes and then, since he appeared only to be interested in the women's professional football leagues, Jesse agreed to an interview, at which a photographer would be present. It never occurred to the reporter that Roddy was telling the truth. He didn't even try to talk to me. I just horned in on the interview when I heard about it. Not that I forced myself on Jesse that way. She asked me if I could be there for it and it turned out I could.

The interview was on Wednesday night at a restaurant in Washington called Iron Mike's. I got there a little early, carrying Jesse's Redskins contract in my coat pocket.

Jesse was sitting at the bar sipping on a beer, dressed in a long blue dress and blue sandals. She wore a white pearl necklace and pearl earrings. She had a small, black purse in her lap. Leaning slightly forward on the stool, one long leg sort of crossed over the other, she looked like a fashion model. I sat down next to her. She flashed a bright smile and said she was glad to see me.

"Where's Nate?" I said.

"I didn't invite him."

I ordered a glass of bourbon. Jesse kept watching over my shoulder at the door and front windows. It wasn't so noisy in the place that you couldn't talk, but music was piped in through speakers in the corners and people were talking fairly loudly. "You know this is Andy's doing," I said.

"Well, it wasn't Nate, I know *that*. I asked him if he told anybody."

"Are you sure of him?"

"What do you mean?"

"I think maybe he wants to be your boyfriend."

She laughed. "No. We're just friends. Nate's got a girlfriend. He's engaged to be married."

I took out the contract. "Here," I said. "I want you to sign this."

She took the contract from me and unfolded it on the bar in front of her. She set her drink down and studied it, looking as if she planned on reading the damned thing cover to cover. The print was pretty compact and there wasn't a lot of light. "It's a standard contract," I said. "Promises a $70,000 bonus. Which you get to keep no matter what. And it pays you $515,000 a year, prorated for however many weeks you stay with the team."

She looked at me. I wanted her to sign it before the reporter got there, and I told her so.

"Why?"

"Don't be suspicious, Jess."

"I'm not."

"I'm trying to give you a lot of money here, okay? But I don't want the reporter to know you've signed it until after your audition."

"That's what you're calling it? An 'audition'?"

I handed her a pen.

"So this is some big secret, then?"

"It's the best day of your life so far," I said. "*That's* what it is. I know plenty of young men who would give everything they have for this one little moment in their lives."

Her eyes looked misty in the low light of the bar; like lake water on a windless morning. I don't think she was sad, or tearing up, but she seemed then just as moved as I'd hoped she would be. She gazed into my eyes, and I could see her thinking, wondering . . . Perhaps she didn't yet fully trust me.

I took out a check from the team, wrote it out for $70,000, and slid it over to her. "Starting today, you will be paid $9,903 a week. You get to keep that, too. As long as you're on the roster."

"Nobody has to approve this first?"

"I have the authority to make this decision, Jess, and I've just made it." I sipped my bourbon, raised my glass slightly toward her. "Congratulations."

And then she signed the thing—the original agreement and all four copies—and gave it back to me. I handed her back one and put the rest in my pocket. "Put that in your purse. This is a famous day. A remarkable day," I said. "I feel good."

"Me too." She stuffed the check and the contract into her purse, laid it up on the bar, then took a big drink of her beer. "When do I report?"

"You can't tell anybody yet."

"I can't?"

"The time will come, don't worry, but for now this has to be our secret a little while longer."

"How long do I have to wait for the money?"

"You don't. That check right there is good. Put it in the bank. Your salary won't begin for at least two pay periods, but they'll make it up with the first check."

The music stopped just then, and people quieted down a bit, before it picked up again. I ordered another glass of bourbon.

She watched me. There was something less innocent about her expression. "You're a pro now," I said. It was just beginning to sink in, what I had done, and my own old heart was beating like a revved-up engine.

"I was already a pro."

"You know what I mean."

"I'm nervous," she said.

She didn't look nervous and I told her that. I said she looked as calm as she ever looked in a game.

"I'll be calm when I play," she said.

"Well, that's all that matters, isn't it?"

After a while, she said, "Are folks going to hate me?"

"Why would anybody hate you?"

She shrugged. "Maybe some of the men on the team? You know, people don't like things to change and . . . this is definitely gonna change a few things."

"You'll get paid a lot of money. Right?"

She nodded.

"Far as I know, the worst thing that can happen's we won't get permission to put you on the field in a game. Even then, you'll turn a few heads, that's for damn sure. And some folks will learn a few things about themselves, maybe."

"That's it?" She put her hands around her half-empty glass of beer, studied it for a minute, then looked at me—looked right through me as a matter of fact.

"I don't want to mislead you, Jesse," I said. "You probably will never really get a chance to play. But if that turns out to be the case, it certainly won't be for any lack of talent, that's for sure." As soon as I finished talking, I wished I hadn't gotten so sensible and matter-of-fact on her. She cast her eyes down a bit, then took another gulp of her beer.

"I don't want to be some kind of sideshow," she said. "Not for any amount of money."

"You won't be."

"I'm going to earn this money, or I give it back."

"Don't even say such a thing, Jesse, you hear? You don't give back one red cent of it."

"Then they'll have to let me play," she said. "That's all." And then she turned back to me and the steely look in her eyes sent a chill down through me. "Somebody's going to have to *tell* me why I can't—that I'm not good enough."

I didn't know what to say to that, and so just gave a chuckle at this marvel of a woman I was sitting beside.

"You get me on the field, Skip."

"I will."

"I'll do the rest."

This woman was a quarterback right down to her toes. I found myself chuckling again.

"What's so funny?"

"No, it's just—you remind me of a quarterback I played with."

"Really?"

"It's just the way he used to talk. They all have confidence; if they lose it, the game is over for them. But some, you'd have to amputate an arm or a foot to get their belief to sag even a little bit."

"Who was he?"

"Jonathon Engram," I said. "The head coach of the Washington Redskins."

I finished my drink and got up. "Look, I'm not staying for the interview. You take it from here."

She nodded.

"Only, remember, it's—"

"A secret. I know. I won't mention it."

"I didn't think you would."

Ten

"THIS BETTER BE good," Coach Engram said. "A woman better than I was."

"Just follow me." I led him out to the practice field, where I already had Darius Exley and Rob Anders waiting for me. I had Dan Wilber, our center, out there, too.

Oddly enough, it wasn't something I had to work very hard to arrange. I knew the players worked out every Thursday from midmorning to early afternoon, so it was easy to ask them to step out to the field with me when they were done so I could show them something. I had called Jesse that morning and told her to be there at 4 p.m. Now that she'd been officially interviewed by the *Washington Post*, it was only a matter of time before the whole thing came out anyway. "Besides," I said. "Coach Engram needs something to perk him up for the coming weeks."

She didn't laugh.

"You aren't nervous are you?"

"No. Well, a little maybe."

"How'd the interview go?"

"He was nice. Wanted to know all about the Divas. Our games, schedules—everything."

"Did he ask you about the Redskins?"

"He mentioned how absurd it would be if what Roddy said was true."

I laughed a little, but there was silence from the other end. Then I said, "How'd you manage to keep from showing him your contract?"

"I wouldn't do that. I promised you I wouldn't."

"Even so, I don't know how you resisted it."

She drove out to the park around three thirty that afternoon. By the time I had Coach Engram on the way out to the field, she had already thrown several dozen or so passes to Rob and Darius.

"You warmed up?" I asked.

She smiled. I introduced her to the coach and he shook her hand. I saw him look at her hand when she let go of his. She was not a limp handshaker. Her hair was a bit matted with sweat. She was wearing a Redskins jersey, black shorts, and high-top tennis shoes. Her eyes looked as if they gave off light.

"Jesse Smoke," Engram said. "Where have I heard that name?"

"I mentioned her to you a while back," I said.

"Really?" He looked at me.

"Well, Jesse," I said, "how about you show us something, then."

She stepped onto the field at the 15-yard line. Darius and Rob lined up about 20 yards on opposite sides of the center, where Dan bent over the ball. She got up under center. I didn't bother to watch much of the action, my attention fixed on Engram. She'd call out a route for Exley, then one for Anders. She'd been doing that for the past half hour or so and at first both were shocked that she not only knew the terminology but understood the routes she called. By now they were used to it. She'd take the snap, drop back, and fire the ball the way she always did. Neither Exley nor Anders had to break stride.

She threw fades, quick outs, quick ins, and hit each receiver where he wanted to be hit. (I had filled her in on that.) The ball never touched the ground, except for when Wilber set it there to hike it again. She hit them from 20, 30, 40, 50 yards. When they got back over to us, they were out of breath. Coach Engram couldn't take his eyes off her.

Then I said, "From sixty, boys."

Exley looked at me.

"You don't have to run it if you don't want to. Walk on down there, and when you're sixty yards away from her, start running, do a post pattern."

But he and Anders both acted like they wanted to see this. They caught their breath, got themselves ready, then stood on the line of scrimmage. Jesse got the snap from center and Darius took off. She dropped back about seven steps and Darius, running full speed, cut at the 35-yard line all the way on the other side of the field, toward the goalposts, at which point Jesse snapped the ball off and dropped it just over his right shoulder, at about the 18-yard line. It was nearly 70 yards in the air. It should have dropped over his left shoulder, so the pass was off and he had to twist himself to get it, but get it he did.

"Over the wrong damned shoulder," she said. She picked up another ball. Then more to herself than anybody else, she said, "Could score on a play like that."

Then Anders took off. He could run, too. She hit him at the same distance, but this time she put it out in front of him so that he ran under it. It had to be 70 yards at least. She was really on. Of all the balls she threw, only one of them was even slightly off target, and the receiver had caught it anyway.

Coach Engram turned to me, smiling. "Goddamn," he said. "You're right. She can throw it better than anybody on this team."

"You owe me a dinner," I said.

"Sign her up." He was making a joke.

"I did," I said.

87

It was priceless watching his face change in the silence that ensued. You could see it hit him—first the shock of it, and then the realization. "You actually *did*?"

"It's on me," I said. "You had nothing to do with it."

But he was smiling. "You son of a bitch."

I thought I'd won. His smile seemed the satisfied kind—as if he was glad I'd taken care of this thing, glad I'd protected him from ridicule. "Okay. Back to the office," he said.

I walked over to the guys. "Not a word of this to anyone. You got it?"

Exley said, "What's it all about?" That was four words more than I'd heard him say in a year.

"Just keep quiet about it until we tell you otherwise."

Dan Wilber patted Jesse on the back. "I didn't hurt your hands did I? Snapping you the ball?"

She gave him a look.

"I didn't do it as hard as we're supposed to, you know."

"So do it," she said. "As hard as you want. I won't drop it."

"Really?"

"My father was a center," she said. "He hit my hands a lot harder than you're going to."

"We'll see."

"How 'bout right now?"

Coach Engram had walked a bit up the path toward his office, but he was close enough to hear this exchange. He stopped and turned to watch. Jesse took snap after snap from Wilber. He kept hitting her hands with the ball as hard as he could. You could hear the sound the ball made slapping her palms. She'd take it, step back, and then flip it back to him. "You can start anytime," she said. You've never seen anybody more calm. She was being tested and she knew it, but she turned it around and after a while, it was Wilber who was being tested. He couldn't even make her wince.

Finally he gave her a sheepish smile. "You can take it, I'll say that."

"Come on, Granger," Engram said.

"Be right there." I turned back to all of them. "Listen, you guys. And that means you, too, Jesse. Not a word of this to anybody. You got it? Until we tell you." I gave Jesse a wink, then followed Engram back to his office. All the way back I could see him thinking. He said nothing. As we were entering the building, I looked back to see Jesse flipping the ball back and forth with Anders and Exley. Wilber stood there watching her, his arms folded. I figured if I got him on my side, the others might fall in line. He was a team captain and the players respected him.

In the office, Coach Engram sat behind his desk and motioned for me to take a seat across from him. I thought we'd talk about how we would spring it on the owner and the rest of the players. The media would be a problem, too. I hadn't realized I still had some work to do.

"Tell me this is one of your practical jokes," he said. "It is, isn't it?"

"Not at all."

He opened a box on his desk and offered me a cigar. I declined, but he took one out, cut the tip off it, and, in the ominous silence that had come over the room, lit it. When he was puffing, he looked at me. "You all right, Skip?"

I nodded.

"You didn't actually sign that—you didn't actually sign a woman to the team."

"I did. You approved it."

He shook his head slowly.

"You did. The very last time I sat in this office. You told me to go to Charley and get a standard contract. A one-year rookie contract."

"How much did you give her."

"The standard."

"And the bonus."

I swallowed hard. Then I said, "Seventy thousand."

"God*damn* it, Skip." He pushed his chair back. Now the cigar looked like a weapon. He held it up, pointing it at me as he spoke. "You realize the trouble you've gotten us into?"

"What trouble? She can play. You saw her."

"I saw her throw a few balls to wide-open receivers with nobody in her face. A lot of people—men, mind you—can do—"

"Not at seventy yards, they can't."

"Come on, Skip—distance doesn't mean a thing."

"Did when *you* were playing."

This quieted him a bit. He puffed, looking out his window.

"I signed her, Coach. You didn't. It's on me. Put the whole thing on me."

"And what do you think we're gonna do with her?"

"Put her out there with the team, let the boys charge at her, watch it. Damn it, Jon, I've seen her under game conditions."

"Where?"

"She plays women's professional football."

He smirked. "Really?"

"I've watched her in rain; I've watched her get slammed to the ground as hard as any linebacker in this league can slam a guy down. I've seen her under pressure, laying it up or firing it on a line. She can do it all."

Now he was laughing. "Have you lost your mind?"

"Did you notice her footwork?"

"Goddamn it, Skip."

"Look," I said. "You'll take the heat for this, no matter what we tell folks—I know that. You just have to trust me."

"It's not a matter of trust."

"What can it hurt to give her a shot? You ever heard of Branch Rickey?"

"What?"

"The guy who put Jackie Robinson on a baseball field and—"

"This is not the same thing."

"Maybe not exactly, but it's sure as hell close."

"Women aren't clamoring to play professional football."

"They got their own leagues. Just like the blacks did."

"You could lose your job, Skip. I do hope you know that. And that seventy grand's coming out of your pocket, too. Did you think of that?"

"I'm willing to take that risk."

"I can't do anything to save you. You gotta understand that, okay? I want nothing to do with this. You sell it. You take the heat for it."

"I'll take the heat," I said, and I meant it. "He can fire me if he wants. I'm not crazy, I've got good sense. She can play. I know it."

He shook his head. He kept shaking it, looking at me. Then he said, "Damn it to hell."

"You once told me I had an eye for talent."

"Yeah, minus some mental faculties, apparently."

"I'm telling you, Jon, she's the best I've ever seen."

"Are you involved with her?" His right eyebrow shifted up a little.

"What? I'm old enough to be her father."

"And that doesn't answer the question."

"No, I'm not *involved* with her. I don't even think she's *got* a boyfriend. Look, she's as good as you were, Jon. And that's the truth."

"Can she run?"

"You bet she can. You should see her footwork. Didn't you notice how smoothly she took the five- and seven-step drops?"

"I didn't, actually."

"Looks like Bob Griese. Or you."

He sat back in the chair. "Shit."

"It might be good for the team," I said. "For sure it'll sell some tickets."

"Selling tickets has never been our problem."

"It will sell tickets in every stadium we go to, every goddamn city. I guarantee you the commissioner will be happy about it. At least once he sees the cash flow he will."

"You think so? Cause here's what I think—I think she'll get killed on the first play from scrimmage. In practice. Soon as we put the pads on."

"She won't. She's tough. And you've seen how strong that arm is."

"An ant's real strong, too. But when you step on it, it's done for."

"Well," I said, almost whispering, "we got some work to do there, I agree. We gotta protect her."

He placed the cigar on the edge of an ashtray on the desk.

"But then, that's true of every quarterback, isn't it?" I said.

I didn't like the way he looked at me, the mixture of sadness and hard-boned assessment—the way one friend might look at another when they're both starving and realizing one of them will have to eat the other.

"It's against the rules, Skip. At the end of the day, nobody's gonna let it happen."

"All right then. But I signed her," I said. "Gave her seventy grand. So what do we do about that?"

He shook his head, staring at me, the cigar swirling smoke above his fingers. "Jesus Christ on a crutch," he said.

"I'll talk to the boss," I said. "Let me take it to him."

He was quiet a long time, still gazing at me. Then he said, "He'll fire your ass."

"Maybe. But what if I convince him? Are you at least willing to work with her?"

He just stared at me.

"Come on, it's innovative, Jon. We'll break new ground."

"The only thing that might get broken around here is that young woman, if we put her on the field."

"Like I said. We gotta protect her."

Eleven

THE "BOSS" AND owner of the Redskins was an extremely wealthy, strong-minded force of nature named Edgar Flores. He'd gotten rich off of that computer program everybody's in love with now called Smite. As you know, it makes use of software and hardware governing every conceivable glitch in a computer. Whenever your computer would hang, or drop you offline for no reason, or behave in a way that made you wait longer than you wanted to wait, you clicked on Smite and it would fix the problem (it really would), but while it was doing that it would also present on the monitor a fully animated picture of your computer that could talk to you. If you wanted to, you could have the pleasure of seeming to cause the computer varying levels of abuse by pressing one of the buttons between F1 and F5. As the numbers got higher, the amount of damage you inflicted rose. You could pretend to spill coffee on its keyboard, or drop it from a small table, or throw it out the window of a tall building and watch it smash to bits on the pavement. The computer would start out saying, "Ouch, that's not real good for me!" and at the highest level, F5, it would be screaming, "Don't do *that*!!" Alternately, at F6 the computer would strive to please you in order to make up for being so much trouble. It might tell you a pretty good joke. At F7 you'd get a song from a Broadway show or, depending on your taste and what you preprogrammed it to do, music from just about any genre. At F8 it would talk to you about great recipes, or terrific wines, or the place to go for the best summer vacations. It would have demonstrations and videos for these programs, and you could update it regularly so it was always fresh. At F9 you'd get previews of upcoming films with showtimes and locations. I don't know how the program operated to fix the glitches, but that little animated computer was always priceless. It would look at you with real sincerity, and the voice was really pleasant. You could request a female or a male voice for the program. (It was always a big company secret where the voices actually came from.)

As you may remember, the program was so successful it spread to refrigerators, toasters, air conditioners, and so on. That's where all those small TV screens came from. Every appliance has one now. Yesterday my refrigerator suggested I cool it down a little so my ice cream would be more solid. Then it told me a joke about penguins. I adjusted the control to colder and it said, "Good job."

It turns out the F6 through F9 portion of the program was the most popular. Eventually, the F1 through F5 got reduced to just the F1 button, and other features were added; folks could sign up for more jokes, children's stories, book reviews, brief bios of celebrities. Nobody seemed to notice the truly positive sign that inflicting pain was never very popular. I always wondered what sort of vengeful fellow would come up with an idea like that, but Flores wasn't really that bad a guy. And he loved football.

He wasn't married and didn't seem to want to spend much time with women. People speculated that he was gay, but he never spoke about it or behaved in any sort of way that might confirm it. He was tall, with a thicket of jet-black hair that he combed straight back on the top of his head. He had a prominent chin and jaw, with a dark five o'clock shadow, bushy black brows, and deep-set, gloomy black eyes. If he'd had a longer nose, he might almost have looked a bit like Richard Nixon, but his nose was short and kind of wide at the end, like a pair of mud flaps. The strongest thing about Flores was his way of disarming you with absolutely meaningless questions in the middle of important meetings. He'd ask so seriously it would set you back just looking into those serious eyes of his. Once, when we were going over our draft plan, I was talking about maybe picking a fullback from Ohio State who hadn't been given the ball very often but who could block like a forklift, when suddenly Flores said to me, "Do you know when a person stops using fractions about his or her age?"

"What?" I wasn't sure I'd heard him right.

"In other words, when do people stop giving their age in halves?"

"I don't know what you mean."

"A kid says I'm three and a half. Whereas, you never hear anybody saying, I'm sixty-two and a half."

I said nothing. I was still pointing at the scouting report on the Ohio State fullback.

"So at what age do people stop giving that half part? I don't think I've ever heard anybody say seventeen and a half, for instance, or even ten and a half, have you?"

I shook my head.

"It has to be somewhere between two and, say, five, that people stop keeping track."

"You spend much time around children?" I asked.

"Sure, when I was a kid myself."

"That was a long time ago," I said.

"What about you? You ever spend a lot of time around children?"

"Never had one. Never wanted one. Even when I was a kid I kept them at arm's length."

"Interesting."

I shook my head again, but thankfully he didn't notice.

When Edgar Flores wasn't working, he sat in a director's chair at Redskins Park and watched the team practice. And he attended every game. It killed him to see the team lose. He'd walk around for days, acting like his country had lost a war and it was his fault. Cheering the Redskins on took all his energy.

Still, he was a busy man and not at all easy to meet with when he was in a business suit, occupied with his business. The Smite Company became Flores Systems, Inc., and he was involved in all kinds of different enterprises by then, though the most profitable of these was still the Washington Redskins. It was the richest franchise in professional sports. Had been that way for a long time. Sellouts since the late sixties at old RFK Stadium. Even when they were bad the Redskins sold out.

Anyway, after a few days of wrangling with Charley Duncan and Flores's administrative assistant, I got in to see him. His main offices were in Fairfax, Virginia, on the tenth floor of an office building he'd built. He occupied the entire top floor, the front half for his assistant and his staff and the other half for his plush, plant-infested, shag-carpeted office and an indoor putting green.

He was sitting behind a big glass-topped desk when I walked in. Three tall, broad windows behind him looked out on the old Fairfax Courthouse. He had a cigar burning in the ashtray.

"What's up?" he said, gesturing for me to sit down.

I sat down in the chair but found it impossible to get comfortable under his poker-faced gaze. For one thing, I was a bit on the soft side, a little curvier in the middle than I am now, and this guy was lean as a cornerback. I always felt as though my shirt might be bulging open around a choking button and he'd be sitting there while my naval stared back at him. He stared at me as though I had dried doughnut sugar all over me.

There's something threatening about a billionaire, no matter how goofy they might be now and then. They don't have the same manners as the rest of us. The ones I've known seem vaguely bored by the whole world, brash and frequently rude; they don't like to waste time in any conversation you may choose to initiate. Everything you say has to be earning something in their estimation, or they break it off. Flores could talk to you about nothing, but you? You'd better not try the same thing with him. Maybe you know what I'm talking about.

He asked me how life was treating me and I said, "Nothing special," then immediately regretted it. "I mean, I'm great. Just great."

"You wanted to see me," he said, a flat statement.

"Oh, yes. Of course," I stammered. "I got a question for you, Mr. Flores, but first I want to ask you something."

"You got a question for me."

"Yes."

"But you want to ask me something first."

I nodded.

"Wouldn't that be a question, too?" He picked up the cigar and drew on it. When he saw I wasn't going to answer him, he said, "Go on. Go on."

"You know who Branch Rickey was?"

Of course he knew, he said. He knew about all the great owners in history. I asked him what Branch Rickey did for the Brooklyn Dodgers and he told me the story of Jackie Robinson. I let him go on with it.

When he was done, I said, "You want to be the next Branch Rickey?"

He put down his cigar and leaned forward. I could see he was interested.

"And, maybe win the next Super Bowl in the bargain?"

Edgar Flores was not a suspicious man, but he reserved judgment on most things, and you could never tell what was going on in his mind, except that he was considering, plotting. And he would not answer a rhetorical question, which was wasted speech as far as he was concerned. He motioned for me to go on.

"I've got a player as strong as Jackie Robinson was. No joke."

"What is he, purple? What's Jackie Robinson and Branch Rickey got to do with me?"

I told him.

I watched Flores's face intently, saw his eyes remain exactly as they were before, saw a very slight convulsion near the corner of his mouth, then saw the line of his lips begin to lengthen a bit. I couldn't quite parse it.

"She's the best pure passer I've ever seen," I said, quickly. "She can do it all. She's big and strong and fast. Her footwork's perfect and she handles the ball like it's a third its actual size." I was in a hurry, racing that growing smile, afraid he'd begin to laugh.

He picked up the cigar again and began to chomp on it, never taking his eyes off me. "What have you got going on with her?"

"Nothing sir. Nothing like that."

"Nothing funny at all."

"No, sir." I was a little indignant, actually. "Look, she *is* beautiful. I won't lie. But she's a quarterback. That's how I see her. I have not looked at her that—the other way." I was telling the truth, mostly. I was drawn to Jesse, of course. But by that time my interests were not sexual, they were purely athletic.

His eyes narrowed a bit, and he glared at me. I could see that he was trying to read me—my soul, my mind.

"I should tell you, I signed her to a one-year deal," I said. "I gave her the rookie minimum. Coach Engram didn't know anything about it."

Flores never did smile. Just puffed a lot of smoke in the air. I don't know how much time went by before he simply dismissed me with a wave of that cigar. "I'll get back to you on that."

I rose from my chair. "You've got to see her throw the ball."

"What's her name?"

"Jesse Smoke."

He turned his cigar, thinking. "Well, now."

"What?"

"When's the next coaches' meeting?"

I told him.

"Tell Engram I'm going to be there."

I turned to leave.

"Granger," he said.

"Yes?"

"Don't hand me that Branch Rickey bullshit, all right?"

I said nothing.

"Branch Rickey," he said with disgust.

"Only, she *will* be the first, Mr. Flores. And I promise you, she'll do just as well as Jackie Robinson ever did."

"And how many will follow her?"

I nodded. I had to admit he probably had a point there. Football was too big, too fast, too injury plagued to be much of a female pursuit. The only way I was going to get anybody interested in Jesse was to show them that she played the game a lot better than any man.

"She's as good as you say she is, and she doesn't look like she might break?" he said now with a fully escaped smile on his face. "Might be fun. Might be a lot of fun."

"Fun?"

"I wonder what old Joshua Bennet will say." He had been feuding with the commissioner over NFL Europe for years. As I'm sure you know, each team in two divisions plays one game a year in England or France. There's a game a week now, and we rotate each year which two divisions will play. The NFC East, our division, was up for the season after next. (NFL Europe is why the NFL switched to an eighteen-game season.) Flores hated giving up even one home game for the long trip to play in Europe. Plus, he never forgave Bennet for talking the league into reinstalling the traditional extra point. Flores always favored the new system the league installed shortly after they stopped numbering Super Bowls: no kicker on extra points. Every touchdown was worth 7 points instead of 6. If you wanted to go for an extra point, you'd line up on the 10-yard line and try to score again. If you made it you got an "extra point," making the score worth 8 points. If you failed, you lost a point and went back to 6. You could decide *not* to go for the extra point, and for years that's what most teams did. Unless they were behind and absolutely needed to, nobody went for an extra point. Fans clamored for the old system. By the time I began coaching with the Redskins, the commissioner had talked the league into going back to it. Kickers lined up at the 33 yard-line, the same place they had all the way back when Flores was in college and Tom Brady was throwing touchdown passes.

"Good old Joshua Bennet," Flores said. "It might be fun."

"But not just that," I said. "I mean, I hope you take this seriously."

Flores glared at me again. Any hint of a smile left his face suddenly, like a light going out.

"I haven't lost my mind, sir, if that's what you're thinking, okay? I've seen her play, and she's better than any quarterback I've seen in my lifetime. That includes our current coach."

"You really think so."

"I wouldn't say it if I didn't."

"What about the rules? Don't they keep her out?"

"Not really. There is no specific reference that says women aren't allowed. In fact, the Jets tried out a female kicker back in 2012 or 2013."

"But it's all about men—man-to-man defense, eleven men on a side . . ."

"Yeah, and the Declaration of Independence says all 'men' are created equal, but that doesn't exactly exclude women, does it?"

He leaned forward, regarding me now with a look very much like cynicism—and very possibly supreme annoyance.

"You just have to see her play," I said.

"Well, hell. Here we are, and it's another season, another year."

"Yes," I said. But I wasn't as keen as he sounded before he stopped smiling. I was just happy as hell to get out of there with what seemed like a kind of approval. I couldn't wait until the coaches' meeting.

Twelve

WE TALKED, AT the coaches' meeting about everything from travel arrangements to zone defenses. Flores attended, as he said he would, but he sat there silently, just listening. We discussed player development and contracts and offense and defense and special teams. We evaluated positions and discussed possible upgrades. I was caught between fear of mentioning Jesse and fear we'd never get to the topic at all.

Finally, near the end of the meeting, Coach Engram spoke up. "I think Skip Granger is right to suggest that we make no announcement concerning our new rookie quarterback."

Flores seemed to give a brief snort of a laugh. But then he said, "I think that's wise." Only he, Coach Engram, and I knew who the new rookie was, but everybody nodded, and the meeting adjourned. That was it. Engram looked at me as though we'd dodged a semi.

So that's how it got started. We didn't need trickery, or any of those things I had been considering; didn't need to scheme or

Robert Bausch

calculate or engineer a damned thing. It was done. Jesse was in. For the time being anyway. It was really a tremendous relief. I had no idea the pressure I had been feeling until it was removed. It felt as though I'd lost a hundred pounds.

We still had players to convince, of course, and there were a lot of other logistics to work on in advance so we could make Jesse's transition to our team as smooth as possible. She would need her own place to dress, and shower, for starters. At Redskins Park that wouldn't be difficult, because the coaches have their own showers and bathrooms, and I could let her use mine, though we'd have to schedule whirlpool time for her alone. On the road, though, it was going to be a problem. She'd have to shower and dress at the hotel; then ride in a taxi with me, dressed in everything but the full uniform with pads. She could get herself taped and put her cleats and pads on in the locker room with everybody else. If she got in a game and got muddy or wet, she'd have to ride back to the hotel the same way. No doubt about it, there were going to be some logistical challenges.

"The little things" is what Coach Engram called them. He was more concerned about how the rest of the league would respond, even if Jesse never got into a game. He was impressed with her talent, he told me that. But she was a woman, which was "three strikes" against her.

Jesse was happy to have the money, but she sure wasn't spending it. She put it all in a savings account and let it accrue interest. When I found out about this—right before training camp was to start—she said, "I'm not going to use much of it, just enough to feed myself and pay the rent. Maybe buy some better furniture."

"But why not?" I said. "It's yours." We were sitting in a Starbucks, sipping coffee. It was early on a Friday morning and I'd promised her a tour of Redskins Park. "I told you the bonus money is yours to keep."

"I haven't earned it yet."

"Oh, you've earned it. For what you're going to have to endure, you're entitled to a lot more."

I know I've mentioned them before, but she had the most expressive blue eyes. They spoke a wordless language that moved anybody that looked at her; except when she was backing up to pass, watching downfield. Then they were as cold as a serial killer's. Anyway, when I mentioned what she would have to endure, she got this surprised, curious gleam in her eyes. "What do you mean by that?"

"You're going to be the best-known woman in the world."

She lowered her head and studied the coffee in front of her.

"And certainly the most famous football player in the world." Anybody else would have been daunted by that notion, or at the very least impressed. I expected to see, even from her, a little stage fright. But when she looked back at me, her eyes had that steely quarterback's glint. "I want to be the best football player in the world," she said. "Not the most famous."

"Jesse, you're going to be the most famous *athlete* in the world. That's just the facts. So . . . you think you can handle the shitstorm that's coming once we announce what we're up to?"

"Long as they let me play," she said. "If they just let me play . . ."

Just before training camp began in July, we announced that the scouting department had signed about a dozen undrafted free agents, and we listed Jesse's name among the others as J. Smoke. When the public relations department and the press wanted the particulars, we gave them—height, weight, position, last school attended, if any, and so on. Jesse was listed as 6'2", 180 pounds. We lied a little about her weight, as she was actually closer to 170, but she was strong and solid even at that weight. No one in the press, not even the reporter who interviewed her, noticed her name on our list. We treated this as just what it was: a serious attempt to line up talent. Coach Engram insisted that none of us act as though anything was funny about it. "You are not to joke about this, not now, and sure as shit not when the whole team knows. Nobody is going to joke about this."

Even *I* saw this as a little bit unrealistic. "You can't expect folks not to . . ."

"There will be heavy fines if any member of this team or this coaching staff makes a single joke. You understand?"

"You bet."

"This thing's going to be enough of a distraction, without us adding to it. The press is going to have a field day as it is. Not to mention the rest of the league. Until they see this girl throw a ball, we're going to be everybody's punch line."

And we were once things got going. The hoopla that followed her first scrimmage shocked even me.

But before we got to that point, we had to deal with the players— locker room issues, pride, camaraderie, and so on. A football team, see, is a collection of individuals who bond in ways most people never understand. They don't just call themselves a team, either. You never hear a football player talking about his "team." It's always "*football* team." They never talk about a "game." It's always "*football* game." (Even the announcers do that, which maybe isn't so surprising since most of them are ex–football players.) And there's a reason for it. These men suffer; they are tested to the limits of their endurance in circumstances where failure is as crushing, spiritually, as a kind of death. The metaphor of going to war is apt. Because it really is like war with the pain and the struggle, minute by minute, to prevail.

A football team, then, is unlike any other kind of team on earth; it's a team where sheer effort and collective will can overcome extraordinary odds. You can't rally any other kind of team to play above its talent, to claw out a win because of sheer emotion and inspired spirit. A baseball team needing to win one game can fall behind by five runs and it's pretty much over. Oh, they might come back, but when they do it's usually an accident of pitching, or maybe somebody commits an error or some other "lucky" circumstance. It's never truly the will of the team that brings them back. Same thing with hockey or basketball. Only a football team can rise up and with brute strength and unified force *take* a victory away from superior talent.

The offense itself is one team, the defense and special teams units are also separate teams. Each of these groups of men has their own language, their own goals and triumphs, but they work together with the other units to make up the entire *football team*.

And each year, we create a new one of these, made up of some players who remain from last year, as well as some new players acquired over the off-season—free agents or players traded from other teams, rookies from the college draft and rookies that were overlooked in the draft. The chemistry between these men that binds them to each other like comrades in a war, must start in minicamp, and it extends into training camp and beyond. But it is absolutely essential. If it's missing, even with a ton of talent, a football team can end up having a miserable year.

So we had to begin with the players.

At the first team meeting, Jesse sat with the quarterbacks and me. Coach Engram took a few minutes to welcome everybody, and then introduced her. He didn't say anything specific about her gender; he simply acknowledged the fact along the way. "This is Jesse Smoke," he said. "She is an undrafted rookie. A quarterback."

Most of the men laughed, thinking it was a joke. Others, I could see, had already talked to Darius Exley, Rob Anders, and Dan Wilber. A couple of them made the mistake of whistling.

"That's enough of that," Coach Engram said, and it got quiet.

"There's going to be a lot of hoopla about this," Engram went on. "But I would like to keep things as low-key as possible. Understand? There will be enough attention when this story breaks. You can talk about it all you want after that. Until then, I want complete silence on the subject. I also want respect for this young woman and her talent. She is a prospect at quarterback."

I looked over at Jesse, who was sitting upright, staring straight ahead. Even cut short, as it was now, her hair curled along the side of her face and down the back of her neck. I expected she might flush with embarrassment, knowing all eyes were on her. But she did not seem to be moved.

Again there was a kind of nervous laughter, and the men started whispering to each other. I heard somebody say, "Is he serious?" I also heard the word "dyke."

Engram must have heard it too. "I won't have any of that, goddamn it. You hear me?"

Somebody said, "Are you serious, Coach?"

A lot of mumbling ensued, even some muttered curses. "This is bullshit," I heard somebody say.

Coach Engram looked at me.

Corey Ambrose sat back in his chair and folded his arms. "Quarterback," he said with disgust. He looked at Jesse. "This—this, *girl*."

"Everybody shut up now," Coach Engram said.

But Darius Exley didn't. He was not a shy man, but he almost never spoke, so when he did speak people tended to listen. At the sound of his voice, everybody quieted down, though no one seemed to hear what he said.

Coach Engram said, "Darius, you got something to say?"

"I say she knows how to throw the ball."

"Doesn't miss, either," Rob Anders said, turning slightly to address the rest of them. "We ran some drills with her and she threw me every kind of pass. Short, long, intermediate. You name it. I never even had to break stride."

"Come on," Walter Mickens said. "Joke's over, okay? Who is she?"

"I mean, no way this ain't against the rules?" somebody said.

Orlando Brown laughed. "We in a fuckin' movie or somethin', Coach?"

Dan Wilber stood up now and it got quiet again. Engram nodded his assent, and then Dan spoke. "I've seen this girl throw a football, okay? I've worked with her, on some of the plays in our playbook. She's passed to Darius and Rob at full speed. I held nothing back—*nothing*—and neither did they. We played hard." He paused, looking around the room. Then he said, "She's the real deal." He sat down. A few people cleared their throats. Jesse, I could see, was smiling.

As for our other three quarterbacks—Corey Ambrose, Ken Spivey and Jimmy Kelso—and most of the rest of the players, they looked as if, well, as if they'd just watched a *woman* get introduced as a quarterback at an NFL team meeting.

Thirteen

EARLY PRACTICES AND DRILLS began rather routinely. To guard against hard feelings, to help Jesse feel comfortable, and to keep a promise I made that first day at Divas practice, I invited Andy Swilling to watch her. I invited Nate, too. He was ecstatic and came with his girlfriend. They were both dressed in Redskins T-shirts and black tennis shoes. Andy came, but was, I felt, very reticent, even distant. I could see he was not going to forgive me for stealing his prize starting quarterback; still, he liked Jesse enough to want to see how she would do and knew it was a good thing for her. Truthfully, I was sort of proud of the guy for being able to see that and for behaving honorably because of it.

Coach Engram's plan was simple enough—let Jesse out on the field for all the reps and drills, without any comment to the press. In the early sprints she showed she could keep up with just about everybody but a few of the defensive backs and, of course, Darius Exley and Walter Mickens. She came close, in fact, to beating Rob Anders in the first wind sprints, but once he saw that potential he found a reserve of speed to make damn well sure he outpaced her. He didn't beat her by much, though. Jesse could run.

In seven-on-seven drills, she excelled, already knowing the play-book inside and out—probably better than Jimmy Kelso, which is saying something. At one point, he dropped back for what he thought was a screen left, and the play was called to the right. Jesse sort of hissed and yelled in one breath, "Right, right, right." Most of the players heard it. Coach Engram did too, though all he did was look down at his clipboard and make a few notes on it.

None of the reporters were interested in the undrafted rookies just yet. It was early. So they didn't notice Jesse. And the players did what Coach Engram ordered them to do. They didn't mention it. When I thanked one of the cornerbacks for keeping his mouth shut, he said, "Are you fucking kidding me? None of us wants *anybody* to know about this shit, man."

One rookie receiver, trying to ingratiate himself with the others, said out loud, "She throws the ball to me, I sure as shit ain't gonna catch it."

"You go ahead and do that," I told him. "And you won't make this team."

Then we had our first full-contact scrimmage against another team.

Normally teams will play at full speed, with the offense going up against the defense, but that doesn't tell you very much about your real development as a team. Nor do you really want to pit teammates against each other, not too often anyway—not when jobs are at stake; it does something to camaraderie and team spirit to force men to fight each other for their own individual survival. The whole idea was always foreign to Coach Engram, in any case, so he didn't do it nearly so much as other coaches. He preferred having at least two full scrim-mages with other teams. So we scrimmaged with the Pittsburgh Steelers and the Baltimore Ravens—two NFL teams that, while not in our division, were plenty strong and willing to give us a game. Our first that year was against the Steelers.

Now, you should know something about scrimmages. The two teams don't play a game, as such, and no one keeps an official score. Each team runs seven to ten plays with its offense against the other team's defense, then they switch and do it again for ten or eleven plays. Teams play hard, going at it full contact with full equipment, with referees and so on, but the ball is always placed on a particular part of the field that the coaches want to work on. You might run ten plays from your own 40 and no matter where you end up—even if you score ten times (nobody ever does)—the ball keeps going back to the 40. Then you might run a few plays from the 30, and then from what is called the "red zone," which is anywhere inside your opponent's 20-yard line. You play offense from those locations against the other team's defense, then you play defense from the same place on the field against the other team's offense.

The teams really do go at it full-bore, except for one hard-and-fast rule: You never hit the quarterback in a scrimmage. If you get to him, you merely touch him and the play stops. A tap on the shoulder will do it. Even if the quarterback is in midmotion, the whistle blows and the play is dead as soon as he is touched. In fact, a defensive player can draw a very heavy fine if he flattens a quarterback in a scrimmage on purpose. Teams don't like it if the quarterback gets so much as bumped. But accidents happen. Sometimes a player will get blocked into the quarterback, or he'll stumble just as he's rushing to touch him. To that extent, it's part of the game.

Jesse got knocked down several times in the scrimmage. Accidentally.

"Is that supposed to happen?" Nate said.

"No, it isn't," I said. "They're not blocking for her."

Nate winced every time he saw Jesse take a blow. She got hit pretty hard, too. Once our right guard backed into her and tramped on the front of her foot as she was falling backward. I thought it had to be broken.

Nate hollered, "Hey!!" and started onto the field.

I had to hold him back. "Don't call attention to that now."

A few beat reporters saw us. Andy held on to Nate's arm. "It's football," he said. "Jesse can take care of herself."

I looked around to see if any of the reporters heard him say "herself," but it didn't appear that anyone had.

"What's going on?" Andy said. He knew the rule, too.

"I don't know," I said.

But of course, I *did* know. Or at least I thought I did, and it's not a very pleasant thing to have to say. As I pointed out, a player is *not* fined for knocking down a quarterback when it is inadvertent. You can't be held responsible for the motion of your body once it's been accelerated to a particular point by somebody else. What the boys out there were doing was playing it that way on both sides of the ball. Our offensive linemen were letting themselves be pushed into her, or they would turn their man just right and with his cooperation, force him onto her in a way that would flatten her. At that point, I assumed it was out of the bag. The Steelers were helping it out, see, which meant they must have known. I'd seen them looking at each other the first time she barked out her signals. Later I discovered that the Steelers hadn't really known, and just thought our guys wanted to get even with the fellow wearing number 17. Three of the greatest Redskins quarterbacks of all time, after all, had worn that number: Billy Kilmer, Doug Williams, and Jonathon Engram. So the Steelers maybe believed it was a kind of early pride that needed to be knocked down a peg.

Jesse took it the way you might expect. She just got up, went back to the offensive huddle, and called another play. But I was furious. I kept my eye on Dan Wilber to see if he was a part of it, and I was glad to see that he did his job on every play, as he always did. It didn't hit him as fast as it did me what was going on. But eventually he started to notice, and when it finally dawned on him what was happening he took action.

And *that* was something to see.

I know you've heard rumors about this and that the story's been told in countless sports magazines and blogs, but now I'm going to tell you what really happened. No one was injured, and Dan didn't pull anybody's pants down or anything like that, although he may have threatened to. No, somebody's pants got loosened a bit, but nobody pulled them off. Here's what happened.

When Dan figured out what was going on, he challenged Jesse to do something about it. Pittsburgh's All-Pro defensive end Delbert Coleman had just twisted off the right tackle and, with his back to her, pretended to fall her way, knocking her down for the fifth time. I saw Coleman tap the right tackle on the back as he went back to his side of the line. They were in it together, our tackle and Coleman, no question, and they were having fun. Dan, I saw, picked Jesse up then leaned real close to her and whispered something through the earhole of her helmet. She looked at him, backing away a bit, and then he said quite audibly, "Do it." She touched her face mask and seemed to nod.

Now, you have to know, Coleman was always proud of his vision on the field, so he wore one of those old Schutt helmets with a low cage on the front of it. Though within regulation, it was really designed for a running back or a wide receiver, not a defensive end. Anyway, it had about a three-and-a-half- or four-inch opening between the top edge of the helmet at his forehead and the top bar of the face mask.

On the next play, Dan cut behind the guard and flattened our own right tackle, whereupon Jesse took a five-step drop, planted herself, and fired the ball right into that opening in Delbert Coleman's face mask. She threw that ball so hard it got stuck there, and made a bloody mess of the bridge of his nose. It was pretty scary, actually, when Coleman went down with the football sticking out of the front of his helmet like that. The medical staff had to deflate it just to get his helmet off, and they did loosen his pants a bit, so he could breathe. But nobody stripped him or anything. And he didn't cry or beg anybody's forgiveness. When the bleeding subsided, he got up and wandered over to the sideline—with no help—and downed a half gallon of Gatorade.

People pretty much respected the "no-hit" rule for the rest of the scrimmage. And that, I think, is when Jesse won over the rest of the offensive line. I've seen the movie about Jesse, and I know the writers give her much credit for her uncanny aim—for putting the ball in the exact spot between the top of the face mask and the edge of the helmet—but to tell the truth, and I don't think she'd mind if I let this out of the bag now, when I tried to compliment her on her accuracy, she laughed. Told me it was a complete accident.

"An accident?"

"I was trying to hit him in the throat. Under his face mask."

"Really?"

"That's what Dan told me to do. Said it would settle everybody."

I laughed. "Well, it worked." We were strolling off the field after the scrimmage. Nate walked in front of us but said nothing. "You got Coleman's attention," I said. "That's for damn sure."

Jesse was not laughing, though. "I was afraid I killed him. I don't ever want to hurt anybody."

"It certainly looked like they were trying to hurt you," I told her.

"Really?"

I nodded.

"I thought it was just the game, you know. You get knocked down in football."

"Not in practice, you don't. And definitely not the quarterback."

Jesse looked off in the distance. The freckles on her nose always made her look a little bit like a teenager. You'd have thought sometimes, when her eyes got this pensive look, that she was hoping for a prom date or something.

A few reporters had seen what happened and started hanging around to watch Jesse play. By the end of practice that day, all hell broke loose. We still don't know who told on us. I guessed it was the guy who interviewed her. But within twenty-four hours Jesse's face was on every newscast in the country. Not just sports news either. The national news. Those guys at practice never saw her with her helmet off, but some researcher got a high school picture of her (from Guam, no less) and that ended up on the web, and then the news itself. Everywhere you looked, there she was with her bright, innocent expression, beaming out from under a curly swirl of dark hair and that splash of brown freckles. Of course there were also a lot of pictures of Coleman lying on the ground with the football jutting out of his face; of Jesse throwing the ball; of Coleman's mangled nose, broken just under the eyebrows in three places.

Interviews with Coleman and the few players willing to talk about it filled every talk show and sports panel. Columnists and pundits wondered at the audacity of the Redskins; at the curious need of our owner to get himself in the news. "This is just Flores making a big splash before the coming battles over NFL Europe," one commentator said. "He's always doing something to thumb his nose at the commissioner." Sportswriters wrote about Jesse's background—whatever they could find, that is. They argued over the rules and whether she would ever be allowed to step onto the field in an actual game. They raved about her success in the women's league. Soon they were interviewing Andy Swilling, who grinned like a real estate salesman and announced that the Redskins had stolen Jesse from his team. God bless him, he also talked about the championship, about her coolness under fire.

I myself refused to grant an interview, and on my advice, Jesse did the same. Reporters got as close to her as they could, but while she was polite and all, she would not talk to them. Was she married? They wanted to know. Did she have a boyfriend? Could she play any other sports? That sort of thing. Everybody wanted to know who this sensational woman was. Some sportscasters actually talked about her skill with the ball. "The passes I saw her throw," one said, "looked as good as any thrown that day by the starters or the backups. Say what you will, the woman's got an arm."

Jesse had thrown all of two dozen balls in practice thus far, and because of her sex, she was already a sports legend. Of course, it didn't hurt that she put Delbert Coleman on his ass. That got some attention, too. But this was just the beginning of one hell of a ride. And we had yet to even discover her other great talent with a football, and it was *that* talent that got her on the field: She could kick the son of a bitch almost as far as she could throw it.

Fourteen

PEOPLE TALK ABOUT the improbability of the coaches and players letting a woman on an NFL team, but to tell the truth, once Mr. Flores saw her kick the ball, it might have been impossible to keep Jesse off the team. She didn't like to punt and wasn't very good at it, but if you put it on a tee, or got somebody to hold it, she could kick it 50 to 55 yards as accurately as any kicker I've ever seen.

We discovered it by accident. She just happened to get to the field early one day, and after doing a few stretches, she opened a bag of footballs and started kicking them around. This was after the first few practices and the scrimmage against the Steelers. In spite of her spectacular "coming out," she hadn't been used a lot. She got a few reps every day, but she was officially the fourth-string quarterback, and even in training camp, they don't get a lot of work with the first team. Not in Engram's camps anyway. Besides, Coach was so frustrated with all the attention he closed practices and workouts to the media and the fans. The league went along with this because, as the commissioner said in an interview on ESPN, most of the reporting was biased and hurtful. "You guys don't let up and it's become pretty humiliating for the players, frankly—Ms. Smoke especially." (That comment got about as much play as a presidential declaration of war. The funny thing was, everybody knew that Commissioner Bennet and Edgar Flores were enemies. They agreed on nothing. If Flores could smite Bennet, he would. So the sudden show of generosity looked suspicious. My own interpretation was that Bennet, who had three daughters who played lacrosse, simply felt sorry for Jesse.)

Jesse was being used so little, to tell the truth, that I was about to say something to Coach Engram about it. But when I got to the field that day, there she was, standing at the 40-yard line with six footballs lined up in front of her about 10 yards apart, each one on a tee. She took two steps and kicked the first one through the uprights. Then she stepped back and over to where she could kick the next one and did that. She kicked each ball through the uprights. It was 50 yards. Then she lined them up on the 30-yard line and did the same thing. Then the 20. I stood there watching this, without her knowing, for more than an hour. She kicked balls from the left hash mark across the middle of the field to the right hash mark. Six balls each time. When she'd kicked the last one and had to go retrieve them, I walked over and started helping her.

"Why the hell didn't you kick for the Divas?" I asked.

"They *had* a kicker."

"Yeah, and she missed half the time."

"So? We only lost one game," she said, stooping down to put the balls back in a sack. "And it wasn't for lack of a kicker."

"But you're so good at it."

She stood up and faced me now, her look almost petulant, like that of a child resisting a chore. "I don't want to, okay?"

I went to Coach Engram and told him what Jesse could do, aware that I had to approach him gently. Already, he was saying things like "Our Lady of the Footballs is getting to be a huge distraction."

He listened with a little less irritation, though, when I told him about the repetitions and how smoothly she made each of those kicks.

"Let's see if she can kick like that when somebody's trying to kill her," he said.

Until that day, I'd never seen her kick at all, but I knew she'd be able to do it. "Trust me, Coach. Jesse's not the nervous type."

But when we approached her with the idea, as I expected, she said no. Oh, she was nice about it, with that fresh-faced kid's smile. "Aww, Coach," she said. "I don't want to be a kicker. But thanks for asking."

Then Coach Engram said, "It may be the only way you can make this roster."

"You let me play more in practice," she responded, "and I think I'll make the roster." She was still smiling—it really was absolutely disarming, that rare mingling of innocence, expectation, confidence, and world-weary hope.

"You think so?"

"Yes, sir."

We were just outside the locker room and I was getting ready to drive Jesse home so she could shower and clean up for the team dinner. Coach was standing there with his hands on his hips, a whistle around his neck and a baseball cap tilted back off his head. He looked down at his black shoes and shook his head slowly. Then he faced her and said, in a low, soft voice, "The league's going to try and block you, Jesse. You do know that, don't you?"

She cast her eyes down a bit, the smile flagging some, but said nothing.

"The players' union's already filing to keep it from happening. The men don't want you out there."

"Really," I said.

He looked at me. "It's something going on between the commissioner and Flores. You knew the NFL would stop this if they could, Skip—but if they can get the players' union to do it, then it's not so much the commissioner picking on Flores again."

"I don't believe it," I said.

Jesse was no longer smiling. You wouldn't say she was disappointed, exactly—at least I couldn't read it in her face. She looked more or less the way she might have looked if somebody had told her she had to wait in another line to make a deposit. But she was looking at me, as though she expected me to say something. Then she said, "Who are they filing with?"

"Pardon?" Engram said.

"Who are the players filing with? A court? The league?" She really wanted to know.

"The league, I guess," said Engram.

"Yeah, they wouldn't go to a court," I said. "That's the last place the league or the players want to be."

"It *could* end up in a court, though," Engram said, "They just don't want to risk having you on the field in a game, Jesse. They wouldn't feel they could play their hardest; they'd be afraid of really hurting you. They believe the integrity of the game would be damaged."

"Integrity?" I said. "What integrity? Those guys don't hesitate a second when they find a way around the rules and the refs don't see it."

Engram looked hard at me.

"It's true, Jon," I said, "and you know it. It's not integrity they worry about."

"Call it purity, then. But they think it would affect the way they compete on the field—that it would create an unfair advantage for us, for the Redskins."

Jesse shook her head slowly, then looked up. "But if I kick? They won't complain if I'm a kicker?"

"Jesse," Engram said, "You're a fan, too, right? Have you ever seen some of the men who have been kickers in this league? You're bigger than a lot of them, and in a lot better shape."

She nodded slowly.

"I really think if we can work you out as a kicker, the league and the players will back down on it," I said. "They don't want lawsuits and they've all seen what happens when they go up against Mr. Smite."

She didn't know what I was talking about.

"Our owner," I said.

So Jesse accepted the deal about kicking and ended up practicing almost exclusively with the special teams unit. In drills she'd make 20 out of 20. That's when Flores saw her kicking. I'd never seen him so excited, though he never said anything to Engram or me directly. It was our team to put on the field as it always had been. He was one of the best owners that way.

When Jesse finished working with the special teams she'd do stretches and work out to strengthen her legs. But I could tell that determined as she was, she didn't like not throwing the ball. She'd be on the ground, pulling her leg up past her ear, stretching her hamstring, and I'd see her watching the passing drills on the other side of the field.

Our resident kicker—not a bad fellow, who the previous year had made 29 out of 34 attempts—injured his popliteus, the tiny sardine-size muscle between the tendons in the back of the knee, and was pretty much useless all through that camp. In two team scrimmages, with folks trying to block her kicks, Jesse went 4 for 4—including a 59-yarder that cleared the uprights by a half a yard. It could not have been more gratifying, watching the ball leave the spot where the holder set it down, sailing high and straight toward the uprights. Something in Jesse's form did not allow for slicing or hooking, so the ball never curved right or left even a little bit; it shot straight down the middle between the goalposts. It didn't matter if she was kicking from the left hash mark or the right one, she got it straight and true.

After the second scrimmage, Coach Engram cut our regular kicker, which I thought meant the job was going to be Jesse's. So did everybody else, and the media storm kicked up all over again.

This time, however, we decided we'd let Jesse speak to the press. The first interview she granted was with Colin Roddy. I wasn't allowed to sit in with her during the interview, but when it was done, she called me and we went across the street from Redskins Park to a coffee shop where we could talk.

"How'd it go?" I wanted to know. We were sitting at a small table near the front window with coffees in front of us. She was stirring hers. Outside, the wind from a passing shower kicked up dust and small wet leaves. She stared out the window while she stirred her coffee, and I remember thinking again how really attractive she was from just about any angle. Not that she was glamorous or anything. If she was beautiful, it was because her face was so trusting, so open to the world, so ready to light up with her own certainty. And, of course, I've talked enough already about her eyes. Large and sparklingly blue, they were entirely unenhanced by any makeup. Makeup would have ruined it; like painting a huge pair of red lips on the Mona Lisa.

"It went all right," she said. "He's really an interesting man."

"You sure talked a long time. Did he write a lot of it down?"

But she wasn't finished. "Charming in a craggy sort of way."

"Charming?"

She gave a sort of half smile. "Yeah. Charming. I liked him."

"What'd he want to know?"

"He wanted to know if I was really a man, for starters—if I'd had a sex change operation."

"Are you serious? I can't believe you didn't slap him."

"I don't know. He seemed just . . . kinda sad to me," she said. "I think he might have been slapped enough."

"He's an asshole," I said.

She didn't like my saying that. "He's odd. I think he has Asperger's or something."

"Then they must have used 'perger' at the end of the word to replace 'hole.'"

She frowned slightly, but then she said, "I told him I really want to play quarterback."

121

I winced. "Well, he'll run with that, I can tell you."

"He also wanted to know how I could get so good at kicking the ball if I'd never kicked for another team."

"Good question," I told her. "I'd like to know that myself."

"I don't know," she said. "Never thought about it. I did it with my dad, though, back in the day, as a way of getting mental control."

I wanted to know what she meant by "mental control."

"It's something my dad believed in. He wanted me to visualize everything. Be able to place the ball right where I imagined it would go. So to help me visualize the ball's path, he'd have me kick it, too. He used to say, 'It's harder with your foot, but if you can get it to go where you want that way, it will be easier when you can hold the damn thing in your hands.'"

It was the first time I'd ever heard her use a curse word. I think she noticed that it registered with me, because she smiled a bit and said, "*His* words."

"But it's amazing you never kicked for anybody?"

"That's exactly what Mr. Roddy said."

"Well it *is* fairly extraordinary."

"I never kicked a ball trying to score points," she said. "But, now that I'm going to do it—not that I'm in for it—the whole idea's kind of exciting."

"Doesn't make you a bit nervous?"

The question was completely opaque to her. "Nervous?"

"About missing, you know, when it counts."

"Oh, I don't think I'll do that."

"Yeah? I hope you're right."

"They *all* count, anyway," she said. "Every one of them counts."

God, it was easy to love her. "You are really something, Jess," I said.

She sipped her coffee and stared out the window again. I could have sat across from her and gazed at that face forever. Looking at Jesse, you kind of understood why art was such a great idea.

Roddy wrote a feature on Jesse that went across the country, calling her a "grand experiment." He'd gotten in touch with other players and coaches and was the first to report the players' union's resistance, the commissioner's having to deal with pressure from just about every corner of the league, and our owner's recalcitrant and continued rebellion against the powers that be. Many, he said, believed that "the Redskins were a laughingstock," and some league sources were certain that the reign of Jonathon Engram had reached its lowest point; that the Redskins were destined to sink to the bottom of the standings once the season started. Some sources (who naturally wished to remain nameless) predicted that the team would not win a single game. "It will be extra incentive," one source said, "for every team to beat the hell out of those guys."

USA Today had a long article about the legal battles sure to ensue. Folks talked about what it means to use the word "man" in the rule book. Some wondered why the commissioner didn't just rule that Flores could not play a woman.

This was all a response to the news that Jesse would be our kicker. I shuddered to think what might happen if we ever planned to play her at quarterback.

Jesse, in any event, took all of it in stride.

She and I went to dinner often during the weeks after her position was announced, and plenty of folks went out of their way to be kind to us. A few of the fans who recognized her wanted her autograph, and after a while she was getting all kinds of offers from local schools to come and talk to their students. She was gradually becoming a symbol—of a number of things, actually. To some, she was the embodiment of the "new equality" between men and women. To others, she represented the end of civilization—an interloper destined to ruin the last bastion of male power. Through all of it, though, she was just Jesse and behaved exactly as she always had, as though some part of her mind did not even grasp the notion of her own celebrity.

"I'm pretty happy," she said one night over a salmon fillet. "Although I'd be happier if I got to play quarterback."

"Don't get your hopes up, Jess," I said. "You know what has to happen for you to get in? Three people have to get hurt."

She nodded slightly. "Assuming he keeps three."

"No, he'll keep all three of them," I said. "Still . . . you never know. Ambrose is always getting hurt, and Spivey's erratic."

"He doesn't know the playbook either."

I nodded. "And then Kelso doesn't have the arm."

"I like him, though," Jesse said. "He's smart. Accurate too." She looked at me then, with this mischievous grin. "He'd be great for the Divas."

I laughed a little too hard.

"Now that was mean," she said. "I shouldn't make fun of Jimmy. He's one of the good guys."

"He sure admires the way you throw a football," I said, which was true. When he first saw her do it, not knowing he was watching a woman, he must have seen the end of his playing days every time she dropped back and sent a ball arching through the air like an electric current.

"I don't want anybody to get hurt," Jesse said. "I *do* want to play, though. Maybe if I have a good year kicking the ball I'll get a chance next year?"

"Maybe," I said. But I didn't believe it. I wasn't even sure she'd get into a game as a kicker.

We had our first exhibition game coming up in a week—against the Oakland Raiders—and I was worried about getting her into that game. Jesse was the only kicker in camp for a while, so everybody assumed it was her job. Then I found out Charley Duncan was scouring the waiver wire looking for another kicker. "Just as insurance," he told me.

Still, I didn't like it much.

"You won't find a kicker better than Jesse," I said to Charley.

"It's not my job to decide who competes. I just do what I'm told."

"Right."

"Look, Engram wants insurance. I go get it for him."

I knew this wasn't true because I'd talked about it with Coach Engram only a few hours before. I wasn't going to call Charley a liar, though. "So you're just following orders," was all I said.

"You got it."

"No wonder Roddy calls you a 'general manager in name only.'"

"Fuck you, Granger," he said.

"She'll get on the field," I said. "I hope you know that. No matter *what* you do here."

"Really?"

"And she'll win the job, too."

"We'll see."

With the Raiders just two days away now, we were done planning what we'd do on the offensive side of the ball. I figured, even if we brought in another kicker, it would be silly not to let Jesse kick at least one field goal. Or an extra point. Why not?

It was a game that didn't count.

Fifteen

YOU'D HAVE THOUGHT it was a championship game. The goddamn stadium was completely packed. Standing room only. Everybody wanted to see Jesse play, even if she was only going to kick off.

But she didn't kick off. She sat on the bench and watched as our newly acquired prospect, a slightly balding ex–Canadian Football League kicker named Justin Dever, handled all the kicking duties. Dever had a strong leg and got it high and deep enough on the opening kickoff that the Raiders barely got the ball out to the 25-yard line. But that opening kick was the only time we needed a kicker in the game. The Raiders shut us out 44 to 0. Except for every single player on the Raiders, nobody played particularly well.

Corey Ambrose completed 4 out of 10 passes, unable to stay on his feet long enough to look for secondary receivers. Walter Mickens had 3 carries for 8 yards. Darius Exley and Rob Anders did not catch a ball. The Raiders played their starters for the first two offensive series, and we did the same thing. The rookies and scrubs went the rest of the way. But while our rookies and scrubs played like it, theirs played like starters.

We were being booed more loudly than I'd ever heard, in any stadium, anywhere in the league. Ninety-four thousand booing fans can make a lot of noise. Nobody was happy.

The thing is, most of them started hollering near the end, "We want Jesse! We want Jesse!" as though she might be able to change the way things were going. This infuriated Coach Engram. "Bunch of boobs only came out to see if we'd put her on the field," he said as we were walking off at the end. Then he looked at me. "It's a goddamn distraction, Granger. And I don't like it."

"Don't put this on her," I said. "She's not why we lost."

"She's a distraction, all right? You hear what they were all yelling at the end there?"

"I heard it."

"I'm not going to let this year get away from me."

"So let her play, then, and they'll shut up."

Engram shook his head and trotted ahead of me so he could get away from the reporters who would have a field day with him anyway in the postgame press conference.

What we didn't know at the time was that, in the fourth quarter of that game, Jimmy Kelso had fractured the hamate bone in his wrist. He didn't know it either, right away. He just had pain there. But after the third game of the regular season, he would have an MRI and discover the fracture. He would miss most of the season.

Right about this time the press was reporting that Coach Engram and I were feuding about Jesse Smoke. She was already being talked about as a "distraction" in the media, which cannot have gotten to them by way of my friend Mr. Engram. That's not how he operated. The word is frequently used whenever somebody thinks that a team is not playing together—it's either "dissension" or "distraction." The two horrible *d*'s. Nobody wants dissension, because there's little that can be done when teammates begin to hate each other.

As I've said before, a team is a human community, with the defense and offense being individual communities within it. The special teams, because many of their players come from both offense and defense, operate as a kind of bridge between the two. There never has been a really great football team—I mean a truly cohesive unit— where the special teams were not up to par. That's just how it works. Psychologically, that is. We had one of the best special teams units in the league, and the guys on both offense and defense really did respect each other. But Jesse put a strain on it. The defense didn't like it one bit, and when we practiced they gave her a hard time. Oh, they knew better than to knock her down by now—which showed that she had earned at least a modicum of respect—but because of her they got really intense, playing like it mattered even in intrateam scrimmages. And that, to Coach Engram, was a distraction. A distraction that could very well lead to dissension. He would not have it. He didn't care what kind of player Jesse was. All he saw was her sex, and that's all the media saw, too. It had become, just as I worried it might, a joke that she was on the team at all.

So I was not surprised when Coach Engram called me into his office the Friday before our second exhibition game. We were going to play the Mexico City Aztecs—or as they used to be called, the Houston Texans. (Houston just couldn't support an NFL team, and they'd had two chances.)

This meeting has been characterized as a knock-down, drag-out battle, two old allies in the football wars nearly coming to blows. But even accounts back then tended to exaggerate things. All the books talk about our battle over Jesse, and some of them even have me as the one bent against putting her in a game. And of course that's not at all how it happened. We raised our voices a little bit, sure, but it was only to be emphatic about a point or two. I don't think either one of us was ever truly angry.

"Collect Jesse's playbook," Coach Engram said with a slight wave of his hand. I didn't even get a chance to sit down. "I'm cutting her today."

"Without even giving her a chance to play?"

He sat down behind the desk but said nothing.

"Seems like a rotten deal to me. I mean not even to let her kick the ball. Why cut her now?"

"She's going to be a source of trouble on this team, that's why."

"You don't know that."

"It's already a problem. I sense it, okay? Don't argue with me."

"Well, I'm not going to ask her for her playbook. She doesn't need it, anyway. She's got it memorized."

"Really?"

"She knows it better than Kelso, Spivey, or Ambrose. Maybe better than you do."

"Get the playbook anyway. I won't say it again."

"Have you at least put her on the waiver wire?"

He looked at me. "You think anybody else wants her?"

I thought for a moment. "What's Flores say about this?"

"Haven't said anything to him about it. It's none of his business."

"Does he know it's none of his business?"

He looked away.

"Have you told him it's none of his business?" I persisted. "It's his team. He approved of that contract. I expect he took some satisfaction in seeing ninety-four thousand fans in the seats for an exhibition game."

"He won't interfere, Skip, and you know it."

"You got to at least see her kick in a game," I said. "At least do that."

"Goddamn it, Skip," he said, standing up, and this is where he got slightly loud. "This is *my* ass on the line. Not yours."

"You think so? Because if you go, I go. And that's not loyalty, either; it's just a fact."

He shook his head.

"You think Flores would keep me around if he fired you? Come on, Jon—what's really bothering you?"

He sat down again and stared at his desk pad for a bit. Then he said, "I can't believe any of this. I feel like we're letting something go here—some element of the game we're not even thinking about."

"You don't want her here because she's a woman."

He said nothing.

"That's it, then, isn't it? It's got nothing to do with distractions or her ability or anything, really, but the fact that you can't stand the idea of a woman playing this game alongside the big boys."

"She can't play this game. That's what I know."

"Look, I'm not trying to force Jesse on anyone," I said, half believing it. "I mean, I know she probably won't ever throw a ball in a real game. But she *can* kick it. We've had kickers that were five feet eight and weighed less than a buck and a half. One of the greatest ever, Garo Yepremian, he couldn't have been five and a half feet tall. She's six feet two. A hundred seventy pounds of solid bone, muscle, and sinew."

"For Christ's sake."

"If she was a man, you'd be licking your chops, Jon, and you know it. And you wouldn't have gone out and signed that Canadian castoff either."

"Dever was just insurance."

"Well," I said. "Keep him, then. But let her kick. Give her that chance."

Now he actually smiled, shaking his head. "This is almost comical. Of all the things to happen this year—this has got to be—"

"Let her kick it until she misses. Tell her one miss and she's out."

"Really?"

"You've seen her in practice. She doesn't miss."

"Anybody can do what she does when there's no pressure on. If I put a six-by-eight plank on the ground, every single one of the men out there, and Jesse, too, could walk right across the field on it without blinking an eye or wavering even a little bit. But I put the same plank a hundred fifty feet in the air? Hardly any of them could make themselves take a step on it, much less walk across it to the other side of the field."

"And I bet Jesse could dance across it."

"Jesus, Skip—you in love with her or something?"

"I'm in love with her ability."

"Ability," he said quietly. You'd have thought it was a word new to him.

"She'll make every kick inside the forty. Fifty yards or less, every time. How much you wanna bet?"

"How much?"

"If she makes every kick, you keep her on the team and list her as the third quarterback."

"I'm not going to cut anybody for her." Neither one of us knew about Kelso yet.

"All right, then just list her as the fourth quarterback."

"And if she misses one?"

"Cut her and I'll hold a press conference to confess it was all my fault."

"I'll take that bet."

"Starting tomorrow night?"

"You got it," Coach Engram said. "But you make sure she knows: One miss and she's out. That's the deal."

"You wanna put the pressure on."

"That's right."

"So do I," I said with a short laugh. "So do I."

"You do?"

"She thrives on it," I said. "Absolutely thrives on it."

"Really?"

"Maybe it's because she's a woman," I said. "You know? She doesn't *have* a pair of balls. So successfully kicking a football through the uprights isn't some verdict on her manhood."

"Very funny."

"You'll see," I said.

Sixteen

IT REALLY WAS something to see. And I don't mean that first game she got to play in either, although that was something, too. No, I mean the look on Jesse's face when I told her the conditions. She didn't blink an eye.

"You know what that means," I said.

"What?"

"You miss and you're out. Engram will do exactly what he says."

We were standing outside the training room after practice. She looked at me with those clear, stony blues. "I'm not going to miss," she said.

There's something about athletes with real talent; I'm not talking about guys who are, you know, better than average, or even the ones who get scholarships and national attention because they've got perfect bodies with no fat to speak of and all the muscles in the right places, along with whatever natural talent, whatever swiftness of foot. That kind of athlete is everywhere. You can find them on any pickup basketball court in America; on any soccer or baseball or football field in any school you care to name. They're everywhere. No, when I say real talent, I mean something beyond mere athletic ability, physical strength, or skill. That's a part of it, obviously. But I'm talking about something else—something internal that integrates all that physical talent and uses it in such a way that it appears almost effortless.

There's a story I like to tell about the great Joe Louis. My grandfather actually saw him fight once and said that Louis could knock a man out with either hand, left or right, and frequently did; he could move and box with the best of them; he was a superb athlete. But here's the thing: so were many of the men he fought. A lot of them were strong, had perfectly tuned bodies, could move with the best of them. For more than a dozen years—until he got old, that is, and started losing to inferior fighters—Louis lost just one fight, to a German heavyweight named Max Schmeling. Schmeling's trainers had him watch film of Louis in the ring, see, and they discovered a flaw in Joe's left jab: Every time Louis threw that left jab, he'd lower it a little as he drew it back to his body—not a lot, but just enough so that if you were watching for it, you could throw your right hand over it and tag him good. And that's what Schmeling did in their first fight. He knocked Louis down in the fourth and twelfth rounds. Some say Louis was essentially unconscious after that first Schmeling right hand. Eventually, of course, Louis stayed down. Schmeling knocked him out.

Hardly anybody saw that first fight, but for the rematch the whole world was interested. This was in the middle of the 1930s, and Schmeling was now a representative of the master race, Hitler's golden boy. (He did not like that role and always hated it when anybody mentioned it to him, but that's how it played in the press.) The story was, a representative of the master race was going to defeat an American Negro. Everybody was sure Schmeling would engineer another slaughter. Most of Germany, anyway, was sure of it. But Americans desperately wanted Joe Louis to win. Even white America wanted Joe to win. And few thought he could.

Right before the fight, Louis said to his trainer, "I'm so afraid."

The trainer was shocked. "You're afraid?" he said. "The way you've trained for this? You're ready, champ. You don't have to be afraid of this man."

"I'm not afraid of him," Louis said. "I'm afraid I will kill him."

The bell rang to start the fight, and it took a little under two minutes in the first round to put Schmeling on the canvas—he'd been hit so many times with Joe's hammering left and right hands, he screamed audibly. People said it sounded like a woman's scream. The fight was over before anybody could say "master race."

That's what I mean when I say "real talent." When Jesse said, "I'm not going to miss," I thought of Joe Louis.

"I love you, Jesse," I said, suddenly. "You're a true champion." It was a burst of enthusiasm that took her by surprise. She smiled a bit, looking down at the ground, seeming to get an idea it would be bad to look at me.

I reached over and gave her a slight punch on the shoulder. She still had nothing to say, but she was smiling.

"You're going to make history," I said. "You know it?"

I'm not sure if my saying "I love you" caused her some sort of alarm, but the awkwardness was kind of embarrassing. I punched her shoulder again so she'd know I wasn't getting romantic on her or anything.

"Quit that," she said.

That Saturday Engram made Justin Dever kick off (as he would all year long—he didn't want Jesse getting blocked or knocked down in kick coverage). The fans booed the kickoff all the way as it sailed high and end over end in the air, but Dever got it inside the 10 and the Aztecs ran it out to their 31-yard line. It was not a great kick. In the second quarter, on third and 9 from the Aztec 37-yard line, Ambrose overthrew Anders on a deep pass to the corner. The crowd went wild, of course, anticipating a field goal. Jesse had been warming up a little by kicking into a net on the sideline. Everybody knew what was about to happen: For the first time in human history a woman was going to step onto a football field and take part in an NFL game. Even if it was just an exhibition game, the electricity of that night was impossible to suppress. You could almost feel the world take a deep breath and watch.

And what a play it was—maybe the most famous play in any exhibition game ever. You've probably seen the film of it a hundred times. It registered in Engram's mind as a missed field goal.

Jesse had been working with Jimmy Kelso, our holder, for only a few practices, and he had a fractured wrist, remember, that we didn't yet know about. What happened caused a gasp to go up from the crowd—I think I even felt the wind of it. I know my own heart stopped. Kelso fumbled the snap and the ball squirted on the ground at Jesse's feet. It looked like Kelso was just nervous and tried to place the ball before he actually got his hands on it. The snap from the center came in pretty low, too. We studied it, believe me.

Anyway, seeing she wasn't going to be kicking the thing, Jesse bent down and picked up the ball. She had only a split second to do this, given the mob of opposing players rushing at first to block her kick, and now to put her on the ground. She held the ball in her two hands and stepped quickly to her right to dodge one guy. Then she stood up a bit, scooted quickly to her left, looking downfield, and saw Dan Wilber, who plays on the end of the line in kicking situations, running behind everybody toward the Aztec goal line. Since he was lined up on the end at the beginning of the play, he was an eligible receiver. Jesse let go a quick short pass about 20 yards or so right into his big open arms. It looked like somebody dropping a pellet into a kettle the way that ball disappeared in Wilber's arms, and he scooted about 15 more yards before anybody could drag him down.

First down Redskins. The crowd went wild.

Jesse trotted off the field, but they wanted more. "We want Jesse!" they started chanting. "We want Jesse!"

Ambrose took us the rest of the way, handing the ball to Mickens, who took it around the left end to score untouched. But the crowd would not let up. Jesse came back in to kick the extra point and you'd have thought that was a touchdown too.

We beat the Aztecs 31 to 10. Jesse kicked a 41-yard field goal in the third quarter and made all her extra points. It was like a big party. The crowd never let up—you'd have thought it was a Super Bowl game.

Engram looked at me when I got to the sideline near the end of the game—I usually occupied a booth up in the stands for games—and I didn't like the look on his face. Jesse trotted off the field with the rest of the players, carrying her helmet by the face guard. They were all patting her on the back and cheering. That one pass had won over the team. She was one of them. Her eyes gleamed, her short hair bounced on her neck, and she stared straight ahead as she went into the tunnel. At least a thousand fans were leaning over the wall at the entrance to the tunnel screaming her name.

"Well," Coach Engram said, as we were leaving the field. "She missed."

"Come on. You're not going to count that."

"It was a miss."

"It was a botched hold. Kelso dropped the damned thing."

He shook his head and smiled. "God*damn* it," he said.

"You hate it that she's doing so well, don't you?"

"She thinks pretty fast," he said. "I liked that quick pass to Wilber."

"It's the kind of thing she can do with her eyes closed."

"Well, then, goddamn it, I wish she was a man." He walked on ahead of me. I was beginning to see what a tremendous strain Jesse's presence on the team was going to be on him. I had no idea, though, what it would do to me, the league, or the rest of the country.

Seventeen

ONCE THE YEAR got started and we were playing games for keeps, things started to settle down a little. Engram kept Jesse on the team, but only to kick field goals and extra points. He held on to Dever, as he said he would, to kick off. His leg was no stronger than Jesse's, but Engram didn't want her on the field in kick coverage. It was risky enough, he said, having her on the field goal team. "She could have been killed on that first kick she tried."

"She didn't get a chance to try it," I said. "And she came nowhere near being killed. She threw a perfect pass to the only open receiver on the field."

"Yeah, well."

I don't have to tell you, it took a while for the media storm to calm down. And a lot of players were openly hostile to us for having the audacity to break the "rules." There was no shortage of strict constructionists in the league angry at our lack of "judicial restraint."

Women, though, loved Jesse, and every cosmetic firm, dress, dish, cooking utensil, and appliance manufacturer wanted her. I acted as her agent at first, but I realized pretty early on that she'd need somebody full-time who knew what he was doing. So I lined her up with an agent to represent her in football—a cocky but honest young fellow named Justin Peck, whom I never minded dealing with. For the commercial endorsements she insisted on using Nate and Andy. Things went pretty fast after that.

You started seeing Jesse in all kinds of ads. She modeled training shoes, workout clothing, camping gear; she was in a toothpaste ad; several times a week, she announced that with her busy schedule she was grateful for her new KitchenAid dishwasher. She drove a Mercedes SLR because it gave her the best combination of hybrid technology and automotive performance. "I get sixty miles to the gallon," she'd say, "and still I have plenty of power when I need it. This car, let me tell you, has got real *kick*."

They painted her face for the ads, put eye shadow and mascara on, so when I first saw her I didn't even recognize her. She was beautiful still, don't get me wrong, only now it was glamorous beauty—a sexy beauty, even. She didn't look even remotely like a football player. In one ad for the NFL about taking care of America's needy I thought she looked particularly silly with that makeup, as she smiled at the camera, lifting her helmet to her head. It was just a total disconnect of identities, and I was embarrassed for her when I saw it.

On the other hand, she was making money in baskets; nearly every day was some kind of payday.

Justin Peck flirted with Jesse a lot, called her way too often to tell her he planned on making sure she collected a lot of money when it came time to negotiate. I told him to leave her alone until that time, but he was determined to cultivate a "relationship." That's what he called it. All Jesse said about him was that he was "cute," though I couldn't help noting that she was a full head taller than Peck.

I kept waiting to see what all that money might do to her. But she just put her money in various trusts and annuities and kept on going. All of this she took care of by herself. She had no advice from me, Andy, or even Nate so far as I know. She never asked any one of us about her money or what she should be doing with it. But I did find out a few things just from being around her.

She bought all new equipment for the Divas, for one thing—helmets, jerseys, shoes, pants, pads, everything. She bought them a gross of footballs, too, and told Andy that in the spring she would make sure the team had a field to practice on and a good stadium to play their home games in. Not that she could afford to have a stadium built or anything, but she could afford to rent Fairfax Stadium, a relatively new venue abandoned by Northern Virginia's only professional soccer franchise, which folded shortly after they'd built the place. It was rarely used except by rock bands and a few remaining high school soccer teams each year. She even paid to have some repair work done on the place.

And for us, Jesse was kicking field goals.

She ended up kicking a good number of field goals in the first few games of the season, as we kept getting stopped on offense. Ambrose just didn't have the same steam in his arm and everybody could see it. A lot of the time, when he'd try to compensate for less arm strength, the ball would just sail on him, flying high over the receiver's hands. We won our opening game 17 to 14 over the Miami Dolphins. Jesse kicked the winning field goal—a 38-yarder. She was on TV all that week—ESPN, the four networks, the NFL Network. She was named special teams player of the week, and of course the late-night talk show hosts had a field day with that. ("She might be the most *special* special teams player on the planet," *Late Show* star Jack Marlowe said.) She was a guest on the *Tonight Show* and the *Late Show*, both. She was more famous than the first lady.

Just before she kicked that first winning field goal, the coach of the Dolphins tried to "ice" her by calling time-out. He wanted her to think about it. She just stood back there, staring at the ground, none of the other players saying anything to her. She might have been looking for a four-leaf clover. Hands on her hips, one leg crooked a bit, she looked, from any angle, like a lithe, strong young athlete. As soon as the time-out was over, she took her place, Kelso patted her on the shoulder and knelt down, and she waited there, arms swinging slightly. Then the center snapped the ball, and Kelso put it down in front of her with the laces away from where her foot would hit it—a perfect hold—and she stepped into it like she was doing a dance step. The ball sailed straight and high, right down the middle, like just about all of them did.

The pandemonium was impossible to contain.

We felt pretty good with that win because we thought the Dolphins were going to be a contender that year. But then we lost the next game—shut out by the Detroit Lions 17 to 0.

We worked really hard the following week to correct some things to get the offense moving. Coach Engram asked me to set a game plan that would take a more conservative approach; more runs with Mickens and shorter passes for Ambrose. I spent two nights working it all out—I mean all night long, with film and our playbook—and managed to design a plan that would take advantage of our speed out of the backfield, putting in some quick slants with Anders and Exley. I even used some plays where Anders lined up in the slot and ran quick outs behind the sharp crossing patterns of Exley. But when we went up to Philadelphia, we lost again, this time 21 to 9. Jesse kicked a 44-yard field goal in the first quarter, 30- and 38-yarders in the second quarter, and that was all we could do. Ambrose got knocked down a few times and hurried a lot. The real problem, though, was his damned arm. He claimed he had no soreness, but it was very clearly bothering him.

After that third game, Kelso had that MRI and we realized he'd be unavailable for at least six weeks, maybe longer. We put him on injured reserve, which meant he was lost for the year. So now we were preparing for Dallas, and we had to get not only a new quarterback, but a new holder for field goals as well.

I am still amazed sometimes when I look back on that year and realize all that had to happen for it to amount to what it did. I couldn't have scripted it better. When Ambrose began to show his age, I suppose I had a little hope in my heart that Jesse might at least get moved up on the depth chart; but it really never occurred to me that she might do better than that. And in spite of what everybody has said since, I never actively lobbied for her. The fact is, Charley Duncan went right out and signed a new quarterback—a guy named Terry Fonseca—who'd played on our taxi squad the year before and knew the offense pretty well. He'd never thrown a pass in an NFL game, regular season or otherwise, but he was always prepared in practice and he knew what he was doing.

And so, we got Spivey ready to play, while working Fonseca on holding for field goals.

One night in the middle of the fourth week, Mr. Flores came to practice. Coach Engram was on the other side of the field, working with the quarterbacks, and I was standing next to the water cooler, watching the running backs' coach flipping balls to Mickens and the other running backs. Flores startled me; he seemed to appear from nowhere right next to me.

"Dallas is three and oh," he said.

"Yes, sir."

"We got a chance to beat them?"

"Oh more than a chance, sir." I meant it. I always believed we could beat anybody.

"How's that rookie playing?"

"She's made every field goal she's tried . . ."

"Not her. Brown, I mean. How's Orlando Brown working out?"

"I think we're going to be really happy with him."

"You do?"

"He gets better every game. That's what I'm told." I wasn't a defensive coach, but I knew Brown was beginning to dominate. They taught him how to lean forward and come in low; how to get his hands up to protect himself. A defensive lineman has to be like a boxer, see—he can't let his guard down. When Orlando first came to camp, he was pretty easy to move out of the way because he let his hands down too low, but now he had them up high and he was pushing people around pretty good. He'd already knocked down two balls and forced a fumble. He also had two sacks. The fans loved him.

"So what's the matter with the offense?" Flores said now, and I knew what he was doing there. My heart sank a little. He really was one of the best owners, because most of the time he left us alone to do our jobs. But every now and then, he'd suddenly take a little more interest than any of us liked. And on that day, he was interested in the offense, which made me squirm. For one thing, it was always my fault when the offense faltered. I helped Coach Engram come up with the game plan, after all, and I usually called the plays.

"There's nothing wrong with the offense, sir," I said. "Nothing, anyway, we can't fix."

"We're going into the fourth game, Granger, and we've scored all of twenty-six points this year."

"We're working on it, sir."

"Why haven't you called for more deep balls?"

I said nothing.

"It looks like you only shoot for five-yard gains, you know? You never go for the works."

I nodded, but I wasn't about to defend myself. Nor would I start complaining about Ambrose or Coach Engram's sway over the game planning or anything else.

"I want to see more creative play calling in the Dallas game. All right, Granger? Go for broke."

I folded my arms and studied Mickens out on the field as he practiced grabbing pitchout after pitchout. I didn't know if Flores was looking at me or not. I didn't care.

"You think you can do that?" he said, finally.

I looked at him. "Sir, we've put together the best damned game plan we can possibly think of; we're practicing it today and tomorrow and in the morning on Friday. We'll walk through it at the stadium again on Saturday. By Sunday at four, we'll be ready to play."

He thought about what I said for a beat, then he said, "I knew a bartender once, and every time he made a Bloody Mary, he'd say, 'That's the best damn Bloody Mary I ever made.'" We were both silent a moment. "You think he was telling the truth every time?"

"I wouldn't know."

"No, but seriously—every time? You think?"

"Maybe *he* believed it," I said.

Flores neither smiled nor frowned. He just watched the practice for a bit, then sort of moved off slowly toward the other side of the field. No way he wasn't going over to complain about me to Engram. I'd hurt his feelings again. Only, it always irked me when he'd start talking football as if he knew anything about it. Because if he *had* known anything, he'd have seen that when we tried the deep ball it either sailed wildly over the receiver's head or fell short and forced the receiver to fight like hell to knock it down. Darius Exley almost broke his hip in the Lions game. As it was, he took a deep bruise that forced him to miss practice all the next week.

I really didn't think that Ambrose's problems "played right into my hands," as Colin Roddy later reported in that book he wrote about all this. He said I believed if I worked at it, "I could get Jesse into a game and then we'd see what our offense was capable of." Another writer for ESPN has said that I was aware that I needed Flores to be pretty pissed off and "putting pressure on Coach Engram before I could engineer" anything like that; that I was "glad that Ambrose was showing his age." So I want to set the record straight right here: I *hated* what was happening to Corey Ambrose. I'm a former quarterback myself. The only person back then who thought of Jesse and what Ambrose's troubles meant for her was Justin Peck. *He* claimed to see the writing on the wall. *He* started hanging around the complex, chatting with reporters about his young client and how great she was going to be.

The truth is, I was just too busy with the day-to-day operations of the offense in the heat of a season to be considering such things. That sort of thing I left up to Charley Duncan and Coach Engram. No, Terry Fonseca came in and I was busy working to get him prepared. I didn't do any lobbying for Jesse. Had what happened that season depended on my foresight and planning, we might have ended up at the bottom of the pile.

But football, like life, is unpredictable. And something completely unexpected happened. Coach Engram benched Ambrose, and we had a really big win with Ken Spivey at quarterback.

Eighteen

THE DALLAS GAME is something special in Washington. Seems like it always has been. And not just since the old George Allen days either. That was a whole decade after the rivalry first got going. Allen salted it maybe, got it even more solidly into the football lore of the city, but the rivalry between the Dallas Cowboys and the Washington Redskins originally got going in the early to midsixties, way before I was born. Anyway, it was as hot back then as at any time, even though the Redskins were perennial losers and the Cowboys had long since become winners. No matter how good the Cowboys got, or how bad the Redskins seemed to be, they still beat up on each other; the Redskins still came back and beat them enough times, and vice versa, that neither team ever felt entirely safe stepping on the field to play the other.

So it was terribly important to Flores that we win this first confrontation of the new season at home.

In the first quarter, on their first possession, Orlando Brown sacked the Dallas quarterback and knocked the ball loose. Drew Bruckner,

145

our middle linebacker, picked it up and ran it 28 yards to the end zone. The new holder was Terry Fonseca, who'd practiced all week with Jesse and promised her a perfect hold every time. He did just what he said he'd do and Jesse kicked the extra point. It was 7 to 0 before the end of the first minute.

On their next possession, Orlando swept into the backfield and knocked the Dallas running back down for a 6-yard loss on third and 2. Brown was playing like a man in a crowd of children. He was so tall and rangy and fast, nobody could stop him. By the end of the first quarter they had a tight end, a fullback, and a tackle trying to block him. This set up some other things on the other side of the line. For the game, our other defensive end—a big, happy-faced nine-year veteran named Elbert James, who was lucky to get to the quarterback five or six times in a year—had four sacks. Bruckner had two. Orlando had two and the forced fumble.

On our first possession, Ambrose drove us down inside the 20-yard line, but then threw an interception in the end zone. We stopped Dallas again, then Ambrose completed two short passes to Mickens and a good over-the-middle toss to Exley and we had first and 10 at the Dallas 18-yard line. On the next play, Ambrose tried to drop it over Mickens's shoulder and the ball sailed on him. A Dallas linebacker picked it off and it was a hell of a race to stop him from taking it all the way back. Mickens caught him at our 33. The first quarter was winding down and Dallas was in business, or so they thought.

At the beginning of the second quarter, driving inside our 20, Dallas lost 16 yards on two successive plays. Brown got his second sack for a 6-yard loss, then Bruckner got one for another 10-yard loss. Our fans went wild.

On third and 26 from our 34, they got called for holding. (The tight end tried to tackle Orlando.) Now it was on our 44. They tried a deep pass in the middle, but our safety knocked it down and they had to punt. That was as close as Dallas got to scoring all day.

On the next series, Ambrose threw two short passes to Anders in the slot, and we had a third and 2. He gave it to Mickens off tackle and he just barely got the first down. We were on our own 28. I remember a cloud passing over the top of the sky and a shadow racing over our huddle, as though god was trying to tell us something. I called a play that had what we call "deep potential." Anders would cross over short, about 10 yards down the field, with the tight end cutting out behind him in the opposite direction. Mickens would block and then fade out on the same side. Exley would stop and then fly up the right sideline. If he was open, we'd hit him; if not, we had Anders or the tight end, or Mickens. Ambrose dropped back, Exley made his move and the defensive back fell down. There was no one within 10 yards of Exley. Ambrose stepped up, looked as if he saw it, but then he went for the tight end who was also wide open, only about 10 yards downfield, and overthrew him by about 10 yards.

That was it. Coach Engram called time-out. Engram said Ambrose was really upset when he got to the sideline. "What'd you call time-out for?"

"You're done," Engram said. "Sit down."

No quarterback can stand words like that. I was in the booth, as I always was, but I heard the exchange through Coach Engram's mike. He doesn't like attitude, and when Ambrose came at him and challenged the move, he really tore into him. "You've completed five of sixteen not counting the two to the Cowboys."

"I've had bad days before."

"Not like this. I'm not waiting for you to come around."

"This is my team!" Ambrose shouted.

"Like hell it is!" Coach Engram was shouting too. "Now sit down."

And so he sent Ken Spivey in. Erratic, emotionally tender, Spivey.

The first thing he did was throw a 44-yard pass, on a line, to Anders, who ran it all the way to the Dallas 5-yard line. Then Spivey flipped it to the tight end in the corner and in two plays we had another touchdown. Jesse kicked the extra point, and we took off after that.

I have to admit, Spivey played a great game. Everything I called worked. It's always a pleasure to see it from up in the booth, when a play you've designed gets run exactly as you designed it and the ball is fired quickly and accurately to where it's supposed to go.

We won going away. Anybody looking at the score—we won 31 to 0—might suppose Dallas had a terrible defense and we had a great offense, but that would not really be accurate. Our defense just shut the Cowboy offense down with the help of our twelfth man—the home crowd, that is, who made so much noise even our own players had trouble hearing our signals. Dallas must have had a half a dozen three and outs—they punted on almost every possession—which meant our offense enjoyed all kinds of time to play out there. The Dallas defense, out on the field most of the game, just got tired, while *our* defense played very well when they had to.

I didn't want our guys to develop overconfidence from that game, though. Dallas had a hell of an offense and their defense was damn good, too. We'd see them again in Dallas on Thanksgiving Day.

I could see already that Orlando Brown was going to be All-Pro. So completely did he dominate, he forced other teams to compensate by putting extra blockers on him. That took players out of the other team's offense and left other defenders on our defense free, and that meant we would have a few other All-Pros on our defense. For the first time in his career, Elbert James got a nickname—they called him "El Train James" because he was getting to the quarterback now as he never had before. Other teams could not put two men on him, they had to block Orlando. Same thing with our defensive tackles, Zack Leedom and Nick Rack, who were stopping the run and breaking the middle of the pocket on passing plays. Our defensive backs could take more chances because opposing quarterbacks had so little time to set up and find a receiver. And all of it started with Orlando Brown. He really was exciting to watch. Even with three men on him, he'd force his way into the play and make things happen.

The day after the Dallas game, Mr. Flores came up to me and said, "One hell of an offense, Coach."

"It wasn't the offense, sir," I said. "It was the defense."

He stopped, seemed puzzled about something. "Well, sure, the defense played well, too."

"And that's why our offense was so good," I said. "Believe it."

He looked at the floor and then wandered up toward his office. No doubt, I'd managed again to offend the man who signed my paycheck.

So we came out of the Dallas game with 2 wins and 2 losses. Dallas was 3 and 1. The Giants, our next opponent, were undefeated. And we would be going up to their home field to play them.

By that fifth game, the fuss about Jesse had pretty much calmed down. She was just our kicker, and folks, well, they got used to it, not to mention her reliability. She was 7 for 7 on field goals and had made all of her extra points. With her uniform and helmet on, you couldn't tell she was a woman either. Taller than Kelso or Ambrose, Jesse carried herself on the field like the professional athlete she now was.

As I've already said, I couldn't spend a lot of time with her after opening day. I did try to keep up, though, with what was happening in her life. I am not the fatherly type, but I guess you could say that I was trying to help her in the same way that a father helps a daughter. The press, for one thing, wanted so much more from her than she was willing to give. Roddy hung around like a forlorn lover. He waited for her after every practice, sought her out after games and even during warm-ups. She would not talk about her family, except to say that her father had taught her how to play and that he was dead. She would not talk about her childhood or anything in her personal life. Several in the press thought that she was my girlfriend, or Nate's girlfriend, or even Andy's girlfriend. She was seen with all of us—the other two a lot more frequently than me once the season got started.

Except for us three, she did not seem to have friends. She was completely into football and the team and her endorsements.

Of course, no celebrity in this culture is safe. I don't know how actors do it. Everywhere you go, people know who you are, or think they do. And the things that get printed in magazines and on the Internet, the claims people get to make in print, are sometimes downright harmful.

The one claim about Jesse that wouldn't go away was that she was a transgender woman—a man who'd had a sex change operation. I don't know where this story first appeared. It's possible some clown wrote it in a blog and then somebody with a pea brain picked it up and forwarded it to somebody. Everybody claims to want the truth, but the "truth" they embrace turns out to be the first bloody lie they hear. Ironic, isn't it?

Roddy had already asked Jesse about it, of course. To which she just laughed. She told me she looked at him like he must be crazy and then laughed.

"He probably believes it," I said.

"Yeah, well, it's not true." We were having coffee outside Redskins Park. I hadn't seen her since the Dallas game and it was the Friday before we played the Giants.

"Of course it's not true," I said.

She shrugged, a knowing grin creeping over her face. "Maybe if Coach Engram thinks I'm really a man, he'll let me play."

I chuckled. "I don't know, Spivey looked pretty good last week."

"I know."

"It's a long season, though."

A few curls had dropped into her view, and she brushed the hair out of her eyes. She frowned. "You think I'll have to prove I didn't have a sex change operation?"

"How would you do that?"

"I don't know."

"Far's I'm concerned, somebody's going to have to prove you *had* one, not the other way around."

"I don't think so," she said.

"Why?"

"People already believe it."

"Yeah, well."

She was right of course. People don't need very much in the way of persuasion to believe a lie; and once they do believe it, they'll hold fast to it in spite of overwhelming evidence to the contrary. I've never understood this phenomenon. There ought to be a name for it. I know. Let's call it "Moon Landing Ignorance." You know how, after the slightest challenge to the 1969 moon landing, thousands of people believed it had all been filmed in a studio; that it never really happened? There is an entire world of evidence, concrete evidence, to the contrary, and yet, even after being presented all of that evidence, these people would still prefer to believe the lie—because they saw a documentary film or read it on the Internet. Think about it. This is what they believe: A conspiracy was launched by more than a thousand people, all of them committed to maintaining a huge, earth-changing, science-affirming lie. Television technicians, film editors, special effects designers, gaffers, key grips, studio staff, sound engineers, Foley artists; all those hundreds of folks in Houston; all the astronauts; the astronauts' families; the news media and all of their staff—a list of people longer than any single article on how the thing was faked—and *all* of them kept the secret; *all* of them refused to leak a single bit of information to anyone outside their vast conspiracy that might tip off the rest of the world about it. More than a thousand people, in other words, kept a secret of that magnitude and are, for some reason, still keeping it even after the landing has been so endlessly challenged. As for the "evidence" that the landing was faked? This comes from observations concerning the flag and the shadow it made on the moon in the pictures that were sent back, the direction of the shadows on the landing craft in relation to the location of the sun.

Yet, here's the thing. Hundreds of thousands of people believe this—believe the moon landing was faked! In spite of the impossibility of more than three people keeping a secret of any scale; in spite of six other missions to the same place. I mean, does anyone wonder if any if those subsequent missions were faked? Whether the photographs taken on those missions had the right sort of shadows? And if all the others were faked, did the same conspirators get in on the act, too, or did they have to enlist new participants in the lie? All seven missions lined up and faked with the same people and they all kept the secret? And did all those people finally decide it was better to fake a failure? Was Apollo 13 faked as well?

You see how utterly stupid some people insist on being?

And so: Moon Landing Ignorance.

The rumors about Jesse didn't hurt her immediately; but then we did not foresee the effect they would have on her endorsements. First, some of the women's products sponsors started pulling back. No reason was ever given; she just suddenly wasn't so important to some of the perfume people or the clothing manufacturers. With the training shoe company she had a one year contract, so those ads continued. But a hair salon dropped out, and then an appliance store. Mostly local people, but . . . you could see what was going on. And all of them would be damn sorry later on, I can tell you.

How could I change anyone's mind about Jesse? For hundreds of thousands of people, she was now a man who had played college football and developed into a great player there, only to then realize he was a woman and get a sex change operation. And who was this mystery man, anyway? That's what the press began to wonder. No one ever posed the question: If this guy played college football so well, why wasn't he famous *before* the operation? And where had this mystery man played college football, anyway?

All of that hoopla and all she'd done for us was kick the ball—and, of course, thrown and completed a *single* pass during a fluke play of an exhibition game. Through everything, Jesse didn't care. "I just want to think about the next game," she'd say.

With Kelso gone and Ambrose nursing a sore shoulder and arm, Jesse got to throw more than a few balls in practice. In fact, during the week we prepared for the Giants, she played quarterback on the practice team—the offense that our defense practices against. I was really busy working with our offense, all the way over on another field, but I heard from a few of the guys on defense that she handled herself like a pro. "Those guys scored on us," Orlando said after practice one day. "No shit."

"Really?"

"She can throw the thing a mile," he said.

Our two backup wide receivers—a kick returner named Jeremy Frank and a quick little speedster named Sean Rice—played especially hard against our defense. Rice frequently got in games with the first-string offense whenever we had three-receiver sets, but in practice he was the one who imitated the opposing team's number one receiver, so he played on the right or left side. It was always a gas for the second stringers to beat the number one defense in the league, which, after four games, is what we had.

"Who's she throwing the ball *to*?" I asked. We were walking on the track, toward the locker room.

"Mostly Rice," Orlando said. "He caught six balls today. Two for touchdowns."

"Really?"

"She hit Jeremy with a few balls, too. She can throw it."

"I know."

"If she *is* a she," Orlando said.

"She *is*, goddamn it."

He looked hard at me, which required that he nearly bend over. I looked up at him with what I hoped was a scowl on my face. "Don't believe any of those lies, Orlando," I said. "Okay? It's just folks who can't accept the fact that a woman might actually play this game as well as a man."

"Well she do," he said. "I mean, I don't know what might happen if she ever get hit really hard, but . . . she quick on her feet and move just like a pro."

153

"And she's got a killer release," I said.

"Sure do."

"Tell Coach Engram about it," I said.

He nodded, a half smile on his face.

"It's all on film, right?" I said.

"Sure is."

"Well, I'll mention it to him, too." Then I told him he was having a great year.

"I got a long way to go," he said. "A long way."

He, too, talked like a champion. Walking up to the locker room, I couldn't help feeling like maybe my job was safe after all, at least for another year. And even if we were just 2 and 2, I was pretty sure we would knock off the Giants.

Nineteen

THE GIANTS CAME OUT running the ball and ran right at Orlando Brown. Their first drive went from their 28 to our 1-yard line on thirteen runs and only one short pass around midfield to their tight end on a third and 2 play. The Giant right tackle was a huge, strong man named Edward Engel who'd been watching film of Orlando all week. On the first play, and many thereafter, Engel stood up like he was going to pass block, only to duck down in front of Orlando's charge. The rookie would put his hands down to get ready to jump over what looked like a roll block, then Engel would hit him square in the gut and just push him out of the way. The fullback and tight end took out the linebacker and the cornerback on that side. The Giants also pulled their guard and their tackle from the left side, the center would take out anybody who followed them, and both of those huge blockers would just smash around the right end. Our cornerback, a very good player named Jerry Walls, who was supposed to force the play back inside on runs around the end, was no match for that herd of blockers coming around that side. The Giant running backs would get to the outside and just dance through the bodies. They averaged 7.9 yards a carry, and the longest run of the day was 18 yards, so you have some idea how many times they wiped us out on that side. Even putting both safeties up close to the line in what is called "the box" was no help.

And all of it was because Orlando got handled so completely. He just wasn't there to clog things up. He got pushed so far back, in fact, he sometimes got credited for the tackle downfield. He just never gave up. It wasn't that Engel was stronger, or even better, than Orlando; he just knew more, had more experience, and could outplay him with that experience. You knew others would try his technique on our prize rookie, but eventually he'd learn how to counter it. By the fourth quarter of that game, in fact, he could already stall that move a little better. He was learning even as we watched him. But it was too late for our game plan.

We scored two touchdowns. Jesse made the two extra points. She never got to try a field goal, though. The Giants drove on us all day, using up most of the clock and racking up a commanding 24 points.

Ken Spivey played well enough but couldn't get it done when it counted. Twice, he had Exley wide open down the sideline. One of those times he threw it out-of-bounds, and the other he threw it clear over Exley's head. He finished with 16 completions out of 28 attempts, for 155 yards and 2 touchdowns. No interceptions. It wasn't a bad performance. But those two missed opportunities hurt.

Nobody was happy on the ride back to Washington. We were now 2 and 3 and in second to last place in the division. And our next opponent was the Oakland Raiders, who in our first exhibition game had already made us look like a high school junior varsity team.

The good news? We'd be playing at home.

The bad news? We'd been playing at home when the Raiders kicked our asses the first time. We'd been shown to be the weaker team, then, and it was only clearer now. The Raiders were undefeated—5 and 0.

And the mystique surrounding Jesse had pretty much worn off. She was our kicker and that was that. Given how badly they'd licked us before, and the way we were playing, it wasn't likely to be a packed house. And nothing irritated Mr. Flores more than seeing empty seats at home.

Not that he didn't always make money; technically, we were always sold out. All the tickets to the stadium were season tickets, and the Redskins had sold out every game since the early 1970s. But folks didn't always come to the games, and empty seats are very bad for publicity and future sales of team paraphernalia. Empty seats mean fewer sales of food and beer and other assorted souvenirs on game day and much less in parking revenues. So it was never good to have them.

We were not looking forward to Sunday afternoon.

In fact, the night we got back from New York, Coach Engram called a meeting.

He wanted all the coaches, but it was clear we were going to be working on the offensive game plan for the Raiders. We were going to run the ball, he said. The passing game was going to be limited. He respected the way the Giants dominated the field, pushed our vaunted, league-leading defense out of the way with old-fashioned sweeps and runs up the gut. "That's football at its most basic," he said. "And we're going to do the same thing to the Raiders."

"I'd like nothing better," I said.

"Dan Wilber asked for it," Engram said. "On the ride home."

"He did?"

"The whole offensive line wants to stick it down somebody's throat."

"You think they can do that against Oakland's guys up front?"

"They think they can."

We talked about the poor showing on the left of our line—the way the Giants continued to run around their right side.

"Orlando was starting to correct at the end there," Engram said.

Our defensive coordinator was a tall, puffy guy named Greg Bayne. He'd been a safety in his playing days, but now you wouldn't put him anywhere but nose guard. He was the one who begged us to draft Orlando Brown and was particularly upset with his prize rookie's play that night. When Engram said he thought Orlando was getting a little better by the end of the game, Bayne said, "Only because Engel got tired of pushing him around."

"Well, he's got a lot to learn yet," Engram said.

"A lot. I think I'm going to play him only when we think Oakland's going to be passing."

"It's your call. Your defense," Engram said. "But I wish you wouldn't do that to him."

"On first and ten," Bayne said, "Oakland runs the ball sixty-eight percent of the time. That counts as a running down. So does second and under five yards to go. They run a lot then, too. When they're third and long—eight to ten or more, Orlando will play to rush the passer. If I think they're going to run the ball, he's coming out of there."

We were sitting around a big table under long, hanging neon lights in the biggest meeting room at Redskins Park. The lights looked like the kind you see dangling over pool tables. Cigar smoke used to fill that room when I first started coaching here, but these days, this evening and every evening, the air was as clean and clear as spring water. Anybody who wanted to smoke had to go outside, or step into Engram's office.

"What will that do to Orlando's confidence?" I said. "Won't take long for him to figure out what you're doing."

"I'll talk to him," Bayne said. "He's not happy with what happened against the Giants either, believe me. But the Raiders will see what the Giants did to him on film. They've got a guy over there— Ruggins, or whatever his name is—who will eat Orlando alive."

It was true. The Raiders had a right tackle who had been All-Pro and who made the Pro Bowl every year since he came into the league. He was almost as tall as Orlando, weighed forty pounds more, and could lift a dump truck. His name was Jon Ruggins.

"So who'll fill in on running downs?" I asked.

"Alvin Parker," Bayne said.

Parker had been our starter for the two years before. He was not a great player, but he played the run fairly well. He'd give Ruggins a battle at least on that side. He'd get in the tangle.

So we were talking about moving some players around. We were discussing the kind of defensive formations we would use to stop Oakland, and then in the middle of it, after a short pause, Bayne said, "What about the quarterback?"

I looked at him. Coach Engram said, "We'll get to that."

"What?" I said.

"Greg's been telling me some things about that girly quarterback of yours."

"Really. What about her?"

"He's got some film he wants me to see," said Engram.

"She plays the second-string offense against our first-string defense and beats them," Bayne said. "They keep scoring on us, and she doesn't miss."

I couldn't help feeling like I should jump up and hug the guy. "She won't miss those long bombs down the sideline," I said. "You give her time and she'll pick apart any defense out there."

"You think so," Coach Engram said.

"And we wouldn't be playing to any empty seats either," I said, thinking again of what that might do to our job security. I'm sorry to say I was thinking about that, but . . . I was. I'd never seen Flores around practice so much, and Coach Engram himself had said a number of times, "This is it, folks. This is the year. We gotta do it." I think we all knew what was at stake.

"Then we're going to have to close practice," Engram said.

I couldn't contain my surprise or excitement. "Are you going to do what I think you're going to do?"

"I don't know. What I *do* know is I'm just tired of missing those open plays downfield."

"So . . ."

"I'll make the announcement on Saturday. Enough folks will know about it after that to fill the stadium."

"You going to do it, then?" Bayne said.

Engram just sat there looking at him. I could see he didn't want to commit to it, even then. But he wanted so badly to win. And those two bad balls Spivey threw were haunting him. He respected me, I knew that. And he believed in Greg Bayne. We were both telling him, as clearly as we knew how, that Jesse could do it.

What was he supposed to do?

Twenty

I STOPPED JESSE outside the weight room early Monday morning, all excited to give her the news. Coach Engram let me have the honor—believe it or not, we did have a discussion about who would tell her. I figured she might just grab me around the neck and squeeze so hard I'd faint. That's how I pictured it. I thought she might want me to pick her up and swing her around like a daughter at a wedding reception. All she did was smile a bit and look out at the playing field. "It's going to be your team, Jesse," I said, confused by the cool of her reaction.

"I know," she said.

"You're not nervous are you?"

She looked at me. "I just wish my father was alive." And by god her eyes were shining with tears.

"I wish he was too," I said and I reached for her.

But she pulled back, raising her hand up, gently. "No," she said. "It's all right." The tears ran down that pretty freckled face now. "I just never thought . . ." she trailed off, looking out over the practice field again. A few players came out of the locker room and trotted down the hill.

"*I* never thought I'd see this day, either," I said, trying to finish what she'd started to say.

And that's when she reached over, touched my jaw with the tips of her fingers, and whispered, "I have you to thank for all this." It was the most womanly thing I'd ever heard her say or do with her football uniform on, her voice husky and sad and beautiful. I really did feel kind of fatherly toward her then, as I noticed how perfect her neck was—the small, fine bones under her throat produced exquisite shadows. Suddenly I was terrified for her.

"I want you to practice that quick release of yours, you hear?"

She nodded, taking her hand away.

"You don't see something right away, throw the damned football into the crowd."

"We're talking game plan right now?"

I laughed a little. "And another thing, Jesse. You can't tell anybody about this yet, all right? Coach Engram's going to close practice. No one can know about this for a while."

"What about Nate?"

"Not even him."

"He said he might come to a practice this week."

"He won't be able to get in. They'll be closed."

She still had the tears running down her face. "Just Nate?"

"You can't tell anyone," I said, feeling bad. "Look, I'm sorry. He'll know soon enough."

She didn't like it, but she wiped her eyes and turned to go into the weight room. "Anyway, thank you," she said again.

"We're going to make history, Jesse," I said, but I don't even think she heard me. She was already through the door.

In spite of my anxiety over her continuing good health, I really was excited about giving Jesse the ball. For one thing, she would be working a lot more with me now. We'd work on the game plan together and be in meetings most of every evening after practice. We'd watch film of the Oakland defense together. She'd have to learn every move they made, every nuance of their defensive alignments.

She already knew our playbook as well as anyone, myself included. She'd memorized every single facet of our offense. I could talk to her about specific plays and she didn't need the playbook in her lap to page through it and find what I was talking about. Even Ambrose had to do that once in a while. And Spivey hardly ever went anywhere without his playbook.

Jesse had the damn thing in her head.

We clicked from day one. I think I learned more about my own plays from her than I had in almost a decade of coaching. I'm not just saying that.

As he said he would, Engram closed practice that week. (Roddy was livid, but he wrote stories about a strategy that might save the season. "This team is at a crossroads," he said.) The players themselves all got behind Jesse, and the offense looked really crisp. We worked on the running game, but there were a few good passing plays sprinkled in. The whole line worked to keep Jesse on her feet. We even ran a few plays against our own defense, promising $200 bonuses to the defensive guy who could lay a hand on Jesse before she let go of the ball. Nobody got to her. Even Mickens blocked his ass off, and he never did like to do much of that. It got to be a matter of honor on the part of the offensive guys: They really wanted to keep Jesse from being hit.

Of course, all of them knew it was a virtual impossibility to keep the quarterback from getting knocked down once in a while. But Coach Engram is wonderful at motivating people. One day he got the offense together and showed films of the greatest offensive line the Redskins ever fielded. And it wasn't that early group of "Hogs" that won those eighties championships, either. The 1991 offensive line allowed just 8 sacks in fifteen games. In the last game, playing in a meaningless contest, they gave up a ninth, but their quarterback that year, Mark Rypien, was as well protected as any quarterback ever was. Engram made it a matter of pride for the whole offense, and Dan Wilber made sure every man on the line knew and understood what they were going for. They were going to be better than that 1991 line.

On the whole, I was happy with how the practices went. So was Engram. He came up to me on Thursday, late in the afternoon, when we were just finishing two-minute drills. "I gotta tell you," he said, grinning, "she looks good."

"Reminds me of you."

"More like a young Tom Brady."

"She stands like him sometimes, but you know when she drops back in the pocket, she actually looks like Griese. You ever see film of him?"

"Really solid footwork. Like she's dancing on air."

"Did you ever think you'd see such a thing? That young woman can throw it as hard as Brett Favre did."

"A woman," he said, shaking his head. "Wait'll I make *that* announcement."

"Look, we've all seen women play basketball as good as any man."

"Spivey's fit to be tied," he said, a slight change in his tone.

"Didn't think he'd be happy about it."

"He's trying to be a mensch. He likes her. They're friends."

"Really?" I said. "I hadn't noticed."

"No, they're friends. *Says* he's glad for her."

"He knows he can play. He'll be ready."

"It embarrasses him. He's 'humiliated beyond measure,' is how he put it."

"Who'd he say that to?" I asked.

"Charley Duncan. *He* thinks it's pretty silly too."

"Duncan's the first general manager to sign a woman," I said. "He should be happy to know he's going down in history."

"It's the 'going down' part I expect he's worried about. Maybe on some level we all are."

I said nothing for a while, then I gave a short laugh. "I guess it *is* kind of humiliating. I wouldn't want to get beat out by . . ." I didn't finish the sentence. "What about Ambrose?"

"I don't know. I put him on the unable to perform list this morning. He's out of it, in any case."

"I feel kind of sorry for him."

Engram shook his head, chuckling to himself. "Man, either I'm delusional and on the verge of being fired or we're about to chart a whole new territory."

"It's new territory, that's for damn sure, no matter *what* happens to you or me. Calling it 'new territory' may be a vast understatement of what we're about to do."

"You got that right."

We both stood there a while, thinking. Then he said, "Let's go have a cigar and talk about how we make the announcement."

Saturday morning at his regular pregame press conference, Coach Engram told the press. What he said was, "I'm making a change at quarterback. All my coaching life I've tried to emphasize that I am always looking for the best player at every position. I have played quarterback in this league, I know what is required, and I am certain that we can improve the play at that position. So I'm going to give Jesse Smoke a shot at it before this season starts to get away from us."

Well, you remember the pandemonium that followed. The whole country seemed to ignite with the news. We were in every newscast, every newspaper, every online news feed. Jesse's face and mine and Coach Engram's instantly plastered all over the world. Almost nobody had ever seen her play quarterback. So maybe it shouldn't have been surprising that what the sportswriters of America wanted to know was: Had Coach Engram lost his mind? Some said it was "a give-up move," that the coach was saying good-bye to the season as flamboy-antly as he could. Some said it was simply a novelty move to fill the stadium, that she'd be benched after the first series. Others claimed it was an affront to the league and the league office, a deliberate attempt to humiliate the commissioner. It was no big deal to let a rookie kick field goals for you, and nothing new about starting a rookie quarter-back, even in the middle of a season. But when that rookie happens to be a female? You'd have thought we'd announced that the president of the United States was going to start at quarterback.

The Raiders came to town Saturday, and most of them said they didn't care *who* played quarterback for us. Delbert Coleman, who the Steelers had traded to the Raiders at the beginning of the season, said he was looking forward to the game. He was asked, "Do you feel as though you have a score to settle with Jesse Smoke for the way she hit you in the face with the ball back in training camp with the Steelers?"

He still had a Band-Aid across his nose. "Yeah," he said. "I feel like I got a score to settle. But I don't really believe they'll play a woman. I promise you this, though: Whoever's at quarterback, I'm going to put *him* or *her* on the seat of *his* or *her* pants." Most of the Raiders were confident, and quietly respectful—they did not make fun of us the way some of the media did—and they were ready to play.

It rained on game day, water dropping out of the sky like it was being poured from a watering can. Even so, every seat in the stadium had an ass in it. And they sold 2,000 standing room only tickets as well. You couldn't find an empty space to move around in. More than 96,000 people waited for the kickoff, in an atmosphere of expectation the likes of which you've never seen, outside of a rock concert, say—or a public hanging.

As in every game up to that point I called plays from a booth upstairs, the best seats in the house. Jesse could hear me and Coach Engram through a headset in her helmet. Our game plan was to run as much as possible to keep the ball away from the Raiders' offense. We won the toss and after the Raiders kicked off, we got it out to the 25-yard line.

On the first play from scrimmage, Jesse gave the ball to Walter Mickens and he ran off tackle for 6 yards. When he got back to the huddle, he was muddy and soaked. On the next play I called a sweep around the left end. It's one of the oldest plays in all of football, and also one of the most basic. Vince Lombardi called it 49 28, and it came to be known as the Green Bay Sweep. It was designed for the running back to "run to daylight." It looks like this:

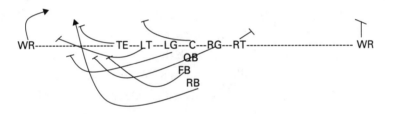

The two guards and the left tackle pull out of the line and run to the left, taking out whoever's in the way; the center blocks the middle linebacker; the sweep-side wide receiver takes out the linebacker or the cornerback on that side; and the running back looks for "daylight" and does his best to run through it.

We had all of a half a dozen running plays in our game plan that day and the Raiders pretty much knew we were going to run them, but our offensive line was strong and good enough to succeed. Our guys were really fired up, see. Engram saw to that. It is so much better in a game if the other team knows what plays you're going to run and they still can't stop it.

Mickens took the ball on the sweep and raced laterally toward the left end, found an opening, and gained 9 yards. (Anders flattened the Raiders' right linebacker.) First down on our 40. The crowd roared as though we'd scored a fucking touchdown. I saw Jesse telling everybody in the huddle to settle down and listen. No question, she was in charge out there.

On the third play, I called a center trap—a play where the center pulls out of the line as though he is going to lead a sweep, and our running back, following the fullback, goes through the hole created by the center when he pulls out. If the lineman across from the center goes with him, anticipating a sweep, the fullback hits the middle linebacker, shoves him out of the way, and the ball carrier gains right up the middle. If the lineman stays put, the linebacker usually follows the center and the fullback has to hit the lineman and get him out of the way. The only time the play doesn't work is if both the lineman *and* the linebacker "stay home" and don't go for the fake. The play calls for a very quick handoff, which Jesse executed brilliantly. The lineman and the linebacker went with the center, and Mickens gained 11 yards right up the middle. First down on the Raiders 49.

On the next play I wanted an off-tackle run again, but Jesse changed the play at the line, ran the 49 28 Red, which was a sweep to the right. This time Mickens found a huge gap, leaped over a diving safety, and ran for 18 yards. First down at the Raiders 31. Now the crowd really got into it.

And I got ambitious. What happened was all my fault, I admit. But I could see the Raider defense gearing up to stop another run, and I knew what our tendencies were in that situation. I always knew our tendencies, see; that was part of my job: Scout our own offense so I could see what other teams might be guessing about us in certain situations. Another run to one side or the other was precisely the kind of play we might run 95 percent of the time in a driving rain, from inside the opponent's 40 on first and 10. So I called Double X2, Red22M, Quick Z. It was a play fake and quick pass to one of the wide receivers. All Jesse had to do was fake a handoff to Walter Mickens, then stand up and hit either Darius Exley on the right or

168

Rob Anders on the left, each running a quick slant to the middle. The receiver was to take the ball, turn up field, and run like hell. With the defense piled in close to the line to stop the run, that kind of play might gain 50 yards or more. The play called for Jesse to drop back only three steps, after she made the fake to Mickens, and then to let the ball fly. Jesse knew it well, had hit it perfectly every time we tried it in practice that week.

I saw her walk confidently up to the line as the offense took their positions. From up in the booth you couldn't even tell she was a woman. She was just a quarterback, built like most of them, tall and lean. She stood behind center looking over the defense. Both the Raider safeties were right up on top of the linebackers, and both corners crowded our two wide receivers. They had eight men in the box—eight men, that is, within five yards of the line of scrimmage. It was absolutely perfect. They might stop a run, but what we had called, if we could hit it, would gain big yardage.

Jesse took the snap, but just as she was pulling back, Dan Wilber, who was taking his position to pass block, accidentally stepped on her left foot, sending her squirming down in the mud. She got back up as quickly as she could, but she missed the fake to Mickens, who went on by and hit the line, trying to fake a missed handoff. Jesse stood for only a few seconds looking for Exley or Anders downfield, and just as she saw Anders break into the clear about 10 yards behind the line, she got hit in the middle of her back by the Raiders left corner, who had blitzed on the play. Her head snapped back, her helmet flew off, and the ball sailed free. She went down hard on her chest into the mud with the cornerback on top of her, while Delbert Coleman, the Raider defensive end on the right side, picked the ball out of the air and raced 61 yards for a touchdown.

I know everybody in the world has seen that highlight film—it is always called "Delbert's Revenge"—but I can't look at it. The sight of her getting hit like that, on our first pass play, still makes me weak in the knees. It was 6–0 Raiders before we'd played 3 minutes, but I wasn't thinking about any of that. I didn't even see Coleman score. I watched the Raider cornerback get up and strut away and then I saw Jesse turn over slowly on the field. She lay there a while, not moving, then Dan Wilber reached down and offered his hand. She reached for it, and I gave a sigh of relief. She was definitely conscious. He pulled her to her feet. She picked up her helmet and trotted to the sideline, staggering a bit as she got there. I thought of those fine bones in her neck and got sick to my stomach.

I picked up the phone and called down to the sideline. Usually either my offensive line coach or Jesse would answer the bench phone, but this time I got Greg Bayne, the defensive coordinator.

"Where's Jesse?" I said.

"They're looking at her."

On the field, the Raiders were lining up at the 33 to kick the extra point, which, to a smattering of boos, made it 7–0. I saw Ken Spivey warming up behind the bench. "Is she hurt bad?" I said into the phone.

"I don't know. She fell down when she got back here."

I hadn't seen that. I told Bayne to put Ken Spivey on the phone so I could go over the plays we would try to run when we got the ball back, but I also needed to talk to Jesse. When Ken got on the phone he said he was ready.

"You think she's going back in?" I said.

"I don't know," said Ken. "I can't tell what's going on. She's on the ground, I think."

The Raiders kicked off and the ball bounced through our end zone for a touchback. We'd be starting on our 20-yard line. There was a long TV time-out, and I watched the field to see what was happening over on the sideline. I saw a crowd around Jesse. The offense trotted on the field and waited in a sort of standing huddle for the end of the time-out. Spivey was at quarterback.

The crowd really started booing.

I heard Spivey's headset start to crackle.

I called another running play. He put his hands up to the ear holes on his helmet to let me know he'd heard me. The referee blew his whistle, and then Spivey and the offense leaned down in the huddle.

I still couldn't see through the crowd around Jesse.

Twenty-One

THEY TOOK JESSE to the locker room and X-rayed her back. (Seeing two of our medical staff walking her to the locker room, I felt something cold stab me in the heart; it was real fear for her, and it shocked me.) The X-rays turned out to be just a precaution. The doctor was afraid of broken ribs, but there was no fracture. She'd gotten the wind knocked out of her and she'd have a hell of a bruise, but . . . she was going to be okay.

After Jesse went out, as you may remember, the game just got away from us. Our defense spent a lot of time slogging in the mud, chasing Raider running backs and wide receivers. They didn't run it on us much—although they certainly tried that move against Orlando that had been so successful in the Giants game. He got pushed out of the way a couple of times, but he'd learned to stay in his lane and fight for position. The trouble was, the Raiders were throwing short dump-off passes to the running backs in the rain, slicing through us like our defense had their feet planted in the mud. At one point, I was half afraid Orlando would break a leg, the way he lunged out of the muck to throw himself at those dark, ghostly, little backs speeding by him, just eluding his grasp.

Spivey couldn't hit a thing. We had the running game going pretty well, but eventually we needed him to hit something. A few times he lost his footing, too. He threw an interception in the second quarter that was a direct result of his front foot slipping out from under him as he was releasing the ball—the kind of thing that can happen to anybody. The ball, sailing too short and high, was, of course, picked off by a linebacker.

By halftime, it was 23 to 0. (The Raiders kicker had slipped in the mud and missed an extra point.) I'd gotten a report from Bayne early in the second quarter that Jesse was going to be all right. When she came back out of the tunnel, the crowd cheered for her, but Engram told me she was done for the day.

We were heading for another loss, though it would be no shame. The Raiders were favored to go all the way that year. And they'd already shown us they could whip us pretty bad in the preseason.

Still, any loss really takes it out of you. And we were losing very badly.

In the middle of the third quarter, the Raiders drove the ball 70 yards and had a first and goal at our 3. They missed a quick pass to the tight end, who was wide open and dropped it. Then they tried to go up the middle on us, but Drew Bruckner and Zack Leedom stuffed it good. No gain. It was third and goal from the 3. They tried to go around Orlando's end, but he knifed through and dropped their running back for a 6-yard loss. The crowd cheered then, glad for something to cheer about. But the Raiders kicked a field goal, and now it was 26 to 0. Eight minutes to go in the third quarter.

Here's the thing: If your game plan is to run the ball and you're down by more than two scores late in the third quarter, you got to adjust. The game plan? That goes out the window. We had to pass, and we had to pass with Spivey.

What we'd practiced all week was short, quick passes to the wide receivers and running backs. We only had one or two long balls in the plan. Spivey could throw it hard and he could be pretty accurate, actually, but with only 6 minutes left in the third quarter and the ball on the Raiders 37-yard line, he got knocked down. He'd completed a 16-yard pass to our tight end to get to the 37, but the same cornerback who had dropped Jesse put Spivey's face into the mud and he got up swinging. He hadn't fumbled, but he wanted to kill somebody. Dan Wilber got a hold of him and sort of danced him back toward the huddle, but there was no calming Spivey down once he lost his temper.

On the next play he dropped back and then fired it toward Exley. It hit their left-side linebacker right between the numbers, but he didn't have the hands to hold on to it. The ball popped into the air and a few people batted it around but it landed on the turf.

I called a draw play, but Spivey changed it at the line. He tried a deep pass to Anders on the left, but it sailed way over his head and out-of-bounds. The crowd was starting to chant, "We want Jesse! We want Jesse!"

Now it was third and 10. I called the same play we'd hit earlier to the tight end, only this time I wanted it run on the other side. The tight end goes in motion and runs the pattern from a yard or two off the line of scrimmage. It looks like it could be a running play to that side and that's what I hoped the Raiders would be looking for, even if it was third and 10. Everything worked to perfection; the tight end was wide open, but Spivey, his face red as a football, hit him in the ankles.

Now it was fourth and 10 from the Raiders 37. We could try a 54-yard field goal, but our kicker was sitting on the bench with a badly bruised back. So Coach Engram, wanting to spare Jesse, sent in Dever. He missed it short and wide left.

Four minutes left in the third quarter now, and the Raiders had the ball near midfield with us still down 26 to 0.

You could feel something essential sapping out of everybody. Even up in the booth I could feel it. When you get to that point in a game, nothing keeps you playing but pride and heart. It's not stubbornness. If it was just that, there'd be more violence; nobody would bother to play by the rules. Most of the time players stay out there and do what each play calls them to do, giving every single ounce of energy on each play, even when it's completely useless. The game is over. What keeps them playing is heart and pride and a refusal to admit defeat even in the certain face of it. That's what makes football so heroic. Only sometimes, when you're not playing well and you know you can play better, and the weather's in your face, and you're beaten down so far you need to take a deep breath just to regain the energy to take another one, you can get to a place where defeat is in everything you do—the way you walk; the way you carry your head; hell, the way you stand on the sideline.

I could see that was happening to us. Head down, Coach Engram kicked the mud clods at his feet. Normally he paced, but not now. Now he just stood there. And when I said through the mike, "Keep your head up, Coach," he ignored me.

Bayne was exhorting the defense, standing on the field sometimes, signaling to them. But the Raiders kept the pressure on, moving down the field, eating up the clock with short passes to their running backs, quick strikes over the middle to the tight end. They marched it all the way to our 12-yard line.

And then, something rather extraordinary happened. Orlando Brown intercepted a pass.

They had their tight end wide open again, but Orlando jumped into the air, knocked the ball back, then ran under it and pulled it in. He galloped 88 yards the other way for a touchdown. Nobody could catch him, as he galloped nearly 10 yards with each stride.

Dever kicked the extra point, and suddenly, with all of 1:30 left in the third quarter, we had a little life in us.

We kicked off (short, unfortunately; Dever was still out of his groove from that missed field goal), and the Raiders kick returner broke through our special teams and ran it out to their 48-yard line. Coach Engram threw his clipboard down in a fit of disgust. Two plays later, our cornerback on the right side, Colin Briggs, fell down, and the Raiders hit a 52-yard pass to their All-Pro wide receiver Jeremiah Stubbs. Briggs had been corralling Stubbs all day; held him to two short receptions, but he slipped in the mud and that was that. Now it was 32 to 7. The third quarter ended after the Raiders kicked the extra point.

We trailed 33 to 7 going into the fourth quarter. The crowd was still chanting, "We want Jesse! We want Jesse!" I was surprised how many of them remained for this debacle. Usually, most fans filed out midway through the third quarter if the team had fallen behind by more than three touchdowns.

And then I saw Coach Engram go over to Jesse. She got up and started throwing behind the bench. The crowd went wild.

"What's going on?" I said into the mike.

Coach Engram said, "Can you get your ass down here?"

"Sure. What's up?"

"She's going back in, damn it."

"Is she all right?"

"She wants you down here. Bring your mike and transmitter."

As I rounded up what I'd need and headed for the door, everybody in the booth was wishing *me* luck.

Twenty-Two

COACH ENGRAM CALLED the plays while I was on the way down to the sideline, having to go down several long switchbacks and stairways deep in the bowels of the stadium to get out to the field. My headset on, I heard him tell her to hold on to the ball. At some point, as I ran along, though, I realized my reception was going out. Still I could hear the crowd roar when Jesse trotted onto the field—it shook the building—and then the public address speakers bellowing her name. I ran down the "up" escalator steps because they were the first stairway I came to, and the elevators, which I had no intention of waiting for anyway, were all the way on the other side of the stadium. There was a long hallway I had to get to before I could even begin to descend all the way to the field. Through the headset, badly breaking up now, I could just barely hear the first play Coach Engram called. Knowing the Raiders would be expecting us to pass, he had her run a quick draw play. I heard the public address announcer say that Mickens got 15 yards.

Now the crowd roared again, even more deafening. The announcer said, "Pass to Anders complete for five yards." So he had her throwing. It was her first completion in the NFL and I'd missed it. Not that I didn't see it a hundred times on ESPN later. Hell, they *still* play it, even these days.

Adrenaline pumped through me so hard, I felt I could fly down those stairs. It's a wonder I didn't fall and break my neck. The headset I wore was now useless. I could not hear a thing. The crowd roared again. "Pass complete to Mickens for ten yards," from the sound system. "First down Redskins."

As I got to the ramp leading down to the first level my headset came back. I heard Engram say, "Coach Granger's coming." Then he called another sweep to the left.

Again the crowd cheered. "Mickens off tackle for seven yards," the announcer said.

Finally reaching the tunnel, I sprinted out to the field and saw through the players lined up on the sideline that, though the front of Jesse's uniform was almost black with mud, the back was spotless. Clearly nobody had knocked her down.

She must not have known I was there yet, as she hurried the team up to the line and called a play of her own—a quick out to Anders that gained 12 yards.

I was surprised to see how hard the rain pelted down. Jesse had us at the Raiders' 38-yard line, second and 10. She'd overthrown Mickens coming out of the backfield. They were in the offensive huddle, and as I walked up the sideline, I tried to signal her. She brought the team to the line again, called the signals loud and clear, dropped back, and looked downfield. Exley flew up the right side-line, and Jesse, planting her back foot, looked to the left of the field first, to freeze the safety, then fired it on a line right to Exley's left shoulder. It was like that first time I saw her on the beach, when she hit that guy on the jet ski. Exley just reached up and gently pulled the ball down, never even breaking stride, and ran it right into the end zone. We had 12 minutes left and after Dever kicked the extra point it was 33 to 14. The crowd was really into it now. You couldn't hear yourself think.

Jesse came back to the sideline, not even slightly out of breath. She took off her helmet and we screamed over the crowd noise at each other about what we'd try to do when she got back on the field. "We gotta be quick," I told her. "Use the middle of the field."

"I know."

"They'll expect us to try for quick sideline passes to get out-of-bounds and save time. The middle will be open."

Engram went to Bayne and told him to get the defense to play, by god, and then he came over to us.

We talked about another deep ball to Exley, or maybe a quick slant to Anders and a lateral to Exley or Mickens. The excitement was so frantic and noisy, I can't really tell you which plays we talked about with Jesse. Those baby blues of hers were on fire, though, I can tell you that. Her blood was up. I suggested a screen to Mickens might work, and Jesse said she wanted to throw the Double XY Corner, though she had to yell it twice before we realized what she was calling for.

Now, even if you're not interested in football, you have to pay attention to how this play worked. Essentially, it's a deep corner route to Exley. He and Anders would run deep post patterns at first, both bending to the middle deep, so that it looked like a crossing pattern. Then, just as the corner and safety committed to that move, Jesse would throw it high, way behind Exley—in fact, the ball would be over the wrong shoulder, so that he had to turn back, which he could do on a dime, and break to the ball. Sometimes, when that play worked, the defensive back and the safety would fall on their asses. It was a dangerous play, though, because Darius would have to be sure-footed as a doe in that slop, and the quarterback had to throw it exactly right so that it dropped down out of the sky at the right spot near the corner, at just the right moment, as the wide receiver got to

179

it. When it works, it's one of the prettiest plays in football, but we'd only run it in practice a few times, and I wasn't even sure we'd ever practiced it with Jesse.

We were still talking about what we'd do when Drew Bruckner intercepted a short pass and ran it back to the 5-yard line. In the din of the cheering crowd, Jesse put her helmet back on and went out with the offense. I donned my headset and turned on my transmitter, but before I could even start to talk, Jesse'd called a middle trap fake and rollout pass to Gayle Glenn Louis, the tight end. He was wide open and she flipped it to him for a second touchdown pass in less than 5 minutes. This time, Jesse kicked the extra point bringing the score to 33 to 21.

Only people who were there can describe how loud it got. I don't think I'd heard that many people screaming all at once. Or ever have since. You just have no idea. The crowd's roar seemed to have wind; you could almost feel the breath of all those people screaming for Jesse.

With 9 minutes left in the game, we kicked off. There was some talk of an onside kick, but Coach Engram didn't want to take a chance in that mud. The Raiders got the ball at their 23 and started up the field, trying to take some time off the clock with a few sweeps and rollout passes to the backs. In six plays they were at midfield, and the crowd had quieted down a bit, which still left the stadium plenty noisy.

On second and 6 from their own 49, the Raiders tried a flare pass to their fullback, a play they hadn't run all year. It was definitely a smart thing to do, but the back sort of flipped the ball up in the air, almost as if he wanted to cradle it, and it jumped up out of his arms right into the waiting hands of Orlando Brown, his second interception of the day. He fell down at the 16-yard line, trying to get to the end zone, but now we had the ball deep in Raider territory again.

Jesse went back out there, and this time I could talk to her. I called a quick slant to Anders on the left. The play is designed to free up either Anders or Mickens, who runs to that side out of the backfield.

But Anders was so quick and Jesse got the ball to him at the 5-yard line. He hit the safety, kept his feet, and spun his way across the goal line. Again the crowd exploded. Jesse kicked the extra point, and now, with 5:15 left, the score was 33 to 28. Jesse had thrown only seven passes. One she overthrew. One was intercepted. She completed five. Three went for touchdowns.

Now the Raiders showed that they were champions. They took the kickoff out to the 31-yard line. Then they started moving the ball methodically down the field. With short runs, quick passes to the backs, and a 12-yard completion on third and 8 near midfield, they used up most of what was left of the clock and we had to use all of our time-outs.

With 2:30 left they were on our 18-yard line. It was second and seven. They ran another sweep toward Orlando and gained another 3 yards. Then they let the clock get down to the two-minute warning. On third and 4, they ran an off-tackle play that got awful close, but Rack and Leedom stopped it only inches short of a first down. They let the clock run down as far as they could and then sent the field goal team onto the field.

I thought it was over, and so did everybody else. But the kicker slipped in the wet turf and shanked the ball to the left of the upright.

It was our ball, first and 10 on the 20-yard line.

Jesse looked at me with those icy blues, put her helmet on, and trotted onto the field. The crowd held its breath, it seemed. Or maybe it was just me. Coach Engram came up next to me. "She going to run it?" he said.

"Not yet."

"What'd you call?"

"Nothing. But I know what she's going to do."

I did know. I could tell by the look in her eyes. The Double XY Corner wouldn't work from that place on the field. She had to get us out to near midfield. So she called two plays in the huddle. The first play was a three-quarter post to Anders. She took a seven-step drop, set up, and the line blocked furiously, forming a very nice pocket around her. She stepped up when Anders made his move and fired the ball on a line, 25 yards downfield, right into his hands. He dodged the safety and ran another 5 yards before the cornerback dragged him down. The ball was on the 50. Everybody ran to get in position for another play. The clock was under a minute now, ticking away. We always practiced getting back in position in a hurry and the men knew how to do it, but it seemed to take an eternity. Some had to drag themselves up out of the mud; some had to gather themselves and run after such strenuous exertion they could barely stand up.

Anyway, they got into position. Jesse came to the line and spiked the ball to stop the clock. One of the offensive linemen wasn't in position when she did that and we were penalized 5 yards. Coach Engram shook his head and glared at me in frustration. I nodded, but I was smiling. I think it was beginning to hit me right then what I had been witnessing; what had happened to me and our team and the NFL and America. I was smiling like a man who's won the lottery.

After the penalty we were on our 45-yard line. It was first and 15 with 38 seconds left. Jesse came to the line and started calling signals. I could see she didn't like what she saw—the two safeties were playing in a deep zone—so she changed the play. She tried a quick out to Mickens about 10 yards down the field, but the pass got to him too quick and bounced off the edge of his fingers and hit the turf. It didn't even bounce. It just plopped into the thick mud and roiled grass.

Second and 15. Jesse took her time in the huddle this time. I still had not called a play and she didn't communicate with me at all.

On second down, she dropped back three steps and fired it to Exley on a quick out right. It should have gotten about 10 or even 15 yards, but he slipped as he was making his cut, and fell down just after the ball got there. He got hit almost immediately but managed to get out-of-bounds. The play only gained 4 yards. It was third and 11. We had no more time-outs and now only 26 seconds remained in the game.

Again Jesse took her time. The rain started to ease off a bit, and a small hole in the clouds let in some late afternoon sunlight. I'll never forget how that light glistened off those wet, dark burgundy helmets as the offense broke the huddle.

Jesse walked up to the line, bent over center, looking at the defense. This time she stuck with the play she'd called, and I knew what it was. At the snap of the ball she dropped back, a full seven-step drop. She stood there, her feet planted, hopping slightly, watching downfield. The pass rush was furious—a blitz from the middle linebacker that Mickens picked up beautifully—and Delbert Coleman, who bull-rushed then twisted away from our tackle and came free, lunged at Jesse, but she quickly stepped to the side a bit, then up into the pocket and Coleman went by. Just as another Raider lineman reached for her, she released the ball so quickly it looked like it was shot out of her arm. But it didn't go on a line. It floated in a high, sweet arch toward the corner of the end zone, and Exley, all alone, trotted under it and let it drop into his hands. It was like ballet. One of the most beautiful things I ever saw. Both the cornerback and the safety had slipped down in the mud, and Exley only had to make sure he got to where the ball was.

What followed was bedlam. I thought that crowd would stay crazy for the rest of their lives. To this day, I've never heard such ecstatic noise. It was louder than it had been that whole day. Fans came from out of the ground it seemed. They covered the field, and the players all stood around wondering what to do. Jesse had trotted back to the bench after the throw and a bunch of players gathered around her to hug her and protect her from the onrush of fans.

It took nearly a half an hour to clear the field so Jesse could kick the extra point. Coach Engram never would let Jesse kick off, so with 16 seconds left Dever kicked it deep—his blood was up, too—and the Raiders didn't get it out past their own 20. Our defense trotted out and held for two desperate plays and the gun sounded.

We won the game 35 to 33. Dan Wilber picked Jesse up on his shoulders and with the others crowded around walked her off the field. Even Coach Engram tried to get in on it. Jesse was high on Dan's shoulders, waving her arms at the crowd and the players all crowded around her. You'd have thought we won the Super Bowl.

And thus began the brief, heartbreaking career that became the legend of Jesse Smoke.

Twenty-Three

BY WEDNESDAY OF that week, Coach Engram was on the cover of *Sports Weekly* with Jesse under his arm—under his arm, like his girlfriend—and in big yellow lettering underneath the photo a banner read: REDSKINS SWEETHEART WORKS A MIRACLE. Under that, in more conventional lettering: COACH JONATHON ENGRAM AND HIS COURAGEOUS DISCOVERY.

Sports Weekly always liked that sort of ambiguity; they might be saying Jesse was Coach Engram's discovery and that she was courageous. Or that he was courageous for discovering her. No matter how you looked at it, the magazine was giving him credit for "finding" the "jewel that is the first female NFL player in history."

I confess to you now, I was pretty bothered by all that. Not that I ever said anything directly to anybody, of course. And I was happy to see that Coach Engram credited me with the whole thing in his book on Jesse. I understood how those things worked, how they could be misunderstood; still, it bothered me. I'm not saying it took courage for me to bring her to the Redskins, or to sign her to a contract without letting anybody know what I was actually doing. Anybody might have jumped at the chance to sign her once they saw her play. Look, if anybody in all of this had courage, it was Jesse. What she was doing, to put it bluntly, and no pun intended, took one hell of a pair of balls.

We were now 3 and 3. Next, we had the Los Angeles Rams on the road. They were 1 and 5 on the year and fighting both injuries and age. They had made the playoffs the year before with a 10 and 8 record. In the first game of the season they lost the entire right side of their offensive line to injury. Since their protection was not very good, they lost their quarterback to a fairly grizzly knee injury in week three. Their stadium was a noisy place to play, but we went up there and Jesse started her second game. We made her wear an extra pad under her flak jacket to protect her bruised back. She already wore pads that encased her chest and protected her ribs in front. The hit she took in the Raiders game gave her a sore neck, but she claimed the big bruise between her shoulder blades didn't hurt at all.

In Los Angeles she looked terrific on the last artificial turf field in the NFL. She moved around in the pocket, dropped back as swiftly and keenly as any pro. We ran the ball a lot—handed it to Mickens and sometimes the fullback Jack Slater, who bulled into the line like a water buffalo. Mickens rushed for 158 yards and scored a touchdown. Jesse had no interceptions, no fumbles, and she did not get knocked down even once. She went 11 for 14, for 266 yards and 3 touchdowns—2 of them to Exley. We won 28 to 3.

Now we were 4 and 3, and everywhere we went, the stadium was packed. People wanted to see Jesse play.

The Giants were still undefeated at 7 and 0. Dallas was tied with us at 4 and 3. Philadelphia had won 3 and lost 3.

The rest of our schedule looked like this:

Week Eight (October 16)	Kansas City Chiefs
Week Nine (October 23)	at Mexico City Aztecs
Week Ten (October 30)	Bye
Week Eleven (November 6)	at Cleveland Browns
Week Twelve (November 13)	Philadelphia Eagles
Week Thirteen (November 20)	at New York Jets
Week Fourteen (November 24)	at Dallas Cowboys
Week Fifteen (December 4)	Cincinnati Bengals
Week Sixteen (December 11)	Tampa Bay Buccaneers
Week Seventeen (December 18)	at San Diego Chargers
Week Eighteen (December 24)	at Green Bay Packers
Week Nineteen (December 31)	New York Giants

The best team in the league was probably the Oakland Raiders, but there were some real powerhouses on our schedule. As I mentioned earlier, the Cowboys were better than the score indicated in our first win against them; the Giants were going to be hard to beat, even at home. They were running on everybody, and it wasn't just trickery; they were very good at pushing people out of the way.

I worked with Jesse all week as usual on the offensive game plan. Monday was usually an off day for the players, but Jesse came in to work with Coach Engram and me on the game plan for Kansas City. At our first offensive meeting, she asked if we could have a talk.

"Sure," I said. "When?"

"How about right now?"

We were in one of the smaller meeting rooms and we'd been watching films of the Kansas City defense. Coach Engram was not there yet, so it was just the two of us.

"What's the matter?" I said.

"I've heard from my mother."

"Really?"

187

"I got a letter," Jesse said, slouched in an office chair. She wore sweats, as usual, and I saw she'd gotten another haircut. She always wore it in tight curls, close cropped but just slightly unruly. It didn't cover her ears which, maybe, were a little too large for a face so perfectly structured. When she told me she'd heard from her mother, there was no tone in her voice. "She saw my face on the cover of that magazine."

"Hunh," I said. "I mean, your face has been out there, all over the media, for a long time."

She nodded, considering.

"You sure it's your mother?"

"It's her. I'd know that handwriting anywhere."

"Didn't you tell me you didn't remember her?"

She sat forward. "I was young when she went away."

"Can I see the letter?"

"I gave it to Coach Engram."

"What the hell'd you do that for?"

Her eyes widened a bit, and I realized I had been a little too loud and emphatic. I didn't want her to know how I felt about how Engram had taken her "under his wing," as the *Washington Post* had phrased it. At the time, though, I admit I was kind of touchy about it. She said, "*I* didn't tell him about it. She wrote to *him* too."

"You're kidding."

Her face was impassive, expressionless. Even her normally bright blue eyes seemed muted. There wasn't a lot of light in the room and it was early in the morning. I didn't want Jesse thinking about anything but the Kansas City Chiefs, but this was an issue I knew we couldn't just brush aside. Coach Engram would join us soon, so I lowered my voice. "Do you know what she said to him?"

"No."

"He wouldn't tell you?"

"Why are you whispering?"

188

"No reason."

"He said he'd go over it with me after our meeting today."

"What did she say to you?"

"Just, you know, how proud she is and all. Stuff like that."

"She's not asking for anything?"

"No."

I sat back. "She will," I almost said, but thought better of it. No need for cynicism before it was totally necessary.

"She lives in Tennessee," Jesse said, and now her voice sounded kind of sad.

"You all right?" I said.

"Yeah." But she didn't sound convinced. I wanted to put my arm around her and give her a good squeeze. I'd seen her frustrated and determined; I'd seen her angry, ecstatic, and happy. I'd seen her when her blood was up and she was so focused you'd have to hit her with a two-by-four just to get her attention, but I don't think I'd ever seen her looking sad.

"Don't you want to respond to her?"

"She loved my father once."

I nodded.

"She knew him when he was young. I don't know. After she left she kept sending me letters and e-mails. For years she wrote to me. I never answered her."

"Why not?"

She looked at me, as if I should know. Then she said, "I hated her for leaving my father."

"How old were you, Jesse?"

"I was eleven."

And then Coach Engram poked his head in the door. "Be right with you." I noticed Jesse smile brightly when she saw him. When he closed the door she looked at me. "Have you seen Darius Exley's dolls?"

"I think he prefers 'action figures,' no?"

189

"Pretty amazing, aren't they?"

I studied her. "You like Coach Engram, don't you?"

She shrugged.

"He's forty-four years old, you know."

"What do you mean?"

"I mean . . . he's pretty old."

"Older than you?"

"I'm fifty-one."

She crossed her legs and leaned back in the chair almost luxuriously. I wondered sometimes if she knew how beautiful she was. A woman built that tall—with angular bones and small breasts, not much in the way of hips and all—could easily have no sense of just how attractive she really is. She was not masculine, Jesse—not even slightly—until, of course, when she stepped onto a football field. As I said earlier, with her uniform on, the flak jacket and her helmet, she looked like a lean guy on the wiry side. She carried herself, I mean, in such an athletic way, you'd never say she was feminine in the traditional sense of that word. She certainly wasn't prissy; didn't scream easily, even when she was pleased. She walked into a room as though she'd just been placed in charge of it, and yet always with a sort of glittery-eyed wonder.

"What do you think of Darius?" Jesse asked.

"Exley's as cool and wily as a cat," I said, smiling. "That's what I think of him. *And* he can catch anything you throw at him."

"What about Dan Wilber?"

"What's with the questions, Jesse?"

She raised her brows a bit and seemed to give a slight shrug. Then she said, "They want to go out with me."

"I hope you don't mean that the way I *think* you mean it."

"How should I mean it?"

"What do you mean 'go out with you'? You mean like a date?"

She nodded, her brow still slightly elevated.

"We can't have that kind of thing on this team," I said.

"Yeah, I didn't think so." She sat forward a little. "I've said no to everybody. Only I kind of like Darius."

"You do?"

"He's smart, and I like the way he carries himself."

"Jesse, if you get involved with any of these players, you know what that will mean."

She nodded.

"Everyone who hates this idea predicts this very thing."

"I know."

"You can't get involved with any of the coaches, either."

"So I'm not supposed to have any kind of a private life?"

"*Away* from this team, sure you are. You have to stick to that, though, Jesse—one hundred percent."

Which is when Coach Engram came back in. "She has to stick to what one hundred percent?"

"Avoid sex with every player, coach, equipment man, administrator, or owner on this team," I said.

Engram blushed as he sat down. "Yeah, that's probably best."

"It's not like any of you have to worry about that," Jesse said, a bit of a smirk on her face. It was as if she knew something we could never know.

It was quiet for a while. I think both of us expected her to say more, but she just sat there, with that half smile on her face. Finally, Coach Engram asked about our game plan.

"I think we can run a few screens to Mickens," Jesse said.

"Yeah," I piped in a little awkwardly. "On the film they're willing to give up a little more than most teams to get to the quarterback. They blitz a lot."

"I noticed that too," Engram said. He was sitting next to Jesse.

I said, "It looks like we can do some real business with a middle screen or shuttle pass behind the center when we get inside their twenty."

"They stunt to the outside a lot down there, don't they." What he meant was that the Kansas City defense sent their tackles in a kind of exchange where they would crisscross over the center, one racing to the right and the other wheeling around to the left behind him. It is a tactic that can confuse an offensive line, but if you block it right, you can open a huge hole up the middle.

And he was right. On film, they had a tendency to run that stunt whenever anyone got inside their 20-yard line. We could run a draw, a center screen, or even a quick underhand flip to the running back cutting behind the center, and if it worked, get some good yardage out of it. Of course the Chiefs knew that play was vulnerable that way, so they'd try to disguise when they were going to run it. We studied the film to look for what we call "keys" to the play—little signs that it's been called and they're going to run it. What Jesse and I had noticed on the film earlier that morning was that whenever Kansas City called that play, their right tackle leaned back a little and his knuckles would raise a fraction off the turf—just enough so you could see a shadow under them. Every time he got in that position, he pulled out to cross behind the other tackle.

When I showed that to Coach Engram, he grinned. "Damn," he said. "This is so much fun sometimes."

"Yes it is," I said. "We should be able to do some business on that play."

There was a long pause while all of us admired the film. We watched that tackle pull out to run that stunt four or five times. Then I looked at Engram. "Her mother going to be a problem?"

"Whose mother?"

Jesse gave a slight laugh.

"Hers," I said, pointing.

He looked at Jesse. "You don't have to broadcast the thing."

"She can tell *me*," I said. "I signed her to this contract. I'm her mentor on this team."

He stared at me, clearly suppressing laughter.

"I'm serious," I said. "I'm looking out for her. I've *been* looking out for her. If something's going on that might—"

"I'd appreciate it," Jesse interrupted, "if we could just concentrate on the Chiefs today? I mean—damn—stop talking about me like I'm in another room."

"I'm sorry," I said. Coach Engram stared at both of us.

"Anyway, my mother is not going to be a problem," Jesse said.

It's a wonder to me now that I believed the *only* problem might be her mother.

Twenty-Four

I MOVED DOWN to the sideline for all the rest of our games. I hated giving up my seat in the booth, but it was just too far from the action, and Coach Engram wanted me to be where I could talk directly to Jesse if she needed it. The day we played the Chiefs, a reporter asked me about the change. I said I wanted to be where I could speak with my rookie quarterback, which got erroneously reported as Jesse needing me down there to play well.

We whipped Kansas City without too much trouble, 35 to 10. Jesse ran the shuttle pass behind the center twice in the first half. Mickens gained 18 yards the first time we ran it—he was dragged down inside the 1-yard line. The second time, right before the end of the second quarter, he went 16 yards for a touchdown. Jesse was cheered like a rock star every time she ran onto the field, every time she completed a pass, as loud as anything I ever heard in that stadium. She completed 18 passes out of 23, for 257 yards and 2 touchdowns. She got knocked down a few times, after she'd released the ball.

There was one really bad sack in the first half—she got hit so hard I worried if she'd get back up again. But she jumped up a moment later and handed the ball to the referee, who had thrown his flag and charged the defense with roughing the passer. (The guy who got charged with the penalty—a pretty good linebacker named Renaldo Kane—complained to the press after the game that it was a bad call. "Those refs feel sorry for her because she's a girl, so we can't even bump her a little bit. I barely touched her." But let's be clear: He hit her in the neck with the crown of his helmet, which is roughing the passer, whether the passer is male or female.) Jesse ended up with a bloody gash across her nose that bled for most of the rest of the half. It was all over the front of her jersey, but the men seemed to rally around her when they saw the blood and the way she herself seemed to ignore it, blocking that much harder. Those men were ready to kill for Jesse. The second half, she did much better. I think she only got knocked down once.

Jesse's most spectacular touchdown pass was to Anders. She dropped back and held her ground for a bit, looking downfield, then she sensed a blitz coming from her right. She drifted a bit to her left, then rolled that way, looking downfield. Anders had run from wide on the left side, a deep post, so he was running across the field, deep to the right, away from where Jesse was going. Just before anyone got to her, while she was still moving those quick, beautifully positioned feet, she threw a 40-yard bomb that dropped over Anders's right shoulder as he raced to the corner. It was a perfect pass, and the crowd could see it coming while the ball was in flight—could see it even before Anders looked back for it. You could *hear* their anticipation. The sound of that—of an entire crowd just beginning the intake of breath ahead of a scream, while the ball makes its arching way to a certain touchdown—it's got to be one of the most wonderful sounds on earth. You have to be in the stadium to hear it. It's as though the ball draws any noise into itself as it spins through the air toward the man running under it, his hands not yet outstretched for it. And when the ball comes down into the man's hands so that he doesn't even have to reach for it—when he takes it as though it's been dropped off a shelf two feet above his head—the noise reaches its crescendo and the place erupts. It's maybe the most beautiful thing in athletics. It beats an ace in tennis, a home run in baseball, a dunk or spectacular three-point shot in basketball. There's nothing close to it.

After the Kansas City game, Jesse wore a Band-Aid across her nose. She was self-conscious about it, but I thought she looked cute. So did the media. The fashion world caught on to her all over again. There was still talk about Jesse really being a man, but now there was a large enough contingent of adults and people with half a brain who ignored that talk. Even the press stopped talking overmuch about it, although Roddy always wanted to know how it made her feel. To which she always answered that she didn't feel anything. "I can't control what people think," she said.

Nate and Andy kept calling her and trying to set up photo shoots and meetings with every kind of commercial venture. The team public relations director—a guy named Harold Moody—bombarded her with requests for interviews from the press, from magazine writers, sports commentators, and talk show hosts. She didn't have enough time in a day to take everything that came her way.

More people knew who Jesse Smoke was than any other human being on the planet. Hell, folks who couldn't remember who the president of the United States was, they knew Jesse Smoke.

It was frightening.

Finally we had a meeting with Andy and Nate and Jesse. We also included Justin Peck, her football agent; Harold Moody; and Coach Engram. The meeting was Engram's idea, but I agreed to it. Something had to be done to stem the tide of demand on Jesse's time. We planned to meet on the Monday after the Kansas City game—an off day for the players.

What we couldn't have predicted was Edgar Flores showing up just as we were all sitting down at the table in the coaches' meeting room.

"Well," Flores said. He wore a white sports jacket, a black shirt, gray slacks, and black-and-white wingtip shoes. His dark hair piled a little higher than normal on his head. He looked tan—as if he'd just walked off a beach or a golf course. He was carrying a manila folder. "Just the folks I wanted to see," he said.

Coach Engram got up and offered the seat at the head of the table, but Flores waved his hand and sat down next to Jesse. She looked at him, her chin a little tucked in and her eyes kind of quizzical, but he smiled and held out a cigar. "I don't suppose you'd want one of these, but would you mind if I had one?"

"I'd rather you didn't," she said. "The smoke makes me cough." She looked like a college student in her large blue turtleneck sweater, black slacks, and sneakers. Sweet and smart and feminine. She reached up and touched the Band-Aid across her freckled nose, and then she turned to face the table. There followed a very long pause while Flores stared rather forlornly at his cigar before putting it back in his pocket.

"Here's the thing," Flores said, leaning forward with the folder in front of him and both arms on the table.

We all sat there in silence.

"Jesse's mom has written me a letter. She's also written the commissioner, the head of the players' union, and Coach Engram here."

I looked at Engram. Jesse was staring at the desk in front of her.

"I think she's written Jesse, too."

She nodded, without meeting his gaze.

"She's expressed concern over Jesse's health."

"You're kidding," I said.

"And her contract. She read in the paper that Jesse is making the minimum salary."

Justin Peck said, "I've communicated with Jesse's mother as well, and I've worked out what I think is a very reasonable—"

But Flores went on, without even acknowledging that sound was coming from Peck's position at the table. "What I've got here is a very handsome insurance policy, in Jesse's name."

"Insurance," both Coach Engram and I said at the same time.

"Health insurance *and* life insurance. I've also got a considerable proposal for a contract extension."

"Really," Coach Engram said.

"Wait a minute," Justin Peck said. "I'm her agent in these matters . . ." He was a curt little man, who always paired gray suits with brightly colored shirts and ties, always neat and pressed and positively glistening. "If *there's* a new contract being proposed—"

Nate, who sat on the other side of Jesse, suddenly raised his hand to silence the agent. "Who does the insurance protect?"

Flores said, "Jesse, of course."

"How?"

"Any injury, permanent or otherwise, will be fully covered by the team. This policy will insure her well-being in perpetuity—until, of course, she dies."

"Insurance won't *prevent* an injury," Nate said.

"No. No, it won't, young man. Nothing will do that." Flores suddenly turned to Coach Engram. "Who is this fellow?"

"He's my friend," Jesse said.

"What about the life insurance?" I asked.

"Goes to her mother."

Jesse looked at him now. "I don't *have* a mother."

This surprised Flores.

"Look, I haven't seen her or spoken to her since I was eleven years old," Jesse said. "As far as I'm concerned, we've never met. I don't even remember my mother, if you want to know the truth."

"You don't have pictures?"

"Just a collection of letters. That's all."

Nate said, "It might be in your interest to let her back in your life."

"Why?" she said.

"Might put to rest all those rumors about you really being a man who's just had a sex change operation."

She turned away from him. I met her gaze briefly and was ashamed that she must have seen the agreement on my face. I didn't say anything, though.

"I don't care about that," she said. "Anyway, I haven't made up my mind about her. I don't know *what* I want to do."

Flores didn't seem bothered by this. He pushed the folder a bit in her direction. "Well, you can just look these over and decide for yourself about the beneficiary for the life insurance."

"Why does she have to *have* life insurance?" Nate said. There was a silence. Everybody looked at him as though he was asking the most obvious question, but he persisted. "No, really. You know what I mean. Do the other players have life insurance policies paid for by the team?"

"Good point, actually," Peck said. "The team may be paying for this insurance, but that does not count as part of her compensation."

"Excuse me," Flores said. "My general manager is not here. We cannot discuss Jesse's compensation without him in the room. So would you kindly shut up?"

Everyone at the table took in a bit of air at that. Coach Engram made a very slight clicking noise in the back of his throat. As for Justin Peck, he got up, picked up his legal pad and pen, and quietly left the room. He didn't even look at Jesse, but she got up and moved to follow him.

"Where are *you* going?" Flores said.

"I'm going with my agent."

"You don't have to." He looked at me. "Skip? Explain to her how this works?"

"Jesse," I said, before even knowing what else I might say to her.

"Look, *I'm* paying for your insurance," Flores said. "All right? Nothing comes out of your pay. Your contract extension is for another year, at double your salary, and a substantial signing bonus. You get every penny of it."

She was standing over him now, looking down, while he was turned around, looking up at her, his hands still on the table. It had the appearance at least of a very odd reversal of power.

"Every penny of it is guaranteed," he said.

"Except, if my agent is right," she said. "Double my current salary is not nearly what an average starting quarterback in the NFL makes."

"Come on, the signing bonus puts you well in that range," Flores said. "And let's face it, we can't commit to you like we can to a man."

"Why not?"

He seemed exasperated. "You might want to play football now, Jesse. But you got this clock ticking, you know what I mean?"

"No," she said. "I don't know." She wanted him to say it.

"I don't want to use an old cliché, but you won't *always* want to play football. I need to plan for that."

"This is about her being a woman," Nate said.

Flores looked at him for a second, as if not even quite believing the notion of sound coming from Nate's place at the table. Then he said, "Of course."

"I'm not trying to be difficult, Mr. Flores," Jesse said. "But you'll have to negotiate a new contract with my agent."

"Okay, then—go get him. We'll all sit down and—"

"This meeting isn't about the contract," Nate said. "We have to work everything else out."

"Work what out?" Flores asked.

"About the demands on Jesse's time, for one thing." He pointed to the folder on the table. "This business about insurance."

I think it was at that moment that Jesse may have begun working out in her mind who really cared about her. It was probably not anything she had ever considered before. She looked at me, and I said, "You do what you think is best."

Then she looked at Engram. He stared at her, thinking. Flores turned back to the table and slowly placed the folder where Jesse had been sitting.

"What we were *going* to talk about here," said Harold Moody, "was how to manage the demands on Jesse's time. She can't be in more than one place at a time."

"I want her concentrating on her job," Coach Engram said.

As Jesse moved back to her chair, I got up and went outside to find Justin Peck. Whatever we talked about, I wanted him there for it. Not that I was being that much of a gentleman. In future negotiations, I knew, he would remember that I'd looked out for him that way.

As the meeting went on with all parties at the table, it finally became clear what Nate meant by his question about the insurance. He was worried about what life insurance for Jesse would say to the rest of the team, and what that meant for Jesse's future. What he wanted to know was: How expensive was that insurance? Did anybody really think that she might *die*? Was that somehow truer of her than the other players?

Flores assured him that he was only trying to think of everything with Jesse; most players had the same kind of insurance, although it was true, not everybody had it through the team. If Jesse's policy was so lucrative, it was because she was, after all, and according to the insurance underwriters, "of the slighter sex" and might incur an injury that would be, well, worse than a man might suffer under the same circumstances.

"Are my bones more fragile than yours?" Jesse said.

"They're smaller," Flores said.

She wrinkled her face. "No they're not."

"Look, you possess a reproductive apparatus that may be vulnerable. That's what the underwriters are telling me. Okay? And that insurance happens to cost more for you than it does for any man."

Jesse let a wry smile cross her face, but she said nothing more.

After that the meeting went pretty smoothly. It became fairly clear that one of the reasons Edgar Flores had upped Jesse's contract and provided such an expensive insurance policy was that in return he expected her to be available to the media as much as possible—prefer-ably wearing a Redskins sweatshirt or hat. He wanted that logo every-where in her ads and commercials. He'd even approved two ESPN camerapeople and a film crew from NFL Films—both of which would follow Jesse around just about anywhere she went at the compound and even to her apartment. Both crews were making docu-mentaries. They wanted her to wear a mike in one of her games, too, but we wouldn't allow it. "She's got to call signals, for Christ's sake," Engram said.

Besides, it was bad enough getting Jesse's chords to the level where everybody could hear her on the field. Coach Engram joked that the "high pitch of her voice would blow the little transmitters all to hell."

Still, Moody was using her for all she was worth. And you couldn't blame him. Jesse brought in fans unlike any other player in the history of football. Everybody from the beer-drinking macho crowd that wanted to see her get her head knocked off to the real aficionados of the game, who wanted to see her play. And women from every walk of life wanted to get in and see her. What had once been a sport in which lots of women were interested up to a point became a national phenomenon that interested virtually every woman. *The Atlantic*, the *New Yorker*, and *Vanity Fair* ran articles about nearly all aspects of Jesse's existence. She was the "mystery girl from the Far East." The "legendary daughter of an unknown coach." There were no pictures of her as a young player, smiling at the camera, holding a football helmet under her arm; no pictures of her with her father, or in the uniform of any high school team. But the American high school on Guam released a transcript of her grades (except for Cs in golf and calculus, she was almost a straight-A student) and old news-paper articles about her prowess on the field when she played in a women's league there. There were a few published pictures of her in action in the women's league, and *Vanity Fair* ran those, only she looked exactly like a young man in a uniform, running with or throwing a football. You couldn't tell it was her, except maybe for the long legs and that whiplike arm moving so fast it only registered as a blur in the photos.

Ladies First magazine did an article about her presence in the locker room. On the road she frequently had to dress in a hotel room then ride to the game in a cab provided by the team. After games, she'd walk out of the stadium and take a cab back to her hotel room. It didn't take long for the press to realize they could talk to her immediately after the game on the field, or in the lobby of the hotel after she'd showered and dressed. At home games, I gave up my office in the locker room of the stadium. There was a shower in there, so she could clean up, get dressed, and then meet the media in the press room. So she never had to enter the locker room where the men showered and dressed, either at home or on the road. The magazine ran detailed pictures of her equipment—the flak jacket she wore that protected her upper body, for instance—explaining that you could pound on it with a baseball bat and she wouldn't feel a thing. The piece showed her knee pads, her thigh pads, her shoulder pads, the headset she wore inside her helmet so she could hear Coach Engram or me.

Sport magazine ran her vital statistics, 6' 2", 175 pounds; her score in agility drills; her speed in the 40-yard dash. (At 4.33, she was the third-fastest player on the team—a virtual tie with Rob Anders. Her feet were so quick she could outdo all of them, even Darius, in the agility drills.) All of that was very plainly laid out for the world to see and know. Still, there were stories on the Internet about how she walked around the locker room naked. How the men ogled her after a victory. How they held her up, naked, and celebrated with her in the shower. If you believed what was being said on the web, Jesse had daily sex with Coach Engram, me, Dan Wilber, Darius Exley, Orlando Brown, and even Rob Anders. She was Edgar Flores's secret lover in one tabloid that ran a picture of Jesse's bright-eyed face inside a bright yellow oval border and next to it, Flores, standing by a small plane with a cigar in his mouth. He flew her to exotic places of the world, the story had it, so they could have their "romantic trysts" in private. Everywhere she went, somebody was taking her picture.

I did what I could to protect Jesse from all that, but the tabloids are right out in the open on supermarket aisles where you check out. Pictures of Jesse and everybody she was supposed to be involved with. It made me sick.

There was even a story about a former husband who wanted to reconcile with her, but whom she was coldheartedly ignoring.

The funny thing was, nobody mentioned a single thing about a long-lost mother.

Twenty-Five

WE WENT TO Mexico City to play the Aztecs. The Aztecs had a pretty good defensive line and not a bad group of linebackers. The thing was, they'd blitz more than a few times with a cornerback, a safety, and all three linebackers at once, and they were very good at disguising when and how they were going to do that. You could never predict when it was going to happen and where it was going to come from. To protect Jesse we installed a game plan that called for her to roll out more—usually to her right since she was right-handed, but we put in a few to her left too. That kind of play is called a "quarterback waggle." We had her throw short passes to the backs and wide receivers on some plays, trying to set up deeper balls later on. We weren't going for anything deep right away, and we planned on running the ball a lot.

What a lot of people missed because of all the attention on Jesse was the great year Walter Mickens was having at running back. He rushed for more than 250 yards against the Aztecs and we won the game pretty easily, 24 to 10. The most spectacular play for me was a hurried field goal that Jesse kicked with only seconds left in the second quarter that made it 17 to 0. Up to that time in the game we'd been running the ball so successfully she hardly threw a single pass. Mickens kept slicing through the line for good yards and we owned the clock. But near the end of the first half we had to get down the field in a hurry, so we started passing it more. Jesse drove us up the field on quick passes to Mickens and the wide receivers. She could get back, set up, and release the ball so fast, I don't know why Coach Engram was so worried about Mexico City's pass rush. She hit Darius with a quick slant that went for 15 yards. On the next play she rolled a little to her left and flipped a nice quick-out pass to Anders. Then she hit Darius again for 18 yards. In five plays, and less than 30 seconds, she drove the team all the way to the Mexico City 36-yard line. Then, with no time-outs and the clock running, she stood back while the kicking team raced onto the field and got into place. She waited for the snap and then, as the time reached 0 on the scoreboard, kicked the ball high and far and right through the uprights. Fifty-three frigging yards. The ball cleared the crossbar by at least five or six feet. As we were trotting off the field, Coach Engram said, "That would have been good from sixty-three."

"I know," I said.

In the second half, we opened it up a bit more. Or I should say Jesse opened it up. She kept changing the play at the line. We'd call an off-tackle run, and she'd get the team up to the line and change it to a pass play. She kept the offense moving with short, quick passes—as we had set up in the game plan. But on one play she dropped back 10 yards behind the center into what is called the "shotgun" formation. She took the snap and drifted a bit to her right, and the Aztecs had a double blitz from the corners. They came at her fast, and she planted her foot, looking downfield. Darius was streaking down the right sideline, and she released the ball just as one of the cornerbacks slammed into her lower legs. The ball sailed high and Darius leaped for it but it was out-of-bounds. Jesse's legs got knocked from under her and she went forward onto her face. I thought I saw her knees buckle in the wrong direction and all of us sort of gasped when she went down. Even the folks in the stadium seemed to take a deep breath. But she got up, pulled a little on the pads at her knees, and then walked back to the huddle.

There was no flag. On the next play she read a corner blitz on the right side and hit Anders with a quick 15-yard pass, and when the safety missed him he went for another 10 yards or so. Jesse, walking up the field after that gain, pointed right at the cornerback who had hit her in the knees. It was like she was saying, "That's what you get." He started talking back to her, bad-mouthing her and everything. She ignored it. She came out of the huddle and changed the play at the line again. "Run what's called, Jesse," I hollered into my mike. But she called another pass play, this time a quick out to Exley on the left. She fired the ball to him so quickly, the Aztec linemen barely got out of their stance before the ball was on its way. Darius snatched it out of the air and ran for 11 yards. Again, Jesse pointed to the cornerback on that side. She was not listening to me with her headset, that much was clear. I looked at Coach Engram, and he called time-out. Jesse came to the sideline and I asked her what she thought she was doing.

"I'm having fun," she said.

"Are you hurt?"

"I said I was having fun." But the look in her eyes was as dead calm as a bank robber's. And the cut on her nose, I saw, had started bleeding again. She took her helmet off and one of the medical staff put a better bandage on it.

As she was putting her helmet back on, Engram said, "Run what's called."

She shook her head a little I think, so he said it louder.

"We're hot," she said.

"I know it's working," Engram said. "But run what's called. That'll work too."

"I want those people good and embarrassed," she said.

I'd never heard such vehemence in her tone before and it surprised me. "You *are* hurt, aren't you. They hurt your knees."

"I'm all right." She wouldn't look at me. It was noisy as always, but it seemed like we were the only ones making noise; like the only conversation was between me and Jesse and Coach Engram.

"You're acting like Spivey," I said.

She looked at me.

"Don't lose your cool."

"I'm fine," she said. She couldn't see the fire in her eyes, but I could.

Coach Engram said, "Stick with the game plan, Jesse." It was an order.

I told her to run Mickens at the corners. "Take it at both of them, one after another. It embarrasses them just as much to get flattened on running plays."

She nodded, then trotted back onto the field. On the very next play, she faked a handoff to Mickens and threw it 30 yards to Anders on a quick post. The ball went on a flat, straight line to him—like a rocket—and he caught it in stride and kept running up the seam for a 55-yard touchdown.

When she came back to the bench after kicking the extra point, she stayed away from Engram and me. I wasn't really angry, and probably Engram wasn't either, but it was a problem both of us didn't want to have. This was not the kind of discipline that either one of us liked. It was one thing to have her calling plays when it was clear to her that what we'd called wouldn't work, but she was just doing whatever she wanted out there, calling her own plays like she was one of the old-time quarterbacks; like a real field general.

Coach Engram didn't like field generals.

I know it sounds kind of petulant and adolescent—the coach wants his own plays called and not somebody else's—but the truth is, a football game in those days was a fully practiced and rehearsed series of perfect performances. You prepared for every contingency, but you also made sure what you designed was employed to its fullest potential; it's the coach's plan put into action in the exact sequence that the coach has scripted it. There's always a little wiggle room, but if the quarterback takes the plan away, the coach ends up standing on the sideline not knowing what is going to happen or what is called on the field. He gets to be like the guy playing a video game who sets the game so the CPU plays itself, and then stands back and lets it unfold without using the controls. He just watches the game do what it's going to do. Nobody likes that. Least of all a head coach in the National Football League.

And once Jesse started calling her own game, a lot of things broke down. We should have won that game going away—we could have scored 50 points—but we started getting a lot of penalties on offense. Five false starts in the second half alone. The offense started milling around on the field and didn't always know what was happening. I realized Jesse had started calling plays from the playbook that were not in the game plan and that we hadn't practiced. I liked it that everybody tried to execute, though—they were listening to her. That's a very good thing. The problem was she wasn't listening to Coach Engram or me. And that's a big problem.

At the end of the game, as we were walking off the field, Coach Engram looked at me with real concern and sadness on his face. "We need to have a serious talk with Jesse."

"Don't worry," I said. "I'll talk to her."

"She keeps that up, I don't care *how* famous she gets or how good she is, I'll sit her right down."

He'd do it, too. Football is teamwork to the highest degree humanly possible. Everybody has to be disciplined; they have to move exactly as planned, with absolutely unerring precision at exactly the same time. It's a clockwork human community that explodes into action and struggles against itself for brief moments of gorgeous fight and flight, and you can't have one maverick deciding to change the pattern or direction of the flight seconds before takeoff. Not all the time.

You just can't have that.

Twenty-Six

THE MONDAY AFTER the game, I told Jesse I wanted to take her out to dinner and celebrate her continued success. What I really wanted was to talk to her with no other person around. I wasn't just going to address the problem at hand either. We hadn't talked about anything but football since the big meeting, and I didn't know if she'd accepted the insurance policy or what was going on with her mother or how she was managing her time now that she was an international celebrity.

We agreed to meet at a place in Herndon, Virginia, called Rally Round that served steaks and good beer. I met her outside the place, expecting she'd show up in her usual jeans and sweatshirt. She came up the street wearing low-heeled black shoes and a long low cut black dress. She was wearing a deep auburn shoulder-length wig. It looked like she had a great mane of hair, curled just right down both sides of her face and down her back. She wore deep-blue sapphire earrings that almost matched the color of her eyes and a necklace with blue stones in it. I didn't recognize her until she walked up and held out her hand. She was wearing eye makeup, which she didn't need, and some sort of foundation that covered the brown freckles across her broad face. I could still see the dark line of what was left of the cut on her nose. Dark red lipstick made her teeth look as white as pearls.

"Well, look at you," I said.

She nodded slightly and I took her arm and escorted her into the restaurant. I was proud to have somebody so beautiful and tall and young on my arm. I'm pretty tall too. We were a very big couple so of course we garnered a lot of attention as we made our way to our table. When we were seated I said, "What's the occasion?"

"No occasion," she said.

"Why the getup?"

"It's not a getup. It's a disguise." The paparazzi had been following her everywhere she went. "I get chased no matter where I go, so I went to a hotel not far from here. Then I showered, changed, put on this costume—how do you like it, my wig?" She turned her head to side and modeled it for me.

"It's nice," I said.

"I walked out the front door like anybody else. Nobody noticed."

"Come on. How could they not notice *you*? I mean . . ."

"I walked right by 'em. Nobody's interested in a long tall Sally like me."

"You have no idea, Jess."

She sat back, and the way the light shone on her collarbone and neck, I thought right then she was the most beautiful woman I'd ever seen.

"You really do look beautiful, though," I said. "Something I never thought I'd say to an NFL quarterback."

A young man came to the table. I thought he was the waiter, but before I could ask him for a wine list he said to Jesse, loud and with no small amount of wonder, "You're Jesse Smoke."

Jesse nodded.

Immediately other people seated around us began to pay attention. I could hear them whispering. Somebody said, "And that's Skip Granger."

"Are you Skip Granger?" the young man said.

"Are you the waiter?"

"No, sir." Then he turned back to Jesse. "Can I have your autograph?"

"Sure," she said, smiling. Even without the freckles and *with* the eye makeup, it was a winning smile. She just looked darker, and—I hate to say this, but—downright sexy. She did not look innocent, I can tell you.

I watched her sign a dozen autographs. The entire waitstaff of the restaurant also got autographs. Only two of them were actual football fans. But they all knew who Jesse was, that was for sure. One guy said, "Great game Sunday."

"You're, like, just the most amazing athlete in history," another said.

Jesse shook her head modestly.

"Certainly the most famous athlete in a long, long time," I said, after the man had gone off.

"I guess," she said.

Eventually we got to eating and people left us alone, although I could still feel their eyes on us. To have any sort of normal conversation we had to whisper, which wasn't easy or fun. But people will listen to what you say—they'll try very hard to hear every word, and they don't try to hide it either.

The place was dimly lit, and in the candlelight, Jesse's eyes and the jewelry sparkled. I ordered a steak and Jesse had the salmon. I ordered a bourbon and water with my steak, and she had a glass of white wine. We ate pretty much in silence and then she started talking about Darius Exley's action figures.

"I just think it's so cute he has so many of them, you know? And that he keeps buying them."

"You don't think it's kind of . . . childish?"

"It's just him."

"You see much of him?"

"No. Not outside practice."

"So when did you see his collection?"

"After the Los Angeles game."

"Really. That long ago."

She pushed her plate back and wiped her lips gently with a napkin. She took a sip of her wine, looking at me with something that might have been suspicion. She waited to see what I would say next.

"Dan Wilber teaches yoga," I said.

"I know."

"You've seen that, too?"

"No. But I heard about it." She put her glass down and smiled. "He's famous for it."

"You think that's cute, too?"

"I think it's weird. But listen, I've come to depend on him. He's my damn Rock of Gibraltar."

"He's a real gentleman is what he is. You can bet the players wouldn't have warmed to you so quickly if it hadn't been for him. That and the football you threw into Delbert Coleman's face mask," I added, chuckling.

"I think it's when I cut my nose that I won them over."

"You do?"

"Dan told me the guys really admired the way I didn't, you know, let it bother me. They liked the way I kept going with blood all down the front of me."

"Hitting Darius with that winning touchdown against the Raiders helped, too."

We ate in silence for a while, then I said, "So, heard any more from your mother?"

Her eyes sank a little. "She sent another letter." She started pushing the remaining salmon around the plate with her fork.

I watched her, waiting for her to go on. When she didn't I said, "You going to tell me about it?"

"She's afraid I'll get hurt."

"We're all afraid of that."

"Edgar said I should—"

"Edgar," I interrupted her. "You call him Edgar?"

She nodded.

I shook my head.

"He insisted."

"He doesn't let anybody call him that. He makes us *all* call him Mr. Flores."

"Guess I'm prettier than the rest of you."

I didn't laugh.

She looked away. I had the feeling I was making her uncomfortable. I raised my glass. "Anyway, this is supposed to be a celebration."

She lifted hers as well.

"To you," I said. I took a good swallow of my bourbon and water, and she took a small sip of her wine. "Jesse," I said. Did you ever dream we'd actually be doing this? You know, what we're doing?"

Now she smiled. "I dreamed it a lot. But . . . It was only ever a dream. I never actually thought it would happen."

I couldn't keep my mouth shut. "I know I've said this to you before, but I have to say, I'm worried about all the men pursuing you."

"All the men?"

"You are not just really smart, Jesse, you're attractive. You know that."

She said nothing.

"I mean, you just joked about being prettier than the rest of us."

"I can take care of myself, Coach."

"It's not *you* I'm worried about," I said. "I'm worried about the men around you."

She looked truly puzzled.

"Think about it, Jess. This is a team, right? And I just worry that some of the men pursuing you will begin to see each other as rivals. That kind of thing can be truly destructive."

She looked sullen as she forked up some salmon and chewed, staring down at the food on her plate.

"You have to guard against forming attachments. That's all I'm saying."

She did not like that I used that word. "I'm not *attaching* to anybody, all right?" She glared at me, straight into my eyes, and I felt as though I'd just tried to seduce her myself. "You make me feel like a mollusk," she continued. "You know? I mean, I understand you don't like the idea of me dating anybody on the team, but . . ."

"I'm not just trying to protect the team," I said.

"What do you mean by *that?*"

"I didn't mean that the way it sounded."

She looked at me blankly.

"I just . . . don't want you to think I'm jealous myself, or something."

Now she really seemed puzzled. "You don't have to protect me, Skip. And, really, I don't *care* if you're jealous."

"I'm just interested in keeping you safe," I said. It was the truest thing I could think to say.

She ate some more of her salmon, and I decided to quit while I was ahead. I was wondering how to change the subject to her play calling when she took things in her own direction (it was becoming a signature). "My mother wants to come out here."

"I thought that was already arranged."

"No. I don't want it."

"Why not?"

"Edgar says he'll fly her out here and give her the royal treatment. All I have to do is give the word."

"So why don't you want her to come?"

"I don't know." She put her fork down and laid her hands flat on the table. "It's just—what does she want now? She walked away from us—my father and me."

"And you haven't seen or heard from her since?"

"I told you she wrote to me a lot after she left. E-mails. Letters. Sent me gifts for Christmas. My birthday. Things like that."

"And you ever answer her."

"Nope."

"Why?"

"I hated her for leaving my father. For leaving me."

"Did you keep the gifts she sent you?"

She wouldn't look at me directly, but she slowly nodded her head.

"You kept them?"

"Yes."

"And you never answered any of her letters."

"I hated her."

"You might have communicated that if you'd sent back those gifts, don't you think?"

"I never used any of them."

"Really?"

"Well, not right away at least."

I took a sip of my bourbon. I forgot that I was supposed to broach the subject of play calling, but at a time like that it would have taken a pretty awful breach of decorum to start talking about football.

"What would you have done if your mother *did* call you?"

"I don't know."

"You think you would have hung up on her, or maybe talked to her? What do you think?"

"I said I don't know."

"What was she to think? You never responded to any of her letters, or her e-mails. She probably knew you hated her."

"What does it take to write an e-mail?"

"About as much as it takes to make a phone call."

"She could have called."

"Maybe she was waiting for you to respond to the e-mails first. She might have called you if . . ." I didn't finish the sentence, though, because of the hard-boned and steely look she gave me right then. I went back to my steak. "Look, it's none of my business, Jesse," I said as I cut a piece off the corner of it. "But I think if she's family, you have to give her a little bit of the benefit of the doubt."

"She *still* hasn't called, though—there's the thing."

"Did you save any of the letters?"

"I have some of them."

"Someday, you may be glad that you do." I took the last gulp of my bourbon and water just as the waiter came back with a drink on the house. He had the manager of the restaurant with him, who wanted to shake both my hand and Jesse's. They sat around the table and we talked football with them a bit. I drank the bourbon the waiter had brought, and then another. Jesse had two glasses of wine. We were all laughing after a while—as if we were old friends. We heard tales of the other celebrities who ate at the Rally Round; of deadbeats and drunks, wives and lovers; people who gave fantastic tips. Then the owner had one of the waitresses take a picture of both of us, then one with Jesse and him. Jesse was a full head taller than he was, but he wanted the picture with his arm around her shoulders. She leaned down and the waitress took the picture. I was feeling slightly sick from all the food and the bourbon and my nerves. I didn't like the light in that room, or all the eyes on us. And the truth was, I was worried about Jesse.

The manager would not hear of us paying for our food. I thanked him and shook his hand, then he gave Jesse a big hug. One of the waiters wanted to hug her, too, and have his picture taken with her. We obliged him that but then had to back away and thank everybody noisily as we elbowed our way out.

In the street I took Jesse's hand and walked with her down to where she'd parked her brand-new Mercedes.

"Nice car," I said. I wondered if she still lived in the sparsely furnished apartment, but I didn't know how to ask about it without being pushy, and certainly didn't want her to think that I was trying to finagle an invitation. She stood by the door of the car and looked at me.

"You see much of Andy or Nate these days?" I asked.

"Just on business."

"Sorry to hear that."

"I'm just too busy," she said. "When I'm not in meetings with you and Jon, I'm playacting in television ads or, you know, at practice."

"So he's 'Jon' now, Coach Engram?"

She gave a short laugh.

"What do you call me?" I asked.

"Skip."

"You do?"

"Of course."

I don't know why that made me feel so proud, but it did. I felt like one of the boys. Was I one of the boys I'd need to protect her from, I wondered. I patted her on the shoulder and she smiled. "Good night. Thanks for dinner."

"I didn't buy it," I said.

"Well . . . thanks for the idea."

"There was something else I wanted to say to you," I said.

"You think I should let my mother back into my life, don't you?"

"Well . . ." I averted her gaze, but she moved in so that she could get a good look at my expression.

"You do, don't you?" She stared at me a moment longer, then shrugged.

"Look, Jesse," I said. "I'm no expert, but I can tell you, if I had children and I was trying to stay in touch, I'd probably send e-mails or letters, too. And I'd hope for a response. A hell of a lot better than calling and being rejected outright, you know? It's so final when a person hangs up a phone. I'd just think, eventually I'll get a response, and try to remain hopeful. Some people would say it's harder to write an e-mail than pick up a phone."

"That is so lame," she said.

"Maybe," I said. "But it was pretty shitty not to return her gifts if you wanted nothing to do with her." I was, I now realized, a little drunk and felt bad for saying that the minute it left my tongue. But I could see it hit home.

"You don't know what it was like," she said, quietly.

"I know you were hurt. I know that."

"It was the most devastating thing in my life. And I think it may have hastened my father's . . ." she stopped. "I think now all she wants is to get in on the big money."

"Well, if *that's* what you think."

"I don't know. I don't know what I think."

"I'm sorry, Jess," I said.

People driving by had started to slow down now, and some folks emerging from the restaurant across the street were laughing loudly one minute and then suddenly quieted down. I was pretty sure they noticed us standing next to Jesse's car.

"Did you say you had something else to say to me?" She waited for a moment, but now I couldn't even remember what it was.

Finally I said, "You'll have to get a better disguise next time, for one thing. And, uh, lose that wig. Didn't fool anybody."

She laughed, then got into her car and drove off. I stood there for a while, watching the red of her back lights pass out of view. It seemed like the world had gotten so much bigger on us, all of a sudden, without either of us even noticing it. Or maybe, in a really sad way, the whole thing was getting smaller and we just didn't know it. I felt sorry for her mother. I'd certainly never failed anybody like that, as fucked up as my own life might have been. Sometimes I wished football had not taken over my life so completely. I was married once—back when I was a player. I thought I was happy. The woman I married was beautiful and smart and kind. She tried really hard to make it all work. But she wanted children and I didn't. I used to say to her, "I'm gone most of the time. I can't be an absentee father. Wait until my career is over." I bought her a dog, thinking that would do it, but it only made her more determined to change her life. When I retired, life just sort of broke us down. I got into coaching, and with the late hours and moving so frequently, and traveling with the teams I coached, it was pretty easy to let things disintegrate.

Once my wife was gone, I didn't have time to truly miss her. Oh, I had my moments, but . . . nothing lasting or crippling. I don't think I let her down, either. Just like she didn't let me down. I was glad to be able to say we'd remained friends. On the other hand, what would it have been like to care enough for somebody that betrayal meant something. It's hard to explain and I shouldn't talk about it in this venue, but . . . I guess I'm just trying to describe how it felt that night as I watched Jesse's car disappear up the dark street.

Twenty-Seven

WE HAD A bye—a week with no game scheduled—after the Aztec game, so the players had the first four days of that next week off. They still came to the complex and worked out and all—some of them checking in with the trainers or the medical staff to work on bumps and bruises. Except for Jimmy Kelso and our first kicker, we'd had no serious injuries thus far. Sure, Jesse had her bruised back, and Orlando had broken several fingers and had a slight hamstring strain that, without treatment, could easily get worse. Darius had a strained knee and Walter Mickens suffered from bruised ribs. And there were a few other minor complaints. But luckily we had made it almost halfway through the season and only Jimmy Kelso was out for the whole year.

We rested the tight end for a week before the bye, fully expecting he'd be back for our next game, which was in Cleveland, against the Browns. I haven't introduced you to the tight end, but of course you know all about Gayle Glenn Louis. He was only in his second year back then, so nobody really understood how great he was. Tall, fast, with really quick feet, and strong as a Clydesdale, Louis had hands as good as Anders and Exley. If you got it to within his reach, he caught it, no matter who bounced off him. He absolutely loved playing for Jesse; and he could block like a goddamn bulldozer. For sure he'll make the Hall of Fame on the first ballot.

Jesse, in spite of her back injury, came in every day to run laps and work with the weights. (She could bench 175 pounds, which was almost exactly her weight.)

We were 6 and 3 after nine weeks. The Giants lost their first game of the year to the Raiders, 16 to 10, and they were now 8 and 1. The Cowboys were also 6 and 3, tied with us for second place. Philadelphia was 5 and 4. So the NFC East looked like this:

TEAM	W–L	PF	PA
New York	8–1	173	66
Washington	6–3	193	132
Dallas	6–3	164	133
Philadelphia	5–4	171	164

For those of you who don't know, PF stands for "points for" and PA stands for "points against." We'd scored more points than anybody in the conference—193. On the other hand, we'd given up 132 points on defense. Overall, it looked like we were giving up almost as many as we scored, but those numbers were misleading. See, in the games where Jesse didn't play quarterback, our offense averaged 14.2 points a game and our defense surrendered about 15.2, and we'd won 2 and lost 3. But since she'd taken over, a space of just four games, our offense had come to average 30.5 points a game, with our defense giving up only 14 points a game. And of course we were undefeated.

Everybody was happy except for Coach Engram. "She's got to run the play that we call," he said to me again. And then he told me he expected me to make sure Jesse understood it. "She'll listen to you," he said. "At least I hope she will. And I don't want to take the chance that she *won't* listen to me."

Our next opponent, the Browns, were leading their division with a 7 and 2 record. They were fast, hard-hitting, and prided themselves on their defense. Still, we looked forward to playing them. Our schemes were working on both sides of the ball, and it would be a real test for the whole team. Of course the offensive line was under intense scrutiny because of who they had to protect. The Browns made a point of telling the press that their defense did not have any "gentlemen" on it and they were looking forward to making Jesse's acquaintance. (Sometimes, football players demonstrate an appalling lack of originality. The standing joke, of course, was that Jesse was not going to get any special treatment just because she was a lady. Just about every team made some remark like that. Or somebody would say something about "Big Mama" and her "brood." Of all the names she garnered that year, that was the one she hated most, "Big Mama.")

Coach Engram was unhappy about Jesse's "autonomy," as he called it—but, hell, he was always unhappy about something, except for the first few minutes after a good win as he was walking off the field. He hated the world when he was preparing to play another team, and above all, he hated the other team. He always saw the potential for disaster and tried to plan against it, but of course life does not let you get away with too much of that, so most of the time he was frustrated and pissed off. As for those things he *could* control? Or ought to have been able to? By god, he'd better have control over them. All of this just to say: He was not about to let this thing with Jesse get out of hand.

I'd forgotten to reason with her about it at the restaurant, or even to ask her about the insurance or what she was planning to do about the new contract, so I knew I had some unfinished business that I had to take care of during the bye week. But that wasn't the only thing I had to do.

Jesse's mother flew into Dulles Airport at a little past six in the morning on the Thursday after the Mexico City game. I met her at the entrance gate, having been handed the responsibility by Coach Engram and Mr. Flores. I stood by the gate in a big Washington Redskins sweatshirt, holding a sign that said, LIZ CARLSON. When she saw me, she raised her arm and strode across the flow of people like somebody intending to choreograph a dance. She was tall—even taller than Jesse—with the same curly black hair, the same blue eyes. She was similar in form, too, with athletic legs, a thin waist, and a fairly slim-figured upper body. Her arms had real definition, I saw, like a bodybuilder's, and the effect was astonishing. She looked basically like a sinewy tall guy in a curly wig.

"You Mr. Granger?" she said.

"Hello." I don't know what my face might have been giving away right then, but whatever it was, she noticed it.

"You the only one here to meet me?"

"Jesse isn't . . ." I didn't know what to say. I almost said that Jesse isn't ready for this yet, but I couldn't do that. Finally, as Liz just stood there staring at me, I said, "Jesse isn't here."

She looked puzzled, and then crestfallen.

"She said she wants to take it slow," I said. But that was a lie. I hadn't heard from her about any of it. When Flores told me Liz was coming I couldn't get in touch with Jesse. It was Flores who told me Jesse had okayed the thing.

"What's she afraid of?" Liz asked.

"Jesse Smoke? Nothing *I* know of," I said.

She shook her head but smiled sweetly.

"Shall we get your luggage?"

"Sure," she said. Her eyes were definitely Jesse's. Or I should say you could see Jesse's eyes in her face. Also the same flat nose, same full lips.

No one was at Redskins Park except a few of the permanent staff and one or two workers from building and grounds. I took Liz to my office—where, only four hours before, I had been watching films and getting ready to install a game plan for the Browns. I told her to sit down and she took a chair across from my desk. "Would you like some coffee?" I asked.

"Had some on the plane."

"You hungry?"

"Where's Jesse?"

"She'll be along." It was a lie, but I was told to keep Ms. Carlson as happy as possible. I picked up the phone and called Mr. Flores. Liz stared at the film disk on my desk, but she didn't touch anything.

"Good morning, sir," I said when Flores answered the phone.

"She here?"

"Yes."

"And Jesse?"

"Not yet."

"You've talked to her about coming?"

"I will today."

"Put her mother in the Hyatt. The top-floor suite."

"That's done. But, they won't let her check in until after two. So—I thought you might want to meet this morning,"

"Sure," Flores said. "We'll have lunch together."

"Yesterday you said breakfast. I've got her here right now, in my office."

"I mean breakfast. Of course. I'll be right over there. Call Engram."

I hung up the phone. "Wouldn't you like to meet the owner and Coach Engram over breakfast?"

"I want to see Jesse."

"I'm going to try . . ." I said. "She may be able to join us."

She brushed a wisp of hair off of her forehead. "Does Jesse know I . . . Did she know I was coming?"

"Yes."

"But the team—I mean, you had to arrange everything?"

"Well, the team's paying for it."

She seemed to nod a bit and then we both fell silent. I stood behind my desk, flipping through the papers lying there, not looking at her.

She got a compact and some lipstick out of her purse and touched up her lips. Jesus, how I wanted somebody to knock on the door. Outside the sun had just started to peer over the rim of trees next to the practice field.

Then Liz snapped her compact closed, threw it and the lipstick back in her purse. "Jesse doesn't really want me here," she said. "Does she?"

"Pardon?"

"She didn't arrange any of this, did she?"

"I'm sure she knows about it."

Liz stared out my window. Her eyes looked kind of sad. "Does she make a lot of money?"

"You better ask her."

"I will if I ever get to talk to her."

"Well," I said. "I'm sure she'll come around."

"What's this funny-looking thing for?" She pointed to the deck for the film disk.

"It's a kind of projector. We use it to show game films." I walked over to the bookcase behind my desk and drew down the screen.

"Doesn't *look* like a projector."

"Well, it's a little more technically advanced than your average. Uses disks and digital projection. I can manipulate film frame by frame with it." She seemed truly interested, so I said, "You want to see a demonstration?"

"I want to see Jesse." She was calm and said this without malice or *any* affect, really. She might as well have said she preferred tea to coffee.

"Look, she may meet us for breakfast," I said. "But even if not, she'll be here in a few hours to work out. She has to."

She smiled. "I can't wait to see her. Only she doesn't look healthy in the photos I've seen."

"Oh," I said. "She's healthy."

"Can I see this thing work?" she said, pointing to the film disk projector.

I turned it on. It's a flat device with control knobs on top, and the film projects from a small aperture on the front of it that you can zoom in with. I'd been going over the film of our offense in the last game, so that is what I showed Liz. I let it run through a few offensive formations and running plays, but she seemed to be studying Jesse's movements.

"She's so light on her feet," she said.

"I know."

"Don't you have film of her throwing it?"

"Sure. This was just set up so I could look at our running plays."

I shifted the machine to pass plays and as soon as I did, Liz said, "That's an offset I- formation, isn't it?"

"You know football?"

"My husband was a coach. I've seen probably as much football as you."

"I doubt that," I said, chuckling.

"Well. I've seen a lot, anyway. That," she pointed to the screen as the film switched to another play, "that's a single back, three-wide formation."

I nodded, impressed. "Sometimes we run the tight end in the slot on that play," I said. "He's real shifty."

After a while I was talking with her about football. She knew a lot. I shouldn't have been all that surprised, because most women had gotten into it by then—but still, Liz knew the game intimately. She knew the names of defenses and formations and a lot of the less obvious plays.

"You learn about football through Mr. Carlson?"

"God, no." She laughed. She had really white teeth and I liked her laugh. "Anyway, there's no Mr. Carlson. I took my name back after the divorce. No, I learned all I know from twelve years with Kevin Smoke."

"Tell me about him."

"Well, he was devoted to football, and to Jesse."

228

I waited.

"That's it, though. That was everything for him. I was not a real part of his life once Jesse got to quarterback age."

"And how old was that?"

"Oh, she was throwing the football with him when she was just a little thing. He gave her a full-size ball when she was maybe six or seven. That football was almost bigger than *she* was," Liz said this with a slight, soft kind of sadness in her voice. It was a pleasant memory, you could tell, but she was clearly feeling sad about how long ago that all was. "They spent every day together, and all that time," she said, nodding, "he was teaching her."

"Was he a quarterback?"

"No. I don't think so. He was just a coach. He was a coach when I met him, and he was a coach when I . . . When we split up. He was a coach when he *died*."

We watched films for a while, and she saw her daughter from a variety of angles, delivering passes. At one point, on a quick pass to Mickens in the flat, she said that Jesse looked a little flat-footed.

"Yeah, she did there a little maybe," I said. It wasn't true. Jesse's footwork was always perfect. "You ever play quarterback yourself?" I said.

"In a women's league," she said. "When Jesse was real small."

"Where?"

"Guam. At the base. We had a league."

"Really?"

"I thought Jesse's father would pay more attention if I was a player." She looked at me with a wry smile and I turned away, slightly embarrassed. "Didn't work," she said.

I thought it would be better if we didn't go any further into the subject, but then she looked at me as though she was making up her mind to tell me something. Only she didn't, and after a long pause where I was feeling hot and stupid, I said, "I'm divorced, myself."

"Jesse's father, he was a legend in the islands."

"Yeah, we had some publicity about him in the local papers when Jesse . . . You know, at the beginning of all this."

"I left him for Ray Anne. That's who I was with until last year. She passed away."

"Oh," I said.

"I'm a lesbian, case you were wondering."

"No," I said. "I mean, I don't wonder about things like that."

Back then a lot of gay people, women especially, felt compelled in the most public and unnecessary circumstances to announce their sexuality. I understand how it was back then. Even after gay marriage was legal all over the country, people were still pretty damn mean about it. All of the most liberal and well-meaning folks still made jokes about gays or being gay that made you see there was still a long way to go. Most of the humor was based on being mistaken for gay, and it was a punch line that came from the expectation that it would always earn a laugh. It was beyond me, how anybody could really believe that the work was done when gay people remained the butt of so many jokes in just about every venue. Still, it always embarrassed me to no end when I was confronted with a person's sexual identity. It was none of my business or anybody else's business either.

Anyway, when she said that about being a lesbian, I was too embarrassed for words. I mean, what *do* you say when somebody announces that to you? "I never would have guessed" sounds about right, but then you're sort of making it clear that you make a *point* of guessing about those things; or, you know, that you have some idea what the hell a lesbian looks like. Or you might say, "Really. How's that working out for you?" Or, "What a coincidence—I prefer women, too." I felt like telling her that I liked to floss regularly, or that I preferred sea salt to the regular kind. Finally, I simply said, "I'm heterosexual, myself."

"Jesse was just a little girl when I left," she continued. "Twelve or thirteen."

"You don't remember?"

"Twelve."

"She says she was eleven."

"I guess she was."

Again I didn't say anything. It was quiet for a while, except for the whir of the fan on the film disk, but then the phone rang, startling me pretty royally. I picked it up and Coach Engram was on the other end. "Flores there yet?" he said.

"No."

"Well, when he gets there, tell him we're going to meet in the café across from the compound. Jesse's coming, too."

"She is?"

"She's with me. We'll be there in a few." He hung up the phone without saying anything further.

"Jesse's coming to breakfast, too," I told Liz.

She seemed to straighten with apprehension when I said that.

Twenty-Eight

As it turned out, I really liked Jesse's mother. She had a sense of humor and could talk to almost anyone. I don't think anybody else much cared for her, though. Not even Jesse. Especially not Jesse. She was polite, but . . . there was no embrace, no real reunion. This didn't seem to bother Liz a bit. She reached out her hand and said, "Hello," and Jesse nodded, shaking hands with her briefly. Just another fan to handle. Or business acquaintance.

"I'm very glad to see you," Liz said.

Flores arrived then, and we all walked into the restaurant. The café was not much, a little breakfast and lunch hole-in-the-wall across from Redskins Park called Huddle Up. They quickly put some tables together so we could all sit down. Jesse sat next to Engram and across from me. She was wearing a long gray skirt, a white blouse, and flat black shoes. Her hair had started to grow out a bit so the curls were more pronounced and covered her ears and forehead with little dark ringlets. She wore sunglasses up on her head, held there on the strength of her curls. Liz was on her left. Next to me was Edgar Flores, natty as ever, in a blue blazer and white pants, white shirt, and a yellow tie. All this he topped off with a yellow fedora hat and in his hand he carried a cigarette holder with no cigarette in it. Coach Engram said later he looked like a pimp from the islands. I thought he should be in the winner's circle at a racetrack, standing in front of a big horse, with a couple of tall, shapely brunettes and framed by an array of bright flowers. Engram himself was in his usual coaching sweats, as I was, the two of us looking like Mr. Flores's stable boys. We were definitely a unique-looking crowd, but there were so many of us, folks left us alone.

Flores went on and on at first about what a great player Jesse was and how glad it made him to bring her to the NFL. He seemed to want to impress Jesse's mother, who listened politely enough. He really had no idea what he was dealing with, though. He appeared to expect some kind of Kleenex-teary reunion, some heavily emotional scene of renewal for which he could collect a little gratitude. He leaned back after the waitress brought us all coffee. "Well," he said, beaming. "You two are the main reason for this little get-together." A long silence ensued, and he looked at both of them as if they had suddenly frozen in front of his eyes. "So, here we are."

Then, in a perfectly even voice, Jesse asked Liz, "Where have you been?"

"I've been in Tennessee, honey, with Ray Anne."

Jesse turned away. Then Liz leaned over and started whispering to her. But Jesse wouldn't have it. She faced her mother now with a petulant scowl on her face. I hadn't seen that look since the Aztecs had bloodied her nose. "I don't care about your lesbian *friend.*"

I saw Flores set himself back a little—as though he recognized a powerful odor in the room.

"What's that mark on your nose?" Liz said, after a moment.

"Where have you *been* all these years?" Jesse pressed again.

"Where have *you* been, Jesse? Huh? I wrote to you every week or so for years. You never wrote back."

Jesse looked down. I thought for a moment this was because we were all sitting there listening, but then she looked back at her mother. "You could have called me," she almost whispered.

"I would have, Jesse. All you had to do was answer one letter, you know? One note from you and I would have been on the phone so fast . . ." she paused, looked around the table. I was so embarrassed for both of them right then, but I could see it was Liz who was feeling the brunt of it. "We don't have to discuss this in front of the whole world, do we?"

All of the men at the table sat completely still.

I decided to step in. "Perhaps it would be better if we let you two discuss this in private," I said, hoping Coach Engram and Mr. Flores would get up with me, but they just sat there looking at mother and daughter.

"Why are you contacting me now?" Jesse said.

"You're famous. I didn't know where you *were* for a long time. Who wouldn't want to get in touch with a member of their family—"

"*Family*," Jesse said. "Right."

"Yeah, family."

"So you're after my money."

"Heavens, no," Liz said. "Of course not."

"The first thing you said there was I'm famous."

"That's how I found you, I mean—"

"So what do you want then?"

"I want to make sure, you know, folks don't take advantage of you."

"Really?"

"You keep every penny if you want, Jesse. I don't want any of it." Liz by now appeared profoundly embarrassed. She kept looking around the table at each of us as she talked. "I just want you to know I'm *here*. I'm proud of you, okay? Proud as I can be. And I want to protect you from the vultures . . ." She stopped and surveyed the room beyond us a moment. "Not you gentlemen, of course." I saw Engram cover a smile that threatened to overtake his lips, unlike Flores who gave a hearty old chuckle. Liz turned back to Jesse. "But, see? You can't be taken advantage of if *I'm* with you. I can make sure of it."

"I already have three agents," Jesse said. She glanced at me, and I thought she might point out that I had been taking care of her, too, but sadly she didn't. "My head coach played for sixteen years in this league and he knows the business. I'm taken care of."

"Agents can be crooks, too," Liz said. "I have my real estate license. I've studied business law at community college. *And* accounting." Her voice broke a little, here, and I felt truly sorry for her.

Jesse shook her head. "I can take care of myself."

Flores started talking about the insurance policy, what it covered, how Jesse would not want for anything if something should happen. He spoke mostly to Liz, and she listened, perhaps relieved just to be rescued from the hard angles of her daughter, who simply finished her breakfast and then sat there sipping her coffee.

It was a long morning. The waitress cleaned up after us and we sat in silence a while. I drank more coffee and watched Jesse's mother. In her own way she was quite stunningly self-possessed and attractive. She wasn't sure who she should look at for a moment and the silence was getting to her a bit. Finally she asked Jesse again, "What happened to your nose?"

"It got cut in a game."

"Liz," Coach Engram said now. "It still isn't clear what you want."

"That's between Jesse and me."

Mr. Flores leaned forward. "You know that this can be bad publicity for your daughter, don't you?"

"What could be?"

"Look, we're in a precarious position, Liz. We have to be perfect with Jesse. Absolutely perfect." He talked as if he knew something the rest of us didn't.

"I still don't know what you mean," Liz said.

"Your— Your . . ." he paused. "Your lifestyle, okay? It could be a problem."

I couldn't believe he'd just used the word "lifestyle." As if a person's identity—a person's *being,* her whole *self* could be reduced to such a silly notion. "Life style." For Christ's sake. Even back then, I'd thought, we might have gotten past notions like that. Flores's words seemed about as retrograde as his fashion sense.

"I'm going to move to this area," Liz said. "I will *be* here if Jesse needs me."

Jesse would not look at her mother. She just sat with her hands in her lap, staring down at them, saying nothing.

"It's not a good idea to reveal too much to the media," Flores said. No one said anything. "It wouldn't do to have this out there."

"Aren't we past that kind of silliness?" Engram said.

"No. Not in this case. There's already talk about her"—he gestured toward Jesse and paused before finishing—"sexuality. As I'm sure you all know, the media, well, they can make a person's life pretty miserable."

All in all, it was about the most awkward breakfast I ever attended; by the end I think even Flores's yellow tie had started to fade.

Twenty-Nine

IN OUR FIRST offensive meeting after the bye week, I finally spoke to Jesse about calling her own plays. I told her it was okay to change the play now and then when it was clear that what we had called wouldn't work, but that the rest of the time she was to do what we asked of her. It was the one way, I said, besides injury or playing badly, that she could end up on the bench.

She nodded and seemed to hear me, though she didn't have much to say by way of a response. I could tell she was preoccupied, but I didn't want to press her just then. As usual, Engram was working with the defense on our first day of preparations, having already worked with me to sketch an offensive game plan for the Browns. He wouldn't join Jesse, Spivey, Ambrose, and me until the second day, when we were actually scripting things and setting up the sequence of plays for the first quarter and the beginning of the third.

I should mention a bit of what was going on with Ambrose. He claimed a shoulder strain and went around outside Redskins Park with his arm in a sling, but there wasn't anything wrong with him. Coach Engram kept reporting him on the injury list as "doubtful," and Ambrose himself told the press he was still not ready to play, but the truth was, he was done. With Ambrose's arm strength gone, Coach Engram wouldn't have dreamed of putting him back in a game. Still, he was listed as the third-string quarterback, and though he never got a chance to work with the starters, or even with the scout team, he dressed for all of our games. Spivey was our second-string quarterback now, and everybody on the team knew it.

It was sad to see somebody as great as Corey Ambrose had been walking around trying to maintain his dignity with some stupid lie about his physical condition. Then again, he made himself useful; I can say that. He was always helping Jesse when he could, spent a lot of time with her on flares and quick outs, showing her how to look a safety off or move her throwing arm a few times before she let go of the ball. Moving her arm, faking the beginning of a throw, like only Johnny Unitas used to do, that was something Jesse really wanted to develop. It's a lost art. Unitas would drop back to pass, his throwing arm moving up and down—just a hacking motion from the elbow to the wrist, with the ball there waiting, like he might launch it any second, and every time he moved his arm a defensive player would leave his feet, jumping high in the air to block a throw that didn't come. And here's the thing: Once a defensive player leaves his feet, he's about as effective as a little cloud. You can push him in any direction you want and he goes down. The move almost always gave Unitas enough time to pick out a receiver and hit him. Unitas played before I was born, and he may have been the greatest ever to play the position, but almost no one imitated that feature of his play. Now, Ambrose helped Jesse to learn the art of the "pump fake"—which is what that move was called. Most quarterbacks don't use it unless the play calls for a fake to a tight end or a quick out to the receiver or a stop-and-go that's supposed to draw a defensive back up so the receiver can then turn and run by him. But, by god, Jesse started using it like Unitas did. Every time she dropped back to pass, her arm was moving a bit, up and down, as though she needed to cock her arm before letting the ball fly. It made her that much more difficult to defend. To Coach Engram's credit, he didn't cut Ambrose. They were both old quarterbacks, of course, allies in that particular trench, and he must have known he could count on the old veteran to help prepare Jesse for each game.

So we worked out exactly what we wanted to do against the Browns. They had a running game like ours—a big offensive line and a running back named Delroy Lincoln who was as good as anybody in the game. Strategy here was key, but we were kidding ourselves if we thought the distractions were over.

The following week, when everybody was back for practice, the press got wind of Liz. Colin Roddy cornered Jesse in the parking lot after the first day of practice and said, "Jesse, are you gay?" Others had asked her the same thing, but I'd always thought Roddy was above that. Jesse just looked at him and kept on walking. "How long have you *known* your mother was a lesbian?"

"Leave her alone," I said. She was walking a little ahead of me, and when I spoke up she looked back at me and stopped. Roddy stood there with his pad and a pen in his hand. "Do you have a comment, Jesse?" he asked her.

"I don't."

"Did your mother teach you how to play quarterback?"

"My mother didn't teach me anything," she said, and started moving away.

"Come on, Jesse, talk to me," Roddy said. "Put all the rumors to rest."

"Look, anything I say . . ." she started to say, but seemed to think better of it. "I don't have any comment, okay? Gimme a break here."

She disappeared into her Mercedes and drove off. Roddy walked back toward the compound with me. "What's going on, Skip?" he asked.

"Getting ready to play the Browns, that's what's going on."

"Come on, what's the story with Jesse's mother?"

"Who the hell have you been talking to?" I asked, stopping to face him. I couldn't imagine how he could have found out in so short a time. Was it Flores? Engram? Somebody in the café? How on earth did he already know?

"Can't reveal sources," he said.

"That's a lot of horseshit, Roddy. I'm no judge and this is no courtroom."

It was a beautiful day for early November. I remember thinking how the warm air felt almost balmy. We walked along the path toward the practice field a while and I admired the smell of pine needles, determined to say nothing more. But then Roddy said, "We've been talking to Liz Carlson nonstop for the last two days, if you really want to know. And well, she's given us so much, I just thought Jesse might want to give *her* side of it."

"Her side?"

"Yes."

"There's a side?"

"Liz says she tried to keep in touch but Jesse would have nothing to do with her."

"I don't know about that."

"What does Jesse say?"

"Jesse would rather have had a phone call, as I understand it."

"See? That's what I mean. Tell me about that."

"Nothing to tell. They didn't have anything to do with each other for, I don't know, something like twelve years."

"Because Jesse disapproved of her mother's lifestyle?"

"I didn't say that, Colin. That's not it at all. And, I mean, what *is* that, anyway? What is a 'lifestyle?' Would you say your 'straight' life is a kind of style?"

He pretended not to hear my silly question. "I need to talk to Jesse."

"You *don't* need to talk to her *or* her mother. You're a sportswriter, why don't you write about sports, for god's sake."

My voice must have got a bit loud there because this stopped him. He studied me a moment, then smiled. "Look, I'll do my job, Skip, and you do yours."

"Really? Cause you never fail to tell me how to do mine."

"Well then, now we're even, I guess."

The week of the Browns game, the *Washington Post* printed an interview with Jesse's favorite wide receiver on the Divas, Michelle Cloud. Michelle was not gay, but she said she had been approached by Jesse at a Washington hotel. "I didn't think anything of it at the time," she said. "Hell, a lot of the players in this league are gay." She claimed that she never could get used to the idea and resisted Jesse's advances. Then an "unnamed player on the Washington Redskins confirmed" that Jesse had engaged in sexual activity with at least two players. This "source" was, he said, "defending" Jesse. But of course all this news did was fan the flames about Jesse and her sexuality.

The news that Jesse's mother was in town, that she was a lesbian and was anything but reticent on the subject of her sexuality, well, it made things even more complicated. Suddenly Jesse was not only the most famous woman in the world; she was at once the most revered and hated woman in the world. The conservatives and the Christian right (which phrase, as a matter of fact, has always interested me; I mean, is there a Christian left? And if so, do they ever say anything to offset the stupidity of the Christian right? Why do they let the Christian right give the entire faith such a bad name?) immediately called for Jesse's dismissal from the league. "A woman like that exerts just too much influence," said one. Another called for her endorsements to be pulled across the board. "The very idea that this woman represents Modesty Perfume," one commentator said, "when she, herself, is an example of sexual promiscuity and largesse, is beyond the pale."

Taking the other tack, *Out* magazine named Jesse the most admirable woman on earth.

All the talk shows made jokes about her; innuendos, intended, one hoped, to poke fun more at the rampant disapproval of Jesse than anything else. Still, it brought her name to the fore in so many venues and in so many ways that after a while even jokes that were in support of her ended up hurtful and sad. ("Where there's Smoke there's a 'flame'"—that sort of thing.) There is no such thing as "enough is enough" in the media. Only when public interest itself wanes, when the money starts to dry up, do they back away from a feeding frenzy, and that's what this was.

You must remember how hard it was back then to pick up a magazine or a newspaper that didn't have a picture of Jesse and/or her mother on the cover. It would go on, I knew, for the rest of the season, and I wondered how long Jesse could withstand it before it started to wear her down. How could she or anyone keep playing through it all? Even Harold Moody, our public relations director, stopped taking calls.

She came to practice every day with her head high, but you could tell it was all in her mind, simmering. Nate started appearing to pick her up after practice, and he, Dan Wilber, and Orlando Brown ran interference for her through the nest of reporters waiting outside the park. Those three guys formed a pretty big offensive line to block for her as she tried to make it to the parking lot and her Mercedes.

Charley Cross of ESPN wanted to interview her just before the game in Cleveland. He was a former protégé of Bob Costas and, like Costas, about the only educated, intelligent sports reporter in the business. It also helped that, like Costas, he had a soul. He wanted to talk to Jesse about the sport, not the "scandal" concerning her sexuality and her background. She asked me what she should do, and I told her, "He's been doing this for almost a decade. Cross is the best there is. Doesn't play games, and he doesn't go for anything but the truth. He's a human being so . . . if you're gonna talk to anybody, talk to him."

She promised him an interview after the Browns game.

That Sunday morning the *Washington Times* speculated that Jesse had been brutalized by her father, which was what drove her to "lesbianism." He'd forced her to be "the son" he always wanted; forced her to learn football, and made her into the "anomaly" or, "in some circles," the "freak" she was. She was described as a "tortured, driven woman" so confused about her own sexuality that she was almost predatory toward other women, and probably "fairly promiscuous with men" as well. The *Times* worried about the "unity" of the Redskins.

Jesse, she took it all out on the Browns.

In the first half she completed 16 straight passes. Four went for touchdowns. The Browns were down by 28 before scoring a single point. Just before the end of the half, they got a field goal. We enjoyed such a big lead they'd stopped trying to run the ball and went strictly to their passing game. (We stopped Delroy Lincoln, who rushed for only 16 yards on 12 carries. That was part of it.) Orlando Brown had four sacks. Nick Rack and Zack Leedom had two each. The only unfortunate thing that happened in the game was that Drew Bruckner strained his knee pretty badly. We had to plug in a rookie there named Talon Jones who was a strong special teams player but essentially untested at middle linebacker. He'd practiced there with the second team, and Coach Bayne liked him, but you never know with a rookie. He was 6' 2" and weighed around 230—fairly light for a linebacker in those days—but he was strong and smart. Just the same, Bruckner was a hell of a player to lose.

In the second half, Jesse was no less effective. It really was something to watch her drift back, find a receiver, and whip the ball right to him, laser sharp with every pass. She went 11 for 13 in the second half. (Gayle Glenn Louis dropped one, and Rob Anders turned the wrong way on a play and the ball sailed over his shoulder before he realized it.) For the game, Jesse completed 27 of 29 passes, for 340 yards and 6 touchdowns. Walter Mickens ran for 103 yards and scored the other touchdown. We won the game 49 to 3.

Not only was it Jesse's first 300-yard game, she tied a Redskins record for touchdowns with six. Only Sammy Baugh (two times) and Mark Rypien had ever done that.

I didn't give a damn about her personal life. She was the best quarterback, the best pure passer, I ever saw.

Coach Engram had taken over the play calling during the Browns game, and Jesse ran the plays he told her to call. It was like he knew what she needed. I kept waiting for him to tone it down, to go more completely to the running game, but he kept feeding Jesse those passing plays. He must have read the *Times* article himself, and been as pissed off as Jesse was. Twice, I saw her nod toward him when I told her the play he'd called. Coach Engram stood there, carrying his clipboard like he was a third-string quarterback, not the coach, his face inscrutable, saying nothing except what the next play should be.

The Browns were supposed to be championship material, but we made them look like a badly coached high school team. The papers said the next morning that we'd "humiliated them." Nothing they tried worked, on offense or defense. Nothing. While for us, it was the opposite. At the end of the game, Dan Wilber, Orlando Brown, and Darius Exley picked Jesse up and carried her off the field.

I was so proud of her right then. I understood, maybe for the first time, what it meant to be "brimming." Hell, I thought I might sprout wings and lift up like something attached to a hot-air balloon. I bet I didn't weigh more than twenty pounds or so at the end of that game. Talk about walking on air.

Jesse, though, she had a look on her face as though she'd just plundered a village, or pulled off the most perfect, most massive heist. Something in her, something in her soul, was being fed by frustration, anger, resentment, even hate. That kind of thing can't last for long, but . . . while it does? People move mountains.

I wish love had the same power. It's the better thing, love, don't get me wrong. I truly believe that. Hatred is potent, see, but it's small and finally constricting—even suffocating. Man, though, it sure can feed skill and will for a little while. Yes it can.

Thirty

IN HER ESPN interview with Charley Cross, Jesse did not appear even slightly nervous. She was just Jesse: sweetly ironic, not too forthcoming, but blunt and willing to laugh at herself. As usual, she was conservatively attractive, in a white blouse with a thin gold necklace around her neck. Cross, a broad-nosed, raspy-voiced man who came off a little like Bill Clinton, wanted the world to see her as a "woman." He opened the interview by saying he was going to be giving America its first true glimpse of an "extraordinary young woman named Jesse Marie Smoke."

Throughout the interview, the camera shifted from a close-up of Jesse's face as she answered questions to highlights of her throwing the football. At one point, the film showed her getting hit from behind in her first pass attempt against the Raiders. Even in slow motion it looked like her head had been knocked off when her helmet flew up.

Cross asked, "Did that hurt?"

Jesse gave a broad smile. "A little."

"Were you injured on that play?"

"No. I didn't really feel it until later, actually." In the studio light, Jesse's curly hair glistened, looking almost wet.

Cross spoke to her gently throughout the interview. "Talk about what it feels like to be the only woman on a field with such violence."

"It's not violence to me, you know? It's competition."

"Pretty violent competition."

"I think it can be violent, but . . . It's all controlled," she said. "Violence is chaotic, like, mostly random. I know it looks chaotic on the field, especially during the heat of a play, but most of the people in a play—they're doing exactly what they're supposed to be doing; and the force you see, that's just part of that." She got this thoughtful look on her face then, and Cross let her think for a second. Then she picked up where she left off. "A football play starts with what I know *looks* like confusion and chaos, all the players struggling and pushing and running to specific places, but then one player begins to emerge in the distance and another one lofts the ball over a crowd, in a perfect arch, to that one player breaking free and the ball and the player come together like some . . . some elegant *fact* of the universe. You know? It turns out all that confusion is really precision. Artistry."

"Artistry?"

"To me, it is. There's no other word for it."

"Do the players on other teams ever talk to you on the field?"

"Sometimes. They say things when they can't get to me. But the blocking is always so good. I've only been sacked twice this year."

"You've been knocked *down*, though, quite a few times."

"Not that many. Anyway, I'm usually watching the receiver I've thrown the ball to. I don't even notice it."

"You don't notice it?"

"Not really."

"But you say sometimes players say things to you."

"Sure."

"What kind of things?"

"Nothing important."

"They call you names?"

"Oh, they taunt and stuff. Sometimes they might call me something."

"Like what?"

"I don't want to get into that. Just, they get frustrated sometimes, but like I said, I got a great offensive line in front of me."

"Talk about your father. He teach you how to play this game?"

"He taught me everything. But—it wasn't like he wanted me to be a boy, you know? Some of the newspaper people—some have tried to make it like I was a disappointment to him because I was a girl, but that's just . . . not true. Let's put it this way. He loved the game and he loved me. He wanted me to know it. It's not like he hoped I'd play professionally, though."

"That was your idea."

She looked directly into the camera now and laughed. "Actually, it was Coach Granger's idea. It never really crossed my mind." My heart brimmed over, of course, when she said that.

"Do you feel like a role model for other young women?" Cross asked.

"Look, I just want to play football. I don't want to be anything to anybody."

"Does it bother you that other girls are getting involved in the game now?"

"No."

"Other girls are trying out for football teams across the country, did you know that?"

"No, I didn't." She got a bit of a serious look on her face. "I guess that's okay. I mean, if a woman wants to play football, then why not? I played in a women's league. Women can play any sport they want. I just think it's not fair to suggest that because I'm a woman I can't do as well at something as men do. If I'm strong enough, if I have the talent, if I move fast enough, then . . . why not?"

"How about the danger?"

"It can be dangerous for anybody who plays it."

"Have you ever been hurt? I mean really hurt?"

"Not really."

"Ever had a concussion?"

"Once, in a game against the Philadelphia Fillies in the women's league, I got slammed down pretty hard and bumped my head. I was dizzy for a while after that. I had trouble sleeping and I had a headache for most of the rest of that week. I guess that could have been a concussion. I know I was hurt on *that* play more than any play so far playing against the men."

"Talk about your relationship to the men on the team."

"They're my teammates. We all work together."

"Did you have trouble in the beginning, getting them to listen to you?"

She looked a little puzzled. "You mean on the field?"

"In general."

"I call the plays," she said patiently. "Or, I let them know what play has been called. We practice all week together. They get used to running the plays I call, the way they would with any quarterback."

"How do you get along with the other quarterbacks on the team? Ambrose? Spivey?"

"Fine. Corey helps me a lot, actually. He coaches me about things."

"What things?"

"Reading defenses. How to mislead the safeties. That kind of thing. He's been a big help."

I thought she was kind to say that. As for Spivey, she didn't say anything about him, except that he was a terrific competitor and never missed getting the ball where it needed to be on kicks when she had to try a field goal.

Except for the news that she might have had a concussion during that game against the Fillies, no really earth-shattering revelations came out of the interview. That's what I liked about Cross, though.

He wasn't adversarial, or interested in pushing the sensational. He was interested in the human side of things. He didn't want to embarrass or expose anybody; he just wanted the audience to meet the person he was interviewing. More than once he gave players who were maligned a chance to defend themselves. And he was a good listener. The whole interview only lasted about a half an hour. Near the end of it he playfully asked Jesse if she was dating anybody.

She got this modest smile on her face. "Not right now, that's for sure. Too busy."

"But do you have a love interest?"

"I'm not exactly . . . free for that, you know?"

"What do you mean?"

She blushed. I could see she had let out more than she intended. But she maintained an expression of concentration, taking her time now to find the right words. Finally she just shook her head and laughed. "Nobody wants to go out with me."

"Is that really true?" Cross said.

She was smiling again. "I won't be going out with anybody until the season is over."

"But then?"

"Are you interested?" She laughed, again.

And that's how it ended, with music and her smiling face, and then a slow-motion film of her launching the ball, in top form. Even in slow motion her release was a kind of blur.

We had the Eagles next. In our first game against them, in Philadelphia, they'd beaten us 21 to 9 and nothing much happened in that game that would make it into team highlights, except for the fact that Jesse kicked three field goals. But the Eagles were always tough. It didn't matter what kind of season we were having, they still managed to give us a hell of a game, and it was no different in

Jesse's first year. Of course for this second game, they had to play on our field.

It didn't help that on the day of the game it rained. It was a damp drizzly November day, and the offense couldn't get the ground game going. The Eagles stuffed Mickens pretty badly, and when Jesse tried to get the ball downfield, they seemed to have a dozen defenders around the ball no matter what play we ran. Jesse got knocked down a lot, but always after she'd let the ball go. Once she got hit so hard the whole stadium gasped, but she kept getting up. At one point when she came to the sideline for a time-out, she had bloody snot hanging from her nose. She got it all over her sleeve and the equipment manager held a wet cloth over her face for a bit, then wiped the blood off her uniform.

"Jesus," she said. "That's embarrassing."

"You okay?"

"I wish they didn't know what we're going to do on *every* play."

"Sure seems like it, doesn't it?" I said.

Coach Engram told Jesse we were going to keep trying to run the ball. By the end of the first half, we still had not scored, while the Eagles had already kicked two field goals.

Jesse completed only 5 of 22 passes in that first half, her worst outing. Some she missed, some got dropped or knocked down. She just couldn't seem to settle down and play to her natural talents, always being forced to move and dodge before she threw the ball. On the opening play of the third quarter, she ducked under a 300-pound lineman and ran the damned thing right through a big hole up the middle. She dodged to the outside when she saw a linebacker coming for her and gained 13 yards before a safety threw his body at her and knocked her out-of-bounds. She flew into the air and landed on her neck and shoulders. I thought every bone in her body might have broken. It looked like a deliberate attempt to hurt her and you could see how angry every player on our side was. The refs didn't like it either. They called an unnecessary roughness penalty and tacked on another 15 yards, which put the ball on our own 41-yard line. Jesse got up and shook her head, then trotted back onto the field.

"Jesse! Jesse, you all right?" I hollered into my headset.

She didn't respond. So I called the next play and tried to get her to look my way. "Jesse, let me know you're all right." She brought the team out of the huddle; I could see she had them in the formation I had called. She glanced over the line, shook her head a bit, then leaned down and called the signals, her voice high and girlish—it had no bass in it at all—and when the ball was snapped, she dropped straight back, looked to her right, then her left, bodies flying all around her. She hit Gayle Glenn Louis going up the seam about 30 yards downfield and he raced up the numbers just outside the hash marks all the way into the end zone. The crowd went ballistic. And all the more so when Jesse kicked the extra point.

Now we were leading 7 to 6. The Eagles took the ensuing kickoff out to their 30. On the next play, Talon Jones batted a pass into the air, snatched it, and took it to the house. Suddenly and very finally, we were ahead, 14 to 6.

The rain picked up shortly after that, and for most of the rest of the game both teams ended up just pushing each other around in the mud in the middle of the field. The Eagles had, I think, one first down in the second half. Again, Orlando Brown made riotous incursions into their backfield, and Talon Jones looked like he had learned a whole lot from Drew Bruckner. Maybe he couldn't rush the passer the way Bruckner did, but he was sure something to see in pass coverage. He knocked two other passes into the air and almost intercepted a second one.

We were glad when the final whistle sounded. As Jesse came off the field, I noticed she was limping a little bit.

"I'm all right," she said with some exasperation when she saw me staring at her. "Don't make a big deal of it."

"Why are you limping then?"

"I'm sore. Okay?" She was in a bad mood, so I let her alone.

. . .

Coach Engram said all the usual things in the postgame press conference. How hard the Eagles always are to beat; how we just played as well as we could. Somebody said, "So, when Jesse Smoke got knocked out-of-bounds on that run play, did your heart stop?"

Engram stared at the questioner, a sardonic smile on his face. "Jesse's tough," he said. "All right?" It got quiet in the room, and he looked around at the others. "You people ought to leave her alone."

"But Coach, was she hurt? I saw her favoring one leg as she came off the field."

"She's okay," he said. "We'll see what the trainer says."

"You said we should leave her alone?" a reporter asked.

"Look, I'm not going to let this business go on anymore," he said. His voice was utterly cold. "I've watched you guys—not just in this room, and not *all* of you *in* this room—but I've watched a lot of you guys hound her and distract her from what she should be doing. She's a great football player; a great quarterback. I ought to know, because I played the position myself pretty well for a few years."

A chorus of voices went up—all starting with "Coach," for there were other questions, but he raised his hand to quiet them. "I'm closing practices from now on. And Jesse's informed me she will no longer grant interviews. I expect you guys to honor that."

"Isn't closed practices prohibited by league rules?" somebody said.

"No, it isn't. I can do it *occasionally* as conditions demand. Well, these conditions demand it every week from now on. Or until I say otherwise." He looked around the room one more time, again with the voices raised and thrown at him, and then he bent the microphone in front of him down and away from his chin, turned, and walked out of the room. Naturally, I followed.

The first reporter to come to see me was Roddy, of course. He had a female from the *Washington Times* with him—a woman named Debbie Croft who was short and lean and wore a business suit that accentuated her waist and hips. Her hair was tight and formed to her skull with curls around her ears, and it bounced when she walked. She did all the talking and Roddy listened. I realized she had no questions for me but a kind of proposal. "You get Jesse to talk to me and I promise she won't regret it."

"What about me?" I said.

"Pardon?"

"Will I regret it?"

"See? I'm a woman, also in a man's job."

"Come on. Women have been doing your job for more than five decades," I said.

"And it still does not feel like a woman's job."

"I'll grant that."

"I think I can help her."

Roddy nodded agreement.

"What makes you people think she needs help?" I asked. "Do any of you even know her?"

"Well, we don't know her like you," Debbie said.

"*I* don't know her," I said, with some energy. "You understand that? I discovered her and I don't know her, really. I'm not sure anybody does. She's her own person, Jesse. She is entirely self-possessed. I know what she wants me to know and nothing more."

"So I'm wondering if maybe she would open up to me."

"She opened up to *me*," Roddy said. "I mean, she told me things."

"She gave you nothing, okay," I said, immediately regretting it. Now he thought I knew something shocking, or at least intimately revealing. The look in his eye would have made a housefly sick.

"What'd she tell you?" he said.

Debbie looked at him oddly.

"She didn't tell me anything," I said. "I just meant she didn't tell *you* anything either."

"Come on, Coach," Roddy said impatiently. "You *know* something. I can tell."

"What's there to know? Goddamn it. Why does there always have to be a worm in your apple?"

He blinked. The question was completely opaque to him. "It's the world."

I said nothing. It was quiet for a moment, then Debbie said, "Is it true about the sex change operation? That she's really a man?"

"You know who spreads rumors like that?" I said, not even bothering to contain my anger. "Men who can't stand the idea that Jesse can do things with a football that have always been the province of men, and she can do them better than any man *ever* did them."

"Can I quote you?" Roddy said.

"You always strive to tell the truth, Roddy, don't you?" I walked away from them and didn't look back.

Thirty-One

OUR NEXT GAME was against the Jets. They had a pretty good offense, but their defense was weak against the pass. Their record was 6 and 5, and they needed a win to stay in the race for the AFC East title. They trailed Buffalo, at 7 and 4, by one game, so a victory against us would certainly help their cause. We were now 8 and 3, having won six straight—all six games Jesse had started—and trailed the Giants (9 and 2) by only one game. So we needed a win pretty badly as well. Dallas, meanwhile, was coming on behind us at 7 and 4. Philadelphia was out of it, having fallen to 5 and 6. Eleven games into the season, the standings in the NFC East looked like this:

TEAM	W–L	PF	PA
New York	9–2	214	89
Washington	8–3	256	141
Dallas	7–4	204	160
Philadelphia	5–6	205	219

While we were playing the Jets in New York, the Giants were going to Dallas to play the Cowboys, who had split their last two games but were starting to execute very well—they were talented and they'd had to play some really solid teams. Oakland barely beat them, 17 to 13, following which they beat Cleveland 27 to 10. They were healthy, too. Whereas the Giants were hurting in the secondary, having lost their starting free safety and their weak-side linebacker for at least six games each. They had to bring in a new punter because their starter broke his leg. Their best wide receiver had suffered a slight ankle sprain, but he was due back for Dallas. Sometimes, the league schedule was so good I set my DVR to record several of the games so I could watch them later. I really wanted to see how the Giants did against Dallas. And not just as a coach either. As a fan.

We would have to go to Dallas and play on Thanksgiving Day, and even during the week before the Jets game, we were already beginning preparation for that. It would be a real grudge match, especially if Dallas beat the Giants. Then again, if the Giants won, Dallas might even be a tougher place to play, with the Cowboys that much more desperate. We'd beaten them pretty handily in Washington, of course, so either way, we figured they'd be about ready to kill when we got down there.

In practice that week, Jesse still had a very slight limp when she walked from the huddle to the line, but once the ball was snapped you couldn't notice it. She finally admitted that she'd twisted her ankle slightly, but an MRI showed no structural damage. Still, we let her rest it on Wednesday and Spivey practiced with the first team. It didn't really matter to Jesse—who was always ready to play—and since practices were closed, nobody noticed Jesse wasn't in there.

Back then, as you may remember, the Jets had one of the few open-air stadiums left in the league—we still had one in Washington—and even the Jets themselves complained about how bad the weather could be there. We went to New York on Friday and had a walk-through practice on Saturday. Both days the air was still and the weather only crisply chilled—like the best kind of fall day. Sunday by noon the field was frozen solid and wind slashed across it so hard and fast it looked like it would pick the whole surface up and send it out over the Hudson River. Snow started swirling in the air just before kickoff. It swept in white churning clouds along the hard surface and made the whole field look like the yard lines and hash marks were yielding up their whiteness to the wind.

It was almost impossible to pass the ball in those gusts of wind. Jesse's arm was strong enough to throw a few tight spirals 10 or 15 yards downfield, but anything deep got blown so far off course you couldn't be sure where it would land, or in whose hands. I hated it down there on the sideline, freezing to death in the icy blasts of air. Coach Engram kept calling running plays and sweeps, trying to wear down the Jets. I might have insisted that we take advantage of their pass defense, but I understood what was going on. In those conditions, Coach didn't want to risk it with Jesse. She was wearing gloves for the first time, and twice she almost fumbled the ball on the snap from center. When she took the gloves off, her hands froze so quickly her fingers got stiff and she couldn't grip the ball then either. She kept her hands in front of a heater on the sideline and pulled the gloves on each time she had to take the field. Jesse's got big hands for a woman— not man's hands either. Just a young woman's hands, a little bigger than normal, with long, wide fingers. She usually didn't have trouble gripping the ball in bad weather. But this day was something else.

It was a hell of a time. We couldn't move the ball. The defense played well enough, but we just couldn't sustain a single drive. I don't know how many times the offense went three and out. At the half we trailed 10 to 0.

In the middle of the third quarter, trailing 10 to 3, Andre Brooks, our right guard, went down. He was small for a guard, 6' 2" and around 290 pounds, but he was one of our best blockers, run or pass, and he was devoted to Jesse. Trying to push off on a defensive lineman charging at Jesse, he tore a muscle in his right forearm. He didn't want to come out, but he couldn't play with only one arm. The backup at that position was a fellow named Dave Busch. He was much bigger than Brooks, 6' 6" and 334 pounds; he was strong and we liked him for the position, but he was not the blocker or athlete that Brooks was.

When Brooks came to the sideline Coach Engram looked at me and the serious expression on his face said a lot. He was thinking what I was thinking. Jesse might be in trouble out there with a weak spot on the line.

We couldn't get anything going in that wind, and now Jesse had to throw in more of a hurry. The first time she tried something deeper than 20 yards the wind blew the ball up and away from Anders and the safety intercepted it. It was early in the third quarter, and it didn't cost us anything but the end of another promising drive. The whole game it just seemed like every time we got something started, the Jets would find a way to stop it. They didn't sack Jesse, but they hurried her, and she was not used to throwing a football with gloves on. I don't think she wanted to admit the gloves were a problem, but you could see the flight of her passes had a little too much arch—they were too susceptible to the wind.

On the third play of the fourth quarter, with the wind in our faces and the ball on our 15-yard line, Jesse rolled a bit to her right and tried to fire it in between two defenders to hit Gayle Glenn Louis on a quick slant. Dave Busch had been fighting his heart out and he blocked well for her, but on that play he got pushed flat by the defensive tackle and the cornerback blitzing from that side leaped over him to hit Jesse just as she threw. She went down in a heap on the hard field and the corner landed on top of her. The ball sailed high, Louis barely tipped it into the air, and the same safety grabbed it out of the air for his second interception. This time, he ran it the 15 or so yards to our end zone and made the score 17 to 3.

Jesse was good and angry as she went out after the kickoff. The steam rushing out of her mouth might just as well have been smoke.

Dan Wilber told me she got into that huddle and said, "We are not going to lose this game." She was something to see right then, he said. She told me before she went in, "I want pass plays now. We got to pass." I could tell from the strain in her voice that she'd hurt her ribs when she hit the field with the cornerback on top of her.

Coach Engram started feeding her what she wanted. She threw two quick-out passes to Exley, one for 8 the other for 11 yards. Each time he stepped out-of-bounds to stop the clock. We were down to less than 2 minutes, so on the next play she dropped back, looked left at Exley, let her hand move with the ball, up and down—lots of Jets players left their feet—then she turned to the right and fired it to Anders moving up the sideline. He caught it without breaking stride and ran 35 yards before he got knocked out-of-bounds on the New York 18-yard line. It was so noisy nobody could hear Jesse at the line. She started using our silent count and the team performed it to perfection. (With a silent count, everybody watches the ball. If the quarterback says it's on "three," the center counts to himself, "one thousand one, one thousand two, one thousand three," and snaps the ball. The quarterback counts too, everybody else watches the ball; when it moves, they do.) On the next play, she hit Anders on a quick post just over the goal line. It hit him right between the numbers and she threw it so hard it actually moved him in the air. He'd left his feet to catch it and the film showed that when the ball hit him he got propelled at least a foot farther downfield—just enough to cross the goal line when he came down. I don't think I've ever seen a ball thrown that hard.

We were down 17 to 10 now. There was 1:30 left and the special teams knew what they had to do. We needed the ball back. We tried an onside kick and Talon Jones almost recovered the ball. It bounced high in the air and a lot of folks fought over it—for a second I thought Jones had it, but after the referees sorted out the pile, they gave the ball to the Jets.

We still had a chance if the defense could stop them. The ball was on our 44-yard line. We had two time-outs left. The Jets ran two running plays and gained a total of 7 yards. We called a time-out after the first run, but let the clock go for the second one. Now it was third and 3 on our 37-yard line. The clock ticked down and down but we knew they had 30 seconds before they incurred a 5-yard penalty, so they'd have to snap it with about 50 seconds left. If we stopped them on third down, even if they used up another 5 seconds, we could call our last time-out and still have about 45 seconds to try to move the ball. In that wind, with people running around and hollering on the sideline, our defense getting ready to stuff another running play, the Jets did something pretty amazing. Their quarterback faked a handoff to the fullback then threw a 5-yard pass for a first down to the tight end breaking out of the line on the right. He ran with the ball for another 14 yards before anybody brought him down. The game ended with the Jets taking a knee at our 18-yard line.

We lost 17 to 10.

As we were walking off the field, the Jets quarterback stopped Jesse and congratulated her. Other Jets players crowded around her and shook her hand. I hadn't noticed before that day, but it seemed like she was earning a fair amount of respect among some of the players. A professional football player is a special kind of person, and having the respect of a foe, especially concerning the way you play this game, is as good as it gets between players of opposing teams. Jesse had tears in her eyes and her face betrayed nothing but disappointment and bitter defeat; still, I think she noticed too that she was being given something right then, something precious.

The following Tuesday, after practice, I agreed to meet Jesse for dinner again. This time we went to a restaurant in Fredericksburg, Virginia, called La Rosetta International Cuisine. It was a spacious, pleasant place far away from Redskins Park and Washington. The restaurant was on the corner of one of the main streets in the town. Jesse said she just wanted to have dinner, but I knew something was up. It was a long drive south and east of Ashburn, where Redskins Park is located, so she wanted to get pretty far away from the place. Even at eight in the evening, the traffic down I-95 was pretty thick. I knew it would be bad, so I left myself plenty of time and got there early. It wasn't hard to find but when I arrived, Jesse was nowhere in sight. I was a bit apprehensive that night standing in front of the restaurant waiting for her.

A man emerged from the shadows and walked toward me. He was wearing a business suit and dark glasses. I thought he was maybe a cop. He walked right up to me and stopped.

It was Jesse, standing in front of me, frowning. "Well?" she said.

"Now *that* is a better disguise."

"I can't be talking to strangers tonight," she said, gravely.

We sat in the back, at a small table lit by a single candle. "How'd you discover this place?" I asked.

"Dan Wilber and Darius recommended it. They come here a lot."

"He bring you here?"

"No. It's far from the city, and they said the food is wonderful."

A waiter came to the table with menus and asked us if we wanted something to drink.

"I'll have a bourbon and water," she said, a slight rasp in her voice.

I ordered one, too. When the waiter left the table, I said, "He didn't recognize you."

"Or you."

I nodded. I'm about two inches taller than Jesse and, I have to say, when I saw our reflection in the glass as we approached the front door of the restaurant, I thought we looked pretty good together, even if she *was* dressed as a man.

"I didn't know that was you until you were right in front of me," I said.

"Good."

"You weren't limping, either."

She smiled. A fine gift. I was beginning to relax.

When we got our drinks and had sipped a bit, Jesse said, "How you think I'm doing?"

She was doing wonderfully, I told her. "Were you in any doubt about that?"

"The last two games I was awful."

"We won in Philly, Jesse. You played as well as anybody against the Jets."

"I was wobbly and stupid. Couldn't hit anybody."

"Nobody could. Worst wind I've ever seen." I thought she was above this kind of self-doubt, so it seemed really odd that she was not only talking to me about it, but that it had grown so acute in just two games. I told her what her play meant to the team. "We're all in this together, Jesse, all right? Every time you get knocked down, the offensive line falls all over itself to get better—they've been playing so hard and so well, they may break the record for the fewest sacks ever allowed by an offensive line. We had a line here—years ago now—that gave up just nine sacks in sixteen games. This team? We've given up only five, and since you started playing, only two. These guys play hard for you."

She nodded.

"You saw the film on Dave Busch. He played like a man possessed when Brooks got hurt. You think they go all out like that for somebody who lets them down? Come on, Jesse. You haven't let anybody down."

"How bad is Brooks?" she asked.

"We'll know more on Wednesday. But . . . I think he's done. I don't know. Maybe if we get into the playoffs."

She looked away, and there was an awkward pause. With her hair combed straight back like that, and the tie gripping her throat, she did look like a young man, actually. And oddly kind of homely. With that broad splash of freckles across her face, she looked like a gangly kid, too afraid of his own coordination to lift a glass without letting his hand tremble. "What'd you think of my interview with ESPN?" she asked.

"Just fine."

She shrugged her shoulders and got this scrunched look on her face.

"Charley Cross is one of the good guys," I elaborated. "I think he allowed you to, you know, be yourself."

Suddenly, she put her hands up to her face and I saw tears in her eyes.

"Jesse, what's wrong," I said.

I reached out and put my hand on her wrist. She only slightly moved her hands away from her face, but she waved me off. She seemed to shrink a bit there in the seat, then she picked up her napkin and covered her eyes.

"There's nothing to be ashamed of," I said.

"I'm not ashamed," she said. I waited to see if she was going to start crying in earnest. Finally she looked at me, and the glitter of those tears in her eyes made her look feminine and beautiful again. "It's just hormones," she said. She touched very gently under her eyes with her napkin. People in the booth across from us noticed but politely stopped staring.

"You okay now?" I asked.

"Really, I am. It's just . . . a bad time, that's all."

"Oh."

She looked at me. "What do you mean, 'oh'?"

I said nothing.

"I'm not having my period or anything, if *that's* what you just 'oh'ed about."

"Jesse," I said. "I just need to— Don't talk to me about things like that."

She was embarrassed. "It's just . . . I'm dealing with my mother."

I nodded as if I understood more than she was actually saying.

"And now, the way I've been playing? And my ankle and now my ribs—"

"Your ribs hurt?"

"Not too bad. Just when I take a deep breath."

"You've probably bruised something."

"It's on my left side, so I can't feel it when I throw. I just . . . I don't want to get knocked down again, let's put it that way."

The waiter came back to the table and took our order. He looked at Jesse a little suspiciously, but even now did not seem to suspect who she really was.

We both ordered lobster ravioli and a tossed salad.

While we were waiting for dinner, the waiter brought us each another drink. "So this injury thing," I said when he'd gone. "Is this why you wanted to meet me for dinner?"

"No."

"Then . . ."

"Do I have to have a *reason* to have dinner with you?"

"Well . . ."

"I wanted to talk to you, Coach, that's all. It's just, a lot . . . a lot's going on."

I waited.

"You know my mother came to stay with me."

"No, I didn't know that."

"I felt bad about how things went. I even felt sorry for her in that meeting, so I talked to her over the phone a few times and then— well, she came to live with me."

"I'm glad to hear that, actually," I said.

I felt honored, too, that she trusted me enough to talk to me right now, under the circumstances. I wanted to find a way to express that to her, but then she met my gaze and said, "Yeah, well—don't be. I just kicked her out."

I took this in. "Is that why you were crying?"

"I was not *crying.*"

I could see she hated that I'd seen those tears. She took a big sip of her bourbon and water, made a tight-looking face, and then shook her shoulders. "Forget about it," she said. "It's probably just that . . . I feel like I owe you everything, you know? So now and then . . ." She stopped there.

"You kicked her out?"

"This morning. We had a fight."

I thought she might start crying again, but she only took a sip of bourbon and stared into my eyes, as if she was looking for some kind of judgment or approval. I shrugged. "What was the fight about?"

"Same stuff, I guess. She didn't say it, but . . . I think she was kind of upset that I didn't mention her in the Cross interview. She kept going on about how I talked about you and about my father. Said I sounded like I owed everything to the men around me."

"I don't think that's the way you sounded at all."

"Well, it really got me angry, I'll tell you that. I started yelling. Let her know I owed her absolutely nothing. And then I told her to get out."

"You feel bad about that?"

"That's the thing. I don't *know.*" She shook her glass around a little. "I mean, so—I've been feeling sorry for her all day. She packed her things without saying a word, then sort of skulked out. Before she left, she loaded the dishwasher. She was like a maid cleaning a motel room."

"Know where she went?"

"Back to Tennessee, I guess."

I didn't know what to say. I sat there, letting the silence build and build. Then I said, "Nothing's permanent, Jess." She looked at me, dry-eyed now but still a little red around the edges. "There's no reason you can't get in touch with her in a few days, right?"

The waiter brought our food. We ate silently for a while, then I said, "You know when I was with your mother alone in the office the first day she was here, she told me that she played quarterback once, too."

The look on Jesse's face changed. She seemed to brighten a bit, and for a second I thought she might laugh.

"She said she thought it might get your dad's attention."

"I didn't know that."

"You don't remember it?"

She frowned. "I do have a vague memory of her in a uniform. But . . . I must have been pretty young."

"She didn't play when you were growing up?"

"No. She watched *me* play."

"So she was there for a while anyway."

"I guess."

"For a long while," I said. "Right? I mean, you were almost a teenager when she left. Anyway, I was going to say that I liked your mother. After that conversation, I thought maybe I understood where you got your direct approach to people."

"Maybe she'll start sending me e-mails again."

"Or, you could write to her."

She seemed to agree with that. We finished our pasta and then just sat there for a while sipping our drinks and staring at the high windows in the front of the restaurant. Finally, I started to talk about the Dallas game, but Jesse stopped me. "I don't want to talk about football now," she said. "Do you mind?"

I wanted to tell her that right now, football was the *only* thing she should be concentrating on, but I said I didn't mind one bit. I wished I hadn't seen her tears. She had enough on her plate without a personal crisis. I was certainly glad Coach Engram had ruled out interviews with the press.

Thirty-Two

DALLAS WAS GOING to be really tough. Having lost to the Giants in the last seconds, 17 to 16, they were now 7 and 5 on the year, still one game behind us. The Giants, meanwhile, were 10 and 2 and seemed unstoppable. Even at 8 and 4, we were clearly struggling. The Cowboys needed to beat us, and they were pissed off about that first game, the way we'd manhandled them.

We were going in there on Thanksgiving Day, and we weren't in the best shape to do it. Andre Brooks would not be back—his forearm muscle was not just torn; it had been separated from the tendon and bone. He'd be out for the year. Our left guard, Steve Henderson, was nursing a high ankle sprain he got in the last quarter of the Jets game. If Henderson went down, we'd have two fairly inexperienced players on the offensive line trying to keep Jesse healthy. Worst of all, Darius Exley had strained his hamstring in Monday's practice that week. He couldn't run full speed without risking pulling the thing entirely, which would put him out a month or more, so Coach Engram decided he was out for the Dallas game. Our best backup wide receiver was a guy named Sean Rice. He couldn't block like Exley, and he wasn't as fast, but he was the best alternative for the left side. Though not especially tall, he had decent speed and good hands and he'd been Jesse's favorite target when she was playing on the scout team.

Since we played the Jets on Sunday afternoon in New York, we had basically two days to prepare for Thursday's game in Dallas—which is why we'd started preparing for it the week before, even as we were getting ready for the Jets. Monday is usually a day off for the players, but we practiced that day and Tuesday—then took Wednesday for the flight to Dallas and a walk-through Wednesday night before the game. It was all terribly rushed, but it was the best we could do.

I wanted to run the ball against Dallas—especially to the right, Dave Busch's side. He was a good enough run blocker that if I didn't force him to pull and go across the field, he could handle whoever was in front of him. Coach Engram agreed with that. It would take Dallas at least two or if we were lucky three quarters to figure out we weren't running very many plays to our left and that Busch was going to stay put. Also, in the weekly injury report to the league, we listed Darius Exley as "probable" to play so Dallas would spend a lot of time preparing for him. We put in a few quick slants and fades to Rice, but it would be Gayle Glenn Louis and Rob Anders who would have to carry the passing game. Also, I decided to put Louis in the slot on three-wide formations, and on some plays we'd run a four-wide-receiver set with Anders, Rice, Jeremy Frank, and our fifth wide receiver, a pretty tall, two-year veteran named Jerome White. He was fast, he had good moves, and he knew how to find his way into the open in a zone defense, which is what we expected to see a lot of from Dallas. White didn't always catch what was thrown to him, but he could find his way to an open spot.

Jesse was uncommonly nervous before the game. After those two bad outings in a row, she had something to prove, I think. I tried to calm her down, but she had this look in her eyes—like a man facing a firing squad after he's heard the word "aim." In pregame warm-ups she was happy about the weather at least. It was chilly, but there wasn't much wind, and the sky was an empty, pale blue. Dallas still had a big opening in their roof, which made for odd shadows on the field, but that didn't seem to bother her. In the offensive drills before the game she threw sharp, crisp, absolutely accurate passes—10-yard, 20-yard, 40-yard, and 50-yard passes—all right on the money. The gathering crowd, filing in to take their seats, actually began to cheer each time she launched a ball. (Of course there were a few loud-mouthed rowdies who called her a "dyke" and so on, but we were used to that.)

Things did *not* get off to a good start. We took the opening kick and Frank ran it out to the 28. On the first possession from scrimmage, I called a play that sent Mickens on a sweep to the right side behind Dave Busch. Jesse brought the team to the line, looked over the defense, then changed the play at the line. She faked a handoff to Mickens and fired the ball to the left, toward Rice running what looked like a quick slant. The corner on that side intercepted it. He dragged three tacklers all the way to our 18-yard line.

Jesse came off the field with that look still in her eyes, but now she must have noticed the look in mine. I walked up to her as she was removing her helmet. "What was that?" I said.

She looked at me, her hair all matted down by the helmet. "I thought the corner on that side was playing too close."

"He was close all right."

"If Sean gets in front of him and I put it in there right, it's a twenty-yard gain. Both safeties were rolling toward Anders's side."

"They're going to be doing that all day. They don't have Exley to contend with."

"That's why I tried to hit the quick slant."

"The corner on that side is quite capable of handling Rice."

She said nothing.

"And he *did* handle him, didn't he?"

"It was my fault. I tried to put it in there too early."

"Jesse, their corner would have been in Sean's hip pocket all the way down that side of the field. He's fast, he's good, and he can cover Sean Rice."

She looked down the sideline at her offense as they took their seats on the bench. I think she was afraid Sean could hear what I was saying.

"Hell," I said, "he can do a fair job covering Darius. The guy's a lot better than you think."

She shook her head. "I know Sean. He'll break free."

"Forget about the interception, Jesse. Just play your game," I said. "And run the plays I call."

While we were having this conversation, Dallas drove the 18 yards from the spot after the interception and scored on a run right up the gut. It was 7 to 0 now, and we weren't going to quiet that crowd any time soon.

On the next series, Jesse called exactly what she was supposed to, but again the offense was having trouble moving the ball. I could see it was starting to get to her. Mickens gained about 7 yards on his longest run, and after two first downs, we faced a third and 6 on our 48. I called a fake draw with both wide receivers fading down the sidelines and the tight end and running back cutting to the outside behind them. The fullback on that play is usually wide open in the middle of the field, but if he isn't, then either the tight end or the running back should be open. It's a pretty good play if everybody does what they should.

Jesse dropped back, planted, and then in the face of a heavy pass rush launched it deep down the right sideline toward Rob Anders. The ball dropped beautifully over his left shoulder into his hands, but when he went down it squirted out and was ruled incomplete. It was a beautiful pass, but it was fourth and 6 and we had to punt.

Dallas stubbornly drove it down the field, gaining little chunks of yardage on each play. They converted on third down four times, the crowd roaring louder and louder with each first down. Our defense put up a hell of a fight, but after an 11-play, 55-yard, 12 minute drive, Dallas faced a third and 6 on our 12-yard line. Their quarterback threw a little underhand shuttle pass to the fullback right between Zack Leedom and Nick Rack. Talon Jones was too far to the right, covering the tight end, so the fullback waltzed almost untouched the last 12 yards into the end zone.

Now it was 14 to 0.

Jesse took the offense on a pretty solid drive then. She completed 4 passes out of 5 tries, and Mickens ran behind Dave Busch and our right tackle, James Cook, for good yardage. We got stalled though inside the Dallas 10-yard line. On third and goal, Jesse tried to flip the ball over the right shoulder of Gayle Glenn Louis, but he couldn't hold on to it.

Shaking her head in disgust, Jesse kicked a 17-yard field goal.

We stopped Dallas on the next series, but we still couldn't get anything going on our next possession. We punted, and stopped Dallas, got the ball back. Same thing. Three and out. We kept getting stopped with dropped passes, or receivers falling down, or Jesse throwing it just a few inches beyond the fingers of a wide receiver. On one play she launched a perfect spiral toward Gayle Glenn Louis but it hit a referee in the back of the head and bounced to the ground. (So did the referee.) That stopped another drive, and Jesse kicked a second field goal, but then Dallas drove it down and scored again before the end of the half and we trailed 21 to 6.

The crowd was really into it then.

I should say something about Coach Engram's ability to make adjustments at halftime. You can't change very much about a game plan once you're in a game, but you can do various subtle things to take advantage of what you see during the action of the first half. Of course if you're getting your ass handed to you, the changes you make have to make a difference, and the tendency is to try to make drastic changes. Engram never did that. He always said that panic was not the way to respond to adversity. He'd stick with what we planned and practiced, but he'd change the look of it a little bit, or move players into different positions to see what impact that might have. In the Dallas game he noticed that their defense was almost always playing in a two-deep zone, with the safeties paying special attention to Anders and Louis. So he decided to go with a three-wide-receiver formation in the second half and put Jeremy Frank in the slot. Since Jeremy returned punts for us and was fast and very shifty, Engram reasoned that one of the safeties would have to look toward him on pass plays to that side.

"We'll run him across the front and on deep outs behind Anders," Engram said. Then he looked at Jeremy. "You got to sell it," he said. "Make them believe."

"That will tie up the safety eventually," I said. "But at first they'll try to cover it with a linebacker and maybe a nickelback."

"That's what I'm counting on," Engram said.

Jesse nodded. She knew exactly what he was trying to set up. "Run Sean from the slot, too," she said. "No linebacker out there can cover him."

We talked it over and went into some of the other variations from the three-wide set. We were going to use Gayle Glenn Louis there too. In the first game against Dallas, we killed them with passes to the backs and quick fades up the sidelines. Now we were going to get into the same formations, but we were looking at the middle of the field. We'd split the safeties eventually and if it worked, we'd have something open deep on one side or the other.

Coach Engram worked the last few minutes of halftime with the defense and Coach Bayne. Dallas had been running on us, reading the tackle stunts we ran on running plays, catching both defensive ends by running inside their outside pass rushes. Bayne decided to keep the tackles in their lanes and stop running the stunts. What we gave up in the pass rush would be offset by shutting down the running game. Orlando Brown and Elbert James would take up some of the slack in the rush and we'd give them a little help with Talon Jones and one of the corners. Our defense was good enough that if we could get some points on the board early in the second half, we'd make a game of it.

I was worried about Jesse's confidence. She hung her head a bit when we were heading through the tunnel on the way back out to the field.

"You okay?" I said.

She looked at me. Her eyes were as bright as ever. "I hate this place," she said, and trotted out onto the field, the offense following behind her.

We kicked off in the second half, and Dallas got a good return out to their 36-yard line. But on the two running plays they tried, they gained nothing. On third down, they tried a deep pass down the middle that fell incomplete. Jeremy Frank called a fair catch on a relatively short punt at our 33-yard line. I'd gone over the first few plays we'd run with Jesse before she took the field. We started again in the three-wide set, and Jesse handed off to Mickens who ran behind Dave Busch for 4 yards. On the next play, Anders and Rice went deep, Gayle Glenn Louis ran a quick slant to the right side of the field, and Jeremy Frank cut to the outside and caught a 14-yard pass for first down. The play looked like this:

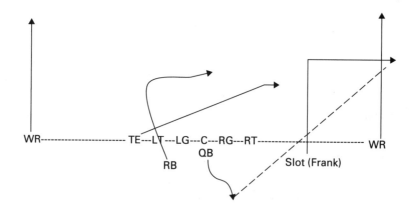

From the Dallas 49, Jesse flipped a quick pass to Mickens in the flat and he gained about 3. On the next play, we were in a three-wide set again and this time Rice was in the slot. Jesse dropped back, faked it to Frank on the left, then hit Rice crossing in front about 5 yards downfield, and he cut to the center of the field and gained 16 more yards. Now we had a first and ten on the Dallas 23. The crowd was still into it, but they'd quieted some because of how quickly we'd marched down the field.

On the next play I called Mickens off tackle. He cut to the outside and gained seven yards, but we got called for a false start. Now it was on the 28, first and 15.

Jesse shook her head and leaned down in the huddle. I called a slot right, corner fade to Anders. Wilber told me later that Jesse said, "I'm not kicking a field goal down here."

I could just hear her saying something like that. Her voice, when she was in the heat of competition was so inspiring I'd almost burst out laughing.

This time Anders was in the slot. Not many teams can run more than one or two players from that position. It's like having four men on a baseball team who can play shortstop. But every one of our guys has to learn how to run patterns out of the slot and every one of them can do it. (That's another quality of Jonathon Engram's coaching.) Anyway, Anders lined up in the slot, and the corner assigned to him man-to-man didn't go to the slot with him—he stayed on the outside. Dallas looked confused on defense. They had shifted to the nickel (which means they had added a fifth defensive back) and played a three-deep zone. Jesse noticed it. She sent Anders in motion to the left, just to confirm it. When nobody in the Dallas defense followed Anders she knew he would be getting a lot of attention on his side of the field from a safety and at least one cornerback. As she called signals, she stood up and looked back at Mickens. Then she leaned over center again and changed the play. Or, I should say, she called a variation on the play I'd called. Anders would still do what he was supposed to do—cut to his right, toward the middle of the field, then run for the corner looking over his left shoulder. The two wide receivers would run long, shallow posts up the seam, and Mickens— who was supposed to block on the play I called—would circle out of the backfield and run to the middle of the field. It looked like this:

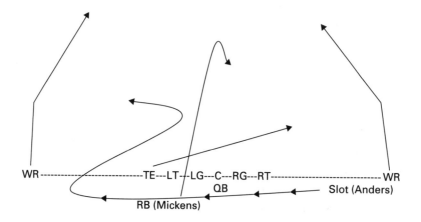

It was wide open. Jesse stepped back, looked downfield, then fired it to Mickens—hit #29 between the 2 and the 9—and he turned around and ran straight for the goal line. He hit the safety in the chest and carried him into the end zone. Jesse kicked the extra point and with 11 minutes left in the third quarter we trailed 21 to 13.

The defense was so fired up by now we stopped Dallas on three plays and got the ball back. This time we couldn't get a first down on a third and 1. Mickens got stuffed by the Dallas right tackle and middle linebacker on the sweep. We punted from our 42 and then, by god, Dallas got moving again. They started on their own 26 and took a lot of time, completed a few short passes, made just enough yards on a few runs up the middle and off tackle, and now with 6 minutes left in the third quarter, they were on our 33 and looking ready to take it away from us.

On third and two, though, Orlando Brown swept into the back-field and tackled their fullback for a 4-yard loss. They had to punt.

They tried for the coffin corner—that is, they tried to put the ball out-of-bounds inside our 5-yard-line—but the ball went into the end zone and we took over on our 20. Things sort of settled after that into a kind of back and forth rut. We drove the ball to midfield and then stalled. (Jesse got sacked, pulled down by a blitzing safety on a third down play.) We punted, Dallas went three and out, punted back. On a sweep to the right side, Mickens fumbled. Dallas drove to our sixteen yard-line and then their quarterback got hit by Orlando Brown and fumbled. From then on Jesse took charge of the game.

It didn't look like that was going to happen at first. I called a play that allowed for a deep pass if it was open. Jesse dropped back, moved her arm up and down the way she does, and then she got hit hard from behind by a Dallas linebacker. She held on to the ball, but she really went down hard. The crowd cheered in an odd way when that happened. Normally when their defense gets a sack, an NFL crowd makes a lot of noise, but this time there were as many groans as there were cheers.

And then Jesse didn't get up, not right away. The crowd got quiet. Compared with the earlier noise, they were suddenly absolutely silent. Dan Wilber leaned over Jesse and after a moment, she turned over on her back, reached for his hand. He helped her to her feet. She shook her head and walked back to the huddle and the crowd cheered. The *Dallas* crowd was actually cheering her.

On the next play, she dropped back again and this time she fired a quick strike to Rice 15 yards downfield on a hook pattern. He turned, caught the ball in his gut, then got creamed by the safety. He, too, got up fairly slowly.

We had the ball at our own 35, first and 10, when the quarter ended.

When Jesse came to the sideline during the commercial time-out between quarters, she had blood running down her cheek. She didn't take her helmet off.

"You all right?" I said.

"Just got the wind knocked out," she said.

"I want the doc to look at you."

"I'm okay," she said. "I want to run that play again."

"Which one?"

"The one I got hit on. Call it again. Anders was open."

Sure enough, on the first play of the fourth quarter, Jesse dropped back, found Anders up the sideline, and hit him in stride. It was a beautiful ball, a perfect bullet of a spiral that arched slightly over his shoulder and fell into his waiting hands. He took it all the way, and now we were just trailing 21 to 19.

Coach Engram decided to go for two points.

Dave Busch came to the sideline with Jesse and Dan Wilber and Gayle Glenn Louis. "Give it to Mickens behind me," said Busch, so fired up his eyes almost clicked when he blinked.

Part of what made Coach Engram a great coach was he knew when to listen to his players. Jesse looked into his eyes and said, "Do it." He smiled and called a simple off-tackle run behind Dave Busch and James Cook. The fullback would punch in between those two, leading the play, and Mickens would run behind him, looking for daylight. It worked perfectly. Nobody got a hand on him.

With 14 minutes left in the fourth quarter we were now tied at 21.

Our defense was still just as fired up as Dave Busch was, but Dallas took the ball and went on a time consuming drive all the way to our five yard-line. With only four minutes to go in the game, they tried a pass to the corner of the end zone, but Talon Jones of all people jumped in front of the receiver and intercepted the ball. He ran out of the end zone all the way to our 42.

Then Jesse trotted back onto the field and I could see I need never have worried about her confidence. There was blood all over the front of her white jersey now, blending right in with the burgundy numbers on her chest, but it didn't seem to bother her. If anything it only served to fire up the men blocking for her. She ran the plays we called, and with Mickens running well on sweeps and off tackle, she threw just three passes on the next drive. One of them was a 20-yard strike to Sean Rice on an out pattern. He moved so convincingly toward the center of the field that the corner, who had covered him so well earlier in the game, nearly fell down for the sudden change in direction. When Rice turned, the ball was right there and he snatched it out of the air just before falling out-of-bounds.

After that, Jesse went on a streak. She looked so good and the line was protecting her so well, we started calling more passing plays from the three-wide set. She completed eleven passes in a row at one point. Sean Rice played like an All-Pro before it was all over. They were double-teaming him, in fact. He caught 8 balls for 154 yards and 2 touchdowns.

We never looked back. In the last 4 minutes Jesse threw two touchdown passes so that we ended up winning the game 35 to 21. Jesse had completed 18 out of 26 passes, for 256 yards and 3 touchdowns. She'd kicked two field goals in the bargain, while Mickens rushed for 113 yards and scored a touchdown himself. All in all, we were feeling like a pretty powerful team again.

At the end of the game, too, some of the opposing players came over and shook Jesse's hand. This in spite of the bitterness of our rivalry, in spite of how much those guys hated losing a game to us. She smiled and nodded to folks. I was so damn proud of her. I guess you could say I was proud of myself, too. Not that I said any of these things out loud, or even thought about them much in those days, but right then I was on top of the world. I had found Jesse, you see, and I had helped her make it in the toughest sports league on earth. It's sometimes not even so humbling as it is exciting when you know you are going to go down in history.

Of course, everybody knows what took place after that Thanksgiving game. But at the time we were pretty well blindsided by it. Not one person, except for a few bastards in the league office and the head of the players' union, expected the law to step in the way it did and threaten everything we were building.

Thirty-Three

WE CAME BACK from Dallas Thanksgiving night to a huge crowd of fans at Redskins Park. For people to leave their homes on that kind of night—it was windy and cold, with occasional salvos of bullet-sharp rain, and on Thanksgiving no less—well, that tells you something about your fans. They all carried signs with Jesse's likeness on them and cheered her when she came off the bus. "We want Jesse! We want Jesse!" they chanted. Then they began to shout, "Smoke! Smoke! Smoke!" She waved and smiled that brilliant, open smile, which somehow was only enhanced by the cut on the right side of her head just below the hairline. (Before we got on the plane from Dallas an internist had put four stitches in it and bandaged her up.) When the crowd saw the small white bandage on her head they cheered even louder. The rest of the players surrounded her. It was such a happy time. The players had Friday through Monday off. They would get a good, long, well-earned Thanksgiving vacation.

On the plane ride back from Dallas, Coach Engram addressed all of us about what we might hope for if the Eagles beat the Giants. "We take care of the rest of our schedule, and we'll have them in our house, with our fans, for the division title." And then on Sunday afternoon in New York, again on a frozen, windswept field, the Giants lost to the Philadelphia Eagles 16 to 14. We were 9 and 4 and the Giants 10 and 3. We trailed them by only one game. I was beginning to think this was going to be our year.

Only on Monday morning after Thanksgiving, this happened: In New York, the league office announced that the Third Circuit Court of New York had issued a temporary restraining order against the Washington Redskins prohibiting us from playing a woman in the National Football League. Jesse would be allowed neither to practice with the team nor to participate in any team meetings or coaching sessions. We were, according to this lawsuit, destroying the "integrity" of the game.

The day the news broke you'd have thought the U.S. had declared war on Canada. We didn't find out about it until around one in the afternoon on Monday. Edgar Flores sent for Coach Engram and the entire coaching staff. I didn't hear anything until it dropped out of Flores's mouth, but Engram heard it on the radio on the way to Redskins Park. It was the most incredible thing I ever saw, the media frenzy at Redskins Park. I mean, I only wish I could describe the confusion and anger that day.

Flores had a sheaf of blue papers in his hand when I walked into the meeting. The room was full. Mostly with guys wearing suits and dark ties. Engram and the rest of the coaching staff and I were in our practice sweats. It was a cold, bright, sunny day, and light cut through the windows in sharp angles. I saw Engram sitting at the end of the table and sat down next to him, still wondering what was going on. The way he looked at me, I thought Flores had sold the team or something.

"What the hell's going on?" I said to Engram.

Then Flores sprang the news on us.

That business about the "integrity of the game," in particular, got me really sore. "She *improves* the integrity of the game," I said. "She improves it every time she steps on that field." Engram put his hand on my arm. I must have gotten pretty loud about it.

"The players claim they cannot go all out against her," Flores said.

"*Who* claims that? Which players?" Engram said.

"It's part of the restraining order. They don't name names."

"Well, who filed the suit?"

"The players' union and the league," Charley Duncan said

"The league is in on it?" I said.

"Yes."

I know I must have cursed pretty loudly right then. Not that it would have bothered anyone. The room never really quieted down for anybody. We were like a band of nitwits discussing our procedures for making coffee on a sinking ship. There was a lot of yelling. Meanwhile, the press was collecting outside. They'd be all over Jesse, too, I knew.

"What does the suit *say*, exactly?" Engram asked.

Flores sat at the head of a long table, but Engram and I were only a few seats away from him. He looked down at the blue papers in front of him and waited for it to quiet down. "The suit asks that she be prohibited from playing any more games for the Redskins."

"Even as a kicker?" Somebody said.

"No playing of any kind."

It got really noisy again, but Engram raised his hand to quiet everybody. "Why?" he said. "What do they mean they can't go all out against her?"

"Players will testify that they have been forced to compromise their game because of her," Flores said. "They say they will produce film of men pulling up before they collide with her, and they will claim this is for fear of hurting her. They also claim the referees give her an unfair advantage. When they *do* hit her, they get penalized for it."

I couldn't believe it. In all the films of our games that we'd studied, I never noticed anything like that. And as far as I could see, the referees had made good calls when they penalized teams for roughing the passer. "That's a lot of horseshit," I said.

"They will *further* claim," Flores went on, "that having her on the field, directing our offense, is a distraction from the intricacies of the game because players are so intent on watching her perform."

This almost made me laugh.

There were three lawyers in the room, right then, but the one who mattered was a short, slightly puffy fellow named Benjamin Frail. He had little fat fingers and an iron gray beard along his jaw, and he was soft-spoken, calm, and polite, and he twirled a yellow pencil in his hand like a little baton. I don't remember the names of the other two, because until registering Ben Frail's name, I referred to the three of them as Curly, Larry, and Moe. Charley Duncan, our general manager, was a former lawyer, too, so I guess we really had four of them in the room. Anyway it was Frail who did most of the talking. He went through the entire legal ramifications of what he called a temporary restraining order, or "TRO." He emphasized the word "temporary." He talked about how things usually moved pretty swiftly with this kind of order. We'd have little time to prepare, and we'd have to show significant reason to have the order quashed.

"But we can get it squashed, right?" Flores said.

"The word is *quashed*, not squashed. The burden of proof is not just on the league office and the players' union. We'll have to do a certain amount of homework, too."

"Why the hell does a court in New York get to tell us what to do?" Engram wanted to know.

"The league is based in New York," Frail said. "It's a suit filed by the league and enforceable because we are part of the league. It's binding."

"Jesus Christ on a crutch," I said.

"There's something else," Flores said.

Now the room got really quiet.

Flores nodded at Frail and he went on. "The suit claims that she's actually a man named Robert Ibraham and that he's in breach of a contract he signed to play in the Canadian League."

Engram looked at me. "For Christ's sake," I said. "She's not a fucking man."

"Well, it's part of the suit," Frail said. "They claim she had a sex change operation. So . . . we'll have to deal with it."

"Why is it even relevant?" Engram asked. "I mean, if she's really a man, then doesn't that tend to eliminate the first part of the complaint?"

"That's a very good point," one of the other lawyers said. "One we may take up in our brief."

"That's not the only problem with that, however," Frail said. "See, the parties contend that she signed a contract to play for the Montreal Alouettes."

"Goddamn," Engram said. He pushed himself away from the table. His chair made a screech on the floor. Everybody was looking at him and he turned to me. "Do you know anything about this?"

"What?"

"This Canadian thing."

"Of course not," I said. "And if *she's* a man, then . . . *I* must be gay, because . . . *I* think she's beautiful."

Somebody let out a little snicker.

"It's not funny," I said. "All right, dammit. Jesse Smoke is *not* a man."

Nobody said anything for a few seconds, then Charley Duncan turned to Flores. "I certainly never thought the commissioner would stoop this far to get at you," he said.

"It's not the commissioner," Flores said. "He had no choice but to join the suit. It's labor peace he's concerned with, not peace with me. He'll take *me* on. It's the players."

"It's not the players either," I said. "It's this goddamned benighted culture."

"And the lawyers," Bayne said.

Eventually we got around to what we were going to do about it.

"I'm going to handle the legal end of things," Flores said to Engram. "How about you?"

"I'll talk to Jesse," I said.

Engram turned to me. "You're going to have to do a whole lot more than that, Skip. I've got to get this team ready to play the Cincinnati Bengals."

"I can work out a game plan for the Bengals. They're not a serious threat."

"I'll take care of the game plan," Engram said. "What I need from you is help working with Spivey."

"Sure," I said, which is when it hit me that Spivey would be our new starting quarterback. "Only . . ."

"Talk to Jesse first."

"You want *him* to do it?" Flores said.

Engram paid no attention to Flores. Still looking earnestly at me, he said, "Let her know we're doing everything we can to fight this thing, that we still want her on this team."

Flores asked, "Is Corey Ambrose still our player representative for the union?"

Engram nodded.

"You think he knew this was coming?"

"Probably. I don't know how he could *not* know it."

"Motherfucker," Flores said. "I don't want that bastard on the field for any game the rest of this year."

"He's washed up anyway," Engram said. "Arm's shot. I wouldn't play him anyway."

This seemed to disappoint Flores. It got quiet for a moment, then he shrugged. "I want film of every play involving Jesse," he said. "I want you to find out about this Canadian thing, too. Somebody get a birth certificate from Jesse, or her mother. We'll meet back here tomorrow morning and see where we are." He and the lawyers got up and started filing out of the room. Engram stopped Charley Duncan. "I might need another kicker. I don't know if Dever is up to it." Duncan nodded and went out.

Engram turned back to me. I was still sitting there, still only half believing everything. I had a million questions. "Talk to Jesse, first thing," he said. "Go there now. Prepare her. Drill her about the media thing and ask her about Canada."

"I'll do what I can."

He looked at me, considered something, then rejected it.

"What?"

"Nothing."

"What? We shouldn't keep things back now, man."

"If we can't get a birth certificate, do you think you can get her to make an appointment with a gynecologist?"

"A gynecologist?"

"Legally we can compel it, but I'd rather she went on her own."

"You mean to prove she's a woman?"

"If she can't produce a birth certificate, we may have to," he said. "Just to prove she hasn't—er, you know—that she's not . . . transgender. It should be easy enough. We have to put to rest all this bullshit about her being a man, or, hell, under contract to somebody else. It's going to be one of the first things the lawyers will want. Fact, I can't believe they didn't mention it today."

"I'll talk to her," I said.

"And then get a hold of Spivey."

"You want to see him today?"

"You're going to be studying film. Lots of it."

I must have looked puzzled, because he got this impatient look on his face. "What?" I said.

"You're going to collect the film. Every time Jesse's dropped back to pass. Study the rush. Isolate every time she got knocked down. She hasn't been sacked much, but she's been knocked down enough after she let go of the ball."

"They've almost killed her on more than one occasion," I said.

"Which is how we'll prove she wasn't treated any different from any other quarterback in the league."

"We don't have to do that," I said. "We got film of Ambrose and Spivey in there. *They* didn't get sacked very much either, right? So . . . all we have to do is show that all of our quarterbacks got the same treatment on the field."

I wasn't worried overmuch about that business of players not going all out when they faced her. I didn't see how that could be her fault, nor how that could impact the "integrity" of a game that regularly touted the "success" of coaches and players who didn't get caught bending the rules. Our main concern was that business about her being under contract to the Montreal Alouettes. It didn't matter if she was really a man, if she'd had a sex change operation or not. What mattered was that alleged contract. If it was true, Jesse's career in the NFL was over.

I left the big meeting on Monday and went right to Jesse's apartment. Of course I had to fight my way through a mob of reporters and journalists and microphones and cameras when I got there. I called her from my cell to tell her I was standing on her front porch. She let the machine get it but when she heard my voice, she picked up right away. When I told her where I was she opened the door a crack so I could slip through. The yelling was almost as loud as inside a stadium. Everybody asking questions at once—as if any living being could understand a single sentence in so many droning voices. You might as well have tried to discern the buzzing of one bee in a frigging hive.

Thirty-Four

Jesse appeared to have been stunned into a kind of angry trance. When I got my way through the door and forced it closed against all those invading microphones and cameras and hands, she had already retreated into the kitchen of her apartment—the only place in there with windows one would have needed a ladder to look into—where she had barricaded herself behind the center island, right in front of the refrigerator. She had her hands tucked into her waist, but she could not stand still. She still had the bandage on her forehead. The phone was ringing, bleating relentlessly.

"Jesse," I said. "We're taking care of this, okay? I want you to know that." Thinking she needed me to be near her, I approached the other side of the island, but she recoiled. In her sweatshirt and jeans, she looked like somebody's teenage daughter, her physical presence diminished to nearly nothing. Each time I moved toward her, she backed farther away.

"What?" I said.

"Don't. Somebody might . . . get the wrong *fucking* idea."

"It's going to be all right, Jess. We'll work something out."

"How?" She cast her eyes down. She could throw herself into such a pure sadness, it was almost frightening. Not to mention deeply feminine. In spite of those husky, well-formed shoulders—because she had very capable upper-body strength, just like she had good solid legs—she just radiated it, womanliness, almost softly feminine at times. I'm no expert on these things, but she always seemed to have this kind of nurturing quality—a strange amalgam of kindness and care. She wasn't the *new woman*, as just about everybody wanted her to be. She was a true woman—the kind that has defined the sex for thousands of years. She was not a temptress, or a Madonna, or an innocent child-like virgin—the only three possibilities in the minds of most men—she was a woman, a person. You know what I mean? And right at that moment, she was a person who was awful confused, pissed off, and clearly feeling cornered.

"I asked Nate to come over," she said.

"Good."

"He's bringing Dan, and I think Darius is coming, too. I told him not to, but . . . he insisted."

"Hell, the whole team might show up, Jesse. They can clear your front porch for you." I took a chair by the kitchen table. By this time she had filled the apartment with furniture. It was a home now, of sorts, a comfortable place, warm and neatly arranged. She had two couches, a recliner, and bookcases full of neatly stacked books. Sunlight broke in lovely angles through drapes in the dining room and crossed the room in a diagonal toward the living room. Her bike was still leaning against the far wall by the fireplace.

"It's nice here," I said.

"Yeah . . . my mother did all this. Before I kicked her out."

"She's got nice taste."

Jesse made this sound in the back of her throat, and I wasn't sure if she was getting ready to cry or laugh. Only, when her eyes met mine, I saw something I'd never seen there before. Her mouth was a straight line, and her wide-eyed look now suggested stark, agonizing fear.

"You all right?" I said.

She didn't look away, but her head gave a very slight shake, from side to side. Then she said, "Right. We should be getting ready for Cincinnati. Hell, I *knew* somebody would keep me from playing."

"Jesse, you *have* been playing," I said. "And better than anybody I ever saw."

She glanced toward the door where the noise had not in the least subsided. People were calling out her name and pounding on the door; the phone was still ringing. "What's wrong with them?" she said.

"They're crazy."

"It's just a game." She looked down. Something sweetly majestic radiated from the slight movement of her head and a swirl of dark hair that caressed the side of her face. She hadn't gotten it cut in a while and it was not as curly now. It was almost a pageboy, except for the way it formed the curlicues on the top of her head. The bandage made her look wounded and sad.

I told her why I was there. "Do you have a birth certificate, Jesse?"

"What?" Her eyes seemed to shrink.

"Just, you know, to deal once and for all with that business about you being a man."

"I don't have it."

"Well, can you get it from your mother?"

"No."

"Jesse, come on—this is too important. You have to call her."

"She doesn't have it either. I used one to get into Japan once, but . . . I don't even know where that is."

"Your mother wouldn't know?"

She shook her head. "I lost it."

"Okay, then. Write to get a copy."

"I was born in Japan, all right? We're not gonna get one in time for Cincinnati, or hell—the rest of the season, even."

"We're behind you, Jesse. You have to know that. We'll fight for you."

She seemed to take this in. Then she said, "What have I done?"

"What do you mean?"

"I've sort of disturbed something big, haven't I?"

I was not happy to hear her talking like that. "You've broken new ground, sure. And . . . so what? Ever heard of Jackie Robinson? Babe Zaharias?"

The racket outside really was unbelievable. A crowd had gathered in the parking lot in front of her apartment and they were all shouting against each other. "You don't have to answer any of their questions," I said. "But if you *want* you can make a statement. Once they've heard from you, they'll leave you alone. At least for a while."

"Listen to that noise. You think Roddy's out there?"

"I didn't see him."

"What if I call him?"

"You'll make his year, but . . . go ahead. He can take a statement over the phone."

She said nothing, but she didn't look away. She was thinking.

"Jesse, there's something I have to ask of you to help us."

Again, she had no response.

"It's not much, but it'll surely help when we go to court."

She came around the island and settled herself across from me at the table. I asked her if she'd like something to drink and she said no, and then I rudely got up and poured myself a glass of water.

"I'm sorry," she said.

"Jesse, you ever heard of somebody named Robert Ibraham?" I watched her face closely and she revealed nothing. She thought about it for a minute, then shook her head.

"You've never heard that name."

"No."

"He signed to play football in the Canadian League, for Montreal."

"So?"

"You don't know anything about him?"

"No."

"We—I didn't think so. I just wanted to know."

"What about him?"

"Just—Look, if we have trouble getting your birth certificate, we're going to have to ask you to do one thing to help us in this."

She waited, looking directly at me the way she almost always did.

"This is a temporary restraining order," I said, looking away for a moment. What was I doing here—bidding for time? "Temporary. That's all. We'll deal with it."

"But I can't play. They took that away from me."

"We're fighting this, Jesse. But, like I was saying, we need you to do one thing for us. And—this is going to be hard to ask—I mean—if it was me I'd never dream of—"

"What *is* it?"

"Do you have a gynecologist you go to regularly?"

She leaned forward and placed her chin in her hands. "You want me to prove I'm a woman."

I was ashamed to nod. "Just that it will simplify all this if we can get a doctor to, you know—"

"Has any *man* ever had to prove he was a man?"

"Some might say they feel like they have to prove that every day."

"You know what I mean."

"Well, the men *do* get physicals by team physicians every year . . . "

"What about my physical in training camp?"

"You know how that was. It wasn't—uh—the doctor didn't . . ." She wouldn't help me out here. "The team doctor is not a gynecologist," I said finally. "He didn't *really* examine you."

"He could tell I was a woman."

"Well, of course we'll get him to testify, but . . . Look, Mr. Flores thought if we got the final say from a gynecologist, who could report unequivocally that . . ." I stopped. I felt so much like a lawyer now, or Charley Duncan—rather than what I wanted to be, which was Jesse's friend. There I was, almost begging her, doing my best to manipulate her into doing this thing because I wanted what I wanted—which was for all the bullshit to just go away as soon as possible. I wanted to get Jesse back on the field where she belonged. "It would put to rest all this talk about a sex change."

She folded her arms across her chest and stared past me at the bright windows. She never said she would do it, visit a gynecologist, but I had at least put the idea in her head. And was that so wrong?

Somehow, though, looking into those clouded blue eyes, I got the sensation that she knew what I was thinking, and that something essential between us had just been compromised, and perhaps even destroyed. I felt like the fellow behind the curtain saying, "Pay no attention to that man behind the curtain."

Not long after that, Dan Wilber, Darius Exley, and Nate showed up. As they gently moved folks off the porch, Jesse sat at the kitchen table to write out a statement. The press set up in the parking lot at the bottom of her front steps. People came out of the other apartments and watched. It looked like a mini–Vatican City just before the Pope comes out on the balcony to bless everyone.

By the time Jesse and I emerged, the lights were so bright it blinded both of us. Standing next to her, I did my best to fend off all those voices and questions, held up my hand, mostly just to shade my eyes, and said, "All right, if I can ask for some quiet—Jesse has a statement that she wants to read to you all."

It took a while for the noise to subside, but then Jesse held up the paper she'd written her statement on and began to read. And as she did so, it got very quiet.

"I am a woman," Jesse said, in a very even, unemotional voice. "I did not have surgery to become a woman. I am playing this game because I love it. I love the competition, the teamwork, the miracle of people working so completely together. The last thing I have ever wanted to do is ruin the integrity of the game, and I do not think I am doing that. I never asked for any special treatment. I play as hard as I can on every down. I assume others are doing that as well. If people are *not* going all out, it's not my fault.

"I don't know how it is possible, or fair, that I should be held responsible for the sexist attitudes of others. If people are afraid to hit me, that's their problem.

"I have been hit. I have been hit very hard. I've faced the same pressure as other quarterbacks in the league. I am under the impression that when a defense cannot get to the quarterback it has something to do with the blocking they face, not with the defense's fears about injuring the quarterback. I can't help it if my offensive line is one of the best in the business. I am proud of the work they do on every play to protect me. I think the integrity of the game will be damaged if men who cannot get through my offensive line, blame their weakness and lack of skill on gender. I have nothing more to say, and I do not wish to answer questions. Thank you."

She looked at me, nodded her head slightly, and went back inside.

Thirty-Five

THE FOLLOWING SUNDAY, we had to play the Cincinnati Bengals. It turned out to be one of the strangest weeks of practice I've ever been a part of. I spent every day in the film room, with most of our scouting department, trainers, and coaching interns, putting together a video and tracking the number of times our quarterbacks got knocked down during the season. We traced the numbers for Jesse as opposed to Corey Ambrose and Ken Spivey. We studied those films so hard I began to see the world in flickers of light and stop-motion photography.

Each night, I'd go to Coach Engram's office and work with him on the game plan; he still wanted me on the sideline calling the plays, or if he took over as he sometimes did, relaying the plays during the game. So I had to know everything the team was preparing. We'd study film of our practices each day—something I've never done before but that turned out to be a good idea. I gained considerable insight into what we were running that might work. We selected the plays that ran most smoothly—where everything clicked and there were no screwups—and cut out all the rest. We watched films until very late at night—sometimes until three or so in the morning. I'd go back to my office, sleep for a few hours, then get up and start back in studying the films of every one of Jesse's passes.

When I was done, I gave everything I had to Charley Duncan and Harold Moody and they prepared the video—it was as professional as a commercial. Jesse had been knocked down after releasing the ball an average of 3.8 times a game. Ken Spivey, 4.8. Corey Ambrose, 4.3. Jesse had been sacked three times so far. Ken Spivey only once, and Corey Ambrose twice. Of course, those averages are pretty misleading if you consider that Jesse got knocked down seven times and sacked pretty savagely once in the Oakland game. The other two sacks were not so bad. Some of the knock-downs were worse. In two games, nobody touched her. Still, it's the same with any quarterback. Not all defenses are equal; some are strong and quick and hard to keep off the quarterback, and others you can push around any way you want.

Charley also calculated that Jesse's release was almost twice as fast as Spivey's, and about a third faster than Ambrose's. The time that elapsed between when she began her throwing motion to when the ball left her hand was literally, on the average, only 0.86 seconds. From the moment Spivey started his motion to the ball leaving his hand was a full 1.6 seconds. Ambrose was at 1.1 seconds. All three had fairly quick releases, but Jesse's was by far the quickest. Only Sonny Jurgensen and Dan Marino in their heyday at 0.87—and, believe it or not, a Pittsburgh quarterback named Joe Gilliam, who had a world of talent and drugged himself right out of a great career, at 0.88—came even close to Jesse.

All of us thanked our lucky stars that we had the Bengals coming to our place, so at least we wouldn't have all the preparations for travel getting in the way. During that hectic week, Charley Duncan gave our Canadian kicker Justin Dever an immediate raise. And Coach Engram, while he kept Jesse on the roster, elevated Terry Fonseca from the taxi squad to second string. Fonseca already knew the offense better than anybody else Charley might sign and he'd been with us since Kelso went down, so he would be ready to play if he had to. But the team released Corey Ambrose. There was no room for him on the roster once we elevated Fonseca, and he knew he was now the odd man out. Coach Engram said nothing to him. His release was announced, and that was that.

The team was unanimous in its support for Jesse. They got down to business in practice, sure, but they were all angry and you could see it. Orlando Brown announced to the media that the players' union didn't represent him, or anybody on the team. "They don't know nothing about what we got here," he said. Dan Wilber said, "I haven't noticed anybody laying back against us; we work just as hard blocking every down as when a man's playing quarterback. And none of us support this lawsuit." Rob Anders said, "They're just pissed because they can't get to her. Have to blame *some*body."

Darius Exley refused to talk to reporters, at first, but on Wednesday of that week they accosted him outside of Redskins Park on his way home from practice. "I'm playing," he said. "My hamstring's fine."

A reporter said, "You going to miss Jesse?"

"Hell," he said, "*you* all will, that's for sure." He paused for a moment, then glared into their faces. "Look, I'd rather play with Jesse, but if we got to go with somebody else, we'll do it. Ain't nobody afraid to hit her on the field *or* off. That's what it looks like to me."

"Have you had a date with her, Darius? Can you verify she's really a woman?"

Darius shook his head in disgust, walked to his Mercedes, and drove away.

Some players talked about how unfair it was to take away one of our best weapons at this time of the season, with the playoffs on the line. A lot of them also wondered what *that* might do to the integrity of the game. All of them, when asked if they supported the players' union, said no. I was as proud of those guys as I ever was. And watching Darius speak with such contempt for the lawsuit and for the media—hearing more words from him than in all the time I'd worked with him—that brought tears to my eyes.

Flores and Charley Duncan and the three lawyers went to New York on Wednesday for a preliminary hearing. Needless to say, the press went with them and followed them all over New York. All Flores kept saying was, "We will deal with this and respect it as we should, but everyone should understand: This is a frivolous attempt to stop our team from achieving its potential. That's all."

The judge in the New York court ordered closed hearings on the case, which angered just about everybody, but I myself was glad. I just wanted the damn circus to end, and nothing turns the jackals away better than a stripped carcass. Cause that's all they had now with the doors closed: nothing but bones.

I have to say, Flores was pretty amazing. He didn't want to rush into the courtroom unprepared, but he also didn't want us to have to play too many games without Jesse. His "staff," which I should mention is considerable and goes well beyond football, they pretty much came to our rescue, enlisting help from both the National Organization for Women and the American Civil Liberties Union. These two groups got a groundswell going on the Internet with blogs and petitions and postings to what seemed just about everybody in the world. Flores found out from Jesse's mother which hospital in Japan Jesse was born in and sent a guy all the way to Tokyo to see about getting her birth certificate.

I'm sure you remember all the fuss. Even the president talked about how "advanced" the Redskins were in the realm of human equality. He wondered how the integrity of the game could possibly suffer from the addition of a player of Jesse's skill. "I think she has increased interest in the sport," he said. But he's a politician, and he also made a point of saying that he worried about her, that an injury in the toughest sport on earth might be "fatal to a young woman." That's what the TV and the blogosphere and the press paid most attention to, of course—the *Washington Post* headline, for instance, read: WHITE HOUSE SAYS JESSE COULD SUFFER FATAL INJURY.

We'd always understood the dangers of the sport, for anybody playing it. But for Jesse, from the start, we in fact took extra precautions. She wore a full-body flak jacket that made her almost invincible—you really could pound on her with a baseball bat and she wouldn't feel a thing. It covered her entire upper body, that thing. Her arms were free, of course, and her legs—but they were well padded, too, and as long as she didn't get twisted too badly the wrong way, she'd be able to play for years. She had not undergone a concussion protocol yet. She was strong and smart and quick and immensely talented. I'm being truthful when I say that, except for that first time she got hit and fumbled, I never really worried about any significant injury. It just wasn't something any of us thought about. Certainly no more than we did with any other players.

Jesse's worst injuries that year, before the lawsuit, were a bruised back and cuts to her nose and forehead. And she'd slightly sprained her ankle. That was it. And in the course of all that, she'd thrown 213 passes in 8 games, completing 186—that's an 87.3 completion percentage, which was unheard of in those days—for 2,364 yards and 27 touchdowns. She'd only thrown 3 interceptions, and her passer rating was 146.6. The best in the business, by far.

No, if the league didn't want this woman playing, it was because she was doing better than any man had ever done. That was the *only* reason, and everybody knew it.

Our defense, when the Cincinnati game began, was angry, and our offense, even angrier. The whole team went into that game in one helluva bad mood. They thought they were going to take it out on the Bengals, who were coming in with a 3 and 10 record and some real problems on offense and defense. Problem was, our guys were so intent on beating the stuffing out of the other team, they kept making stupid mistakes. On several plays, they took themselves out of position to knock somebody on his ass and ended up getting taken for big yardage. It took the whole first half to calm them down, by which point, we were trailing 14 to 10. Dever made one field goal from 23 yards out but missed two others. His first attempt, from 46 yards, went wide right. The second one, from 42 yards, went wide left. That kind of inconsistency, well, it's a pretty bad sign. If your kicker's going to miss, you want him to miss either one way or the other. That, you can work on. When he misses wildly in more ways than one, though—you've got yourself a problem. Nobody spoke to Dever when he came back to the sideline after those misses. You had to feel bad for the guy. After all, everybody knew that Jesse would not have missed even one of those kicks.

Spivey played well, stayed within himself, determined and flinty, but he was rusty and you could see it. He missed the first five passes he tried, and then, when he started hitting them, he was just a little bit off—a bit high one time, a bit behind his man the next—and, when they managed to catch the ball our guys were getting creamed. Darius was screaming at Spivey to get it to him; Spivey tried a few deep passes, but we only got one touchdown out of it. Mickens kept hitting the line like he wanted to batter somebody into powder.

Engram was something at halftime. I walked off the field with him, but in the confusion of everybody piling into the locker room, I lost him. When we were inside, and it quieted down, I realized he wasn't there. Everybody took a knee or sat on a bench and waited. The rest of the coaches and I looked into their tired, angry faces. Finally I took the floor myself. "You guys *know* you can play better than that. We kick ass in this league *together*, as a team, all right? No one guy is going to make up for Jesse with a hit in this game. We *all* have to do it, by playing together, staying within ourselves, and executing."

A few acknowledged what I'd said, and I looked around for Coach Engram, who still had not appeared. I stepped outside looking for him. Time was running out. I figured we could stick to the offensive game plan and do fine once we got them to start playing as a unit instead of an angry gang of individuals. But if we were going to make any defensive adjustments, we'd have to hurry. To be honest, everybody knew we should have been ahead by several touchdowns already, and we all expected that Coach Engram would come at us with a vengeance. When he let loose—when his temper came into play—he was as eloquent as a poet, and scary too. He could motivate men, for sure. And that is what I thought he was going to do at halftime. But time ran out and he still had not shown up in the locker room. None of us knew where he was. Then, just as everybody was preparing to go back out on the field, we heard him coming down the hall, whistling. I made the men wait. They watched the door.

He got to it, swung it open, and started in, but then he stopped and looked up at all of us. "Oh, excuse me, boys," he said. "*I* thought this was the *men's* locker room." Then he backed out matter-of-factly and closed the door behind him.

Nobody said a word. We went back out on the field and those guys played like one beast; they hit and tackled so completely, it was a clinic to watch it. Spivey was like an engineer out there, directing the offense down the field every time they got their hands on the ball. He completed 13 straight passes in the third quarter and finished the day with 18 completions in 31 attempts, for 266 yards and 3 touchdowns. Mickens ran for 233 yards on 17 carries and scored 3 touchdowns himself. We won 52–14.

The only thing I hated about that weekend was the headline on the front page of the *Washington Post* the next day, which read, JESSE WHO? And then, under it: REDSKINS DOMINATE BENGALS WITH SPIVEY, MICKENS.

I liked Spivey. He was a good guy, if you didn't push him around too much. And he had a good, accurate arm. But he never saw the day he could play with Jesse. If she had been on the field that day? The damn Bengals would've had to call the police to stop it.

We were 10 and 4 now, and the Tampa Bay Buccaneers were coming to town the following Sunday. We didn't know if Jesse would be with us or not, though. She wasn't even allowed to watch the Cincinnati game from the sideline, but Mr. Flores had her in his box—his guest of honor. She cheered with everybody else, and reporters who saw her wrote that she seemed to be having a good time. But after the game, as I was leaving the stadium, I saw her ahead of me walking toward the player's exit. We were in a long corridor under the stadium that everybody called "the tunnel," and she was far up in front of me, but I knew it was her so I called out.

She stopped and waited for me.

"Hanging in there?" I said.

"I'm fine." Her face revealed nothing. She was in a business suit and shiny black pumps, her hair curled and framing her face like black smoke. She wore just a little bit of lipstick, though she had clearly smeared something on her face to obscure the freckles. As I've said many times, those freckles were the best thing about her face; and that delicate, broad nose of hers, perfect for their display. Without them she looked a little like a good-looking prizefighter with lipstick on.

"We kicked their asses," I said.

She nodded.

"Our guys played like they were up against the players' union."

She put her arms around my neck, then rested her head on my shoulder. Taken aback, but happy for the contact, I wrapped my arms around her. Was she crying? I couldn't tell. Then, after a moment, she let go of me and stepped back. "In case this is finished," she whispered. "Thank you for all of it."

"It's not finished, Jesse."

302

Now she did have tears in her eyes. "I'm not going to a damned gynecologist, Coach."

I had no response to that.

"It's just . . . too much to ask, you know?"

"Jesse, it'll put half of their case in the can."

"I'm not a man, okay? I'm not Robert Ibraham, whoever he is. I shouldn't have to prove that."

"But if it's the only way . . ."

"No one else in this league has had to undergo that kind of— of . . . scrutiny. It isn't fair and it sure shouldn't be legal."

"Jesse, it could take weeks for our guy to get back here with that birth certificate. The last I heard, the hospital was having trouble locating it. They've sent him to some census bureau. By the time it gets here, the judge will have made his ruling. If he lets this go forward . . . it's going to take months, and your season's over."

A few of the players came out into the hall now. Jesse smiled and they all passed by to shake her hand, tell her how much they missed her.

"Yeah," she joshed, like the good sport she was. "I could really *see* you guys missed me."

When Spivey came by, she grabbed his hand with both of hers. "Great game, Kenny."

"You'd have buried them in the *first* half," he said. "Took me a while to figure them out. But I had a good second half." He wasn't such a bad guy, Spivey. And if we had to go with him, we'd make do I guess. But right then . . . I hated him. I did not want him feeling so smug about beating one of the weakest teams in the league. He did say something very kind to Jesse as he was leaving, something truthful. "You'll be back in there, Jess. Everyone knows you're the best player for the job."

When he was gone I said, "The video we've made, Jesse, *proves* you have not been treated any differently than any other quarterback. All we need is to put to rest this talk about your—about this Ibraham fellow."

"Who says I'm him?"

"Somebody in the league office is supposed to have traced you back to him."

"How?"

"You think your mom had anything to do with this?"

Her eyes seemed to widen then, as if recognizing the idea for the first time; she was seriously considering it. But then she said, "No. She wouldn't do that."

"Well, you did send her away . . ."

"I didn't tell her to leave. Not like that. I told her I just needed some space, to think."

"You told me you broke her heart."

"She'll get over it."

I said nothing.

"Hell, she broke *my* heart."

"I know. You said that." We started walking toward the door. I could see her thinking as we walked, staring at the ground in front of her. "We'll work something out," I said.

"Not even fingerprints."

"What?" I said, looking up, confused, and then nodded.

"Nobody else has to do it. You think that's fair?"

"Jesse, who cares if it's fair? The world's not fair."

"*I* care," she said. "*I* do."

"I just want you back on the field," I said. I couldn't believe that, with so much at stake, she would not give in to the simple demand that just this one time she allow herself to be treated differently than any of her teammates. But this was a principle she held in her heart for herself. She was not thinking of women, or the rights of the players or any other thing but her will to be treated as she thought she should be. And she was stubborn. By god, she was stubborn. But I loved her. Hell, I still do. It didn't matter to me then and it doesn't matter to me now, the pretty big lie she continued to tell.

Thirty-Six

THE JUDGE WAS an elderly gentleman named Joshua P. Lorenzo. He announced he would hear both sides and then decide for himself the merits of the case. Which meant it would be up to him if it went any further than his courtroom. He could rule that the league and the players' union had a valid case and let it go forward as a lawsuit, which would effectively end Jesse's season, or he could decide that the case was frivolous and dismiss it, which would put Jesse back on the field immediately. What he was going to hear, therefore, was pretty much the entire case as the lawyers had prepared it. And what we would have to do is present our case as well.

Who was Robert Ibraham? Everybody on both sides wanted to know. Flores said we had to find out, had to find this guy if we could. As far as I knew, the lawyers on both sides were looking high and low for him. What the plaintiffs had was film of him at the Montreal tryout camp, some from fairly close up, and then film of Jesse to contrast it with. They also had players who said they knew him and who had seen pictures of Jesse and believed she was, in fact, the man they knew as Ibraham.

Ibraham, we learned, had played college ball at a small two-year school in Alberta, then tried out for Montreal. He was good enough in tryouts that they signed him to a two-year contract. Then, shortly after that, he disappeared and nobody ever saw him again. All of this happened the year before I met Jesse. The players who had seen Ibraham in camp would testify and, if possible, identify Jesse at the hearing.

In the meantime, we had another home game to prepare for. While we were doing that, again with Spivey at quarterback, the news broke online that Jesse was my lover and that I had discovered that she was really a man during a "lost weekend" in Belize. A *Post* gossip columnist printed that rumor while disingenuously denouncing it as "almost certainly untrue," which "almost certainly" guaranteed that half the population would believe it, implicitly.

Nothing's more stupid than a crowd, sometimes. We have become a culture that responds almost exclusively to crowdthink—to the unruly reaction of the mob—everything we do now predicated on popularity and audience approval. Nobody really cares anymore what the truth really is; only what everybody *thinks*. After all, if everybody thinks it, then, hell . . . it must be true.

I had no contact with Jesse while I was preparing the game plan for Tampa Bay and conducting practices with the team. She was not allowed at Redskins Park, and she would be needed in court anyway, so she went to New York with Edgar Flores and his legal team. At some point, I knew she was supposed to testify at the hearing.

Judge Lorenzo began hearing the case the Monday after the Bengals game. It seemed like everybody was in New York except for me, Engram, Bayne, and a few assistants, and of course the players themselves. We tried to concentrate on Tampa Bay—a pretty solid team that had sustained some very bad injury problems early in the year. Now they were getting healthy, though, having battled back to an 8 and 6 record and a chance at the playoffs. After winning five in a row, these guys were not going to be easy to beat.

Coach Engram didn't want any of us distracted by what was going on in New York, so he wouldn't let us check in with anybody during the day. Thus, I knew about as much back then as you or anyone who read the newspapers what the players' union and NFL lawyers were planning to say on those first days of testimony. But once the case got started in court, Charley Duncan called Coach Engram and me almost every night to let us know what was going on. First, the lead lawyer for the league, a flat-faced, round little man who spoke very slowly and, according to Charley Duncan, bent forward as if he were about to tip over, presented the case of Robert Ibraham, drawing upon films, as I said, and the testimony of four witnesses, all of whom played for the Alouettes.

The films, Charley said after that first day in court, were pretty amazing. "This guy Ibraham? He looked just like Jesse throwing the ball, I'm not kidding."

"Really?" Engram said, sighing. We sat at his desk, listening to the speakerphone. He looked at me, his right eyebrow slightly raised.

"Same motion, you know? Same footwork. He was as tall as she is. And what a release. Just like Jesse's."

"But it couldn't have been Jesse," Engram said.

Duncan let a long silence develop. "I really don't know. In those films," he said after a moment. "Those films were just . . . a little more persuasive than I'd 'a liked . . ."

"This is crazy," I said. "Has anyone been able to *find* this guy Abraham, or whatever his name is?"

"Ibraham," he corrected me.

"Okay, goddamn it, *EEbraham*," I said. "Anybody know where the hell he is?"

"No. That's the thing. Even the league can't locate him. The Canadian League says he disappeared right after they signed him. But they've got these guys who played with him in a few practices and saw him in drills. Tomorrow morning, Jesse's going to be there, and they'll have a chance to identify her."

"You think I should come up there?" Engram said.

"Nah, Coach. Team needs you in Washington. We're handling it."

I asked him how Jesse was taking it.

"She just sits in court all day and listens. Doesn't say anything. Just sits there with Flores and me and the lawyers."

"What do the Canadians *mean* this guy disappeared?" Engram asked.

"Just that—he walked away, I guess, after they signed him, and nobody's heard from him since. We got 'em on the contract, though."

"How so?" Engram sat forward, listening intently now.

"So they claim he was still under contract to them, right? And if Jesse is really a man—if she really *is* this Ibraham fellow—she's under contract to the Alouettes, but our guys pointed out the contract was for two years and since that time has passed and no money has changed hands—the contract is null and void."

"You think the judge'll buy that?"

"Why not? It's common sense. And it's the law. They didn't pay him—or her, right? After the first full practice they never paid any money." Duncan seemed pretty certain we had them on that point, and he was a lawyer, too. He said our guy had pointed out that according to the law, since neither party executed any part of the contract, there *was* no contract. "Even if she was Ibraham, she signed the thing, see, but never got paid one penny for it. They didn't pay and she didn't play."

"Well that's good news, at least, isn't it?" Engram said, rubbing his temples.

"Far as it goes, yes, absolutely."

"I don't care if Jesse is really a man," I said now. "I want her playing for us."

"We're doing our best," Duncan said. "Flores has got our boy in Japan looking for a birth certificate that says Robert Ibraham on it."

"He couldn't locate Jesse's?" Engram said.

"The Japanese don't believe she was born there. Flores says if she's really a man, it's fraud, pure and simple."

"So what if she's had the operation?" I said. "That kind of thing is— I mean technically and literally, she'd still be a woman now. So how can it be fraud?"

"I just know Flores won't like it," Duncan said. "And let's face it, guys, it's bad for the league."

"Come on," I said, but Engram nodded his head.

"I don't mean the integrity of the game," Duncan said. "We're going to win that with the video I put together. But it's just . . . real bad publicity, you know? For the league."

"What's bad publicity is this stupid lawsuit," I said. "They should have thought of that before they went on the attack."

"Folks didn't like it," Duncan went on. "A woman playing quarterback. And now this . . . This is just one hell of a publicity clusterfuck, no two ways about it . . ."

"She's the best I've ever seen at reading defenses," Engram said. I stared at him, trying to figure out where he was going. "She's got a cannon for an arm, she can run almost as fast as Rob Anders; she's got feet quicker than Darius Exley's, and she can kick it a goddamned mile. Fuck them."

I was so glad to hear that right then, to hear him talk like that. Engram seemed as much in her corner now as I was. Despite this tremendous distraction, Jesse was one of us, and the league had gone after her. We were all in it together.

Tuesday afternoon, we had a mishap in practice. Orlando Brown sprained his right knee. He limped off the field and we wouldn't know until Wednesday or Thursday how bad it was. The backup over there was Dave Schott. And Carey Epps, too, could step in and play there. Both were capable players, but you couldn't lie: Neither one of them could hold a candle to Orlando, who was a bona fide superstar now. In just the fourteen games he'd played as a pro he'd accumulated 16½ sacks, 7 forced fumbles, 4 fumble recoveries, 2 interceptions, and 1 touchdown, all with two and sometimes three blockers working on him. Orlando was everybody's choice for Defensive Rookie of the Year and All-Pro honors. His loss would be very, very costly.

Feeling none too good about how things were going, I was not looking forward to the kind of ball-control offense I knew Coach Engram would want to run in the absence of Orlando. I wanted to eat alone that Tuesday night, but I got a call from Nate. I was in my office when he called, just getting ready to give up on the day.

"What's going on?" he wanted to know.

"Nate, I don't know any more than you do," I sighed.

We talked for a while about the lawsuit, then he asked if I would meet him for dinner at a restaurant and bar near Redskins Park called PJ's. I was hungry and needed to eat anyway, so I agreed.

I tried to find out if there was any word on Orlando before I left that night, but there was nothing. He was home resting his knee and he wouldn't see an orthopedist until the next morning. In some ways that was good news. If he could wait to see a doctor, it was probably not a very bad sprain.

When I got to PJ's, Nate was already there. We had a drink at the bar while we waited for a table. Nate talked about how ridiculous everything was and about the stupidity of the players' union and the league. "She's good for the game," he said. "More women than ever are watching."

"I know."

"Jesse's a hero to women all over the world. Men too."

"*Some* men," I said.

"Most men."

I shrugged.

"Everybody *I* know."

After a while a waiter came over and led us to our table. I just wanted a salad, but Nate ordered up a huge steak. I drank a few glasses of wine, and Nate had a shot of whiskey and two Bass ales. Something was eating at him, but I wasn't ready for any more problems, so I didn't ask about it. I told him about Orlando's injury and what I thought it would do to our game plan.

"I don't mind running the ball," I said. "Fact, I like it when it goes well. But I hate to play keep-away; I hate to run the ball and keep running it because I don't want to play defense. That can backfire. You don't score enough points. You're still vulnerable in the fourth quarter, and then if your opponent gets something going, you can end up losing."

Nate continued to gnaw on his steak and I thought again about how odd it was that he and Jesse were only friends. If I was this guy's age and had his physique, I'd have been chasing Jesse around like a rutting buffalo. Not that his own girlfriend wasn't attractive or anything, but . . . come on.

After dinner, he sat back and looked at me. I was sipping coffee. "You talked to Jesse?" he asked.

"Not this week."

"She calls me every night." He sat there for a while, thinking. I had the impression he was trying to get up the nerve to tell me something, but then he just shrugged. "Jesse's so grateful for everything you've done," he said.

I didn't see the need to respond to that. I *had* done a lot for her and she'd told me before that she was grateful.

"She thinks it's over," he went on.

"Really?"

"She feels as though she's been caught in a trap."

"What sort of trap?"

He shook his head slowly. "She's afraid of losing your respect, Coach."

"Impossible."

"Well, it's the team she's thinking about. This kind of distraction, so late in the season . . ."

"Nate, did she tell you something I should know?"

"Just what I told you. But . . . she's worried about what's going to happen."

I took a sip of my wine. "You two are pretty good friends, aren't you?"

"Sure."

"How long have you known her?"

"She was just a girl when we met." He smiled to himself. "Lent her my jacket because she was freezing."

"In Guam?"

"No."

"I thought it was in Guam you met her."

"Yeah—the *first* time." He looked around as if he was afraid somebody would overhear us.

"What do you mean the first time?"

"See, I met her in Guam the first time. It was in the school, the high school there."

"And what about the second time? That wasn't Canada was it?"

"The first time I met her was in Guam. But yes, later I ran into her on a ski trip to Canada."

"Where in Canada?"

"One of the ski lodges. Near Toronto. I can't pronounce it."

"Really."

"Why?"

"So maybe she *did* play in Canada," I said.

"She played in Guam. A women's team in Guam. Just for the last year of high school."

"Coached by her dad?"

"Yeah."

"You play football too?"

"Not really—I mean, I played a little."

"Nate I need the truth here, all right? Are you telling me the truth?"

He looked offended.

"I thought you said you never played football."

"I never played *well*. I don't think I ever said I didn't play at all."

"But you knew Jesse when she was a young girl."

"Well, a teenager. In high school."

I nodded. He got this look on his face. "She's not a *man*," he said. "Jesus Christ. Anybody can see that."

"I know. We're going to have to prove it, though."

He shook his head, but he had nothing more to say.

Thirty-Seven

THAT THURSDAY, WHILE the team went through its last full-contact practice for Tampa Bay, Flores sent his private jet to Dulles Airport at six o'clock in the morning to pick me up and fly me to New York. It was an emergency, he said. Jesse had refused to appear in court Wednesday afternoon, and when he'd tried to persuade her, she'd insisted she had to talk to me.

Flores himself met me at LaGuardia at a little after seven in the morning. It was barely a day yet—the sun seeping weakly through low clouds over the East River.

"What's going on?" I said, surprised to see the boss as my welcoming committee.

"There's no birth certificate. Not for Jesse *or* Robert Ibraham." It was a long walk from the gate out to the car line, and as we walked he told me what had gone on the day before. Four former Alouette players had apparently identified Jesse as Robert Ibraham. "They were sure," he said. "They testified that *his* hair was different back then, looked right at her and said that *his* hair was blond when *he* played with them, that *he* wore it in a close-cropped crew. They kept calling her a *he*. It was goddamned insulting, you can't imagine, and Jesse just sat there staring at them."

"I don't believe it."

"Not that their goal was to be insulting. They all commented on how they wished they could have played with him, how much they admired his skill at quarterback: his quick feet, instantaneous release, his accuracy. His toughness. Not one of them knew him personally. All of them talked about how *shy* he was." Apparently, according to Flores, the Alouette players testified that Robert Ibraham had stayed away from all of them. Didn't talk to anybody, and didn't spend much time in the locker room either. One of them testified that he had heard from one of Ibraham's friends—he couldn't remember who— that Ibraham had already started the procedure to make himself a woman, so he skipped out after those early drills in his sweats and never did shower with the men.

"Well, they sure did a good job then," I said. "Making her into a woman."

"Level with me here, Skip. Have you ever had sex with her?"

"Of course not," I snapped, offended at the question.

"You know anyone who *has*?"

"I don't know. She may have dated a few of the players at first. You'd have to ask them."

"This is getting to be more trouble than it's worth," he said. "The very day the Canadians identify her in court—the very day!—she refuses to testify." Flores was wearing a gray suit, a dark brown scarf around his neck, no overcoat. When we got outside, the frosty wind sent his hair flying. "We managed to get a recess until this morning at ten a.m." He kept brushing his hair back with his hand as we walked to where his limousine waited for us. "You get her to that courtroom today, you hear me? She's going to answer these charges."

"I'll do what I can," I said.

When we were seated in the leather backseat of his car, he said, "This could be our whole season, Skip. You got that? We'll lose her for good if this lawsuit is allowed to go on. So just—*do* something."

"Sir, we'll win the Super Bowl *with* Jesse or without."

He could see I didn't believe it.

"But we'll get her back," I said.

"You better. Or both you and Engram'll be hunting down some new jobs."

I couldn't help myself. "Is that a promise?" I said

Again, he withdrew into himself. He was sitting right next to me in the backseat of that huge limousine, but it was like he took his mind and went somewhere else. I was just sitting with this well-dressed, intrepid mannequin.

It was a little past eight in the morning when we got to the Ritz Carlton, where Jesse was staying. I had one hour to talk her into testifying, and if she didn't show up then, Judge Lorenzo could declare her officially in contempt of court or simply rule that the case could go on and extend the temporary restraining order.

I left Flores in the lobby. On the ride from the airport the new day had emerged more fully; it was a clear, bright morning, the sky blue and fresh looking, the air shifty and cold. I thought it might be a good idea to get Jesse out of the hotel, take a walk maybe. But when I got to her room, I realized she wasn't prepared to go anywhere. She was wearing jeans and a sweatshirt as always, but her hair was flat and dirty looking and her face had a wrung-out look to it—as though she'd trekked a great distance without water.

"You all right?" I said, as she backed away from the door.

"Sure. Come on in."

I was glad to find Liz sitting in a comfy chair next to the television. She was sipping some sort of fruit drink. She looked up and smiled when she saw me.

"What's going on?" I took a seat on a chair by a desk in the room. Jesse sat on the edge of the bed.

"I guess I'm done with all of it," Jesse said.

Her mother gave a loud, exasperated sigh. "Talk to her. Would you?"

"You're *not* done, Jesse," I said. "You're too good."

"No?" she looked at me. For the first time I saw defeat in her eyes.

"Jesse," I said. "I don't care if you're a man, or you *used* to be man, or if you're planning on being a man. None of that matters to me." She smiled a little but said nothing. "It doesn't matter to anybody else on this team either, okay? We just want you to continue playing for us."

"I don't have her birth certificate," Liz said. "But I brought a video of when she was a little girl, throwing and kicking the ball. I can walk into that courtroom tomorrow and—"

"You have a video of her?"

"At nine years old, when she won the Punt, Pass, and Kick competition. In two categories. *She* doesn't want to use it."

"I'm not going to show them that film. It's irrelevant. And it's humiliating, dredging up my little kiddie films."

"How on earth could it be irrelevant?"

"It just is."

"*I'd* sure like to see it," I said.

"I knew something like this would happen," Jesse said. "I just . . . I just wanted to get through this season before it did."

"We haven't lost yet."

"That video of you," Liz said. "It proves—"

"It proves nothing, Mother." There was no softness in the way Jesse said this, but at the sound of the word "Mother," Liz could not hold back a little smile of satisfaction.

"The tape is irrelevant," Jesse went on. "It doesn't matter what's on it."

"Except, how could you be this fellow Ibraham if your mother testifies with the video and proves you've always been a girl?"

"The tape's irrelevant," Jesse said again. "So is my mother's testimony."

"Why?" I said.

"I'm not a man and I never *was* a man," she said. "But, let's put it this way—I know who Robert Ibraham is."

That stopped me cold. Liz and I both looked at each other and almost in unison said, "You do?"

And then Jesse met my gaze with the saddest eyes I've ever seen. They were almost gray with sadness. "I lied to you about him."

My mind reeled a moment. "Well, who *is* he?"

She folded her arms across her chest. "How much trouble *would* I be in if I—if I . . ." She stopped. I waited. She took a deep breath, then she said, "*I* am. I'm Robert Ibraham."

It didn't register with me at first, what she was saying. I thought at first she was confessing to the whole thing. There was a long pause where none of us seemed to be looking at anyone. Then I said, "So . . . you *were* a man once?"

"I *pretended* to be a man. It was the only way I could play football."

"You're kidding," I said. Liz, eyes wide in amazement, just stared at her.

"I used the name of a guy who really did play college football. Robert Abraham took over my father's team in Guam when— Anyway, he was the coach there when I left and . . . I didn't think he'd mind if I used his name. I changed the spelling to *Ibraham*."

"I'll be damned," I said.

"I just thought—I just thought, you know, I might fool everybody and get to play. And maybe when they saw me play I'd . . . Only then I had to leave. Right after I signed that contract, one of the players— See, I had a fake ID with Ibraham's name on it and my picture. I was so scared all the time, I finally broke down and told one of the other players on the team. He convinced me I'd never get away with it."

"That was Nate?" I said.

She nodded. "How'd you know?"

"Just a guess."

"He was a backup tight end."

I started to laugh.

"How much trouble am I *in*?" she said.

"I don't know," I said, still laughing. "Kinda funny, though, isn't it? And ironic to boot. I mean, here they are, trying to prove that you're this man, and that you've had this operation and all, and you—you . . . Do you see how *funny* that is?"

"I guess." She clearly didn't.

"I'm surprised this isn't killing you."

"Glad *you're* having fun." Now she did laugh a bit.

"Don't worry about it," I said. "We'll blow this town before the end of the day. I don't think they have a case."

"But then . . . haven't I committed fraud?"

"Jesse," I said. "There's not a damn thing that's fraudulent about you. You're *the* genuine article. You're about *the* most genuine article there is in the world. It's the rest of us—the league, the media, the players and coaches, hell the whole damned world—that's guilty of fraudulent behavior."

"What do you mean?" Liz asked.

I turned to her. "The bullshit that gender means a damn thing. That women are the weaker sex and need to be coddled and protected. Because, all along, right under everybody's nose, it's pretty clear, isn't it?—which gender has had to be coddled and protected . . ."

"You got *that* right," Liz said.

"To tell the truth," I said, "we are all of us—from the moment we're born until the minute we die—pretty well and truly in the shit." I laughed a bit more, and then I said, "You and I are going to court right now, Jess. Okay?"

She gave me a sad smile as she nodded yes.

319

Thirty-Eight

"COURT" TURNED OUT to be a large, rather plush conference room in the judge's chambers. But there was a big table in there and we all sat around it—our people on one side and the plaintiffs on the other. I was not surprised to see Corey Ambrose there, as a representative of the players' union. I couldn't even look at him. The commissioner sat directly across from Edgar Flores, and next to him was the attorney for the Montreal Alouettes—a very gray, jowly faced old man with wire-framed glasses, named (and I'm not kidding) Crook, who kept making notes on a legal pad in front of him. The head of the players' union was a former offensive lineman named (improbably) Judy Harold. The guy was still in great shape, his sports jacket bulging in the upper arms and chest, and to his credit, he seemed ashamed to be there. Next to him was the players' union lawyer, a lean, snakelike fellow named Zabriskie who was constantly rubbing his hands together on the table in front of him. On our side were Charley Duncan, Ben Frail, Edgar Flores, Jesse, and me. Jesse had changed her clothes and brushed her hair, but she still looked a little washed out. She was clearly tired and oddly pensive. She didn't see the thing as I saw it.

Judge Lorenzo sat at the head of the table. A great tall window loomed behind him and sent angled beams of light over his shoulder and across the table. He looked like a deity preparing to establish justice. He was dressed in a gray business suit with a black bow tie. He wore gold cufflinks and a gold ring on his pinky finger, and like his attire, he was all business.

Across from the judge, at the other end of the room, was a disk projector and whiteboard screen and next to that a table and chair for witnesses. Enormous blue curtains surrounded the windows on both sides and the curtains behind the screen were closed. Apparently they had already watched a lot of the film on previous days, but the whole apparatus was still there for our side.

Ben Frail, too, had laughed when we told him the full story that morning, but the humor of the situation did not distract him from what he saw as certain real legal problems remaining. Jesse's integrity was going to be on trial now and he didn't want any of us to forget that.

The first thing Frail did, with Jesse's permission, was show the Punt, Pass, and Kick footage. Then he asked me to tell Jesse's story. I did so, fighting laughter the whole time.

Lorenzo did not laugh. In fact, when I got to the part about Jesse pretending to be Robert Ibraham, he leaned forward and gave her what can only be described as a scathing look. But he said nothing. Then Frail brought up the issue of the contract with the Alouettes, and Judge Lorenzo interrupted him. "You've already presented your case on that counselor."

"Yes, Your Honor. But I wanted to address this new issue, as regards the original contract."

Lorenzo nodded. "Go ahead, but I won't take it kindly if you waste any of our time here."

"All I wanted to say was, even though Ms. Smoke was pretending to be a man, no damage pursued from her deception."

Judge Lorenzo said to Jesse, "How did you get through the physical exam?"

She looked at me first, which only would have told her that I wanted to know that myself.

"A friend," she said, quietly. I'd never heard her voice sound so timid.

"Speak up," Lorenzo said.

And suddenly, she was Jesse again. She sat straight up and looked at him directly. "The Alouettes did not have a full-time team doctor, Your Honor. They had a nurse. She gave me a physical and then promised not to tell anyone. Far as I know, she kept her promise."

Zabriskie, the players' union lawyer, said he had a question for Jesse.

"Go ahead," Judge Lorenzo said.

"Did you *pay* this nurse anything to keep quiet?"

"No. Like I said, she was a friend."

"You knew her beforehand?" Zabriskie said.

"No."

"She just *became* a friend."

"Yes."

"Just like that."

"She was a woman," Jesse said, as if that explained something.

"And she did this for you, even though it meant she might be fired."

Jesse shrugged. "I knew I could trust her. She seemed to like the idea, actually. Said she hoped I could make it work."

"And how did you know you could trust her?" Zabriskie said. "Was this some sort of fellowship of the womb?"

"Like men don't have their own good ol' boy networks?" Jesse snapped.

Judge Lorenzo leaned back in his chair. "Point well taken."

"Your Honor," Frail said, "I think the contract the Alouettes gave Jesse to sign should not be at issue. She never deceived them once she signed it. She did not play. She accepted no money. In what way, then, is it a valid contract that bears any level of scrutiny?"

"And I said: We've been over that."

"She signed it," Zabriskie said. "The Alouettes have a signed contract."

"No money changed hands," said Frail.

Judge Lorenzo looked at Jesse. "Did you expect you could dress in the locker room? That somehow none of the other players would see you? How on earth did you imagine you'd get away with it?"

"Well, I came to see I couldn't," she said. "That's why I just—that's why I *left* the team."

Judge Lorenzo shook his head in what seemed like wonder. "Remarkable," he said.

Crook, the Alouettes' lawyer, said, "You still signed a contract to play for two years with—"

"I don't want to hear any more about that contract," Judge Lorenzo said, sharply.

"Your Honor," Frail said. "I only want to make it clear that the contract Ms. Smoke signed with the Alouettes—"

"The one she fraudulently signed as Robert Ibraham," Zabriskie said.

Frail ignored him. "I just don't think it would be fair for them to make an issue of this new information, since that contract was never fulfilled, regardless of *whose* name was on it."

Lorenzo said nothing, but he nodded in agreement. I realized what Frail was up to. He wanted to limit any damage that might accrue from Jesse's original dishonesty—which is how the Alouettes characterized it. I was a little worried about what the league would do about it. More than any other sports league—or even any other corporation for that matter—the NFL monitors and disciplines players for off-the-field behavior. Regular drug testing is only the tip of the iceberg.

If you're going to work for the NFL, you'd better have a spotless history, no question. They would not like what Jesse had done. Our only hope was that it would be overlooked because of the special circumstances. At best, we hoped the league wouldn't discipline her until next year.

Now Frail began to present our side of things concerning the integrity of the game. According to Charley Duncan his questions and reactions all week to the allegations of the other side had been brief, to the point, and sharply defined. So he didn't have much to say. But the video he put on spoke for itself.

First, he showed players seeming to pull up as they approached Jesse—using many of the exact same plays that the other side had used as their evidence—only he let the film run a bit longer now, to show that one of the things they were pulling up from was an oncoming block from one of our behemoths on the offensive line, or from Walter Mickens, who could flatten just about any player he wanted to. Several of the players who had claimed to "pull up" got flattened.

Then, using a split-screen technique, Frail showed those same players against Ken Spivey and Corey Ambrose—in films not only from this year but also from the previous one. (This was something Charley Duncan arranged that I wasn't even aware of.) On each play, the players in question looked exactly the same. Frail paused several of the clips at the same moment and showed that each time a player claimed he had "pulled up," his motion was not pulling up at all, but in fact bracing for a hit, or jockeying for better position on the quarterback.

Finally the film went to the hits Jesse herself had taken, including that first one that bruised her back, knocked her helmet off, and resulted in a touchdown for the other side. All the evidence was there. Frail presented a chart that showed roughing the passer penalties against the Redskins were roughly equivalent to the rest of the league. He showed film of each one of those penalties and pointed out how each infraction occurred.

Looking over at Charley Duncan, I gave a thumbs-up. Much as the guy always irritated me, I had to admit, that video was a masterpiece. I'd given him literally hundreds of hours of film—virtually every passing play Jesse was involved in, not to mention Spivey and Ambrose—and he and Harold Moody had edited the thing perfectly, and added some of their own. Working through the night, they had put it all together, and then they presented it to the lawyers in New York so they could prepare to manipulate it to the best advantage.

When we were done, the folks on the other side of the table visibly started to squirm. Judge Lorenzo said he wanted to hear from Jesse.

"Yes, Your Honor?" Jesse said.

"What do you have to say for yourself?"

She looked across the table. "Well, to the players' union, I don't have anything to say," she said. "Maybe they have something to say to me. To the Alouettes, though, I do apologize."

"You think you could have gotten a chance to try out if you'd just admitted you were a woman?" Lorenzo asked.

Jesse fixed the man with a stare now, but then seemed to think better of it. "No, Your Honor. I do not."

"The Alouettes wanted him under contract," Crook said. "That's why they signed him for two years."

"Did the Alouettes know they were signing a woman?"

"We did not consider it, Your Honor."

"Well, you got the paper," Lorenzo said. "But you didn't pay her, like her counsel says. So it wasn't in fact an active contract, was it?"

It got real quiet in the room. Judge Lorenzo looked around at everyone, then took off his glasses and rubbed his hands over his eyes. Somebody on the other side started shuffling papers. The judge put his glasses back on and sighed, heavily. "Gentlemen," he said. Then he paused, looked at Jesse. "And lady." Jesse nodded. "I might have taken some time with this. In the past I have always given myself at least a day between hearing a case and rendering a decision. But here, I'm afraid I don't have much to consider."

Now everybody leaned a bit toward him. My heart thrummed along with everybody else's. This was going to be it.

Judge Lorenzo put his hands out flat on the table in front of him. "This case is brought before me in this jurisdiction in an attempt to cause the Washington Redskins to refrain from employing one Jesse Marie Smoke. The arguments advanced—that she is under contract to another team as a man, that she is a detriment to the integrity of the league because of the inability of some players to hit a woman as hard as they might hit a man—have been . . . subtle and persuasive."

Uh oh, I thought, but then he went on.

"They also happen to be frivolous. I cannot think of a single legal case in our whole history where one side sought to limit an individual's right and ability to play a game. Nor do we have a very healthy or happy history when one side seeks legal means to prohibit a person from a particular field of endeavor because of gender or sex. It is frivolous. The claims of the plaintiff are clearly unreasonable and not worthy of consideration by this court or any other court in this land. My ruling is that I will not allow this case to go forward. The temporary restraining order is hereby revoked." Then he looked at Zabriskie. "You fellows ought to be ashamed of yourselves. This is the twenty-first century, by god."

We started celebrating, while the other side began putting their papers in briefcases and folders. I gave Jesse a big hug. She wrapped her arms around my neck and as we were standing there gripping each other, she whispered in my ear, "This means I can play, right?"

"It sure does," I said. "Maybe even this weekend."

The commissioner came around to our side of the room and congratulated Edgar Flores. "Really am glad it turned out this way," he said in a low voice. "She's good for the game."

I was elated to hear him say that. It gave me hope that he wouldn't discipline her for what she did to the Alouettes. Though, in truth, I

326

couldn't see why he would want to do anything about that. All she did was use up a little practice time and convince them she could play. It was their fault that her sex, and their ingrained attitude about it, caused her to withdraw and prevented her from giving them exactly what they'd wanted.

I couldn't wait for the press conference.

Thirty-Nine

I BEGGED FLORES to release Charley Duncan's video to the media, but he didn't want to embarrass the league or the commissioner any more than he had to. No, he was gracious at the press conference in the grand ballroom of the hotel. We walked out, all of us—Duncan, Flores, Benjamin Frail, Jesse, and me—onto a sort of stage with a bank of microphones in front of us and the usual assortment of bright lights and cameras, Liz Carlson stepped up to join us. She and Jesse embraced, and the crowd gave a cheer.

At first, Flores went to the microphones and spoke for all of us, answering each question with patience and sincerity. I don't think I'd ever seen him so serious. He said he was glad it was over, glad we could get back to what we were all about, which was playing football. Our goal was still, as it always had been, to win our division first and then go from there. No, he had no hard feelings toward the commissioner, *or* the players' union. In any unprecedented event, in any sea change to what has been, you had to realize there would be disturbances and upheavals until people had a chance to get used to the new circumstances.

"Jesse," he said, "may be a groundbreaker. She may not be. Who knows if there'll ever be another like her? She may be just an anomaly—a onetime phenomenon that we should all enjoy and revel in. Delight in. Either way, I'm awful proud to be a part of it."

It would have been a terrible mistake, he went on to say, to end what promised to be "one of the wonders of our time." It was the closest he came to criticizing the league or the players' union.

Finally, he said he would like to show everyone a home movie of Jesse, if she would allow it—a home movie of her, at age nine, winning the Punt, Pass, and Kick competition in Guam. He turned to her, and Jesse nodded. It was just the right thing to do for making peace with the league office. The whole room broke into loud cheers.

The hotel staff, clearly prepared for this, set up a large screen at the back of the room, and as the press conference went on, the film ran for everyone to see. Within twenty-four hours, every TV in the country had that film of the young Jesse—standing all of five feet six inches, already—kicking the ball high and far; throwing it almost as far as she could kick it; punting it high and deep. As many sportscasters pointed out, even at age nine, she was as good as any high school player. Had there been any room left for her legend to grow? You wouldn't have thought so. But it did. I think the whole country was in love with her.

Flores narrated as the film played. He talked of her athletic skill and prowess even at such a young age. You'd have thought it was Flores himself who had taken the footage, that he'd been there from the beginning, helping her compete. He spoke like a proud father.

Finally, he let Jesse herself step up to the microphone. Blinking those deep blue eyes in the lights, she gave that innocent, childlike smile of hers, just as the film looped back to the beginning and started playing again. Jesse leaned over to the microphone. "I'm just happy this is all over," she said.

Questions flew at her now. "Are you ready to get back to playing?"

"Yes."

"Do you think you can play this Sunday?"

"I haven't practiced," she said.

"Ms. Smoke, have you cheated anyone, do you think?"

"Not the Redskins."

"But you cheated the Alouettes?"

"No. Not really. I cheated them out of telling me I couldn't play, maybe. The two-year contract I signed, though, that didn't count because I never took any money."

"What were you doing for those two years?"

"Traveled a lot. Then, as some of you know, I spent a year in the Independent Women's Football League."

Behind her, in the film, (they let it play over and over again during the press conference) she kicked a ball high into the white sky. It was quiet for a minute while everyone in the room concentrated on the grainy image of Jesse Smoke taking a ball into her hands and throwing it high and far. Everybody clapped.

"What would that little girl say about the woman you've become, Jesse?" somebody asked.

Jesse just smiled. "You know, it's funny," she said. "Sometimes, even now, I feel like I'm only nine years old."

Then Colin Roddy stepped out of the crowd, carrying a microphone. There were as many cameras on him as on Jesse. "Do you think the players' union should apologize to you, Jesse?"

"I do, actually."

"Are you a member of the players' union?" A woman in the back row asked.

"We all are."

"Did any of your teammates join in the effort to keep you from playing?" asked Roddy now. Leave it to this guy to look for the worm in the apple.

She hesitated. I saw her look a bit back in the crowd. Was she looking for Ambrose, for some sign of what she should do? But then she just said, "No. Everyone on our team was behind me."

"Did you watch the game against the Bengals?" another woman asked.

"Yes. I was in the owner's— I was in Mr. Flores's box." She glanced at Flores and he raised his hand a little, smiling like a politician.

"You think Ken Spivey did a good job?" Roddy asked.

"Of course. Ken's a great quarterback."

"But you'll be glad to get back on the field?" said another voice from the crowd.

"If that's what coach wants. I just want to win."

"But you do want to be number one again." Roddy was persistent. He leaned forward, his microphone held high.

"Sure I want to play. Of course I do. I haven't practiced this week, though. I don't even know what plays we're going to run . . ." she stopped. "But, look, we'll figure it out, and I'll do whatever I have to do to play."

Somebody asked then if she'd reunited with her mother. I was surprised that anyone in the press was even aware of their troubles. Liz looked at Jesse, smiling, and for a moment they seemed to really see each other, to understand something the rest of us could scarcely guess at.

"We're fine," Jesse said, turning back to the cameras and lights, smiling that broad, freckled smile. "At least my mother never doubted I was a girl."

Liz had bright tears in her eyes, and the laughter in the room was loud and full of genuine affection. Even reporters, collectively and individually, can be moved to empathy and warmth on occasion, you know? With all their lights and cameras and notepads and recorders, they can still be human beings at times.

Jesse ended the press conference by stepping down off the stage, and we all followed her into the crowd. On the way to the exits some

331

of the more hardworking reporters wanted to know if I was going to try and get Jesse ready to play in three days. I just said I'd have to see where we were. I really didn't know if it was realistic for her to play so soon. Sometimes it's possible for a player to run through the plays we've put in, participate in the walk-through, and then manage to get it to work on the field. But Spivey had put in a full week's work preparing for this game, and I knew our coach.

Forty

I WAS RIGHT about what Coach Engram would do that weekend. We had a walk-through on Friday and he let Jesse go through a few things with the first-team offense, but for that week, it was Spivey's team. Tampa Bay came in as fired up as any team we'd played that year. They *had* to win.

Spivey started and did well enough. He finished with 13 completions in 28 attempts, for 244 yards and 1 touchdown. He threw two interceptions, one of which led to a Tampa Bay field goal. Walter Mickens rushed for 159 yards on 33 carries. We pounded him into the line over and over again, trying to keep Tampa Bay's offense off the field. But our defense was really incredible. With Orlando Brown sitting it out, Dave Schott played the game of his life. He was always good at stopping the run, but in this game he even pressured the Tampa Bay quarterback and caused a fumble. He didn't get a sack, but he was in the guy's face all day. He must have learned something from watching Orlando all year.

We won the game 17 to 13.

The following week we had to travel to San Diego. With a full week to prepare, Coach Engram announced that Jesse would take over the number one spot again, though not without complimenting Ken Spivey on the job he'd done in her absence. Spivey really had come through for us, even learning to control his famous temper. (It didn't hurt that, with our crack offensive line, he wasn't getting bumped very often.) Asked how he felt about being demoted for Jesse, he said, "She's the best player at the position. Look, I want to play, and I'll be ready. But Jesse's our number one and I'm behind her. I'll say it." I was really beginning to like the guy.

All week in practice, Jesse seemed a bit rusty. Her passes sailed a bit on her—either too high or just a little bit out in front of where they were supposed to be. Darius was fully recovered from his injury, as quick and fast as ever, but we were afraid he'd get hurt leaping for those high throws in practice, so we let him sit out the last day of full-contact drills. Rob Anders also sat out a while, and Jesse got used to throwing to Sean Rice, Jeremy Frank, and Jerome White. Coach Engram said we would have the hottest corps of receivers in the play-offs, if we got that far. Happily, near the end of the week, Jesse started to settle back in and throw more accurately.

Every day after practice, she went through several field goal drills—the same ones she'd been doing when I first discovered she could kick, only this time she had her long snapper and holder on each one. On Friday I stayed out there and watched her. They worked from one side of the field to the other, with the center snapping it from the 7, the 17, the 27, the 37, and even at the end from the 47-yard line. At the 47, it's 63 yards to the goalposts. She made 7 of 10 from that distance. All of them went right at the opening. Two of her misses bounced off the crossbar, and the last one fell short. While I was out there, Edgar Flores sidled over to me. He was more relaxed, wearing a tan leather jacket and black slacks. I only glanced at him and looked away, afraid he'd notice the expression on my face when I saw him coming.

"What's up?" I asked.

"Just watching, like you."

"Really?"

"She's something, isn't she?" he said, just after Jesse made one of her 63-yarders.

"Never seen anything like her," I said. "Male *or* female."

"She's certainly big enough to be a man. I couldn't stand to be with such a horsey woman."

For some reason this really hurt my feelings. I can't explain it, except to say that I was always very protective of Jesse—not that she needed it—and Flores's remark was so rank and insulting it infuriated me.

"Come on, she's a beautiful woman," I said. "You're pretty nuts if you can't see that."

He didn't seem to notice my ire. "Is it true that she never dates anybody on the team?"

I looked at him. "Is there something on your mind? I mean, you already asked me that."

"And she pretty much hangs around . . ." He didn't finish the sentence.

"She hangs around the wide receivers and her offensive line," I said. "If that's what you're asking. They're all pretty close."

"Well, birds of a feather."

"Yeah," I said. "Don't blame 'em either. They're better people than most of us."

He glared at me, but he had nothing more to say.

We were going to have a battle on our hands with the Chargers. They were 11 and 4, just like us, and leading their division. The flight to San Diego was long and bumpy. Jesse slept next to Dan Wilber up in front of the plane with me, Coach Engram, Walter Mickens, Darius Exley, Rob Anders, and Edgar Flores. Before Jesse fell asleep, all of us went over the game plan again, briefly. The hope was that we could take advantage of San Diego's rather light defensive line, and their corners, who were a bit shorter than most. It was probably a good thing, I said, talking about how to play them, that Jesse's passes had been a bit too high during the early part of the week, as it prepared our receivers for leaping and catching balls over the hands of defenders.

"My passes won't be high in the game," Jesse said.

"Even so. Wouldn't hurt if they were," I said.

She smirked. "If you *want* them high, I'll throw them high . . ."

"Just run the plays called, Jesse," Engram said. "And throw it like you always do."

I don't know whether our game plan was wrong or what, but in the first quarter we couldn't seem to get anything going. We kept stalling on third down and soon fell behind 3 to 0. A dropped pass here, a holding penalty there, several blown assignments and lost yardage at crucial times—all of that kept us scoreless for the entire first quarter. Luckily, early in the second, Jesse managed to tie things up with a 33-yard field goal.

There was no scoring for the remainder of the first half. Jesse drove us downfield on a couple of very long drives, but Mickens fumbled on the San Diego 12-yard line on one of those, and on the other, Jesse tried to hit him in the flat and the ball got knocked into the air by a linebacker and intercepted by the safety. The interesting thing on that play is that Jesse ran the safety down and collared him from behind. Took him down like a damn coatrack. He was really surprised, and the crowd—the San Diego home crowd, mind you—went wild for a while.

At the beginning of the third quarter, San Diego got a drive going. Orlando was sitting out again and they started running to that side. Dave Schott was usually great against the run, but his success the week before rushing the passer made him a little too aggressive that way in the second half. Twice they ran right by him while he was

336

taking a wide rush to the quarterback. Each time they used that play it was third down and their running back gained enough yardage to keep the ball.

On the sideline during a commercial time-out, Coach Bayne showed Dave a few pictures so he could see what they were doing. They kept running that play by him, showing pass and then running it. Bayne got him to see how they were doing that, and with his help the defense stiffened inside our 30-yard line. With a little less than 3 yards to go, San Diego showed pass again and handed off to their running back, but Dave held his ground and hit him just as he cut toward the line of scrimmage. They had to go for a field goal, which they made.

Now the score was 6 to 3. It almost stayed that way. Their defense was really good, and everything we tried they seemed to have the answer for. Their defensive backs kept knocking balls out of the air and their pass rush forced Jesse to hurry on several plays. She didn't dance a lot, she stood her ground and got hit plenty of times, but they were on her so fast a lot of the time she was forced to throw it before she was ready. The clock just kept ticking away, and we kept punting back to the Chargers.

On the scoreboard we could see that the Giants had beaten up on the Patriots 38 to 3. They were now 12 and 4. We needed a win to keep pace in the division race.

Early in the fourth quarter, Jesse started clicking on short, quick passes to Gayle Glenn Louis and Walter Mickens. Then she hit Sean Rice on a crossing pattern about 15 yards downfield. He caught the ball, ducked under a tackle, and raced to the San Diego 9-yard line. On the next play, Mickens ran around the left end and scored. Jesse kicked the extra point and we had the lead 10 to 6.

On the next series the Chargers went three and out. We took over on our 26-yard line. I called a trap on the right side with Mickens and he gained 7 yards. On the next play I wanted another run up the gut, but Jesse changed the play at the line, dropped back into the pocket, drifted a little to her left under the pressure, and threw a perfect pass, 40 yards in the air to Sean Rice racing down the right sideline. He took it the rest of the way for a 67-yard touchdown pass. Jesse kicked the extra point for a 17 to 6 lead, and that's how it ended. The Chargers never crossed midfield after the third quarter.

I don't just credit Jesse with this—although she had to be a part of it, because everybody seemed to play harder and pull together so completely after the lawsuit—but for the first time since I got into coaching, I was with a team that was playing together on every level. We were like a college team—full of fight and emotion and true comradeship—only a helluva lot more seasoned. Our defense was every bit as good and dominant as our offense. And we were putting everything together at just the right time of year. This was football as I'd never seen it played before.

After the San Diego game a lot of the Charger players came up to Jesse, wanting to get close to her and pat her on the back. Most of them said, "Great game," or "Good job, QB," or something like that. They seemed to want her to know they hadn't been in favor of what the players' union had done on their supposed behalf. San Diego's quarterback, a guy named Jake Pauley, said, "Congratulations, Jesse. We'll see you guys in the Super Bowl."

I thought he might be right about that.

We had to fly to Green Bay the following week for a game on Christmas Eve, and then we'd have the Giants at home.

The plane ride back from San Diego was a loud and happy celebration. Our only injury was to Dan Wilber, who got kicked in the shin late in the game and had to limp off the field for a few plays. He had a pretty ugly bruise but said not to worry. He'd be ready the following week.

Green Bay could be tough if the weather was bad, but, at just 7 and 9 they'd been decimated by injuries. Coach Engram announced on the plane that Dave Schott would continue to play in Orlando's place.

338

Meanwhile, Talon Jones was knocking people into oblivion at linebacker and Drew Bruckner was now getting good and healthy. Everybody was beginning to believe in us. Even if this *didn't* turn out to be our year, it was already a season that no one would forget. I couldn't wait to see Jesse in the playoffs.

Green Bay was easy. The weather was unseasonably warm for that time of year, sunny and in the low 40s, with almost no wind. Jesse had a great day throwing. She completed 18 of 22, for 351 yards and 5 touchdowns. Exley caught two—one from 40 yards and the other from 36. Anders caught one for 81 yards (Jesse put it in the air more than 55 yards before he caught it), and Sean Rice caught two—one from 15 yards and the other a 31-yard pass and run on a short wide receiver screen. Walter Mickens ran for 144 yards on 16 carries, scoring a touchdown. Jesse kicked two field goals, a 28-yarder and another from 34.

As for defense, we held Green Bay to 109 yards of total offense. They didn't get the ball on our side of the field all day. Damned if we didn't shut them out. Our defense had eight sacks. The defensive line had four (even Dave Schott got one) and Talon Jones, still playing middle linebacker, had three sacks of his own. Colin Briggs, our right cornerback, had a sack and two interceptions. The final score was 48 to 0.

That same week, the Giants beat the Seahawks 27–14, making us both 13 and 4, tied for first place in the division. Here's what the NFC East looked like going into the last week of the year:

TEAM	W–L	PF	PA
New York	13–4	330	173
Washington	13–4	435	212
Dallas	8–9	315	297
Philadelphia	7–10	316	368

On New Year's Eve, the Giants would have to come into our place and beat us for a second time. They whipped us pretty badly early in the year, when we had Ambrose at quarterback. Now, they were going to face Jesse.

Did I mention that she was named Offensive Player of the Week after the Green Bay game, for the third time, no less. Again she was on the cover of *Sports* magazine and *Pro Football Times*. There was talk that she might be named NFL Man of the Year.

And thus began the most unforgettable period of my life as a coach. And the most agonizing.

Forty-One

EVERYBODY KNOWS SOME version of the story by now, of course—
ESPN, NFL Films, and even a few sportswriters have told the story.
Believe it or not, though, one of the most accurate accountings of the
last game of the season and our run at the Super Bowl was in that
Hollywood movie, *The Eyes of Jesse Smoke*. The only thing really
lacking in that film was Jesse herself. They were wise to use a lot of
footage of her playing the game, and I have to say, the actress who
played Jesse was athletic enough. But, not to take anything away from
Jennifer Bradwell—she's about the only actress who *could* have played
Jesse; she was the right height and she had the flat nose and brown
freckles—only Jesse could be Jesse.

I can't express, even after all these years, how glad I was to be
involved in all of it, especially being in on it from the beginning. In
some ways I felt as though I'd created Jesse out of thin air. I found
her, and helped her find a way to play. I don't think I taught her a
thing about football, but I helped her prepare. From the start, see, it

was just about doing that for her, getting her prepared. She was always grateful for every drill, every session we spent together getting her ready to try out for the team.

I worked with Jesse Smoke almost every day of those last few weeks of that great first season. We were pretty worried about what the Giants would try to do to upset Jesse's rhythm, as they called it. A few stories had been appearing in the New York media about how the Giants would have to rattle her, find a way to get into her head.

On offense it was clear they were going to try and run the ball against us as they had in that first game. Edward Engel was still their right tackle, and, like last time, he'd be working on Orlando Brown, who had recovered enough to come back at defensive end. But as long as there was no residual pain from his knee injury, Orlando was not the same player Engel had faced in that earlier game. Not only were we getting back to full strength—almost everybody else was pretty healthy, too—our run of injuries had forced us to uncover other talented players. Dave Busch had developed into an outstanding offensive guard. We even ran a few plays that required him to pull and run like hell to the other side. Dave Schott was a capable end on either side when Orlando needed a breather, and Talon Jones was almost as good at linebacker as Drew Bruckner had been. Drew was doing so well we listed him as probable. He would get to play a bit, but we wouldn't put him in there for the whole game.

What worried us most was the Giants quarterback, Scott Hempel. Strong and fast, he could run as well as pass. He moved around in the pocket as well as anyone in the league and he could throw just as accurately. At the other end of his heat-seeking passes, you may remember, was none other than six-foot-six wide receiver Taylor Price, who could jump like a kangaroo and had great hands. Even double-covered, the guy could make the most dazzling plays.

It was not going to be an easy game, no, but we were confident we could do better than we'd done in the first go-round. With Jesse at quarterback.

Jesse wanted to throw the ball, of course—and that was part of our game plan—but our main concern was stopping the Giants enough to *get* her the ball. Of all the teams we'd faced that year, the Giants had the best offense. On the ground or in the air, they could dominate a game. They might not have scored as many points as we did all season, but it wasn't because they didn't have the firepower; it was because they took their time going down the field. And when they got close, they usually scored. They led the league in yardage and time of possession, by a long shot. Whereas, even with Jesse's passing and our more-than-capable running game we were rated fourth.

Further, the Giant defense, too, was the best in the league. They'd given up all of 173 points all year—an average of a little over 10 points a game. Everything these guys did was precise, deliberate, machinelike. Even the games they lost were close and could have gone either way.

All that week the weather was warmer than usual, so we got in some very good practices. Jesse and I worked on the game plan together with Coach Engram. He spent a lot of time with the defense, though, so most of what we finally installed for the game was what Jesse and I had worked out. She watched film with me all that week after practice, and stayed out with the wide receivers to work on timing and quick patterns. She wanted to be sharp. The players stayed after sometimes to watch her working with Darius and the rest of the gang. If anything, it looked like her release was getting even quicker. Sometimes she'd get to firing balls as they were tossed to her and the people watching would gasp at the speed of it: The balls would just get to her and then they'd be on their way, as if they bounced off of her and she didn't catch each one, put her hands on the laces, and fire it downfield. Her release was that quick.

On game day—New Year's Eve—the air was cold and white. The temperature at game time was 12 degrees, and what little wind there was sliced through your skin like something made of steel. The sky was empty, unforgiving.

Our game started at 4:00, so there was not much light left and it was only getting colder as the sun disappeared behind the U.S. Capitol. The field was as hard as a concrete parking lot. We won the coin toss, and since there was no wind to speak of, we decided to receive the opening kickoff. Sean Rice ran it out to our 22-yard line.

On our first play from scrimmage, Mickens was stopped for a 2-yard loss. I called a quick slant to Gayle Glenn Louis, but when Jesse dropped back, Dan Wilber accidentally stepped on her foot and she fell down. As she scrambled to get back up, we saw what the Giants were going to do with her all day. Two of them broke through our offensive line and knocked her to the ground just as she released the ball. Louis caught it and ran for about 4 yards, but now it was third and 8, and Jesse was shaking her head in disgust getting back to the huddle.

On the next play, she dropped straight back and hit Darius for a 12-yard gain. Again, just as she released the ball, a Giant lineman plowed into her and threw her to the ground. He drew a 15-yard penalty for roughing the passer, but it didn't seem to matter. They were going to put the pressure on, and if they couldn't get to her before she passed, by god they were going to knock her down even after she released the ball if they could get away with it.

Our drive stalled at midfield and we had to punt.

It went like that the whole game, a struggle between the big fellows at midfield. Our guys stopped their running game, and we had one of our cornerbacks, Colin Briggs, and strong safety Doug Harris, shadowing Taylor Price all over the field.

At halftime, the score was Giants 6, Redskins 3. Jesse had kicked a 31-yard field goal. But she had spent the better part of that first half flat on her back. She got knocked down on almost every play. The Giants were penalized for roughing the passer four times, but it didn't help. Our line was as good as ever, but the Giants pass rush was furious, relentless, and determined. Even on running plays, they came. I was worried they'd kill her.

She came to the sideline, frustrated and angry but under control. She wanted to solve what they were doing but couldn't take even a few seconds to look downfield before they were on her from every possible direction. In spite of the strength of our offensive line, it was almost impossible to figure out how to block a pass rush that almost always consisted of a blitz from somewhere—a cornerback, a line-backer, a safety. Sometimes they'd zone blitz—that is, rush a safety and corner and let a defensive lineman back up and get into pass coverage. On any given play the line had to predict where the rush was coming from, and even when they got it right, the Giants came at Jesse and tried to knock her down. Twice they actually batted her pass to the ground before it went five feet. They only sacked her once, but on almost every play they knocked her down after she'd released the ball. Quarterback knockdowns and hurries—that was what they were after, and that's what they got. I never heard a crowd boo so loudly. Every time they knocked Jesse down it sounded like the stadium might actually explode from the noise. If I had been a Giants player, I would have been shaking in my boots.

Finally, near the end of the third quarter, we downed a punt on our 45-yard line, and Jesse suggested we try a few rollout passes. It wasn't something we'd practiced, but I let her go ahead. She started rolling out a little, flipping the ball almost as soon as she got it. The first time she tried it, she hit Mickens with a 5-yard swing pass and he gained 13 yards to the Giant 42. She handed off to Mickens on the next play and he gained 5 yards off tackle. Then she took the ball from center and moved a little to her left, reading their defense, and threw a 10-yard strike to Sean Rice, who twisted his way to the Giant 27. Now we were in range for a tie.

On the next play, the Giants stuffed Mickens for no gain. I could see them out there, getting ready for another furious pass rush. Jesse's uniform was covered in field lime and dirt. I told her to call a draw play. They broke the huddle. She leaned down under center, calling the signals. Steam shot out of everyone's mouth. The Giants jumped too soon and got called for encroachment, a 5-yard penalty. Now it was second and 5 from their 22. I called the same play. Jesse walked to the line, surveyed their defense, and then changed the play at the line, calling instead a quick seam pass to the tight end. It looks like this:

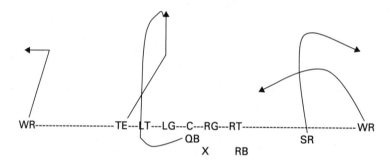

WR---------------------TE---LT---LG---C---RG---RT--------------------------------WR
                                QB   SR
                                   X   RB

Well, Gayle Glenn Louis ran it perfectly. The Giants tried an all-out blitz up the middle and the seam was wide open. Jesse rolled slightly to her left and then flipped the ball to Louis just as she was flattened by their safety. She never even got a chance to see Louis strut into the end zone, untouched.

She got up, shook it off a bit, and then, kicking the extra point, raised her hands in the air. We were ahead 10 to 6. When she came off the field, there was blood trickling down from her nose and mouth. Those points simply could not have been more hard-earned. While the Giants had the ball, the team doctor ran Jesse through the concussion protocol. I held my breath, in fear we'd lose her the rest of the game, but in spite of the bloody nose and mouth, she was fine.

· · ·

Our defense had done a spectacular job all through the game, but early in the fourth quarter, Elbert James twisted his ankle and had to come out. We put Dave Schott in to replace him and the defense continued to hold the Giants off, but with about 3 minutes left, Hempel started marching them downfield. The drive began on their 18-yard line. Two quick passes later and they were at their 39. A 2-yard run, a 5-yard pass to their tight end, and then a 15-yard pass to Taylor Price put the ball on our 39. They called their first time-out. Now there was just 2:15 left. On first down they lost a yard on a quick-out pass. Then Hempel completed a 5-yard pass over the middle, just before the two-minute warning. It was now third and six at our 35-yard line.

We were getting frantic on the sideline. While Coach Bayne called defensive plays and exhorted the defense, Coach Engram, Jesse, and I were going over what we'd have to do if the Giants went ahead of us with so little time remaining. We talked over the various emergency plays we'd practiced; our two-minute drill, our strategy for every contingency. I couldn't tell what was going on beyond our little circle, but the crowd noise was deafening. I knew it was not going our way.

On third down, Hempel completed a 10-yard pass to their tight end. First and 10 at our 25-yard line. The next play was an incomplete pass into the end zone. Second and 10. With 1:31 left, Price caught a 14-yard pass over the middle that put the ball at our 11. Then, believe it or not, the Giants called a time-out. It was clearly a mistake, but we were elated. They gave us time to prepare before the next play. On first down Hempel tried another pass into the end zone, but Doug Harris knocked it down. Now it was second and 10 with 1:23 to go. Orlando Brown came limping off the field. It wasn't his knee this time, but he'd got kicked in the shin pretty badly. Dave Schott, though, couldn't take his place because he was playing on the right side for Elbert James. Coach Bayne sent in Mack Grundy, a special teams player, third stringer on the defensive line, who hadn't played much all year. On the next play, the Giants sent their running back on a sweep to Grundy's side, trying to take advantage of him. Grundy threw himself into the play, broke up the lead interference, and tackled their running back for a 3-yard loss. The Giants called their last time-out amid a blast of noise from the crowd. Grundy stood there at the end of the line, his hands on his hips, waiting. He looked like an All-Pro, god bless him, like he'd been playing that position all his life.

Now there was 1:10 to go: third and 13 from our 14-yard line. New York came to the line. They were in a three-wide set. For the first time in the game, Taylor Price was in the slot. They tried to run a quick fade to the corner with him, but he was covered by Briggs and Harris, so Hempel hit their tight end for a 6-yard gain. It was fourth down now, the ball on the 8-yardline, with 55 seconds to play. With no time-outs, the Giants had to call a play, bring it up to the line, and run it. Over the deafening noise of the crowd, Jesse, Coach Engram, and I were screaming to each other about how, with less than 50 seconds left, our offense could get down the field and score. We *had* to be ready in case the Giants made good on their final push.

Hempel called a quick-out pass to the right corner of the end zone to draw at least one of our safeties over there, and Taylor Price ran a quick slant over the middle from the other side. Hempel tried to throw it high so the magnificent Price could leap right over everybody for it. It seemed like a year that ball was in the air, but Doug Harris, like an NBA player fighting for a rebound, jumped right up and ripped it out of Price's grasp for an interception. He came down in the end zone and went right to his knees for a touchback. We took over on our 20. Jesse went in and knelt down twice and the game was over. We won 10 to 6, our lowest scoring victory in almost fifteen years.

But we won the division title, and throughout the playoffs we were going to have home-field advantage. We'd compiled our best record under Coach Engram, 14 and 4. With Jesse at quarterback, we were 10 and 1. She made us a true team, Jesse. Her presence, the way the offense played for her. Oh, those days, man, those days. What I would give to go back there, just for an hour.

Forty-Two

ALONG WITH ARIZONA, we drew a first-round bye in the playoffs. The Giants, finishing in second place in our division, were the wild card team and so they had to play New Orleans. San Francisco, the other wild card team, would go up against Minnesota.

We began preparation for the Giants during that bye week, thinking we'd see them again, and, sure enough, they beat New Orleans handily, 28 to 0. But with San Francisco beating Minnesota 19 to 10, the 49ers came to play us here, while New York traveled to Arizona.

San Francisco gave us a hell of a game. We held on to win, but it wasn't easy. Jesse got the wind knocked out of her, and Spivey had to finish up for a final score of 27–21. Also, the 49ers tried the same tactics the Giants had used: all-out blitzes from so many different angles we'd have to study film for a week to chart all of them. They didn't have near the success the Giants did, but Jesse still got knocked down seven times, chased out of the pocket twice, and once got thrown back on her head so hard I could hear it on the sideline. That was the play that knocked the wind out of her. She lay there a long time, and when she got up and came back to the sideline she seemed so wobbly on her feet, we had to put Spivey in. Jesse went through the concussion procedure again, and although she did okay, we decided to keep her out the rest of the game. We were already leading 27 to 14 at the time. Our defense had to hold out again against a furious rally at the end.

In the 4:00 game that afternoon, Arizona shocked all the experts and stopped the Giants cold, 24–7. It wasn't even a contest.

That week *Football* magazine ran a collage of pictures on their cover of Jesse after various knockdowns. In one, Dan Wilber was helping her get up off her back while three dark blue shadows of Giant players loomed over her; in another, a huge 49er lineman was throwing her to the ground and you could see a grimace on her face; in still another, Jesse was flat on her back after getting the wind knocked out of her and hitting her head. Two 49er players stood over her, one of them gesturing as if he was a boxer who'd just taken down his opponent with one punch. Superimposed over the photographs was white lettering that said: THE GLOVES ARE OFF. Under that, in smaller text: JESSE SMOKE GETS BACK UP, BUT HOW MANY TIMES? NEW ATTITUDE PUTS REDSKINS QUARTERBACK AT RISK.

Coach Engram was of course furious when I showed it to him. "It's not a new attitude, idiots. It's called a new strategy. Fucking press always gets it wrong."

"Guess it makes for a better story that way."

"Like they weren't trying to knock her on her ass all *year.*"

"Yet they all still believe it, that the guys had been laying off her because she's a woman. Maybe it's a good thing."

"Thing is, I *am* worried about her." He wasn't smiling anymore. "She's taken a hell of a beating the last few weeks."

"She say anything to you?"

"I think she's in some pain. A lot of pain."

I'd been with her almost every day, and I hadn't noticed she was in any trouble.

"In our meeting yesterday," Coach Engram continued, "she suddenly coughed up a clot of blood into her hand."

This sent a cold sensation into the top of my heart.

"She was embarrassed," Engram said. "Said it was nothing, but I could see it hurt her. Then her nose started bleeding, right there at the table."

"You take her to the doc?"

He nodded. "He said it was nothing. Just the dry air. He listened to her lungs and they were clear. Apparently the bloody nose dripped back into her throat before it came out the front."

"Jesus," I said.

"I don't want her getting hit so much in games. We gotta stop that."

"I mean, it's not like they don't know by now that the strategy doesn't work," I said.

"Look at her numbers against the Giants and 49ers. *It* works."

Jesse had not had a banner day in either game; that was true. In the Giants game she'd been knocked down a dozen times, hurried eight times, and sacked once. She completed 13 of 44 passes, for only 166 yards and 1 touchdown. She only had one interception, but a lot of her passes just got knocked down. It was a miracle she didn't have more. Against the 49ers, she completed 17 out of 30, for 215 yards and 1 touchdown. She had no interceptions, but again she had balls batted down.

"Everybody's going to be trying some version of that defense now," Engram said.

"Except they don't have the Giants' personnel now, do they?"

"Look, we'll switch to zone blocking up front—that'll slow some of it down. But what I want to do is practice this week to take advantage of it; I want to fucking *slaughter* that kind of defense in this next game."

"Hit it hard," I said.

"We'll see how long it takes the rest of the league to catch up."

I didn't say anything to Jesse about her bleeding episode. You can bet I watched her closely all week in practice, though. We rehearsed only three-step drops preparing for Arizona. With her quick feet and quick release, we could hit some short passes just behind the line and in front of the linebackers before the defensive line could get fully out of their stance. It would put a little more pressure on our wide receivers, but running patterns that close to the line they'd be able to take advantage of a few picks that would be impossible to detect. (A pick works to get a man open. We might run Rob Anders and Gayle Glenn Louis in a crossing pattern and have them just run into or get in the way of Darius Exley's defender, which would leave Exley suddenly wide open.) Like this:

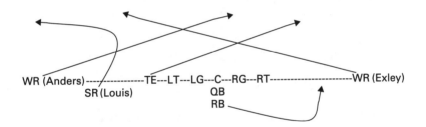

We could do that with both receivers. Technically it's illegal, but when you run it close to the line with the confusion of players in there, the penalty is rarely called. We could work it with Darius picking off Anders's defender, too. Jesse could read defenses well enough to know when she was facing man-to-man. That's when picks really work.

Jesse would have a lot of choices on every play, and we would have as our goal that she not get knocked down even once. On most plays we'd have her drop three or four steps and fire it to one of the wide receivers on a quick in or a quick out. Or she might hit the tight end. The fans would be treated to the quickest passing game they'd ever seen.

To win the NFC championship, we were going to have to beat the Cardinals. They had a defensive line and set of linebackers as hard-hitting and powerful as the Giants, so we'd make sure we were ready for them. I was disappointed, though, not to be facing the Giants again. For one thing, we couldn't be sure the Cardinals would try that same defense. They were smartly coached and they had handled the Giants' defense so easily; they were favored to beat us by 3 points.

The night before the big game, Jesse called me and insisted she had to see me right away. I drove over to her apartment a little worried about what might be up. She'd been practicing every day without any evident pain, or much of it. Fact, we were finally so confident in her condition, we hadn't even listed her on the injury report that week.

At the door she smiled and took my hand. She did not have the porch light on, so I stepped out of the darkness into a well-lit hallway. She closed the door then led the way into her living room. She gestured for me to sit anywhere, so I took a seat on the couch. Jesse sat on the love seat across from me. "You want something to drink?"

"No."

Liz came down the hall from the bedrooms there and installed herself in a chair by the fireplace. She took a deep breath and smiled. "Hello," she said. "It's good to see you, Skip." She looked as if she'd been working hard.

"This is serious," I said. "Isn't it?"

Jesse cast her eyes down, then looked at me. "I wasn't going to say anything about this, but this afternoon my mom said I should— I think I have to let you know."

"Let me know what?"

"I've been spitting up blood, Coach."

Forty-Three

I'M NOT THE sort that panics, but I insisted that Jesse go with me straight to the team doctor. I would have rushed her to an emergency room, but if we did that it would be all over the news before midnight, and none of us wanted that kind of publicity. The team doctor was a general practitioner named Ron Bryan, but everybody just called him Doc. He met us in his office at Redskins Park. I thanked him for coming out so late to see us.

"What's the problem?"

"She's bleeding again," I said.

Jesse looked at me.

"Coach Engram told me about the other day," I said. I was pretty scared. I think Liz was, too. Jesse was simply Jesse. Curious maybe, but not especially alarmed. Doc listened to her describe her symptoms, then asked her if she felt any pain in her chest.

"No," she said. "Not recently."

"Recently? When did you have pain there?"

"Back when I got hit so hard in that first game. When my back was bruised."

"Have you been coughing?"

"No."

"Any fever? Night sweats?"

"No."

He watched her with serious eyes. She said she had frequent headaches.

"*How* frequent?"

"A lot, lately," she admitted.

"Since the other day?"

"Yes."

"Bad headaches?"

"No. Not even very painful—just, well . . ." She looked at me. "Just sort of an achiness in the center of my head? Nothing I'd even take an aspirin for."

He made her stand up and close her eyes and extend both arms to the side. "Now, bending only at the elbow, touch your nose with each forefinger, one at a time." She did this. "Okay," he said. "Now put your arms down to your sides. Close your eyes again, and raise both arms up, palms down, so they are exactly parallel," She did this too.

"Okay," he said.

She opened her eyes. "Did I pass?"

"You did." Then Doc said he wanted to take her back into an examination room and have a look in her mouth.

"You want us to come along?" I said.

"No, you wait here."

"What do you think it could be, Doc?"

"I don't know."

"Is it something bad?"

I wanted him to tell me there was no cause for alarm, but he didn't do that. He didn't look worried, but neither was he being very sanguine about it. All I could get him to say was that the list of possible causes was as long as his arm. "Look, let's just take things one step at a time," he said.

"Doc," I said. "We got a game tomorrow."

"I know that."

"If there's any chance she won't be able to play . . ."

"I'm playing," Jesse said. "And stop talking about me like I'm not here. I hate it when you do that."

I nodded in apology.

"We'll see what this might mean," Doc said. "It's probably nothing. But it won't do any harm to be sure of a few things. I want to listen to her chest again."

While I waited in the hallway with Liz, I called Coach Engram, and he came down to join us. After a while, all three of us were pacing. I asked Liz if it had been a lot of blood.

"No. Just a little. In her handkerchief."

"Was she coughing?"

"No."

I didn't know, but thought maybe that was a good sign.

At one point, Coach Engram broke the nervous silence. "I thought you were going to tell me she was pregnant or something."

Liz looked at him.

"I took her to Doc a week ago for the same thing, the bloody nose," Engram said. "He said she was fine."

"It got worse," Liz said.

"I just hope she's all right," I said. "I don't give a damn about the game anymore. I want her to be all right."

Finally Jesse came out, looking none the worse for wear. Doc was behind her. When he saw Coach Engram he moved over to talk only to him. But we were all there listening.

"She's got nothing going on in her chest," he said. "Her lungs are clear. I listened and this time I took an X-ray. Her teeth look fine. Nothing I can see in the back of her throat."

"So what's the problem?" Coach Engram asked.

He shrugged. "It could be high up, in her nose. The sinus area we can see—'Little's area' it's called—that's clear. Higher up, though, she could have a polyp, or even an injury that's bleeding down into the back of her throat."

"She had a bad bloody nose during the game Sunday," I said.

"And after the Giants game, too," Jesse said.

"I don't remember that," I said.

"I do."

"So what do we do here?" Engram said.

"I want her to get some rest," Doc said. "Have a CAT scan on her head as soon as we can arrange it."

"What about tomorrow?" Engram said.

"Well . . ." He didn't finish. He looked at Jesse kind of sadly, then at me. With a short wave of his hand he said, "I don't think she should, but . . . I left it up to her."

"I'm playing, " she said.

"Is there any danger of permanent harm?" I asked.

"I'm playing," Jesse said.

"My best guess is, it's safe," Doc said. "I'd rather she got this taken care of first, certainly, but . . . there's no concrete danger."

"Should I keep her out, Doc, or not?" Engram said, flatly.

Doc paused a minute before speaking. "I've left it up to her," he said, quietly.

So on Sunday, Jesse walked onto the field with the rest of the offense and the crowd cheered like they always did. We kicked off and the Cardinals went three and out. They punted and Sean Rice, catching it on our 24-yard line, broke through the first line of defenders, slipped to the sideline, and ran it back for a touchdown. Jesse trotted out and kicked the extra point. Before she even took the field for our offense it was 7–0. Over the next 5 minutes or so the Cardinals held on to the ball, got it down to our 15, but then stalled. They kicked a field goal and it was 7–3.

Then, after they kicked off to us, Jesse began one of the most incredible shows I've ever seen. As it turned out the Cardinals did try a version of the Giants strategy against us, blitzing from a variety of formations, but they never laid a hand on her. Time and again, she just dropped back three steps and fired the ball—or flipped it, or gently lofted it—to Exley, Anders, Louis, Rice, Mickens, Frank, and White. Everybody got into the act. She completed 20 of her first 22 passes, for 244 yards and 4 touchdowns. It was uncanny to watch, actually. These were passes of 5 to 15 yards, mostly. I think her longest completion that day was an 81-yard pass to Anders that started out as a quick 8-yard toss over the defensive line and two blitzing linebackers. The cornerback on that side fell down, and Anders was free to jog his way to the end zone. We led 35–3 at the half.

In the locker room, Jesse spit a lot of blood into a white towel, and Coach Engram said he was going to let her take the second half off. "If we score again, you can do the kicking. But you're done for the day." He announced it to the whole team.

She didn't like it, but when he told her it was to keep her fresh for the Super Bowl, everybody got into it, cheering and hollering Jesse's name. It was a sweet thing to see. She put her hands up over her face and rubbed her eyes. Everybody stepped past her and patted her on the shoulders as we went back out for the second half.

The Cardinals scored on their first possession of the third quarter, but we took the ball on the following kickoff and ran it on them—a long, time-consuming drive that took up most of the third quarter. We kept the ball for 14 plays. Mickens ran it in from the 4. He gained 128 yards on 24 carries in the game, and he had 11 of those carries in that one drive. They couldn't stop us. Spivey mopped up, completing 5 of 7 passes. Winning the game 42–10, we were headed for the Super

Bowl. The next day all the papers and sportscasters in the country were calling us a "powerhouse." One article suggested that we might even be able to beat the Oakland Raiders, who had also "waltzed" into the Super Bowl.

On the Monday after we won the NFC championship, Jesse woke up and found a mass of blood on her pillow. She told her mother about it, and me. I insisted she go to the doctor, but by noon she felt okay and refused to do it. "I know what I'm dealing with," she said. "Okay? Please don't ruin this chance for me." She wanted so badly to play in the Super Bowl I believed it clouded her judgment. I even asked her, "Do you want to risk your life?"

"I'm not 'risking my life.'"

For two weeks, while the press chased after her, desperate for an interview with the First Woman to Play in the Super Bowl, she carried a red handkerchief around to spit blood into, as necessary, making sure nobody noticed.

She was sharp in practice, though—threw the ball like she always did—and she studied film of the Raiders, preparing for the game as though she *knew* it would be her last game on earth. Gradually, over those two weeks, the bleeding got worse. She was sick from swallowing it. In spite of how she played in practice, she started to look ill. Roddy wanted to know if she was losing weight. "She looks a bit thinner to me, Skip," he said. "She okay?"

"She's fine," I said, but I didn't really believe it.

The night before the game, she checked into a hospital for further tests—and *that*, we couldn't keep from the papers or the television people.

I'll never forget the hours I spent in that hospital waiting room. I've never been so terrified in my life.

Forty-Four

WELL, OF COURSE you know the story. It's been told a million times. But you don't know the truth. What really happened.

Jesse wasn't "rushed" to the hospital for emergency tests. I drove her there. I stayed at the hospital as long as I could, but it was the day before the Super Bowl. We were in Los Angeles and I had to get to the Coliseum by 9 a.m. I left Jesse there with Andre Brooks and Jimmy Kelso—two of our injured-reserve players, still a part of the team, who were attending the Super Bowl.

The doctors didn't tell her she could die. No one suggested anything like that. They just told her they didn't want her to play. She had an unexplained "mass" high up in her nasal cavity, apparently— just at the point where it bends down toward the back of her throat. They wanted to operate as soon as possible, and she told them they could have at it *after* the game.

But they kept her there a good, long time. As game time approached, she got more and more anxious. When they finally let her go, we were already in warm-ups. She had to race back to the hotel and get dressed, then make it to the locker room to don her equipment and her uniform.

She didn't rise from a hospital bed at kickoff time and sneak out of the hospital, like in the movie. And she wasn't forced to hail cabs and ride buses to get to the stadium. Brooks and Kelso were with her the whole time and they drove her to the game. But she couldn't get there in time. She was fifteen miles from the stadium at kickoff.

Meanwhile, Spivey started. Everyone agreed the Oakland Raiders were the league powerhouse that year. At 16 and 2 they had scored 596 points, the most of any team in the history of the NFL, averaging a staggering 33 points a game. Only the '98 Vikings, the '83 Redskins, and the 2007 New England Patriots had ever averaged more, but that was in a sixteen-game season. The only teams the Raiders had lost to were the Giants and us. Our first game against them—one of the most thrilling contests I ever saw, and Jesse's first start—felt like years ago. And the idea of duplicating that effort seemed impossible, certainly without Jesse.

It was bright and sunny—no wind, and no clouds. Cool as a fall day in Vermont. The Raiders kicked off and things sort of went down from there. Spivey couldn't get anything going. Suddenly, the Raider defense, which wasn't the best in the world—they'd given up 334 points during the year—was playing like the Giants. They didn't even seem to care that Jesse was not in there; they used the same multiple blitzes and defensive packages that had been designed to put our quarterback on her ass. This was an all-out rush, mind you—with no quarter. The object was to knock the quarterback down, no matter if the ball was still in his hands or not.

Now, Spivey had gotten better with his temper, but, as I said about him in the beginning, he didn't take kindly to being shoved or pushed around. He started to lose his cool, and his passes wobbled, sailed high on him, lost velocity. Or, on the short swing passes to Mickens and Jack Slater, our fullback, he'd throw it right into the ground.

The Raiders were quick to take advantage, but our defense was at full strength. Orlando Brown, Drew Bruckner, and Dave Schott played like madmen; and Talon Jones, who came in on passing downs, covered the middle of the field like an entire trio of linebackers. He was that fast and that unstoppable.

So we held on. It was nothing like the first game, though. Nobody scored in the first quarter. Both teams kept struggling to get first downs. There were six punts in the first quarter alone. About midway through the second quarter, the Raiders pushed the ball to our 10-yard line. They tried to run it in from there but gained nothing. On third down, their quarterback, a really great player named Darren McCauley, threw a looping pass into the corner of the end zone to their tight end and suddenly we were down 7 to 0.

Jesse still hadn't come into the game, but by the time McCauley threw that touchdown pass, she was already at the stadium. She didn't see the pass on television in the hospital, as the story goes. In fact, she was dressed and could have gone in on the next series, but Coach Engram would not let her on the field. He told Kelso and Brooks to keep her in the locker room, by force if they had to. He'd decided not to risk it; as he says in his book about Jesse, he was going with Spivey.

Spivey gave the ball to Mickens for two plays, but he only gained 4 yards. Then, on third and 6, Spivey missed Darius Exley on a crossing pattern and we had to punt again. We still had plenty of time in the first half, but we had to get the damn ball back.

This time the Raiders moved it a little more quickly. McCauley hit his best wide receiver, Jeremiah Stubbs, for a 31-yard gain on the first play from scrimmage after the punt. Now they were at our 33-yard line. He hit his other wide receiver, the great Aaron Crow for 15 yards. Then they ran a draw play up the middle that gained 11 yards.

It was first and goal from our 7. The defense dug in though and held them to a field goal.

Now, it was 10 to 0.

On our next play from scrimmage, Spivey threw it at the feet of Rob Anders on a quick slant. Then Delbert Coleman, the Raiders' superstar defensive end, slammed him to the ground and he fumbled. Dan Wilber recovered at our 15-yard line.

Our punter, Jack Clue hit a terrifice kick that put the raiders all the way back to their 28 with 4 minutes left in the first half.

Coach Engram paced the sideline. I couldn't concentrate on the game knowing Jesse was in the locker room and that she wanted to play. But I didn't say anything to him about it. I was worried about Jesse, about what was wrong with her. I couldn't believe they'd let her leave the hospital.

We both watched as the Raiders marched the ball to our 17-yard line. They missed a third and 4 with a shuttle pass that dropped out of the running back's hands before he could take it up the middle. He would have had a first down and a lot more, if he'd held on. They kicked another field goal and made it 13–0.

The stadium was quiet mostly. There were a lot of Oakland fans there, don't get me wrong, but they just didn't make that much noise. It was like they expected much better; despite the points the Raiders had racked up so far, the fans seemed disappointed in their team's performance; and of course they didn't like it that Jesse wasn't playing. Boring and sad, it seemed like the whole game was being staged as a kind of retreat to a world where there was no Jesse. Hell, I was the offensive coordinator on a Super Bowl team and I could hardly focus on what was happening out on that field. It might as well have been a high school soccer game.

The fans knew Jesse was coming out before I did, and in no time the noise was deafening. You've seen the films of Jesse trotting out of the tunnel behind our sideline and approaching the bench. We wore white jerseys in that Super Bowl because that year the NFC was counted as the visiting team. That bright burgundy number 17 on her back glittered against the white jersey. She carried her helmet, her curly hair bouncing in the lights, and just as the offense was taking the field, she cut through the defensive players standing on our sideline and ran out on the field.

Spivey slapped her hand as she passed him and he came to the bench with a kind of wry smile on his face.

"What the *fuck*?" Engram snarled at him. "Get back out there."

"It's her play," Spivey said.

That part of the story is true. Spivey *was* willing to let her take over. "I was having a lousy day," he said later. "I knew she'd get it going."

It's also true that Coach Engram didn't want her in there; that she took the field on her own. But she wasn't spitting blood, or running a fever. She didn't hide among the players on the bench and vomit into a bucket either. I don't know how that story got started.

Here's what she *did* do:

First, she settled the offense down. "This defense isn't that good, all right?" she said when she got into the huddle. "And the way our defense is playing?—we should be kicking ass."

Now, the Raiders were running those random blitzes, so some running plays would get stuffed pretty embarrassingly, but if you hit a hole where the lineman was pulling out to get into pass coverage, or where they might be stunting to let in a linebacker, you could break some things. Jesse called a trap play with Mickens going off tackle, and he gained 5 yards. Then she dropped three steps and hit Anders with a perfect strike for 8 yards. It was like watching a clinic on quarterbacking. She commanded the huddle, walked to the line surveying the defense, then leaned over center and called the play she wanted. I didn't even bother trying to call things from the sideline. It was her game and we both knew it. She had practiced this offense for almost two weeks before she became ill. If this was going to be her last game ever, she wanted to make the best of it.

She hit Sean Rice for 15 yards and a first down at midfield. Then she ran a quick draw play with Mickens. He got 7. She ran him again off tackle for 13. She faked it to him and hit Darius for 22 yards. Then she hit Gayle Glenn Louis at the 2. Not one Raider laid a hand on her.

On first and goal she dropped back a second, faked a throw to the right, then took off up the middle untouched and scored a touchdown. The fans erupted. It was positively deafening. Even the Raider fans cheered for her. Could they, too, have sensed this might be Jesse's last game?

She kicked the extra point just as the second quarter ended: 13–7 Raiders. When Jesse came off the field, blood was all around her mouth, running from her nose. She took a wet towel and wiped it off. She sat on the bench with her head back until the halftime whistle sounded. Then she trotted with the rest of us into the locker room.

Coach Engram tried only briefly to get Jesse to sit for the second half. I looked at her point-blank and asked, "Are you okay?"

"I got a bloody nose," she said.

"Jesse."

The other players gathered around her. I couldn't stop them. It was so close in that room. I'll never forget the feeling of oneness—a powerful sensation of being a whole person, all of us, with one aspiration, one will, one hope. All eyes focused on her, and she turned her baby blues away for a moment, caught up perhaps for the first time with true awareness of a shared soul. She was not a woman then, and we were not men. We were simply human, a collective of one. I put my arm around her and said, "We love you, Jess."

The men cheered.

She wiped her whole face with a white towel. When she put it on the bench next to her, the image of her face captured in blood and sweat, it looked like the Shroud of Turin.

Coach Engram surveyed his team quietly a moment, and then said, "Let's go out and finish this thing."

But for all of the team's renewed sense of purpose, and true game day fury, they left that locker room in silence, as if headed for an execution.

The Raiders took the opening kick of the second half and started down the field, playing with confidence and pride. They had no idea what they were in for. Our defense settled in after they let the Raiders complete a 12-yard pass for a first down. Then, like some sort of iron trap, the defense clamped down hard. When they tackled McCauley for a 10-yard loss, they didn't make any demonstrations or do any dances. When, on the next play Colin Briggs, our right cornerback, flipped Isaac Crow head over heels and caused him to drop the ball, they did not jump for joy. On third and 20, when McCauley completed a short 6-yard pass over the middle and Talon Jones leveled the receiver before he could gain a single yard more, the defense trotted silently off the field. They were all business and the Raiders had to punt.

Jesse took over on our 22-yard line and handed off to Mickens four times in a row, with the offensive line pushing everybody out of the way. Mickens gained 8, 13, 11, and 22 yards. Then Jesse faked a handoff to Mickens, dropped back, and hit Rob Anders on a shallow post for a 24-yard touchdown. She kicked the extra point and we were suddenly ahead 14–13.

We kicked off and the Raiders kick returner cut through a break in our special teams and ran it back for a touchdown to make it 20–14.

After that, it was like watching something staged; something rehearsed. The defense just would not let that vaunted Raider offense stay on the field. Orlando played in a quiet fury. Drew Bruckner stopped the run, and Talon Jones broke up passes to running backs.

Zack Leedom and Nick Rack, Elbert James, Mack Grundy—it didn't matter who was in there—they played as if they knew in advance everything the Raiders were going to do.

Near the end of the third quarter, Jesse led the offense on a long march down the field, managing that team like a cardsharp. She'd walk to the line, look at the defense, then run the play with absolute precision. Short drops and dump-off passes. Handoffs to Mickens or Slater up the middle. Exact passes to the wide receivers just before they stepped out-of-bounds, or just as they turned on the post or on a buttonhook pattern. The Raiders tried to get to her, to knock her down, but they were almost helpless.

Twice she broke the huddle and walked to the line with blood on her chin. The players all noticed it. She'd spit through her face mask, and it, too, dripped blood. At the end of that long drive we were on the Raiders 16-yard line, first and 10. They still held on at 20–14. Jesse threw a quick slant to Gayle Glenn Louis and he caught it, charging toward the goal line, but he dropped the ball. The Raiders recovered inside their 5-yard line. Jesse came back to the sideline and grabbed another towel. I looked into her eyes.

"Don't look at me like that," she said.

Gayle Glenn Louis came over now and said, "I'm sorry, Jess."

She was coughing blood into that towel. When she could talk, she said, "We'll get it next time. You caught three balls to get down there."

When he saw the towel he turned to me. "That's a lot of blood, Coach."

"Jess," I said. "We got to sit you down."

She wouldn't look at me.

Our defense stopped the Raiders again near their 31-yard line and they had to punt. The third quarter ended and they still led 20–14.

Coach Engram called for Spivey to go in at the beginning of the fourth quarter, but Jesse ran out anyway. She went fast, as if she knew we were going to try and stop her.

"Goddamn it," Engram said. "Spivey get out there." But he was already moving out onto the edge of the field. A referee came over to Engram.

"Coach," he said. "Your quarterback's bleeding, did you know that?"

"Yeah, we know it."

Jesse was already in the huddle with the offense. I yelled into my headset. "Jesse, get back here."

Now only part of the story as presented in the movie is true. We *did* do everything we could to get Jesse off that field. Coach Engram called a time-out, and then we went out onto the field—Engram, me, even Coach Bayne. In the movie they play up the power of Jesse's defiance, and they've got her ordering us off the field. Don't get me wrong—she was a commanding presence most of the time, and I won't say that if she *had* ordered us to leave her out there, we wouldn't have done so. Certainly makes a better story. But Jesse was not defiant, right then. She was sad and her voice was less commanding, than, I don't know . . . full of longing. "Don't do this," she said. "Okay? Just—please, don't do this."

"We'll take care of her, Coach," Dan Wilber said.

"I may never play another game," she said. There were tears in her eyes—only the third or fourth time I'd seen that. But these were big, glistening tears.

Engram started to reach for her, then thought better of it.

"Let me do this. Just this one time," Jesse said. "I know I can do it." Blood dripped out of her nose.

Engram turned and started back for the sideline. Bayne and I followed. I didn't look back at Jesse.

Bringing the offense to the line at the beginning of the quarter, Jesse started another one of those long drives down the field: Short crossing patterns to Exley and Anders; a beautiful 15-yard pass to Gayle Glenn Louis on third and 12. She got them down to the Raider 9-yard line before the Raiders stopped us, knocking down a quick corner route to Exley. Mickens dropped a certain touchdown inside the 1-yard line. On third down, with nobody open Jesse had to throw the pass out of the end zone to avoid being sacked for a loss.

She kicked a field goal to make the score 20–17, but we still trailed by 3.

The Raiders got the ball out to their 32 with the kick return. Now it was really up to our defense, though the crowd kept chanting Jesse's name. There were about 12 minutes left in the game.

Jesse stayed away from us when she came to the sideline, but she didn't hide among the offensive players, like they had her doing in the movie. We knew where she was, and we knew what she was up to, too—sitting with them, talking strategy. The whole time she had that towel, and she was wiping her face with it.

Our defense once again stopped the Raiders on three plays and they punted to our 18-yard line.

Jesse ran back onto the field with the offense and put on one of those displays people still rave about. I know in the movie they have her driving us down the field and scoring the winning touchdown at the last minute, and it's awfully dramatic that way, no question. But anyone who actually saw that game knows the truth of it.

Jesse completed eight straight passes as we marched down the field. Mickens caught one for 28 yards up the middle and was tackled at the Raiders 2-yard line. On the next play, Jesse faked it to Mickens then ran it around the right end herself for a touchdown. Eight straight pass plays. One run. When she faked that handoff, everyone in the stadium thought Mickens had the ball, until they registered Jesse herself waltzing around the end for that touchdown. We had the lead now, 24–20.

Just as they had been doing for the entire second half, the defense forced the Raiders to punt, this time to our 19-yard line.

Before Jesse trotted onto the field, she said, "You want to get in on this, Coach?"

"What do you mean?"

"Why don't you and coach Engram call the plays." It was so sweet. She was grateful that we left her in, and she was thinking of us, of what the game meant, and how we'd feel if we were more involved. I could hear laughter in her voice. She was so happy—enjoying herself so much—I was suddenly elated that we hadn't taken her out of the game, no matter how sensible that would have been.

I called two running plays. Mickens up the middle for 8 yards, then the Green Bay Sweep around the left end for 12 more. We were on our 39-yard line. Jesse called time out and came to the sideline. I asked her what the hell she was doing wasting a time-out.

"Excuse me, Coach," she said. Then she spat a huge gobbet of blood at her feet. "I didn't want to do that on the field."

"Jesus, Jesse."

"Just keep calling the plays," she said.

"I'll let Coach Engram do that," I said.

Coach Engram glanced over and half smiled, hearing me say that. He might even have winked at me, for all I can remember. "Leave it to Jesse," he said. He meant it. She gave a bloody grin, waved at him and ran back out onto the field. That's what happened. There was no argument on the sideline as depicted in that movie. Coach Engram didn't yell at her to let him call the plays. She did call her own plays but that was exactly what Coach Engram and I wanted.

"It's your game, Jess," I said into the transmitter. "Go get 'em."

She called a shallow slant to Anders that gained 8 yards. Then she hit Exley on a crossing pattern for 14 more. The noise of the crowd at this point was unbelievable. Absolutely thunderous. Now we were on the Raiders 39. I was like anybody else in that stadium, cheering as loud as my voice allowed, wondering what the hell she would do next. We weren't coaches anymore, any of us. We were just fans, watching Jesse work her magic.

Jesse called a quick pitchout to Mickens and he gained 17 yards around the right end. On the next play, she faked a handoff to Mickens and hit Gayle Glenn Louis for a 22-yard touchdown. This time he held on to the ball, holding it up over his head in triumph as he ran into the end zone.

Jesse kicked the extra point, putting us ahead now 31–20.

Champions to the last, the Raiders took the ensuing kickoff and tried to make a game of it. I know the final score is misleading, and it was good of the filmmakers to make the ending more dramatic. The Raiders did drive all the way down the field, used the clock as well as they could, and made it all the way to our 5-yard line. They did make four tries to get the ball into the end zone, and that stop by our defense was accurate. The only problem is, the game was almost over by then, and even if they *had* scored it wouldn't have changed much but the final score. What the film left out was what happened when we took over at our 5-yard line with 3 minutes left. Jesse engineered another drive, this one 95 yards in seven plays. She hit Anders for 31 yards on the first play from scrimmage at our own 5. Then she ran a fake draw play with Mickens going up the middle and hit Gayle Glenn Louis for 28 yards down the middle. She was like a magician out there. Nobody knew where the ball was once she got it in her hands. When she faked the draw play to Mickens, all of us watched him thinking he had the ball.

On second down, at the Raiders 36-yard line, Jesse hit Darius Exley with a perfect pass up the right sideline and he took it in for another touchdown.

I know it makes a better story if Jesse is in agony, bleeding out of her nose and barely able to remain upright as she struggles onto the field and rescues us at the last minute, but it just isn't what happened. For one thing, it's pretty hard to convince anybody that when you beat a team 38 to 20, you've been saved by some late miracle.

For the day Jesse completed 19 of 23 passes, for 336 yards—and of the four she missed three were dropped balls. She threw three touchdown passes and ran for two more. Only Doug Williams of the Redskins, years before, ever had that kind of Super Bowl. The rest of the team was at peak performance as well. Mickens ran for

167 yards on 16 carries. Our fullback, Jack Slater, rushed for 72 yards on 12 carries.

We were Super Bowl champions, and Jesse was named Most Valuable Player.

My god, what a year that was. I still get tears in my eyes remembering it.

Forty-Five

So THERE IT is. The legend of Jesse Smoke. Except it's no legend. It is the true story of Jesse Smoke's first year in the NFL as it actually happened. In her rookie year that young woman took us to the Super Bowl and led us to victory. She did call her own plays in the fourth quarter of that last game, and those men played for her as if she were Joan of Arc herself.

In a way, she *was* a saint. She showed all of us a thing or two about being a person; about forgetting just a little bit, our notions about gender; we were all stronger, both as individuals and as a team, for knowing Jesse and playing with her. The men on that team came away from their time with her more determined, courageous, and willing to change and learn. Her one sin—the lie she told to the Alouettes and, indirectly, to me—is completely forgivable when you consider what she was up against, what she wanted for herself. And isn't it what all of us want for ourselves—to make use of our talents? Jesse wanted to earn her bread doing something she loved. And she believed she could earn it, if people would just give her the chance.

Was she a hero?

To me, of course she was, and always will be. Okay, she didn't save any lives; she didn't rescue anyone or prevent the suffering of others. She didn't pluck anyone out of a fire or dive into deep water and drag a child to safety; she never took a bullet for anyone. She played a game—a beautiful game, one that approaches all the values of our culture in times of frightful extremity, only without most of the real dangers of life and conflict, the real potential disasters; a game that calls up that little spot of heroism that might just be necessary in real circumstances. It allows us to act like heroes, even when what we are engaged in isn't really heroic. That is at least part of why the sport— perhaps any sport—is so beautiful.

A week after the Super Bowl, she went into surgery and had a small polyp removed from the back of her ethmoid sinus. It was the cause of all her bleeding episodes and, thank god, it was benign.

She showed up the following year in minicamp, ready to lead the team. The two years she played were some of the most eventful in Redskins history. We went to a second Super Bowl with Jesse at the helm, but in that game she tore up her right knee pretty badly. Both the anterior and posterior ligaments were torn. All of us knew it was a disastrous injury. It didn't even matter that we lost the game.

Jesse had to sit out a year, and when she tried to come back the following year she just didn't have the footspeed or strength in her legs to keep playing. She knew it, too. It was one of the most tragic days when she came to me and said she'd have to give up the game.

"I will be grateful to you for the rest of my life," she said.

"It's funny you should say that," I told her. "Because everybody *I* know is thankful they had a chance to play on the same team with you, or, hell, to see you play." I had tears in my eyes.

375

Coach Engram and I retired a few years after that. We never made it back to the Super Bowl, but we had some good years. When we hung it up, Dan Wilber, who had retired after Jesse's first year and got into coaching, took over as head coach and won two Super Bowls on his own.

Jesse was still the most famous woman in the world when I quit coaching, but by that time there were three other women in the league: one defensive end named Alley Howell, (6' 2", 288 pounds), who played for the Vikings, and two kickers—Justine Brown of the Cardinals and Delia Harmon of the Jets. As for the women's leagues, they are much more popular now than they ever were before Jesse. All eight of the current women playing in the NFL, as I write this, came from one of the women's leagues.

I still see Jesse now and again. She and her mother are best of friends now—and when we get together they both like to gang up on me and point out all my faults. As you no doubt know, Jesse's married to Darius Exley and they have a beautiful little girl they've named after Jonathon and me: Jonna Granger Exley. They are both teaching her how to play football and, thanks to Darius, she already has the largest collection of action figures on earth.

Jesse coaches for the Washington Divas, and Darius is with a Washington law firm. Both of them are in the Hall of Fame, and so are Orlando Brown, Drew Bruckner, Talon Jones, and Sean Rice. For sure, Gayle Glenn Louis will be there and I think eventually Rob Anders, and our strong safety Doug Harris will make it too.

All of those guys played for one of the best teams in history and one of the best coaches. No team ever played with more spirit or unity than that first one, though. And that was because of Jesse. What started out as a dreamy sort of halfhearted practical joke turned out to be one of the best things I ever did with my life; the principle reason I am remembered in my profession.

Not long ago, we all got together to celebrate Jonna Exley's third birthday at their huge Victorian in Potomac, Maryland. Most of the old gang was there—Darius, of course, Rob Anders, Mickens, and Rice. Doug Harris, Gayle Glenn Louis, Dan Wilber, and Orlando; most of the players were there with their wives and children. Jonathon Engram and his wife showed up a little late. The players cheered. We were all in the backyard on a bright, sunny Sunday afternoon in May. Everybody gathered around a long picnic table covered with a white tablecloth dotted with Redskins insignias. Jesse and Darius had rented a twenty-foot-long canopy that shaded the table.

On that day Jesse and I walked up a slight hill in her yard, some distance from the gathering, and I told her I was going to write this book. She sort of grimaced and turned those blue eyes away from me. We'd just sung happy birthday to Jonna, and the kids were all sitting at the table, devouring cake and ice cream. Jonna had followed Jesse and me up to the top of the hill. "Where're you going, Mommy?" she said.

Jesse knelt down, licked her fingers, and started wiping cake from Jonna's mouth. The little one struggled against her. "Mommy, *don't.*"

"Hold still," Jesse said, wiping her hand clean in the grass.

"She's beautiful, Jess."

"She's spiky and stubborn is what she is."

"Inherited."

Jesse looked up at me. "You really going to write another book about me?"

"Not just about you. About all of us."

Jonna pushed Jesse's hands away. "*No,* Mommy."

Jesse brushed the little girl's hair back, kissed her on the forehead, and stood up. "Go on," she said. Jonna ran back down to the table. I watched the curls in her hair bounce as she ran.

"God, she looks like you," I said. "Your hair bounced just like that when you ran."

"Doesn't everybody's?"

"You don't want me to write about you?"

"Oh, I don't care, Coach. It's just all so long ago."

"Don't you think about it sometimes?"

"Only when I try to get up with this knee," she laughed. Then she stared right into my eyes. "Coach, it was a great year in my life—*all* my time playing was terrific. But nothing compares to . . ." she stopped. She tilted her head a little, still gazing into my eyes. "Look, the other day I came home from the grocery store, two full, heavy bags in my arms. Jonna was underfoot, following me into the house, jabbering the way she does. I can barely understand her sometimes when she gets going. I kind of stop listening. Anyway, I put the groceries on the counter. Jonna was at my feet, and I had to step around her to put the groceries away and I felt myself losing patience with her. I just wanted her to be *quiet* for a minute, stop pulling at my slacks and leave me alone, for god's sake. I was so frustrated. Then, I just sat on the floor, leaned back against the counter, and looked at her. She came running into my arms, and I forgot the groceries, the open refrigerator. I just held her there, and I realized I was happier at that moment than when we won the Super Bowl. Just looking into my little girl's eyes was better than all of it."

I never had children. I didn't know how that felt. I was kind of sorry I didn't.

"So, if you want to write about me," she said, "don't forget to include *that*. I'm happier now than I've ever been."

"Sometimes," I said, "remembering your first year, I can get to feeling pretty happy myself."

Coach Engram strode up the hill to us now, bouncing Jonna on his hip. "Three years old already. And isn't she cute?"

Jonna smiled at him, her hand on his cheek. Once again there was cake all over her face.

"Are you married yet?" he said to her.

"Noooooo."

"What kind of car do you drive?"

"I don't have a *car*," Jonna said, laughing. "You're *silly*."

Jesse was laughing, too. It was a nice sound—one I didn't hear very often when she was playing. There was something softly feminine about it. She stood there with her arms folded in front of her, looking at her little girl fending off Coach Engram's attempts to tickle her under the chin. I could see that Jonathon Engram was a pro around children. He'd raised a few of them himself.

"Skip's going to write his own book about us," Jesse said. She held out her arms and Jonna sort of fell into them. "Wow, you're getting so heavy, little girl." She gently put her down.

"Can I have more cake?" Jonna said.

"It's your birthday, sweetie. All you have to do is ask." Jesse took her hand and started off back toward the picnic table where all the other children were still gathered. I watched the two of them walking down the hill, Jesse towering over this little version of her.

"You going to write the thing yourself?" Engram asked.

"Won't be too hard, I think. It's all still so fresh in my mind."

He nodded.

A cheer went up as Jesse and Jonna approached the table again. Jesse waved to the guys, like she was leaving a football field, weary and exhausted, wearing the bruises of yet another triumph.

Appendix:
Roster, Schedule, Final Standings

Redskins Roster in Jesse's First Year (Starters in Bold)

Name	Pos.	Number	Height	Weight	Year (R=Rookie)
Floyd Allen	DT	90	6-1	331	6
Corey Ambrose	QB	9	6-1	215	12
Rob Anders	WR	89	5-11	175	5
Colin Briggs	CB	23	6-2	191	4
LD Breedway	LB	52	6-1	256	8
Andre Brooks	RG	79	6-2	290	3
Orlando Brown	DE	95	6-11	331	R
Drew Bruckner	LB	56	6-0	250	3
Dave Busch	RG	64	6-6	334	R
Jack Clue	P	5	6-0	188	9
James Cook	RT	62	6-7	351	11
Michael Coore	RB	30	5-9	223	10
Riley Corells	LB	50	6-3	245	2
Justin Dever	K	4	6-1	215	4
Ray Drewyer	FB/TE	83	6-3	266	4
Carey Epps	DE	96	6-6	296	5
Jory Evans	DE	91	6-4	312	R
Darius Exley	WR	82	6-6	231	3
Tim Fallon	LB	59	6-2	233	1
Jeremy Frank	WR	85	5-10	188	3
Terry Fonseca	QB	16	6-2	212	1
Chris Gates	CB	41	6-1	195	8
Mack Grundy	DE	92	6-4	301	5
Doug Harris	SS	42	6-5	240	2
Steve Henderson	LG	78	6-3	297	4
Marcus Jackson	RT	72	6-7	316	14
Elbert James	DE	99	6-3	313	9
Talon Jones	LB	54	6-2	230	R

Name	Pos.	Number	Height	Weight	Year (R=Rookie)
Jimmy Kale	DT	97	6-1	330	R
Jimmy Kelso	QB	19	6-1	215	5
Michael Klam	SS	21	6-0	234	2
Edward Kray	LT	75	6-5	354	7
Greg Lavelle	C/LS	46	6-6	289	6
Benjamin Leads	LB	51	6-3	255	10
Zack Leedom	DT	94	6-2	325	8
Gayle Glenn Louis	TE	81	6-4	244	2
Matt McCauley	CB	31	5-10	189	3
Walter Mickens	RB	29	6-0	220	4
Alvin Parker	DE	88	6-4	293	11
Andrew Pauley	RB	28	6-0	191	1
Nick Rack	DT	93	6-1	306	9
Sean Rice	WR	87	5-11	185	2
Trey Ryker	CB	27	5-10	188	6
Dave Schott	DE	98	6-0	278	8
Brian Sears	LT	74	6-6	314	5
Jack Slater	FB	49	6-1	244	3
Todd Smith	FS	25	6-2	214	11
Jesse Smoke	QB	17	6-2	170	R
Ken Spivey	QB	13	6-2	195	3
Greg Stills	TE	45	6-3	231	1
Jimmy Triplett	FS	24	6-3	220	4
Jerry Walls	CB	26	6-0	195	2
Jerome White	WR	14	6-2	213	3
Daniel Wilber	C	76	5-11	342	7

Redskins Schedule in Jesse's First Year

Week One (Aug. 28)	Miami Dolphins	W 17–14
Week Two (Sept. 4)	Detroit Lions	L 0–17
Week Three (Sept. 11)	at Philadelphia Eagles	L 9–21
Week Four (Sept. 18)	Dallas Cowboys	W 31–0
Week Five (Sept. 25)	at New York Giants	L 14–24
Week Six (Oct. 2)	Oakland Raiders	W 35–33
Week Seven (Oct. 9)	at Los Angeles Rams	W 28–3
Week Eight (Oct. 16)	Kansas City Chiefs	W 35–10
Week Nine (Oct. 23)	at Mexico City Aztecs	W 24–10
Week Ten (Oct. 30)	Bye	
Week Eleven (Nov. 6)	at Cleveland Browns	W 49–3
Week Twelve (Nov. 13)	Philadelphia Eagles	W 14–6
Week Thirteen (Nov. 20)	at New York Jets	L 10–17
Week Fourteen (Nov. 24)	at Dallas Cowboys	W 35–21
Week Fifteen (Dec. 4)	Cincinnati Bengals	W 52–14
Week Sixteen (Dec. 11)	Tampa Bay Buccaneers	W 17–13
Week Seventeen (Dec. 18)	at San Diego Chargers	W 17–6
Week Eighteen (Dec. 24)	at Green Bay Packers	W 48–0
Week Nineteen (Dec. 31)	New York Giants	W 10–6
Playoffs (Jan. 15)	San Francisco 49ers	W 27–21
(Jan. 22)	Arizona Cardinals	W 45–10
Super Bowl (Feb. 5)	**Oakland Raiders**	**W 38–20**

Final Standings, Jesse's First Year

Division/Team	W–L	PF	PA	PCT
NFC East				
Y*-Washington Redskins	14–4	445	218	.777
X-New York Giants	13–5	336	183	.722
Dallas Cowboys	8–10	332	351	.444
Philadelphia Eagles	7–11	340	485	.388
NFC North				
Y-Minnesota Vikings	13–5	485	291	.722
Green Bay Packers	8–10	365	394	.444
Detroit Lions	8–10	364	456	.444
Chicago Bears	4–14	256	560	.222
NFC South				
Y-New Orleans Saints	10–8	344	356	.555
Tampa Bay Buccaneers	9–9	379	388	.500
Carolina Panthers	7–11	256	418	.388
Atlanta Falcons	5–13	234	444	.277
NFC West				
Y-Arizona Cardinals	14–4	495	244	.777
X-San Francisco 49ers	14–4	458	198	.777
Los Angeles Rams	8–10	377	296	.444
Seattle Seahawks	2–16	239	588	.111
AFC East				
Y-Buffalo	15–3	468	290	.833
New York	8–10	423	409	.444
Miami	7–11	344	456	.388
New England	1–17	209	545	.055

Division/Team	W–L	PF	PA	PCT
AFC North				
Y-Cleveland	12–6	388	246	.666
Baltimore	10–8	413	342	.555
Pittsburgh	5–13	316	394	.277
Cincinnati	4–14	308	512	.222
AFC South				
Y-Jacksonville	14–4	523	216	.777
X-Tennessee	14–4	558	277	.777
Indianapolis	9–9	412	344	.500
Mexico City	4–14	290	378	.222
AFC West				
★-Oakland	16–2	596	334	.888
X-San Diego	13–5	435	278	.722
Kansas City	10–8	457	313	.555
Denver	1–17	258	435	.055

PF = points for; PA = points against; PCT = winning percentage; ★ = home-field advantage throughout playoffs; Y = division title; X = wild card team

A Note on the Author

Robert Bausch is the author of many works of fiction, most recently the novel *Far as the Eye Can See*. He was born in Georgia and raised around Washington, D.C., and received a B.A., M.A., and M.F.A. from George Mason University. He's been awarded the Fellowship of Southern Writers' Hillsdale Award for Fiction and the John Dos Passos Prize, both for sustained achievement in literature. He lives in Virginia.